Thalassa Ali was born in Boston, Massachusetts, USA, the daughter of two archaeologists, one British. Her husband was from Lahore, Pakistan, and she lived there for twelve years, spending the last three years of her time there running her husband's business following his sudden death. She became a stockbroker on her return to America and, in 1993, turned to writing. She converted to Islam in 1984, and is a member of a Sufi brotherhood, based in Karachi. *A Singular Hostage* is her first novel, the first of a projected trilogy.

More praise for *A Singular Hostage*:

'Thalassa Ali must be one of the most interesting, timely people around . . . sheds new light on a bizarre and little-known event in political history' *The Big Issue in the North*

'Does indeed bear comparison with M M Kaye' *The Bookseller*

A
SINGULAR
HOSTAGE

Thalassa Ali

review

First published in Great Britain in 2002 by Review
An imprint of HEADLINE BOOK PUBLISHING

First published in paperback in 2002

10 9 8 7 6 5 4 3 2 1

ISBN 0 7472 6772 3

Typeset in Perpetua by Palimpsest Book Production Limited,
Polmont, Stirlingshire
Printed and bound in Great Britain by
Clays Ltd, St Ives plc

HEADLINE BOOK PUBLISHING
A division of the Hodder Headline Group
338 Euston Road
LONDON NW1 3BH
www.reviewbooks.co.uk
www.hodderheadline.com

To the memory of
Sayed Akhlaque Husain Tauhidi,
who showed me the Path to Peace through scattered pearls

Samina Quraeshi

Samina Quraeshi

Acknowledgements

Among those who have helped me with this book were my writing teacher Arthur Edelstein, my faithful writing group, and other dear friends in the US, Pakistan and India, including Gillo Afridi, Tony Mahmood, Samina Quraeshi, Deborah Barlow and Diane Franklin, and Riffy Ghani. Jill Kneerim, my agent in Boston, Judy Martin in London, Danelle McCafferty, my first editor, Lois Ames and Peter Scholl took the book seriously. Anne Williams, my editor at Headline, and Zoe Carroll, her assistant, held my feet to the fire, as did the eagle-eyed and determined Kate Miciak at Bantam Dell in New York. I also thank Sophie and Toby, my closest allies of all.

The rest of you know who you are. Thank you all.

Historical Note

This story takes place in the north of India, now Pakistan, in 1838, the second year of Queen Victoria's reign. By that year, Britain, through its proxy, the Honourable East India Company, controlled most of the Indian subcontinent. To the north, the Great Game – the nineteenth-century struggle between Britain and Russia for control of Central Asia – was gathering speed.

By 1838, the British feared a Russian threat to their Indian territories. Determined to outwit the Russians by gaining political control of Afghanistan, Lord Auckland sent his armies to Kabul on a military adventure later known as the First Afghan War.

Before launching his Afghan Campaign, Auckland took the extraordinary step of travelling twelve hundred miles across India to enlist the aid of the dying one-eyed Maharajah Ranjit Singh of the Punjab, whose independent military state lay between the British territories and Afghanistan. That year-long journey, on which Lord Auckland was accompanied by his two spinster sisters, his entire government and a ten thousand-strong army, culminated in the great durbar, or state meeting, at Firozpur, on the border between British-controlled India and the Punjab.

A treaty between the two was essential to the British campaign. Maharajah Ranjit Singh knew this, and delayed signing the treaty for a month, forcing Auckland to send his troops across the mountain passes into Afghanistan in deep winter.

This story takes place during that month.

Lord Auckland, his sisters, his political secretary and his chief of protocol are real historical figures, as are Maharajah Ranjit Singh and his chief minister. The durbar took place much as I have described it, and the subsequent movements of the British camp are generally accurate.

Mariana Givens, Harry Fitzgerald, the baby Saboor and his family, and Saat, the Maharajah's youngest wife, are products of my imagination.

Thalassa Ali

Glossary

abba	diminutive of father
ammi	diminutive of mother
Angrez	English
anna	a coin: one-sixteenth of a rupee
attar	scented oil
azan	Muslim call to prayer: given five times a day
baba	diminutive for a male child
Begum Sahib	polite form of address for a married lady
bhabi	polite term for a young female relative
bhaji	polite term for an elder female relative
bhisti	water carrier
Bibi	polite form of address for a young woman
burqa	woman's head-to-toe covering made of many yards of cotton
caravanserai	overnight stopping place for travellers and their animals
chapatti	flat disc of unleavened wheat bread: the bread of the people
charpai	a bed of webbed hemp stretched on a wooden frame on four legs

dal	lentils
dhoolie	litter for carrying a woman
dhoti	Hindu loincloth
durbar	meeting between heads of state
Granth Sahib	sacred text of Sikh religion
gulab jamon	sticky brown sweetmeat
guzar	quarter, as in a section of a city
haveli	large walled-city house, built around a courtyard
howdah	litter or seat with railings, for riding on an elephant
Huzoor	polite form of address, equivalent to 'my lord'
jalebee	orange, pretzel-shaped sweetmeat
jan or jani	darling
ji	yes; also used after someone's name to denote respect
khabardar	be careful!
kameez	long shirt, usually of cotton, worn over loose trousers (pyjamas or a shalwar)
kukri	knife with a downward-curving blade
luddoo	ball-shaped yellow sweetmeat
mahout	an elephant driver
mehndi	henna paste, used for dying the skin and the hair a russet brown colour
Memsahib	polite form of address for a European woman
Moghuls	emperors of India in the sixteenth and seventeenth centuries, responsible for much of India's finest architecture and design
mohur	gold coin worth 15 silver rupees

muezzin	man who gives the Muslim call to prayer
munshi	teacher, especially of languages
murshid	a spiritual guide or teacher
nach	dancing
namaste	traditional Hindu greeting
neem	tree with astringent bark, used to clean teeth and heal wounds
n'hut	nose ring
nikah	marriage agreement
palki or palanquin	litter carried by bearers, often used for long-distance travel
qamar	moon
qul	third day of mourning, when the entire Qur'an is read for the benefit of the departed soul
Qur'an	sacred text of Islam
reetas	seed pods that are boiled, then used for washing the hair
salaam	traditional Muslim greeting meaning 'peace'
shabash	well done
shaikh	leader of a Muslim spiritual brotherhood
shako	military cap in the form of a cylinder
shalwar	loose cotton trousers worn under a shirt
sirdar	noble (as in Sikh sirdar), or a leader (as in sirdar bearer)
sufi	Muslim who is also a follower of a spiritual path
surma	black powder, used as eyeliner
suttee	Hindu widow who burns herself to death on her husband's funeral pyre, or the practice of doing so
tamasha	show, spectacle

tasbih	string of beads, used to count prayers or the names of God
tulwar	curved sword
ubtan	paste, made of oil and spices, used to soften the skin
wah wah	excellent
zenana	ladies' quarters
zikr	Sufi practice of repeating God's name with special head movements, for the purpose of spiritual gain

Prologue

At 2 a.m., Shaikh Waliullah Karakoyia opened his eyes. Years of offering his prayers at the appointed hours had given him a delicate sense of the passage of time. Sometimes he allowed himself to imagine that, should he be sent to the windowless dungeons of the Lahore Citadel, whose walls shut out the call to prayer, he would still know when to wash himself and stand before his God.

He shivered and reached for his shawl. Moonlight filtered its way through the latticework balcony outside and fell like coins on the prayer rug that lay ready, pointing west to Mecca, its corner turned back to avert evil. Wooden curtain rings clicked softly as he padded through a doorway to the little table that held his water vessel and brass basin. The water was cold as he washed for the post-midnight prayer, a prayer optional to all save those schooled in the mystical traditions of Islam.

God is great, he murmured as he dried his face.

Facing the wall so that no creature might come between him and God, the Shaikh stood straight, his hands folded, his eyes half-closed.

In the name of Allah Most Gracious, Most Merciful:
Praise be to Allah, Cherisher and Sustainer of the Worlds;
Most Gracious, Most Merciful,
Master of the Day of Judgement.
Thee alone we worship, thee alone we ask for help.
Guide us to the straight path: the path of those whom
    thou hast favoured;
Not of those who have earned thy wrath, nor of those
    who have gone astray.

As he recited, he abandoned himself to his dreams: mind pictures so dazzling that he found them difficult to describe, even to the most advanced members of the mystic brotherhood he had led for more than twenty-five years.

Eyes on the mat before him, the Shaikh moved through the slow dance of his prayer. He bent, straightened and bowed, his forehead to the tiles beneath the threads of his prayer mat, as his fellow Muslims had done for thirteen hundred years, the venerable Arabic coming in half-whispered cadences in the moonlight.

By sunrise, the sky was heavy. The rain that had poured in torrents before dawn had nearly ceased, leaving a faint light to shine on the Shaikh's house and on the cobbled square where it stood.

The light strengthened and found its way into the narrow lanes and bazaars of Lahore City. It spread over the wet pavilions and courtyards of Maharajah Ranjit Singh's Citadel, the great marble fort that shared with the city the protection of its ancient, fortified wall.

In an octagonal tower set into the Citadel's outside wall, the Maharajah's youngest hostage was refusing a cup of milk.

Saboor would not drink from the cup the servant girl held out invitingly. Compressing his lips, he turned his head away.

'Oh, Saboor Baba,' the girl crooned, looking about her cautiously as she held out the cup, 'drink this, it is sweet.'

'No,' said the child firmly, and trotted away, his little shoulders bouncing. Reaching the safety of the bed where his mother sat loosening her hair, he crouched beside her and followed the servant with round, anxious eyes.

'What is the matter, my darling?' His mother pursed her lips and made a kissing sound. 'Why don't you want your milk? You love your milk.' Cocking her head, she studied Saboor and smiled. Auburn hair cascaded over her shoulder and lay in a shining coil in her lap.

'Oh, Reshma, is Saboor not the sweetest baby in all of Lahore?' she asked in her child's voice.

'Yes, Bibi,' murmured the servant girl, her head swaying in agreement. The cup she held shook gently, making little waves in the milk.

But Saboor would not have his milk. He crawled beneath the bed, his bare feet disappearing from view. There he sat, obstinately refusing his breakfast.

'Well then, your ammi will have to drink it instead,' his mother said. 'Ammi loves warm sweet milk.' She reached for the cup, heavy embroidered silk falling back from a delicate wrist.

The servant, her eyes widening, tried to take it back. 'No, Bibi. This milk is for Saboor,' she protested, but Mumtaz Bano would have it. She made a polite but commanding gesture.

As his mother took the cup from Reshma's fingers, Saboor crawled hurriedly from his hiding place, his mouth open, his breathing rapid. At the edge of the bed he dragged himself

3

upright at his mother's knee, his face flushing, in time to see her lift the cup to her mouth and swallow.

For a moment there was silence. Then he began to scream.

'What is the matter, my darling?' Mumtaz Bano asked, her eyes wide. She reached out and stroked Saboor's face with her free hand, but he could not answer. He could only scream and shake his head back and forth, his mouth stretched open as far as it would go, his eyes screwed shut.

The servant girl stood immobile, her hands pressed over her ears to shut out the child's cries. Then, mumbling an excuse, she snatched him up and fled.

Without stopping outside the door for her slippers, she flew, the child shrieking on her hip, past other rooms whose languid occupants scarcely looked up. Breathing hard, she climbed a flight of stone stairs to the outer door and ran out across a damp courtyard to the Queens' Garden.

They were alone. A nearby fountain burbled. Reshma set Saboor down on its cold marble edge, then wiped tears and mucus from his face. The grinding, desperate sound of his screams told her that his heart was breaking.

'Why do you cry?' she asked him, her voice trembling. 'Nothing has happened. Nothing.'

The guards sharing a water pipe near the tower door had not looked up. Shielded from their eyes by a cypress tree, Reshma tugged her unclean veil over her head and crouched beside the child, willing him to fall silent. Now, her terrible work gone all wrong, she could only wait until Saboor's mother fell, unknowing, into deadly sleep. Later, when the body was discovered and she was questioned, she would swear that she and the child had been outdoors all along.

Saboor's mouth was still stretched wide, although he gave

only a single, drawn-out cry. Reshma reached towards him, then drew her hand away.

Today's evil had begun a year ago, with jealousy and whispers, after the old Maharajah ordered Saboor and his mother to the Citadel from their home in Shaikh Waliullah's house half a mile away. Saboor's presence alone, the Maharajah had insisted, would protect him from illness and death. Saboor was, after all, the grandson of Shaikh Waliullah, a man whose mysterious abilities were known to all.

A myna bird shrieked in the cypress tree overhead. Reshma wrapped her fingers round her knees. Saboor's mother, whom Reshma had once envied for her beauty and her station, now lay mortally poisoned in her room. If Saboor had been helpless to save her, what use was he to the Maharajah?

Reshma looked down at the wailing child. If he did possess special powers as people claimed, they had done him no good; they had only brought him to his present exile among the Maharajah's queens, and the loss of his pretty mother.

He was quieter now. Reshma lifted him to her lap where he lay hiccuping and listless, refusing to meet her gaze. She bit her lip. What would the Maharajah do when he learned of Mumtaz Bano's death? Aware of the jealousies swirling within his household, would he guess the truth, that the poisoned cup had been meant, not for the mother but for the child, his favourite, his tiny magician, his pearl of pearls?

She looked past the tree at the guards who now dozed beneath a portico, their forearms shading their eyes. The Maharajah, at least, was far away, encamped with his court on the border of his kingdom, waiting to meet the English people. It was his youngest queen whom Reshma feared more, Saat Kaur, whose own infant son had failed to attract the Maharajah's love, and who now waited in a downstairs room for the screams that would herald Saboor's death. How was she to explain her failure?

Reshma wiped Saboor's wet face with a corner of her veil. How different he looked now, his brightness gone, his soft, questioning look replaced by heavy exhaustion. Before today, save for the old Maharajah with his constant demands, Saboor's sole companion had been his lonely young mother. Alone and friendless now, how would he survive?

Reshma closed her eyes against her tears, but they seeped from beneath her lids and trickled down her face. Why had she, who had never deliberately caused harm, consented to be the bearer of the poisoned cup? Was it her terror of the young queen's rages? Had her own deprivation, her bondage, made her hard?

'Forgive me, Saboor,' she whispered. 'Forgive me.'

A new fear clutched at her. Saboor had refused his milk. He had crawled as fast as he could from beneath the bed when his mother had taken the cup. Had he been trying to stop her from drinking the poison? *Had he known?*

She glanced at the silent child. It could not be possible. Saboor Baba, after all, was only one and a half years old.

Chapter One

As a watery light filtered into her tent, Mariana Givens awoke with a start. Overhead, rain whispered against canvas.

She sat up and pushed her hair from her face. Why had she awakened so suddenly? Had an unusual sound, a voice, come from outside?

As she reached for her boots, a familiar scuffling at her doorway signalled the arrival of Dittoo with her coffee. She dropped the boots, flung herself down and dragged the covers impatiently to her chin. Feigning sleep was the only way she could prevent Dittoo from talking to her. Even among Indian servants, Dittoo could win a prize for talking.

She breathed evenly, watching through her lashes as he pushed his way inside, past the heavy blind that served as a door, bringing with him a wave of damp chill and the scent of cooking fires. His bare feet on the striped rug made wet sounds that grew louder as he advanced towards her bed, wheezing a little, the tray rattling in his hands.

She forced herself not to wince as the tray dropped noisily onto her bedside table. Above her, Dittoo cleared his throat. Mariana had thought of asking the advice of the Governor-General's two sisters regarding Dittoo's habit of standing over

7

her while she was in bed, but had refrained, knowing they would only insist he be sent away. Whatever the sisters might think, Mariana was certain Dittoo's behaviour had nothing to do with her being twenty and unmarried.

When he turned away, she opened her eyes and watched him shuffle towards the door, his shoulders bowed under their usual invisible burden, then remembered what had woken her. It had been the silence outside her tent. Where were the coolies who daily dismantled the red canvas boundary wall in her corner of the state residence compound? Where were the shouts of the men, the grunts of their pack animals?

Her tent floor was wet, the air damp and cool. She remembered the sound of rain pounding on the roof in the night.

'Dittoo,' she called after him, making a mental note never to do it again, 'are we travelling today?'

He swung back, beaming. 'That is what I wanted to tell you, Memsahib. They do not know as yet. Everything depends upon the big elephant. I heard them saying—'

'Thank you, Dittoo,' she said, and waved him away.

The blind closed behind him. Mariana sat up. She picked up her boots and banged them upside down against the side of her bed, then looked down, as she always did, to see if some interesting creature had tumbled out of one of them.

The red wall outside her tent would be taken down only if the camp's biggest baggage elephant proved able to carry his load. If she hurried, she might see the elephant for herself.

Hopping first on one foot and then the other, she fought her way into her boots, shrieking as cold water squirted up through the holes in the striped cotton rug under her feet. After flinging off her nightdress and grappling with her stays, she buttoned herself into her favourite tartan gown, pushed

8

a handful of brown curls inside her matching tartan bonnet, and tied its ribbons carelessly under her chin. She ignored the ewer and washbasin waiting on their stand. There was no time to wash her face; she had an elephant to visit.

Leaving her untasted coffee steaming on the table, she hurried across the soaking rug, Miss Emily's voice sounding in her ears. 'How many times must I warn you, my dear,' Miss Emily had said only yesterday afternoon while regarding Mariana severely over her reading spectacles, 'that you must not forget your position. Never allow a native to see you confused, upset, or less than perfectly dressed.'

Mariana took an impatient breath and stepped out into the early morning mist that had replaced the rain.

Her tent was well located. Tucked sideways into a front corner of the Governor-General's own residence compound, it had a clear view of the residence tents and a good, if distant, view of the principal gate, a folded entrance in the red canvas wall that enclosed the entire compound. Intriguing sounds often drifted into her tent from the other side of the wall, causing Mariana to spend much time imagining the various origins of the people and animals passing by on the avenue outside.

Smooth, shiny mud marred only by Dittoo's footprints covered the distance from her modest doorway to the centre of the compound. There, arranged in a square, the three riotously patterned tents of Lord Auckland and his two unmarried sisters, and a dining tent large enough to seat twenty, billowed wetly in the dawn breeze.

Beside Mariana's tent, the red canvas wall stretched away towards the guarded gate. Holding her skirts away from the mud, she began to hurry along the wall.

She should have waited in her tent until the march. That was the rule for ladies travelling in camps. If there was no march, a lady waited until nine o'clock before going across to the dining tent for breakfast. She then returned to her tent to read or write letters until lunch. After lunch, she paid calls, in this case upon Miss Emily or Miss Emily's younger sister Fanny in their tents. Before dinner, she went out for a ride. Mariana knew these rules because Miss Emily had repeated them to her several times.

But Mariana would not shut herself away behind canvas. Ladylike idleness drove her mad. Besides, she would miss everything, and it was her duty to learn all about the camp, and about India. If she did not, her twice weekly letters to Papa would never be good enough.

She risked a glance towards the residence tents. There was no sign of activity there; no tattletale lady's maid carried things across the compound, no English-speaking native manservant stood watching her. If she could get past the gate, then across the avenue and back again without being seen, she would be safe from Miss Emily's glares at breakfast.

She followed the wall, avoiding the stout guy ropes pegged to the ground every eight feet. The wet ropes and the gusting wind reminded her of the dream from which she had awakened. In her dream she had shivered in the prow of an unfamiliar ship as it sailed headlong through a dense fog towards a destination she could not guess. It seemed odd to dream of a ship as she lay in a tent on the flat plain of northwestern India, a thousand miles from the sea, but odd as it seemed, the dream had come twice, perhaps three times, before.

Beside her, the ruddy canvas was dark with rain. High, grimly heavy, designed to keep out thieves, to Mariana's eye the red wall blocked out much of the excitement of living in a travelling camp. Even the Eden sisters felt the same. 'It would be almost worth the horror of discovering a knife-wielding savage under one's bed to be able to see more of the avenue from our tents,' Miss Emily had remarked only last week as she, Miss Fanny and Mariana negotiated the entrance.

By 6 a.m., the folded entrance, like the wall, should have been collapsed on the ground, tended by coolies coiling guy ropes and rolling up sections of canvas. Like the wall, it was still standing.

Ignoring the salutes of the sentries, Mariana passed through the still upright entrance and emerged onto the avenue. A hand to her eyes, she peered up and down the avenue's length, towards the flat open plain at one distant end, and the orderly horse and elephant lines at the other.

The wide avenue looked much as it had last evening, lined with office tents and the tents of senior government officials. Only the great durbar tent had gone from its place opposite the guarded entrance, leaving an empty rectangle of churned mud where several hundred coolies stood watching something she could not see.

She hurried towards them.

The big elephant, Dittoo had informed her, was nearly twelve feet tall. The largest of the hundred and twenty-seven baggage elephants attached to the British camp, he was the only animal strong enough to carry the durbar tent, the great reception tent essential to Lord Auckland for the entertainment of native princes. The elephant's name, Dittoo had said, was Motu. Such an elephant as Motu, Dittoo had added, was born only once in a hundred years.

Rain was Motu's sole enemy. The tent, an enormous weight when dry, became an intolerable burden after a soaking rain. As it was unthinkable for the Governor-General to

11

be without his durbar tent, and as Motu was unable to carry it more than one day's march at a time, the elephant was never left behind. If Motu could not carry his burden, Lord Auckland and his spinster sisters, the British government of India, ten thousand soldiers, thirty-odd thousand government officials, shopkeepers, servants and coolies and countless pack animals waited, squatting in the mud, until he could.

Mariana reached the muddy space and swept to a stop, craning to see over the pushing, half-naked coolies. A few of them turned to look at her. Oh, please let the big elephant be able to carry his load! She could not bear any more delays in the journey; she was on pins and needles to meet Ranjit Singh, the legendary Sikh ruler of the Punjab.

From where she stood, she could see nothing. Hesitating only a moment, she plunged into the crowd.

'*Hattho, hattho*, move out,' she ordered, and the coolies obliged, pushing against each other to open a narrow pathway through their ranks.

She was nearly there. Ahead of her, someone called out orders. An animal grunted. Staccato shouting erupted nearby. An elephant's trunk waved in the air. She had never looked closely at this elephant. How high would twelve feet be? Would he be strong enough to lift the wet tent even after—

'Miss Givens! *Miss Givens!*'

Mariana froze in mid-step. A fair-haired Englishman had appeared, standing on a bale of baggage a short distance away. He waved a blue uniformed arm.

She could not avoid him. Collecting herself, she waved in return. The mist had now become a soft rain once again, which soaked through the shoulders of her gown and joined the moisture on her skin. Why, if she must be caught alone outdoors, mingling with half-naked coolies at six in the morning, must she be caught by Lieutenant Fitzgerald of the Bengal Horse Artillery, the first man she had liked in the whole camp? What would he think of her?

She braced herself and started towards him, tucking a damp strand of hair into her bonnet as she walked. Should she avert her unwashed face from his when she reached him? No, it was too late for that.

Fitzgerald and a dozen young officers had been invited three evenings before to the Governor-General's dining tent, and were all, therefore, suitable marriage prospects. Fitzgerald had sat across from her at dinner. Mariana had seen immediately that he was a possibility, with his square, handsome face and high, Roman nose, his hair smoothed unfashionably back with pomade. After the soup he had put back his head to laugh at someone's remark, and that gesture, the angle of his head, the shape of his mouth, had caught her eye. Later, risking a glance, she had noticed him looking at her speculatively over the chicken fricassee. His expression gave nothing away but his look had excited and disturbed her. For the rest of dinner she had laboured to converse with the man beside her, rationing her glances across the table, but Fitzgerald had not met her eyes again.

'Miss Givens,' Fitzgerald called again, frowning as he climbed down from his bale, smart in his uniform, 'surely you should not be here. If you will wait a moment, I shall escort you to your tent.'

'Thank you, Lieutenant,' Mariana shouted back, over the crowd's noise, 'but I also have come to see the elephant.'

As she approached him, he looked at the front of her gown, then glanced hastily away. She glanced down and saw a telltale bubble of cloth poking up where she had missed a button. Her

13

whole gown must be buttoned wrong. Her hair was coming loose from her bonnet. She bit her lip and raised her eyes to find him smiling at her.

He offered his hand. 'If you have come to see the elephant,' he said, 'you had better climb up here with me. This promises to be interesting.'

She scrambled to the top of the bale, breathing in the rain-soaked mustiness of his uniform, feeling the warm pressure of his fingers.

Steadying her by her elbow, Fitzgerald pointed. 'There he is.'

Mariana looked out over the heads of the crowd and drew in her breath. In front of them, ringed by coolies, a massive bull elephant struggled to rise to his feet, the Governor-General's rolled-up durbar tent creaking and swaying on his back. A mahout straddled the elephant's neck, beating at the huge head with an iron prod, shouting at him in Bengali, while the crowd, already liberally splashed with mud, argued and laid wagers. Ignoring them all, the elephant steadied himself while he searched for purchase in the glassy mud, then, with a fearful, trembling effort, heaved his tottering burden upwards.

At the last instant, a great hind leg gave way. Mariana felt Fitzgerald stiffen beside her. The coolies stilled, then groaned as, overbalanced by the sodden canvas, the elephant rolled, squealing, onto his side, scattering the coolies like so many chickens and sending his mahout scrambling.

What a perfect scene for today's letter to her father! Mariana turned to Fitzgerald, her face alight. 'This is what I like about India – real Indian things, not imitation English things. We try so hard to be English, with our tents and food and furniture, but it doesn't—'

'I'm sorry, Miss Givens,' Fitzgerald interrupted, letting go of her elbow, his gaze travelling past her as if he were looking for someone, 'but I must inform General Cotton at once of the elephant's failure.' He swung himself to the ground and held up a hand, looking both military and apologetic. 'Allow me to help you down.'

She looked at the elephant a moment longer, pressing the sight of him into her memory, then took the hand Fitzgerald offered.

When she reached the ground, he raised an elbow to take her arm. 'I must see you to your tent, Miss Givens. It's too far for you to walk alone.'

His hair gleamed as he bent to her. He had missed a spot on his cheek while shaving. His eyes, like hers, were green. He smiled crookedly.

Tempted to accept, Mariana hesitated. In the ten minutes it would take to reach her tent, they would converse. She could learn much about him in ten minutes; but what of the toppled elephant that breathed harshly behind her in the mud, the tent still roped to a wooden frame on his back? Could he get up again? Was he hurt? Dear Papa, waiting at home in Sussex for her letters, must be told.

'That is kind of you, Lieutenant,' she replied, 'but I shall stay here a moment longer. I wish to have a word with this elephant's driver.'

Fitzgerald took his arm away. 'A word with his mahout?' he repeated, frowning. 'But how can you – ah, of course, you speak their languages.' He hesitated. 'But I should not leave you alone here.' He looked over his shoulder, as if seeking help. 'Surely it is not a good idea.'

Mariana planted her feet in the mud. 'I came here alone, Lieutenant Fitzgerald,' she pointed out. 'But I'm sure,' she added, looking him full in the face, 'that we shall see one another again soon.' She glanced away, certain she had held his gaze too long.

He hesitated, then bowed. 'I am flattered that you remember my name, Miss Givens. And you will be all right here?'

Mariana nodded, her lips pressed together, then offered him her wide, impulsive smile.

He smiled in return. 'Then I shall tell no one I have seen you.'

When she looked back, he had gone.

The crowd was thinning as she made her way to the mahout. The elephant still lay on his side, weighed down by the sodden tent, a grey mountain with one visible, bloodshot eye. The mahout moved around him, crooning as he went, a large, wicked-looking knife in his hand, slicing a rope here and a strap there, expertly loosening the animal's load.

He started when Mariana cleared her throat. He was smaller than she was, and wiry. His shoulders moved awkwardly when he greeted her, as if he were unused to foreigners.

'What is your elephant's name?' she asked, in her slow, unaccented Urdu. Being English, she was entitled to be imperious. She chose to be civil.

'It is Motu, Memsahib,' he replied over his elephant's whistling breath, departing from his own language to answer her. His face was deeply seamed. The whites of his eyes were the colour of old ivory.

She nodded. 'Motu. And yours?'

'Hira Lal.'

Behind Hira, the elephant twitched and raised his trunk. Without an apology, the mahout turned from Mariana and went back to his work.

Well then, she would speak to his back. She raised her

16

voice. 'Why are you cutting all the ropes? Won't they be angry with you?'

'What do I care for their ropes?' Hira's fingers shook as he cut through a thick leather strap. 'I told them we should not try to move the tent today.' His own voice rose. 'I told them Motu would fall. I warned them of the danger to Motu.'

'Danger?' Mariana took a step closer. 'What danger?'

Hira made one last cut and the load fell away like a huge, cold sausage. Motu lay still for a moment, then rolled onto his knees, the empty frame still tied to his back.

The little man turned to face Mariana. She could not imagine how he could bear the chill, wearing only a loincloth and a strip of worn cotton. He was covered, from his carelessly tied turban to his bare feet, in the pungent smell of elephant. 'An elephant's spine is delicate,' he told her. 'If something causes the load to shift, the frame may press upon the spine. Such accidents cripple or kill elephants. An elephant must never fall when loaded.' Now that his face had relaxed, Mariana saw how frightened he had been.

At Hira's command, Motu lumbered to his feet and towered above them both. It was the unusual length of his legs, like four great tree trunks, that made Motu so tall. While Mariana watched, he bent his front legs and lowered his face to his mahout. Hira Lal spread his arms and took hold of the two great ears, then set one foot high on the elephant's trunk, mounted in one sinuous motion and seated himself twelve feet above the ground.

'How long have you been his mahout?' Mariana tilted her head up to him, a hand on her bonnet, not wanting them to leave.

'Since he was small,' Hira replied. The heavy elephant prod

17

appeared in his hand. 'I hope,' he said, 'that we die at the same time. We are used to one another.'

Shivering at the thought, she turned back towards the avenue.

So Dittoo had been right about the elephant's name, Fatty. Perhaps Motu had been a little tub when he was small, like her baby nephew Freddie. Whatever the elephant had been then, he was now immense, grey and wrinkled and covered with coarse, black hairs. Mariana sighed aloud. She would never have enough of elephants.

Freddie must have changed in the year since she had left England. He had been an energetic, sticky-faced little creature then, with pudgy feet and a halo of golden hair standing up all over his head. By now he would be nearing his third birthday.

A large puddle of shiny mud blocked her way. Mariana stopped and stared at it, as the breeze sent a little shower of rain onto its surface. Freddie would be five in two years, the same age her brother had been when he died.

Poor little Ambrose. He had been playful one day, hot and agonized the next, and gone for ever soon after that. For a long time after he died, she had thought she would never recover.

From the moment of his birth, Ambrose had been in her charge. At eight, her sashes untied and dangling at her sides, she had walked the gravel paths in the garden with him in her arms. When he had begun to speak, it had been she who translated his first words. 'He wants another potato, Mama,' she would say. 'He wants to pat the dog.' Later, Ambrose had been her curly-haired companion. He had followed her everywhere, never telling her, as others did, that she was untidy, or too noisy, or that she talked too much. She had shown him her private hiding places in the garden, and they had crouched

18

together beneath the bushes, their clothes speckled with burrs, while she spun stories for him of talking frogs and fairies who lived at the bottom of the garden.

Holding her skirts aside, she circled the mud puddle, ignoring the stiffening breeze. She had been twelve, her sister Charlotte fourteen, when Ambrose died. Whenever she thought of that time, she remembered her mother and her Aunt Rachel standing grim-faced and exhausted at the door to the bedroom where he lay, quiet now, in the sleep that precedes death.

'Come inside,' Mama had said to Mariana and her sister, 'and bid your brother goodbye.'

Together, the two girls had tiptoed to his bedside and found him snoring, his mouth open, his little face wasted, his head, shaved against typhoid fever, ugly and stark upon the pillow. Certain that he would open his eyes for her, Mariana had reached down and taken his hand, but he had not awakened, and his small fingers had felt empty of life. Realizing the truth, sick with pain and fear, she had dropped to her knees and thrown her arms about his small body. 'Do not die, Ambrose, *please*,' she had wailed, while Charlotte sobbed beside her.

Mariana pushed chilled hands into her sleeves as she made her way to the avenue. Ambrose had not been the first to die. Two other Givens children had been lost to measles when Mariana was four: Colin at two, Rachel at six months. She did not remember them well, although she did recall her panic when, after her own slow recovery, she had noticed the silence in the nursery.

The lost children were never mentioned, and Mariana had never seen her mother weep for them. White-faced and trembling, Mama had not wept for Ambrose either. Her silence terrified Mariana, who thought it meant she was to

19

blame. And why not? Talkative and clumsy, she had gone on living while the precious babies had all died.

'But why must we be brave?' Crumpled on a chair before the sitting-room fire, Mariana had searched her mother's still face for consolation and forgiveness. 'Why may I not cry for Ambrose when my heart is broken?'

Her mother's clasped hands had tightened. 'Because, Mariana,' she had said before turning away, 'what we need at times like these are resignation and fortitude. Weeping will only make us ill.'

Her hollow-eyed father had smiled wanly. 'We must sustain ourselves,' he had added, 'with the knowledge that God is good.'

From that day, they had rarely spoken of Ambrose. While Charlotte tried to behave normally, Mariana had trailed about the garden alone, weeping painfully in the hiding places where she and Ambrose had played, Ambrose who had thought her perfect, who had smacked his lips as he watched her spread strawberry jam on his scones.

She kept his favourite wooden soldier, hiding it by day and sleeping with it by night. The sight of strawberry jam sent her sobbing from the dining table.

She found herself noticing other people's pain. She burst into the kitchen and flung herself into the arms of a scullery maid whose sister had died. She often said awkward, truthful things. Mama and Aunt Rachel had fumed at her odd behaviour. Only Papa never said a cross word to her, dear Papa to whom her heart went out even now, as she stood beside the avenue in the rain. Absorbed in his work, he had not understood the deadly swiftness of Ambrose's illness. He had not expected his young son to die.

But now there was little Freddie. Perhaps Charlotte's son

would take Ambrose's place in her Papa's heart. One day, perhaps, Mariana's own babies would do the same for her.

That, of course, would be soon, if her mother in England, her Aunt Claire in Calcutta, and the matchmaking Miss Emily had their wish.

'It is my plan, Fanny,' Miss Emily had said confidentially to her younger sister a week ago as they waited to be handed into the dining tent, unaware that Mariana had moved up behind them, 'to have Mariana meet *every* unmarried officer in camp. They shall sit beside her by turns. If I have my way we shall have a wedding before long.'

Miss Emily's enthusiasm, thought Mariana, must be gratifying to Mama who waited patiently at home in Sussex for news. She herself found it maddening.

'One year,' Mama had said as she packed a newly stitched gown into the largest of Mariana's three trunks, 'is all you shall have until the next lot of unmarried girls arrives in Calcutta. I hope and pray that, in that time, you find a suitable match. If not, people will think you shopworn. It will be too late.'

A string of camels, padding along the avenue at the same speed as the man who led them, their brass ankle bells chinking, blocked Mariana's way. She tapped a fretful foot, impatient to get across the avenue and inside the guarded entrance before she was seen again.

Since her arrival from England, India, not marriage, had absorbed Mariana's attention. Now, her year nearly over, she must find a husband. Lest she forget, letters warning of approaching doom arrived every third day in the mail pouch from her Aunt Claire in Calcutta.

Mariana was only too aware of the progress of the other potential brides who had arrived with her last winter. Aunt Claire's most recent letter had described the engagement of the

21

plainest of them, a Miss Finchley, who had made a surprisingly good match, while one of the prettier girls had become ill with smallpox, and was expected to be disfigured for life by the scars.

'They are sending her home.' Miss Emily had shaken her head as Mariana folded Aunt Claire's letter away. 'What a pity. I understand Miss Ranier was a lovely girl, with every chance of success. Now, if she is fortunate, she will live her life out of a trunk, a kind maiden aunt to one family member after another. If not, she will be forced to hire herself out as a governess.'

Miss Emily had sighed. 'How suddenly things change.'

The camels were still passing. Mariana fidgeted on the avenue's edge. Her year was nearly over and she was not yet engaged, but her position was most enviable, nonetheless. The great moving camp, her home for the past three weeks, was also temporary home to more than half the British government and all but a handful of Calcutta's British-born army officers, most of whom were young and unmarried. It was a good thing, as both Miss Emily and Aunt Claire had pointed out. Had Mariana been one of a hundred girls with only one available man, she would have had no chance, with her inquisitiveness, her untidiness and her unconventional behaviour. Yes, Mama had echoed in her letters from Sussex, what chance would Mariana have, with her unmanageable curls, her too-wide smile, her square shoulders?

But there were disadvantages to being the only young lady among so many eager men. Jaded by too much choice, she now noticed only their missing teeth, their protruding ears, their desire to please her. Her dinner partner last night had looked so exactly like a white rabbit that she had barely been able to make conversation.

Miss Emily and her sister, of course, had their own opinions. They seemed more interested in the men's qualities than in Mariana's affections. Miss Emily's possibility was a lively man with an odd-shaped head whose family was reported to be very generous. 'We must remember, Mariana,' Miss Emily had pointed out, 'that most of these men are second or third sons.' Miss Fanny's favourite was a tall, lugubrious person who had a habit of bursting into tears. 'Nothing,' Miss Fanny had observed, 'is more important in a husband than a kind heart.'

They both liked the White Rabbit.

The camels had gone by. Mariana lifted her skirts and began to dash across the avenue just as a European on horseback appeared suddenly from between two tents.

She stopped hurriedly. Major Byrne, officer in charge of the camp and chief protocol officer, pulled abreast of her, a stout figure, upright in the saddle. His black boot shone at the level of her chest. Spiked brass spurs caught the sun.

He gazed meaningfully down a ruddy nose, first at the departing elephant, then at Mariana. 'Good morning, Miss Givens,' he drawled. 'Out for a walk this morning, are you?' His eyes drifted to the front of her gown.

'Yes indeed, Major Byrne,' she replied. She forced a smile as heat rose to her face. Water dripped from the rim of her bonnet.

He returned her nod with a sharp little one of his own, then spurred his horse and rode away down the avenue, his horse's tail flicking.

She kicked up an arc of mud with the toe of her boot. Why should it matter to Byrne that her gown was buttoned all wrong? Her chin high, she hurried across the avenue. She would cross the avenue when she wanted to. She would look at elephants or speak to mahouts when she chose to. *They* might expect her to sit all morning in her damp little tent staring at the walls, but she would not. She could make no new discoveries for herself and Papa by looking at the openings in those walls, to Dittoo's corridor, to her cramped bathing space, to the space where, terrified of the sudden appearance of Dittoo or the sweeper, she gripped the inner and outer curtains closed while using her chamber pot.

Who was fat Major Byrne to be superior? She did not make honking noises the way he did when he thought no one was listening. She had not missed the honk he gave just now as he rode away. And what of his friend William Macnaghten, who had given her the post of lady translator, with his great bushy eyebrows and his habit of studying his tongue in a pocket mirror? What was wrong with them all?

Lieutenant Fitzgerald, at least, had understood. She marched past the sentries at the gate, her nose at a severe angle. 'Dittoo,' she snapped as she entered her tent, 'bring my riding habit, and tell the grooms to saddle one of the mares.'

Chapter Two

Miss Emily had instructed Mariana to take at least two grooms with her whenever she went out riding. Although she hated being followed on foot over miles of ground, Mariana did not send her trio of underfed youths away at once; but out of deference to Miss Emily, she allowed them to trot behind her past the large tents of senior government officials, past office tents and veterinary tents, until she had reached the horse lines at the avenue's end. There, she reined in her mare and sent her attendants off.

At the lines, hundreds of animals stood tethered in long, orderly rows, tended by a host of natives. Between the horses, guinea hens, natural enemies of snakes, picked at the muddy ground.

Mariana watched the dark-skinned grooms going about their work, wrapped in lengths of cloth against the chill. Her favourite, a tall, bony-faced senior groom, saluted her as he strode by, leading a mare with a cut on her neck. Mariana always looked for the tall groom when she came to the lines. He never hurried and he rarely spoke, but there was something about him that drew her attention. Whatever it was, the other grooms felt it too; they treated him with great respect, although he did not seem to notice.

She sighed. What could be more different from home than this place! Try as she might, she could never capture in her letters one-tenth of what she had seen and smelled of India. Everything was strange here, the sudden dawns and dusks, the feel of the air, the taste of everything.

Modelled after the legendary camps of the Moghul emperors who travelled with their governments, armies, wives and slaves, the British camp was at once grand, complicated and squalid. Mariana never tired of its myriad lanes and tents, its colourful, noisy bazaars. With a population of only forty-odd thousand, it scarcely compared to a Moghul emperor's camp, which, she had learned, would have been three times as large. Nevertheless, the British tents stretched for several miles over what was now a sea of mud broken only by an occasional ruin or stand of thorn trees.

The camp's departure for the Sikh kingdom had taken place at Calcutta the previous October. Mariana, newly added to the Governor-General's party, had missed that exciting event as well as the first six months of the camp's travels. What information she had about the journey came from dinner-table conversation and from Lord Auckland's sisters, both of whom had pointed out that having suffered the journey once already, they had no need to suffer it a second time in recollection.

The camp travelled, as the earlier camps had, at the rate of ten miles a day. Each morning at 6 a.m. sharp, as the last trunks were being loaded onto wagons and pack animals, Lord Auckland and his sisters left for the next campsite, travelling in a carriage in fine weather, in closed palanquins carried by bearers if there was a threat of rain. After some three hours of hard, cross-country travel, they would arrive at the next campsite where, barring disaster, their breakfast, sent ahead in the night, waited for them in the spare dining tent.

Blue smoke from cooking fires hung in the air. Suddenly hungry, Mariana sniffed, enjoying the scent of charcoal and unfamiliar spices. But, hungry or not, she should not expect a lovely breakfast at nine o'clock. By now the breakfast wagons, their drivers alerted by runners, would be on their creaking way back with the brioches and the smoked duck, and would arrive too late to do any good.

On the march, travelling as she did with the Governor-General's own party, Mariana had no need to fend for herself in the great procession that followed after them, prodded by professional camp drummers. Ill or well, in whatever conveyance they could find, everyone else in camp, from the most senior official to the lowliest sweeper, rushed to stay ahead of the dust or mud thrown up by ten regiments of marching soldiers and by the baggage train with its straining bullock teams, laden camels, quick-moving donkeys, and elephants hauling artillery and wagons full of grapeshot and cannonballs.

Thanks to the efforts of thousands of coolies, the camp reconstituted itself at each new site within hours of arriving, with every shop and servant's quarter in its appointed place, and the grand avenue, as if by some miracle, exactly as long and as wide as it had been the day before.

It had taken from October until the end of March for the camp to make the journey from Calcutta to the northwest corner of British India. There, when the raging heat of summer overtook the tents, Lord Auckland, his sisters and his senior officers had abandoned the army and the baggage train to their own devices and travelled up to the hill station at Simla to rest from their journey in rose-covered cottages and entertain themselves with dinners, fêtes and theatricals. It was there that Mariana had made their acquaintance and had been invited to join the Governor-General's party.

Now November had arrived, with its cooler days and balmy evenings, and the camp was travelling once again. Its final destination, Firozpur on the British side of the Sutlej River, was now only fifty miles away. Across the Sutlej, which marked the northwestern border of British India, stood the independent kingdom of the Punjab, home to the old Lion of the Punjab, Maharajah Ranjit Singh, who even now waited on the border at his own lavish camp for the British to arrive.

In less than a week, the camp's long journey would end, and the great durbar would begin: the state meeting for which Lord Auckland, his government and his army had travelled so far. At the end of the durbar, after many military reviews, dinners and entertainments, the moment would arrive when Lord Auckland and the Maharajah signed the treaty sealing their agreement to combine the British and Sikh armies, and together, or 'hand in hand' as the Maharajah had put it, conquer Afghanistan.

Mariana clucked to her little mare. Leaving the horse lines behind her, she began to cross the two miles of open plain separating the British government and army camps. For the next weeks, news of the durbar and the Afghan Campaign would fill the letters she wrote to Papa, while her letters to her mother and her sister Charlotte would be full of the doings of Lord Auckland and his sisters, and of her own prospects of marriage.

She yawned. Her family. The warming air felt moist. She reached up and undid the top button of her riding habit. Today was Sunday, and it was Sundays she thought of when she thought of home, Sunday lunch in the vicarage dining room with its tall windows and everyone at table.

'*Thin* slices please, Wilfrid,' her mother would say in her penetrating voice, as Papa carved the mutton, while at the end of the table Mariana's sister Charlotte exchanged glances with her husband, and baby Freddie squeaked in his little chair beside them.

Perhaps it had been the sight of Charlotte and Spencer, happily married with a son, that had prompted Mariana's mother to send her to India.

'She is nearly nineteen, Lydia,' Aunt Rachel had said a year and a half ago, her taffetas rustling as she and Mama spoke privately in the small sitting room. 'This corner of Sussex has no one to offer but poor Mr Bertram with his four little girls and young what's-his-name who has that dreadful stammer. We have no connections elsewhere, like other families. We all know Mariana's looks are far from fashionable, and much as I love him, her father can give her no fortune. India is full of ambitious young men. Send Mariana to Calcutta, to Claire and Adrian. Her bad habits will matter less there.'

'I suppose you're right, Rachel.' Mama's voice had dropped. From her listening post in the passage, Mariana held her breath.

Renewed rustling meant Aunt Rachel had drawn herself upright on her favourite straight-backed chair. 'Of course I am right. The girl's tactlessness is legendary. Who can ignore her remark about your cousin's twin babies, "two misshapen peas in a single pod", at church, in front of their grandmother? And what of the frights she has given us? What of the time she disappeared when she was sixteen, and came home hours later covered in mud, saying she had fallen into the river?'

'Please, Rachel,' Mama said quietly. 'I thought we had agreed never to mention that awful time again.'

'Of course, Lydia.' Mariana imagined her aunt waving an impatient hand. 'But what of her curiosity? Do you know that Mariana *listens behind doors?*'

29

'Yes, Rachel, I do.' Her mother's sigh washed over Mariana's hiding place.

Mariana did, indeed, listen behind doors. She had done so ever since the summer after they had buried Ambrose, when she had gone to her father's study to tell him dinner was ready.

It had grown late, and he had not appeared at the table. Sent to call him, Mariana rushed across the passage in her usual headlong way, then stopped abruptly, horrified at the sounds coming from behind his closed study door. She had always believed that her father never cried; now his surreptitious, muffled sobbing cut her to the bone. 'My boy, my poor little Ambrose,' he moaned, over and over.

Mariana crept away to tell her mother that Papa was busy and would be coming presently, but the sound of his sobs never left her. From that day, she had never entered a room without first listening outside.

The week after her conversation with Aunt Rachel, Mama broached the subject of India, looking hard at Mariana between rapid jerks of her knife as they cut delphiniums for the front hall.

'I do not know what I shall do without you, my child, in spite of all the trouble you give me,' she announced in her ringing tone, causing two men in the kitchen garden to look up from their hoes, 'but your Aunt Rachel is right. Young ladies do go out to India these days, properly chaperoned, of course. It really is the best thing for you, considering your prospects here.' She shook her head. 'If you had blue eyes and a neat, rosebud mouth like your sister, things might have been different. I know your father finds that great, broad smile of yours enchanting, but subtlety is now the order of the day. As for your hair . . .' She pointed her knife towards the house. 'If you stay here, Mariana, you will spend your life changing the

30

flowers and the library books. Claire and Adrian have not seen you since you were Freddie's age. Having you there will give them pleasure. After all, they have no children of their own. Go to India, darling, and give yourself a chance.'

India. The East. Until that moment, for all Aunt Rachel's advice, Mariana had never pictured herself sailing to India to marry someone there, and perhaps never return. But now that it was to happen, India began to beckon her. There she would start anew, her slate wiped clean, free of the troubles of her past, and of the restrictions of English village life.

During the following six months, while they waited for Aunt Claire and Uncle Adrian's response to her father's letter, Mariana, already missing her family, showered sudden kisses on Mama, Charlotte and little Freddie.

'For goodness' sake, girl,' Mama said, patting Mariana's back, 'stop flinging yourself at everyone. You haven't gone yet.'

But as much as she loved them all, it was the thought of being parted from her dear, soft-hearted Papa that troubled Mariana most.

'I shall miss you dreadfully, my darling,' he had said on her last day, taking her hands in his own large ones, and looking sadly at the three trunks standing ready to be loaded onto the carriage. 'You must remember that we are here, and that we will always love you.'

How would Papa manage without her? Since Ambrose's death, who besides her had undertaken to make him happy? Mama, bearing her loss in tight-lipped silence, had been useless to him. Charlotte, trying her best to be brave, had been too preoccupied to notice his misery. It had been Mariana who had taken it upon herself to cheer her father. She had found a path to his heart in his passion for military strategy, all that

31

now remained of a thwarted military ambition, squashed by his clergyman father twenty-five years earlier. She had read the books in his study and pored over battle plans. When she found him pale and distracted, she talked of the great battles: Marathon, Hastings, Waterloo. Later, as their bond and her own interest grew, she mastered other battles. At the age of fifteen she horrified Aunt Rachel by discussing the Battle of Agincourt in the garden with her father and a gentleman neighbour.

It was Mariana, too, who appreciated her father's sermons.

'How do you expect,' Aunt Rachel had said after church on Mariana's last Sunday at home, 'to inspire people like Miss Pringle and Mrs Brownley to Christian works by citing Alexander the Great, Wilfrid? What do you mean by instructing them always to "attack the enemy's strongest sector"?'

As Aunt Rachel shook her head, Mariana and Papa had exchanged their special look for the last time.

When she was sixteen, Papa, in turn, had kept her secret after Jeremy Harfield nearly drowned in the river.

Jeremy, a tall boy in labourer's homespun, had been picking apart a rope with his fingers when she chanced upon him on one of her solitary rambles along the riverbank.

'Caulking my boat,' he had replied, when she asked what he was doing. He pointed to a little dinghy that bobbed beside him in the weeds. 'I'm stuffing fibre into the cracks to keep the water out.'

Jeremy was only a raw village lad, but she was glad to see him occasionally, glad of the smile he gave her when she appeared, hatless, on the path. He said he did not mind her questions. He seemed to enjoy her company.

One day, several weeks after they first met, he looked up

when she came but did not smile. 'My sister Emma died last evening,' he said simply, after a moment's silence.

Mariana put a fist to her mouth. 'Oh,' was all she could say before her own remembered pain overtook her, and she began to cry, afraid Jeremy would think her weak but unable to stop herself.

He swallowed. 'Three days ago she was took badly,' he added, watching Mariana rub her wet face with her knuckles. 'She had delicate lungs, you see. The doctor came, but it was no use. She died in my mum's lap. She was only two.' He dropped his eyes. 'She was a tiny little thing. I used to wrap her in my muffler when she felt cold.'

Mariana snuffled wetly. 'I'm sorry to weep like this,' she quavered, 'especially when you're being so brave, but I can't help thinking of my brother Ambrose. He died when he was five. I loved him so much.'

'I'm sorry about your brother.' He smiled crookedly. 'I don't mind if you weep. Perhaps you are doing my weeping for me. In any case, I feel better now.'

They met daily after that. A week later, the dinghy was ready. Mariana helped him to push it into the current, then climbed in and sat watching him pull on the oars.

The world looked different from the middle of the river. As he rowed, they talked of heaven, imagining it full of fat babies and small children, and stocked with every possible treat and pleasure. 'I hope to see Emma there one day,' Jeremy said softly.

'And I my brother Ambrose,' she replied.

Forgetting the time, they stayed too long. The sun was setting when Jeremy rowed hurriedly to an overhanging willow tree, then stood up to hand Mariana to the bank. In her haste to scramble out, she overbalanced the little dinghy, causing it to rock wildly. Jeremy cried out, then, arms flailing, was over the side.

Where there had been warmth and enjoyment, now there was only chaos. Why had she jumped so dangerously from the boat? Why had she not guessed that he, a poor labourer, could not swim?

A willow branch stretched over the water, out of his reach. 'Wait,' she called. Her heart hammering, she climbed onto the branch and crawled unsteadily out, fighting her hindering skirts, gasping as she slipped sideways.

Jeremy had stopped struggling. He floated, his arms outstretched before him, his open mouth half submerged in the moving water. Almost too frightened to breathe, Mariana worked her way out along the branch, twigs catching in her hair, sharp pieces of bark tearing the skin from her hands.

The branch dipped treacherously as she reached Jeremy, threatening to tip her into the river beside him. 'Here, Jeremy,' she gasped, reaching out to him while the skirt of her dress trailed in the water, 'catch hold of my hand!'

Somehow, he did. One hand gripping the creaking branch, she tugged him towards her, then crawled shakily backwards as he followed, pulling himself hand over hand towards the safety of the bank.

Later, they sat, panting, among the willow roots. Mariana's clothes, like Jeremy's, were sodden and filthy, but she felt giddy with relief, unbearably happy that they were both safe.

'You look awful,' she said happily, digging him in the ribs with her elbow.

Although his teeth had begun to chatter, he put his head back and laughed aloud.

After her mother had astonished Mariana by bursting into great gulping sobs of relief when she arrived home, chilled and bedraggled, her father called her into his study, then shut the door.

'Early this evening,' he said gravely, 'while walking along the river, one of my parishioners thought he heard someone drowning. He rushed to help, but found that the rescue had already taken place. The victim, a young labourer in dripping clothes, was on his knees, being sick into the river. You were sitting beside him, patting him on the back.'

There was no point in lying.

'Mariana,' her father said gravely, when she had finished her story, 'you are sixteen, and coming out into society. It is most unsuitable for you to be seen with young labourers. I shall not tell your mother of this,' he added, 'but you must promise me that you will never see Harfield again.'

Never see him again? 'But Papa,' she begged, 'Jeremy is my friend. *Please* don't make me give him up.'

He sighed. 'You have a natural curiosity, Mariana, and a quick sympathy for others, but you act far too rashly. You should have known that a friendship like this one would only end in loss. From what you have told me, it was your own hastiness in getting out of the boat that nearly killed the lad. But I must say you showed quick thinking in a crisis. I believe you saved his life.' He smiled wistfully. 'I should not mind having you beside me in battle.'

Mariana kept her promise, and did not return to the riverbank. A few months later she came upon Jeremy on his knees, rebuilding a stone wall in the village. She nodded carefully, and he returned her nod.

It had not occurred to her then to disobey her father's orders, but by the time she reached home, Mariana was so angry with herself that she barely spoke to anyone for the rest of the day.

35

In bed that night she vowed she would never again give up someone she cared for.

A year later, she was leaning on the rail of the *Marchioness of Ely*, watching the English coast glide past, wondering how she would survive the dreary invalid lady who was to chaperone her on the voyage out. After more than three months of listening to Mrs Sumter describe her headaches and her choking feeling, it had been a huge relief to get off the ship and throw herself into Aunt Claire's arms.

After Sussex, Calcutta had seemed tantalizing, wordly and exciting. In spite of the increasingly hot weather and the absence of Lord Auckland and his camp, there had been no slowing of the customary social round. As one of a dozen newly arrived English girls, Mariana found herself invited to everything.

'It is your skin, my dear,' Aunt Claire explained as she inspected Mariana's appearance before a ball. 'Fresh, rosy skin is admired here more than anything else. Our skin turns yellow in this climate, you see. A few good agues and, pouf, you are primrose! Mrs Warrenton next door has survived here for fifty years. That is why she is orange.' She pursed her lips. 'We must get you one or two new gowns. People will talk if you repeat too often.'

Determined to supply her father with interesting letters, Mariana had begun immediately to investigate India. Her imagination afire, she had questioned everyone she met about the natives but had found, to her astonishment, that no one wanted to tell her anything. Calcutta, she began to discover, was as rigid as Weddington Village. Her new life was to be exactly the same as before, only it was to take place in the heat and humidity of the East.

'It's no use, Aunt Claire,' she said crossly a month later, before the third dinner in four days. 'I *hate* Calcutta parties. I

36

have met every eligible man for miles. Not one of them knows a thing about India. All they talk of is their horses and their promotions. The thought of marrying any one of them gives me a headache.'

'Don't be silly, Mariana. The other young ladies like them well enough.' Aunt Claire frowned. 'Do you think you should wear the blue tonight? I think you've worn the rose already this week.'

'And the ladies do nothing but gossip.'

Aunt Claire raised her eyebrows. 'And why not? What else is there to do? Of course you must go to parties. There will be other men. How are you to meet them if you stay at home? And stop fidgeting, Mariana, or I shall stab you with this brooch.'

Later, when Mariana asked to be taken to the native part of the city, Aunt Claire's hand flew to her breast. 'You are not to go there, my child!' she cried. 'Mrs Warrenton's niece insisted on seeing the native city. She was next seen being carried on board a ship for home, swathed in bandages!'

Kind, balding Uncle Adrian took out a map of Bangalore and showed Mariana the route he had taken as a young district officer in the south, travelling from village to village with a tent and a writing table, settling disputes, but he would not upset his wife by taking Mariana to see the natives.

Her efforts to learn about the Black Hole of Calcutta also failed. When she asked an elderly general to describe the tactical errors leading to the disaster, he reacted with horror. 'He treated me,' she complained to her Uncle Adrian, 'as if I had committed murder.'

'One hundred and twenty-three people suffocated in that awful little room,' Uncle Adrian replied. 'It happened a long time ago, and we should have recovered by now, but we have not. If I were you, I should not mention it again.'

'But,' Mariana had almost shouted, 'if we insist upon forgetting them, how can we learn from our mistakes?'

At the outskirts of the army camp, Mariana stopped near a row of nine-pound cannon and shaded her eyes, studying the heavy guns. For all she knew they might be Fitzgerald's.

A troop of native cavalry had stopped to rest in the shade of the gun carriages, their mounts tied to the spoked wheels. Their hairy, buck-toothed officer stared at Mariana as if she were a mirage.

The officer's hungry gaze made her more uncomfortable than the curious stares of the native cavalrymen. She tugged on the reins and turned back towards the horse lines of her own camp.

She reached up under her wisp of veil and wiped her forehead. What an adventure this was, and all because of what had happened twelve hundred miles away in Calcutta, one summer afternoon.

Sitting idly in her window one stifling morning, Mariana had noticed a piece of cloth lying on the ground near Uncle Adrian's front gate. Being the exact colour of the earth on which it lay, the cloth had been nearly invisible, but when it moved slightly, the motion caught Mariana's eye. Ignoring Aunt Claire's instructions to stay indoors until lunchtime, she went outside to investigate.

When she reached it, she saw that the cloth was about the size of a bath towel. Lifting one corner, she found underneath it a creature that must once have been human. She could not determine if the thing was male or female. All she could see in that horrifying moment were contorted black limbs and a death's head face, the lips drawn back in a toothless grimace.

Disturbed, the creature looked up at her through runny eyes and made one gesture, an unmistakable request for water.

She turned and raced into the house in search of a servant to send outside with something for it to drink, but the kitchen was empty. Banging about in the pantry, she found one of Aunt Claire's glass tumblers, filled it with water, and dashed back to the gate.

Mariana had not taken in the condition of the creature's hands. She saw as she offered the water that they were useless, bent double, the fingers twisted inward. Still, it sat up weakly and tried to grip the heavy glass between its wrists. The effort proved too great: with a little moan it fell helplessly back to the ground.

Mariana gritted her teeth. Having come this far, she refused to turn back. She held the glass out at arm's length and gestured for the creature to drink.

For what seemed an eternity, the creature gulped at the water, its neck extended. Then, water dribbling from its chin, it lay back on the dun-coloured dirt and began to speak. It spoke for some time, incomprehensibly, in some native language, its voice a thin whine. Finally, satisfied, it stopped speaking and closed its eyes.

Mariana was immobilized by the sound of its voice and overcome by a sudden desperate desire to know what it had said. She tore herself away and hurried, the glass still in her hand, to the tumbledown servants' quarters behind her uncle's house, where she stood in the dust shouting for Shivji, the servant who spoke English, to come at once and help her.

By the time Shivji emerged from his quarters and followed her to the front gate, there was no longer any sign of the cloth or the wretched thing that had lain under it. At her insistence Shivjii made a half-hearted effort to find it on the road, but returned to report that there was no sign of the creature she had described.

Aunt Claire ordered the tumbler to be smashed. 'It terrifies me to think,' she quavered from her pillow, after collapsing in the drawing room and being helped to bed, 'that native lips, and most especially those of a native in the condition you describe, have touched one of my own English tumblers. The thought of that particular one becoming confused with the others and my actually drinking from it has made me quite ill. How *could* you, Mariana?'

Even Uncle Adrian tried to sound cross. 'I know you only did it to be kind,' he told Mariana uncomfortably, 'but you must understand the danger of getting too close to some of the natives. There are those whom one may allow to come near, such as our own servants, but a creature like that one might easily have given you unmentionable diseases. Promise me you will never do such a heedless thing again.'

That evening, Mariana stood on the stairs listening to Aunt Claire and Uncle Adrian in the drawing room discussing taking her away from the 'bad air' of Calcutta.

'Yes, Simla,' Aunt Claire said, her voice so like Mama's carrying easily to all corners of the house. 'You can always do your work in the hills. You know how I hate travelling, especially such a great distance, but we must not remain one more day in Calcutta in this heat. It does not suit the girl. You know what she is like at the best of times, and now she has begun to behave even more oddly. I will never forgive myself if she does something mad and ruins her chances.'

Even more oddly? Ruin her chances? Mariana climbed the stairs and shut her door with a bang.

*   *   *

40

Four little girls walked in single file beside the rough path, heavy-looking bundles balanced on their heads. Mariana watched them from her mare, envying their grace.

How could she have guessed, when she and her uncle and aunt set out for Simla, that their stay would bear such interesting fruit?

One afternoon as Mariana and Aunt Claire sat drinking tea in the garden, Uncle Adrian had stepped from the verandah, pink-faced with pleasure, rubbing his hands together.

'The most extraordinary thing has happened,' he announced, pulling up a folding chair. 'I have rediscovered the old man who taught me native languages when I was a young man in Bangalore. He was passing in front of the church. I recognized him at once. He looks exactly the same, although it is nearly twenty years since I saw him last. He is a good man. I should never have mastered those languages without him.' He blinked and cleared his throat. 'Mariana,' he said, turning to her, a little frown between his eyes, 'would you like to study Indian languages with the old man while we are here?'

The creature from Uncle Adrian's garden appeared before Mariana's eyes, water dribbling from its mouth, telling her something she could not comprehend. She caught her breath.

'But my dear Adrian,' Aunt Claire protested, turning from her husband to Mariana and back again, her lace parasol clutched in one hand, 'the girl is not interested in studying any subject at all, far less native languages, are you, my darling?'

Mariana did not look at Aunt Claire. 'Yes, oh yes, *please*,' she breathed.

Uncle Adrian smiled at his wife. 'Here is an opportunity, my dear,' he said, 'for the girl to gain real knowledge instead of the silly nonsense one hears everywhere.' He leaned forward and put a hand on Mariana's sleeve. 'The old man will teach you

41

more than languages,' he said earnestly, his fingers closing on her wrist. 'He will teach you poetry. He will give you some understanding of how the best natives think. I know that no one believes it any longer, but one can, and should, learn a great deal from the best of the natives.'

Mariana nodded, unable to speak.

Her uncle stared at the far-off mountains. 'Things have changed since I first came out,' he said wistfully. 'I don't like this new, snobbish attitude towards the natives. They should not automatically be treated as inferiors, regardless of their station or their learning.' He pushed himself out of his chair. 'Mariana, the word for teacher is *munshi*. You should call your teacher Munshi Sahib. I know it is not done any longer, but you must do it. He is not a servant and should not be treated as one.'

He marched off, leaving Aunt Claire upright and quivering in one basket chair, and Mariana beaming in the other.

The following morning as she sat in the drawing room, Mariana heard her uncle greet someone, and realized that her new teacher had entered by the front, not the kitchen, door. A moment later, her uncle entered the room rubbing his hands, followed by a wispy old man.

'Mariana, my dear, this is your Munshi Sahib,' Uncle Adrian said, grandly, then stepped aside.

The munshi, who had removed his shoes outside the door, came forward and stood in his stockinged feet, facing Mariana's chair. His eyes, fixed on hers, were benign. A worn woollen shawl thrown about his narrow shoulders covered the top half of a snowy shirt that fell below his knees over a pair of carefully ironed pyjamas. The white stubble of his beard might have looked seedy on another face, but it gave him a bookish air. His face, an even shade of brown, exactly matched his hands.

42

'I understand, Bibi,' he said in English after greeting her, 'that you wish to learn some languages of India.'

Mariana let out a great sigh of gratitude.

From that day, Munshi Sahib called on Mariana twice daily, once after breakfast, and once in the afternoon. Driven by an unexpectedly passionate desire to learn, she studied day and night, practising the sounds of Urdu whenever she was alone. As helpless as an infant at first, she gained a measure of fluency within three months, astonishing her uncle.

'We must,' he decreed one day at lunch, 'find a way to make use of this talent of yours.'

And they had. In early November, the need had abruptly arisen for a lady translator for Lord Auckland's two sisters. The next day, after being handed over to the care of Miss Emily and Miss Fanny Eden by a proud Uncle Adrian and a tearful Aunt Claire, Mariana left the Simla hills, accompanied by Munshi Sahib and her servant Dittoo, for the great camp that waited below them on the plains.

Her mount shied abruptly on the muddy path. Keeping her seat on the dancing mare, Mariana looked for danger but saw none. Was it a snake? Jackals? Although her little mare still trembled, she could see nothing. She leaned forward to stroke the animal's neck, then started with a cry as a scarecrow of a man erupted from the trees and barred her way.

His hair was matted, his stare hot and otherworldly. He clutched a heavy wooden staff in one hand, and with the other he pointed a knotty finger in her direction. 'You, Memsahib,' he quavered, his body swaying, 'listen to what I am telling you!'

Mariana glanced quickly about her. Was there no one to help? Where were hairy, buck-toothed officers when they were wanted? Why had she left her grooms behind?

43

Very well then, she would have to escape on her own. Her heart hammering, she leaned forward in the side-saddle, preparing to dig her spurred heel into the mare's side.

With a howl, the man dropped his staff and raked the air above him with his hands, causing the little mare to jerk sideways. 'The path you will take requires courage,' he shouted hoarsely, 'but it will bring you peace. Be careful, careful! That is all.'

Before Mariana could move or speak, he scooped up his staff and without another word strode swiftly away and vanished into the tangle of thorn trees.

Light-headed with fright, she stared into the silent trees, then spurred her mare.

'India is full of soothsayers and magicians,' Uncle Adrian had warned her once. 'Everyone who comes out here is exposed to them at one time or another. You must never listen to what they say.'

Afraid to look behind her, she cantered past dusty trees and ruins, past an abandoned well, hearing only the pounding of the mare's hooves, which matched the beating of her heart.

After reaching the safety of the horse lines, she signalled to her waiting grooms to follow her to her tent.

'The natives are a superstitious race,' Uncle Adrian had said. 'They believe all sorts of nonsense. But you, Mariana, must always remember who you are. Do not listen to native fortune-tellers. If you do, you will never be the same again.'

The White Rabbit from last evening bowed eagerly as she passed him on the avenue. Deep in thought, she scarcely nodded in reply. What path had the madman meant? Why should she take such a path if all she would find there was peace? And why should a path to peace require courage? She dismounted in front of her tent and handed the reins to the groom. She wanted all sorts of things: her father's happiness, excitement and adventure, knowledge of India, and an English husband. But she most definitely did not want peace.

'Memsahib, your Munshi Sahib approaches.'

Dittoo's voice broke into Mariana's thoughts twenty minutes later as she sat at her table in the light of the open doorway. Now that she was safely in her tent, her encounter with the madman seemed more dreamlike than real. How mysterious the natives were, appearing and disappearing without warning, offering bewildering advice in strange languages. Had the misshapen creature under the towel been a soothsayer too?

Miss Emily would insist that she pin up her loosening hair before her munshi arrived. Still feeling the madman's hot stare, Mariana raised her arms too quickly, and exhaled crossly at the sound of her favourite tartan gown giving way under her arm.

A discreet commotion outside her doorway told her it was too late to change. If she kept her arms down, the old man would never notice. 'Come in,' she called.

A brown hand appeared, grasping the reed door blind to hold it aside, and her teacher stepped carefully into the tent on stockinged feet. The rug made a small, wet sound.

'Oh, Munshi Sahib,' Mariana said quickly, 'please be careful of your feet. The rug is very wet.'

Her teacher seemed not to have heard. He came and stood beside her, long feet planted firmly. '*As-Salaam-o-alaikum*, Bibi, peace be upon you,' he intoned, as if she had not spoken.

'And upon you,' she replied, returning his greeting. 'I am so sorry, Munshi Sahib,' she added in her best Urdu, or High Hindustani, as Uncle Adrian called it. How stupid

45

to have begun her lesson with a mistake. No matter how severe the emergency, greetings always came first. 'It was just that I—'

Her munshi raised a hand. 'It does not matter,' he said mildly. Water had seeped through the striped rug. The English hose that covered his feet were already turning dark. 'It does not matter.'

She was not to mention his feet again.

He raised his chin and clasped his hands behind his back, signalling that the lesson had begun. 'Today, Bibi, we will talk of Lahore. As you may visit there, you should know something of the city.'

Mariana brightened. 'Oh, yes, Munshi Sahib. I am very anxious to see Lahore!'

'Lahore, of course, is the capital of the Punjab.' The munshi leaned back, his hands still clasped behind him, and fixed his eyes on the curved ceiling of Mariana's tent. 'What, Bibi, do you know of Lahore?'

Mariana arranged her skirts. 'The city of Lahore,' she began, 'is so old that no one knows when it was founded. It is surrounded by a thick wall, which is pierced by twelve gates. The Citadel, which is the Maharajah's palace and fort, and the Badshahi Mosque take up the northwest quarter of the walled area. The rest is occupied by the city itself.'

The munshi rocked a little on his heels. 'That is correct. Do you know that Lahore once stretched far beyond its present boundaries? Two hundred years ago, before invaders came through the northwestern passes, Lahore reached far beyond its fortified walls, with gardens, bazaars and countless houses.' He spread his hands. 'The city, which now has nine guzars, or districts, once had thirty-six. There was a great jewel bazaar called the Palace of Pearls outside the walls. Even today, small

46

pieces of jewellery and gold can be picked up there in the mud after a heavy rain.'

Rain. Water. Mariana looked again at her munshi's feet. His socks were now wet all the way to his ankles.

This was unbearable. 'Munshi Sahib, please forgive me,' she wailed, clutching at her forehead, 'but I have a sudden headache. I beg your leave to rest.'

The old man's expression did not alter. 'Bibi,' he said, after a pause, 'I am sorry you are unwell. I will return when you are able to receive me. In the meanwhile, please remember that there is little time to waste. Your Governor-General's great meeting with the Maharajah will begin very soon. You must be ready.' He smiled.

He knew she had told an untruth about her aching head.

He reached into his clothes and produced a paper folded in four. 'Here is a poem for you to translate. Please prepare it for our next meeting.'

Maintaining his usual distance, he laid the paper on the corner of her table and took a step back. She unfolded it and saw that it contained four lines of verse in his flowing, right-to-left Urdu script.

Mariana practised the salaam, right hand to her forehead, as the munshi, his back to her, grasped the reed curtain and stepped from her tent into his shoes. She watched him stride away, without a backward look, towards the guarded entrance.

Munshi Sahib knew Uncle Adrian well, although no two people could have been less alike. Not one of her teacher's gestures, no turn of his head, no hunching of his shoulders was like that of an Englishman.

Who was he, really? The old man never allowed idle conversation during their meetings. When she asked where

47

in India he had been born, he replied that she would be able to answer that question for herself when she became familiar with the various people of India. When she asked about his family, he said that his family was of no consequence to her study of languages. When she enquired how he had come, genie-like, to be in Simla where Uncle Adrian found him, he had said nothing at all.

She turned back to her desk and picked up the paper again. She, Mariana Givens, was about to translate a poem that looked like this *into English*. She stretched her arms over her head, then brought them sharply down, too late to prevent the tartan gown from tearing past repair.

Bother! She had meant to ask Munshi Sahib about the madman's message: 'The path you will take requires courage . . .'

Chapter Three

After the poisoned milk had done its work in the Maharajah's Citadel, word of Mumtaz Bano's death spread rapidly into the old city beside the Citadel's walls, speeding from mouth to mouth through cobbled lanes until it reached Qamar Haveli, home to three generations of Shaikh Waliullah's immediate family and a score of more distant relations.

Wailing arose at once in the upstairs ladies' quarters of the house, while downstairs the high carved doors swung open to admit the first sombre-faced male visitors into the Shaikh's inner courtyards. As the day progressed, servants from neighbouring houses crisscrossed the narrow streets, carrying vessels of food to the haveli's back entrance, for it is the custom that no food is cooked in a house of mourning. Incense, painful to all, heavy in its associations, made its way on the breeze over the roofs of nearby houses. 'Shaikh Waliullah's daughter-in-law has died,' the incense proclaimed, with more finality than any human voice. 'Mumtaz Bano, mother of the Maharajah's hostage child, is dead.'

The tall doors opened and a square-bodied horseman rode out, his weapons rattling at his sides, his horse's hooves echoing in the brick entranceway. Head down, he passed along curving lanes until he reached one of the twelve gates leading out of Lahore City. Seeing him pass through the Kashmiri Gate, an ironmonger called out, 'Godspeed, oh messenger of the Shaikh!'

From his saddle, Yusuf Bhatti saluted, but gave no reply.

He rode north, taking the ancient road leading to Peshawar then to the Khyber Pass, and Afghanistan, three hundred miles beyond. He coughed at the dust that rose from underfoot, his shoulders hunched beneath the weight of the news he carried. He rode for three hours, stopping only at the appointed times to offer his prayers by the roadside. As he travelled he scanned the crowded highway for a familiar figure riding south.

Near Gujranwala, he found the man he sought. Passing through a roadside village, he caught sight of Mumtaz Bano's husband mounting his horse near a fruit vendor's stall, an orange in his hand, his neat beard and long embroidered coat tarnished with the dust of hard travel.

His jaw tightening, Yusuf spurred his horse.

Hassan Ali Khan's clever, good-natured face lit with pleasure as he leaned from his saddle to embrace his closest friend. 'Yusuf, may you have a long life!' he cried. 'I was thinking of you just now. What a journey this has—'

When Yusuf pulled mutely back, Hassan's smile faded. He drew himself up and sat warily, his horse moving restlessly beneath him, his eyes locked on his friend's face.

Yusuf dropped his eyes and clenched his knees on the saddle.

After a moment Hassan's shoulders sagged. He took a ragged breath. 'Is it my father?'

'No, it is not Lalaji.' Yusuf raised his head and looked into Hassan's face. 'It is not your father,' he said, his eyes filling, 'it is your wife.'

50

'What? When?' Hassan's voice sounded like dry leaves.

Yusuf looked away and wiped his eyes on his sleeve. 'This morning.'

A pair of donkeys pulling a cart loaded with bricks minced past, sidestepping the two riders. Seeing one man's grey face and the other man's tears, the driver spoke aloud to no one in particular. 'So,' he said, 'in this world ill news comes to both great and small.'

A passing merchant grunted his agreement.

'How?' Hassan squeezed his eyes shut.

Yusuf hesitated, then told him the truth. 'They are saying she choked on some food. We do not like the story.'

'We do not like the story?' The reins shook in Hassan's fingers. 'Do they think someone has *killed* her? *Killed* my Mumtaz Bano?'

Yusuf looked at his hands. 'We have no proof,' he said, 'but we think there was jealousy in the Jasmine Tower. One of the queens—'

'What of Saboor?' Hassan interrupted. 'Where is my son?'

'He is still at the Citadel.' Yusuf spoke roughly to cover the additional pain he knew this news would cause. 'The people there have refused to release Saboor without permission, and the Maharajah has already gone south to meet the British. They say they have sent a message to his camp.'

Hassan shook his head. 'I know the court people. They will never dare give this news to the Maharajah for fear of being blamed.' He brushed his fingers across his face. 'My baby is alone there now. Oh, Allah!'

Yusuf's sword clanked as he leaned towards his friend. 'I will ride to the Maharajah's camp myself. I will leave now. I will ask for Saboor to be sent home.'

Hassan raised his head and looked into the distance. 'Home,'

51

he repeated. Abruptly, his still face crumpled. 'Oh, Yusuf, why did I take Saboor to see the Maharajah last year? Why was I so proud of him that I ignored the risk?' Passers-by stared.

'Come,' Yusuf said, pointing to a distant tree. 'We can talk there. Why blame yourself?' he asked Hassan as they left the road. 'None of this tragedy is your doing. How could you have foreseen the Maharajah's passion for Saboor, or that he would order him to live at the Citadel?'

'That moment has never left me.' Hassan swallowed. 'I see it daily: Saboor on the Maharajah's lap, turning his head to look at the bright colours and the jewellery, the old Maharajah peering at him out of his one good eye, stroking him and crooning to him. "This baby has a light in his heart," the Maharajah said to everyone, "a bright, sweet light. He will stay with me and bring me health and good fortune."' Hassan's mouth turned downward. 'My Saboor was only six months old.' He sighed. 'My poor Mumtaz Bano, forced to leave us and live with the Maharajah's queens. They terrified her, with their falseness and their cruel ways. Now they have killed her. I failed her, Yusuf, I failed them both.' He dropped his head into his hands.

Yusuf sat silently. Over the past year Hassan had tried many times, with increasing desperation, to retrieve his wife and son from the Jasmine Tower. He was a skilled courtier and well-connected, but the Maharajah, his health weakening, had refused to give up Saboor. Instead, he had clung to the child as if to life itself. 'Saboor and the Koh-i-Noor diamond are my most treasured belongings,' the Maharajah had said many times.

Yusuf reached for his friend's shoulder, but Hassan straightened with a jerk, and took up his horse's reins. 'We must hurry home to Lahore. 'We must not miss Mumtaz's burial.'

They had been riding in silence for nearly an hour. Yusuf shifted in the saddle. What was Hassan feeling? What did he see at this terrible time? Did the creatures on the road and the villages in the distance shimmer before his eyes? Did the road rise and fall like a live thing before him? Aching to embrace his friend, Yusuf glanced sideways, but saw only Hassan's closed face.

Saboor must be miserable at the Citadel, although that particular misery would most likely end soon, when the order came for him to join the royal camp sixty miles south of Lahore. But who knew what would happen to the child there, alone and unprotected?

Yusuf slapped at a fly. If Shaikh Waliullah, with all his spiritual abilities, had been powerless to protect his own daughter-in-law, it was doubtful that he could help his grandson. People were saying the Shaikh should have saved Hassan's wife with magic. People talked all kinds of nonsense. Like the Maharajah, they, too, claimed that Hassan's baby son had powers, that five minutes of Saboor's infant company could lift a man's darkest mood. Yusuf grunted.

Hassan's grim voice broke the long silence between them. 'I hate the Maharajah,' he said quietly. His eyes were half closed, his face wan above his beard.

Yusuf stared at his hands. A great soldier and statesman, Maharajah Ranjit Singh was loved by most of his subjects. A soldier himself, Yusuf had admired the old one-eyed Maharajah all his life.

'I have told no one, not even you, Yusuf, what I have suffered over this past year,' Hassan went on, keeping his voice low, even though the road was nearly deserted. 'I have worked for the Maharajah, travelled to distant cities for him, collected his taxes, argued with his enemies; and all this time I have hated him more than all his enemies together.' His fist tightened on his knee. 'All this time I thought that if I said it aloud, if I let

53

myself speak my hatred, I would go mad. I had no power to strike back at the Maharajah. He tore my very soul from me, but I could not fight him for fear of causing my family more harm. Today that harm has come, in spite of all my struggle.'

He looked, hollow-eyed, at his friend. 'Allah help me, Yusuf, I never thought I could feel such hatred towards anyone.'

Yusuf tugged on one of his ears, then the other. 'In that case, Hassan,' he said, 'God help us both.'

Three hours later they reached Lahore.

It is sympathy that breaks reserve. At the first sorrowful greeting from a gentle-eyed Hindu blacksmith near the Masti Gate, Hassan began to choke. Yusuf urged his horse ahead, allowing Hassan to follow him, however blindly, to his father's house.

At the periphery of the city, they passed rope makers and coppersmiths. Nearer to the centre, they made their way past cloth sellers, acknowledging as they passed the grave salutes of all who knew their story. They manoeuvred their horses through the congested streets, past spice sellers and goldsmiths, diamond merchants and weavers of the softest silk. At length they reached Wazir Khan's Mosque, home to the most precious of goods: incense, perfumes and illuminated books.

Opposite the mosque stood the Waliullah family's ancestral home.

The tall doors of the haveli stood open. Male members of the Shaikh's family stood outside greeting visitors, all of whom were ushered inside and directed either to the Shaikh's presence or to the main courtyard, depending upon the degree of intimacy with the family. Palanquins with tightly closed side doors passed through on their way to the ladies' quarters. A crowd of onlookers craned to see each new arrival.

'Stand back,' cried a voice from the crowd as the two horsemen approached the gate. 'Hassan Sahib has come!'

The crowd moved aside, staring, to let them pass.

'May Allah Most Merciful grant you patience,' shouted someone. The crowd lent its voice in agreement.

'May the lady's soul rest in peace,' said another voice.

'Yes, yes, may she rest in peace,' answered the people at the door.

Their horses' hooves echoed hollowly as Hassan and Yusuf rode into the haveli's high, vaulted entrance. They dismounted and made their way past groups of men, then through a gate with a carved wooden lintel. There, in his small courtyard in front of a decorated portico, Shaikh Waliullah had already risen from the padded platform where he sat daily among his close companions. He opened his arms to receive his son.

Yusuf stood at the back of the crowd. He had his instructions. Immediately after the burial he was to ride out of the city again and head south to the Maharajah's camp. Once there, he must somehow persuade the Maharajah to return the infant Saboor to his grieving family.

He grimaced at the thought. He was a soldier, quick with a tulwar, the curved sword of his profession, but clumsy with words. He did not have the golden, persuasive tongue of the courtier Hassan, but the task must be done, and there was no one else to do it.

He must not fail.

At the Maharajah's camp two days later, Yusuf made poor headway as he rode along a crowded avenue. 'Move out, move out,' he shouted, fighting impatience as he forced a path for his horse through the throng of merchants and hangers-on. He pushed by a cluster of silk-clad riders who scowled and whispered as he passed. Dandified fools, let them talk.

He skirted a line of carts piled high with blood oranges. He should find food, but he was too angry and disappointed to eat. In his haste to cover the distance between Lahore and the Maharajah's camp, he had bypassed the small walled city of Kasur. Since then he had learned that the Maharajah's chief minister, Faqeer Azizuddin, childhood friend of Shaikh Waliullah and Hassan's patron, had been at Kasur. No one but Faqeer Azizuddin would be able to gain Yusuf an interview with the Maharajah. No one knew when the minister would return.

He had been their best hope.

Yusuf turned towards the Maharajah's horse lines. His mount, at least, should eat and rest. He sighed. If only he and Hassan could rescue the child themselves . . . Yusuf had thought of it, without hope, all the way from Lahore. No one entered the Citadel's gates unnoticed. Even if they could, by stealth, reach the inner gardens, how would they gain entry to the women's quarters? The Jasmine Tower, home to the Maharajah's queens, was walled off from the rest of the palace grounds. Armed sentries guarded its single, low door. Only Allah knew how many eunuchs were within, protecting the inhabitants of the Maharajah's harem.

No, Hassan's baby must be rescued with cleverness, not force.

A naked Hindu mendicant strode along the margin of the camp avenue, a begging bowl in one hand, his body covered with ashes. Yusuf glanced at the man, then away.

He had never seen Hassan's wife. Hassan himself, her distant cousin, had not seen Mumtaz Bano until after the marriage papers had been signed, the blessing given. Only then would the figured mirror have been produced and held at an angle, to show the groom, indirectly, the face of the bride who sat beside him, her head bowed modestly under her scarlet wedding veil. Whatever Hassan had seen that day, it did not matter now.

Yusuf rubbed his eyes. He would make himself eat, and then, putting his trust in Allah, he would go on to his next task.

Leaving the Maharajah's camp behind him, he would continue south across the Sutlej River and travel deep into British territory, searching out the British camp as it made its way north towards the border. There, among the British tents, he must find the man who, like Faqeer Azizuddin, had been a childhood friend of the Shaikh. This man, like the Faqeer, must be told in person of the tragedy at the Jasmine Tower.

With luck, on his return journey, Yusuf would not miss the Faqeer a second time.

Daylight had faded and dense clouds obscured a quarter-moon as Yusuf rode south on a borrowed mount, ignoring the discomfort of travelling without rest. As darkness descended, he followed a pitted track past ragged trees and empty fields to where a fortified mud village stood on a mound of earth, presenting eyeless walls to the outside world. Directed by a boy driving a bony cow, he presented himself, dusty and famished, at the headman's house.

After dining on chapattis and boiled lentils cooked over a dung fire, he lay down to sleep on a string bed in the headman's courtyard. Looking into the blackness, he listened to the grunting of the animals.

Was Hassan, too, lying sleepless tonight?

Within hours of her death, Mumtaz Bano had been buried beside Hassan's mother who had died when Hassan was only nineteen. Nine years ago, Yusuf had been among the men carrying the body of Shaikh Waliullah's wife out through the carved haveli door, wrapped in its winding sheet and decked

57

with flowers, while behind him the family women wailed. He thought of Hassan's wife, of friends and family members bearing the burden on their shoulders as the sound of the final prayers rose and fell behind them.

His bed creaked as he sat up in the darkness. What would happen to Hassan's son? How long could Saboor survive alone at the Citadel?

'Allah-hu-Akbar,' he said aloud, consoling himself. 'Allah-hu-Akbar.' God is great. If God were willing, help would arrive in time.

The only real garden in the Lahore Citadel was the Queens' Garden.

Twenty years before, at the desire of the Maharajah's second wife, the garden, a square space adjacent to the ladies' tower, had been returned to the graceful formality of its Moghul days. It had been a symmetrical Persian garden then, divided into four squares, with a marble fountain at its heart. In each cypress-shaded square, paths led to a smaller fountain between plantings of jasmine, gardenias, oranges and roses, whose perfume was carried by the breeze from one end of the garden to the other.

The central fountain had been set into a marble platform, where on pleasant days the Maharajah's ladies enjoyed themselves, screened from idle onlookers by a row of tall cypresses that cast their shade along the gravel walks. In warm weather the younger ladies played by the fountain, giggling and trying to push one another into the water, while their serving women waited on their pleasure in the shade of nearby trees.

It seemed that this morning was too cool for such games. The Maharajah's thirty-seven wives seemed satisfied to recline on carpets in the garden, leaning against bright-coloured bolsters

58

like resting butterflies, their loose garments falling in silken folds against their bodies.

The senior-most wife rested near the fountain, her hooded eyes expressionless, her two legs spread apart, each one kneaded rhythmically by a serving woman, while the other queens positioned themselves nearby, nudging one another discreetly out of the way, vying to be close to the centre of influence.

The old Maharani grimaced. 'Not so hard,' she said sharply to one of her servants. The woman nodded and went on with her work. The Maharani closed her eyes, ignoring the competition that boiled silently around her.

Crouching under a tree a little distance from the other serving women, a young servant girl glanced down at the dishevelled baby who squatted at her side, his eyes passing from queen to queen, as if he were searching for someone.

Was he looking for his mother? Reshma did not believe so. She was certain he had known the milk was poisoned. She was sure that when Mumtaz Bano took the cup, he had understood that she was about to die. His screams in the garden, she knew, had been screams of loss.

What then, or whom, did he seek? If only his colour were not so poor. If only his cheeks were still plump.

'Look at Saat Kaur,' said a pale woman, jerking her chin without sympathy towards Reshma's own queen, a grey-eyed sixteen-year-old who sat apart from them, a frail baby on her lap. 'That boy of hers is certain to die soon. No child so weak and unhealthy can live for long.' The pale woman waited, picking her fingers, for the senior queen's response.

The Maharani opened her eyes briefly and gave the sick baby an incurious glance, but did not favour the speaker with a reply. Biting her lip, the woman subsided into silence.

Near her in the crowd, a second, harsh-faced woman smiled bitterly.

Reshma shivered. How these queens hated one another! How they feared for their future!

Saat Kaur did not look up, although colour stained the dewy cheeks that had first caught the Maharajah's eye. Yawning deliberately, she lifted the baby, whose skin was as yellow as turmeric, put him down beside her and turned her head towards the row of cypress trees. Reshma shrank into her loose clothes and tried to put Saboor behind her. Oh, please let Saat Kaur not see him . . .

The little queen narrowed her eyes then started, her body stiffening. She reached for a silver tray and took a sugary sweetmeat. 'Send the boy here, Reshma,' she commanded.

Saboor ceased his searching from face to face and looked at the young Maharani. Swallowing, Reshma pushed him forward.

Saat smiled and called softly to the child, the orange sweet glistening in her fingers. 'Come here, take this.'

Saboor hesitated then trotted shyly to the young queen's side. As he stretched out his hand for the treat, she snatched it away and slapped his fingers sharply.

'There,' she said, her mouth curling downward at his tears, 'that is what you get for making yourself a favourite of the Maharajah. Nothing is what you get.' With a disdainful gesture, she dropped the sweet into the fountain where it sank and rested, still tempting, under the water.

Her voice had a knife's edge. 'Who gave you permission to spend hour after hour in the company of the Maharajah while his own son waits here, unnoticed?'

Beside her, his cheeks wet, Saboor gazed uncomprehendingly into her face.

60

'And what is this "light" you are said to have?' Saat Kaur added to his back as he stumbled away. 'I see no light. Pah! I see only a dirty, foul-smelling boy whom no one loves.' She gestured at the child with a finely painted hand. 'Reshma, why do you keep bringing him here? He does not belong among royalty. Take him from my sight, and do not give him food. Why should we feed him?' She had raised her voice. The other queens nudged one other. 'He is no child of ours.'

Reshma scrambled to her feet, tugging her veil forward to hide her face. She caught Saboor up and lifted him onto her hip. 'Of course not, Bibi,' she replied, turning her head away as she spoke. 'Of course we need not feed him.'

She carried him away, away from the uncaring faces around the fountain. Once out of their sight, she buried her face in his small shoulder. A damp spot appeared on his shirt.

'Oh, Saboor,' she whispered, wiping the tears from both their faces, 'how can I leave you alone and attend only to my queen? How can I then atone for my crime? Who will care for you?' She looked anxiously over her shoulder. 'Come, do not weep so. I will find you some dry chapatti while they amuse themselves in the garden.'

Chapter Four

The best horses in the British camp were to be found at the Governor-General's own horse lines. Separated by a hundred yards from the mounts of lesser camp members, the animals stood tethered in glossy rows, resting from the day's march, served by the most experienced of the camp grooms. At the far end of the second row, Yar Mohammad, senior groom, straightened from inspecting a bruised leg on one of the mares and strode towards a nearby cooking fire to have his food.

As he squatted, warming his hands before the fire, he had an acute sensation that something important was about to happen. He closed his eyes and found himself looking at a strange and vivid scene.

He saw a fire before him, much like the one whose warmth he could feel on his face, but the fire in his vision gave off a great cloud of dust and smoke. For an instant he could see nothing more. Then, padding toward him out of the haze, came a lioness. She moved carefully, for she was carrying something heavy in her jaws. Once clear of the fire, she paused and looked about her as if to satisfy herself that she was safe, then deposited her burden on the ground.

Yar Mohammad now saw that she had been carrying a baby,

a boy the same age as his own youngest daughter. The boy's face was fair, broad, and sweet of expression.

He sat on the ground, with the cat watchful above him. After a moment her long body stiffened. In one swift motion, she picked the child up again and moved off, her tail twitching, his small body dangling from her careful jaws. An instant after she had carried him away, a new cloud of dense smoke and dust enveloped the place where they had been sitting.

Yar Mohammad opened his eyes. The campfire with its suspended cooking pots was still before him. Men chatted idly, their hands outstretched to the fire's warmth, their bodies neatly folded like his, their feet flat on the ground, their arms resting on their knees. Yet when he closed his eyes again, the cloud of dust and smoke appeared once more, and once more the tawny cat appeared carrying the soft-eyed child.

Yar Mohammad lowered his head, allowing his turban to shield his face from the eyes of the other grooms. The length of unstitched homespun that served him as a shawl trailed on the ground beside him as he moved his body closer to the fire.

Remembered words came to him as clearly as if they had been spoken moments before: 'If you see or hear something out of the ordinary, you must tell your murshid, your spiritual guide. These events often contain in them instructions or important information. To reveal these things indiscriminately is wrong, but to conceal them from your spiritual teacher is also a grave mistake.'

For all that he remembered those instructions, Yar Mohammad could not obey them. The only spiritual teacher he knew, the man who had once said those words to him, was eighty miles away. He had met him only once, but the meeting remained vivid in his memory. The teacher's eyes had been deep, filled with profound knowledge. He had radiated goodness and strength. He was Shaikh Waliullah, leader of the Karakoyia Brotherhood, one of the five hidden brotherhoods of India, whose members taught and practised the mystical traditions of Islam.

Yar Mohammad looked up and gazed into the distance. His lips tightened. By Allah, there was something he could do. He could tell the great man. He did not know the great man's name, but a few days earlier the mere sight of him, a Muslim stranger passing on the avenue, had caused Yar Mohammad to stop so abruptly that the ladder-carrying carpenter walking behind him had almost knocked him down. The stranger's eyes had reminded Yar Mohammad so forcibly of that spiritual teacher of long ago that he had forgotten the oats he had come for and had followed the elderly stranger from place to place in the camp, watching as he went about his business, marvelling at the man's calming effect upon others, at the kindness with which he addressed a fruit seller, a scribe, children begging on the avenue. When the old man returned to his tent, Yar Mohammad had gone back to the horse lines, convinced that this stranger was well versed in the mysteries of the heart.

Now Yar Mohammad gathered his shawl around him and rose silently, and although he did not change his long, unhurried stride, he took the shortest route, down alleyways, between ramshackle tents, past small bazaars where men stood arguing over mounds of fruit, until he reached a neat tent whose door was just then being propped open by a small boy.

'Is the most respected sahib available?' he enquired.

Gesturing for him to wait, the boy vanished inside, but before Yar Mohammad could sit, the boy put his head out again, beckoning with a raised hand.

Standing shoeless and uncertain inside the doorway, Yar Mohammad saw that the tent was bare except for a single tin box that stood in one corner, and a string bed on which the great man sat writing with pen and ink. He looked up from his task and pointed to the ground beside him.

Yar Mohammad felt once again that he was in the presence of no ordinary person. Although the old man's face and dress were unremarkable, he exuded a calm that poured over Yar Mohammad like honey.

He squatted down beside the bed and began to speak, describing without preamble his vision of the lioness and the child.

The old gentleman listened without comment, nodding from time to time. When Yar Mohammad finished speaking, the old man sat silently for some moments, his eyes closed. When at last he opened his eyes and spoke, his tone carried no trace of superiority. 'You have done well to come to me at once with this information.'

Yar Mohammad's heart swelled. The great man had spoken, not to his station as a groom, but to his soul. It had been years since anyone had addressed him like that.

'The cloud of dust and smoke in your vision signifies an emergency of some kind.' The old man's face puckered in thought as he picked up a tasbih of black onyx beads from a square of cotton cloth beside him. 'Although it concerns an emergency,' he went on, his eyes travelling around the tent as he fingered the beads, 'it does not appear to be a vision that gives instruction but rather one that conveys information. Now tell me why you have come to me with your story.'

Yar Mohammad, his eyes on the ground, considered his answer. 'Seeing you walking on the avenue,' he began carefully, 'caused me to remember someone in Lahore, whom I hold in great respect. I had hoped—'

'And what is the name of this gentleman?'

65

'His name, Sahib, is Shaikh Waliullah Karakoyia.'

The old man nodded several times. After a moment he called the little servant boy. 'Bring this man tea, Khalid,' he instructed, then turned to Yar Mohammad and regarded him seriously. 'I know Shaikh Waliullah,' he said, 'very well.' Yar Mohammad's heart quickened as the old man paused. 'There is no question that this vision of yours is intended as a message to the Shaikh,' he continued, nodding again. 'Otherwise, why would you have been sent to recount it to me? You must therefore borrow from the lines a strong horse that will not be missed, depart at once, and ride north until you reach Firozpur on the banks of the River Sutlej. That is a twenty-mile journey. See if the Maharajah's new bridge of boats is ready. Should you find the bridge unfinished, a barber named Kareem who lives near the great mosque will arrange for you to cross the river by ferry. Once you reach the far bank, you must ride without stopping the sixty miles to Lahore City and there deliver the full story of your vision, with no omissions, to Shaikh Waliullah Karakoyia. Is that understood?'

Yar Mohammad nodded.

'Tell him,' added the old man, 'that I have sent you. My name is Shafiuddin.' He picked up his paper and pen. 'And now,' he said with a little nod, 'Khalid will bring your tea outside. Drink it before you start.'

His heart pounding, Yar Mohammad found himself dismissed by a single, tidy motion of the old man's hand.

He was to see Shaikh Waliullah again. As Yar Mohammad finished the last of his tea, scenes rose before him of the triumph and shame of his other, long ago meeting with the Shaikh. Of course he and his first teacher, the good-natured Abdul Rashid, had both been young then. If he had known better, Abdul

Rashid might have kept his imperfect knowledge to himself, and not tried to show his village cousin the profound mysteries of the Path, but he had tried to teach Yar Mohammad, and the knowledge he so generously shared had made Yar Mohammad the clumsy practitioner he had been in that far-away time. Without Abdul Rashid, he would not have had the vision that sent the two men on the long journey to Lahore from their mountain home six months after Yar Mohammad received his first lesson.

Undimmed by time, the memory of his vision returned. A personage whose name he dared not utter had appeared before him and handed him a ceramic vial that, it seemed, had fitted warmly and perfectly into the palm of his hand.

Yar Mohammad put down the teacup and stood, shaking out his clothes. He must start for Lahore.

After passing rows of tents, each with its group of string beds standing in the sun, Yar Mohammad caught the welcome smell of the horse lines. He walked by the pits where blacksmiths heated iron bars in trenches of fiery charcoal. Two sweating blacksmiths greeted him. He returned their greeting without looking up.

When that vision had come so many years ago, he had been young. He had not yet understood the need for discretion in spiritual matters. Overcome with confusion and a sense of his own unworthiness, he had told his wife what he had seen. In her simplicity, she had run to her family with the news that her young husband had seen a vision of the Prophet Mohammad. Scandal and misery had followed. Some villagers, believing he had developed great powers, had come to him expecting miracles and been disappointed. Others had called him a liar. In the end, he and Abdul Rashid had set out for Lahore to discover the truth.

Seated on his padded platform, the Shaikh had listened to their story. He had then explained to them both, kindly but with great firmness, the importance of disclosing spiritual events only to the proper people. Finally, he had turned his powerful gaze on Yar Mohammad.

'I believe,' he said, 'that the meaning of your vision is that you have been given a gift. It is no small gift, Yar Mohammad. You may not yet know what it is, but when the time comes, you will know. Coming from such an august source, it is a tremendous gift indeed. You are a fortunate man.'

Yar Mohammad had not tried to conceal the tears that ran down his face and dripped onto his clothes. After that, although he had never failed to treat Abdul Rashid with affection and respect, tending him faithfully in his last illness, he had always regarded Shaikh Waliullah as his true murshid.

As he scanned the horse lines choosing his own mount, a horseman approached. Yar Mohammad noted with annoyance the animal's drooping head and uneven gait. The rider was a strong-looking man with burly shoulders, perhaps a well-to-do Kashmiri. Such a man should know better than to ride a horse to exhaustion. Approaching him, Yar Mohammad opened his mouth to point out the necessity of caring properly for one's mount, but the traveller addressed him first.

'I am looking for one Mohammad Shafiuddin who is also known as Shafi Sahib,' he said in a dry voice. His hair and his jutting beard were grey with dust. He dismounted stiffly and leaned, heavy-eyed, against his horse's flank. 'I have important news,' he added, rubbing his face absently with a thick hand.

Yar Mohammad hesitated, studying the weary stranger who had asked for the great man. Should he point the way, and then, without further delay, follow his own instructions and mount

68

quickly for the ride to Lahore? Or should he escort the man to Shafi Sahib's tent?

'I have ridden, with little rest, directly from Lahore City.' The stranger looked as if he might fall asleep where he stood.

No longer hesitating, Yar Mohammad reached for the man's reins. 'Take this horse,' he said to another groom, nodding towards the rows of well-muscled animals. 'Care for him as if he belonged to the Governor-General himself.' He turned towards the visitor. 'Come with me, Huzoor. I will take you to Shafi Sahib.'

Shortening his stride to accommodate the other man's tired legs, he retraced his steps to the tent. When they reached it, the stranger nodded to the little servant boy. 'My name is Yusuf Bhatti. Please tell your sahib that I have come from Lahore, from the house of Shaikh Waliullah.'

The Shaikh's house. As the man shouldered his way inside, Yar Mohammad followed, glancing cautiously towards the string bed as he lowered himself, uninvited, to the floor near the tent's open entrance. He waited without moving, containing his excitement.

His sword clanking at his side, the visitor saluted the old man. The double handles of a large dagger peered from his cummerbund. 'Peace be upon you, sir,' he offered.

Shafi Sahib replied serenely, his eyes on the newcomer's face.

'I have come with unfortunate news.' The visitor glanced at his hands then put them behind his back. 'The daughter-in-law of Shaikh Waliullah Karakoyia of Lahore has died.'

The news fell on Yar Mohammad's chest like a heavy blow. The chill that followed told him there was more to this tragedy than he yet knew.

'Poor Waliullah, poor young Hassan,' Shafi Sahib said mildly, shaking his head. 'May God rest her soul in peace, and grant them all patience.' The visitor lowered his gaze to the floor. The old gentleman looked at him expectantly. 'There is more,' he said gently.

The man called Yusuf was perspiring. He stared at the ground as he spoke. 'Unfortunately she did not die at home, but at the Citadel, where she and her son were being held hostage by the Maharajah. The child, who is only a baby, has not been returned from the court.'

'Ah.' The old gentleman stared thoughtfully in Yar Mohammad's direction, then turned back to his visitor. Unsure of his welcome, Yar Mohammad sat without moving.

'Is the Maharajah still at Lahore?' Shafi Sahib enquired.

'He has left Lahore, sir. He is at his camp, preparing to meet the British officials.'

'Then he may not yet know of this sad event.' Wise eyes looked the speaker up and down. 'And you have come straight from Lahore?' Shafi Sahib pointed to the place beside him on his string bed. Yusuf sat down heavily.

'No, sir,' he replied. 'I stopped at the Maharajah's camp to ask for help in freeing the child.'

'Ah.' The old man tapped his fingers against each other. 'Whom did you see there?'

'No one, sir. I was to meet Faqeer Azizuddin, but he was not there. He had gone away to Kasur.' Yusuf gestured impatiently.

'So you did not meet the chief minister. Did you ask anyone else for help regarding the child?'

'No, sir, those were not my instructions. I have not yet been able to help the family at all.'

In the ensuing silence, Shafi Sahib closed his eyes. His lips moved silently. Yusuf Bhatti glanced sideways at him for a moment, then, propping his elbows on his knees, he sighed and dropped his head into a pair of blistered hands.

It was impossible to tell what the old gentleman was thinking. For long minutes he and his visitor sat silently, side by side on the string bed: Shafi Sahib upright, his eyes closed; Yusuf Bhatti hunched beside him. At length the old man spoke, but not to his visitor.

'Go, Khalid,' he said decisively to the servant boy who materialized out of the shadows, 'and bring this man water and food. Bring him plenty of both. And then show him where to bathe. Yar Mohammad!'

He had not been wrong to intrude. Praise be to Allah!

'Arrange for provisions and for three horses. We will begin our journey as soon as this gentleman has rested and eaten.'

As Yar Mohammad left to do the great man's bidding, Shafi Sahib spoke to his visitor with gentle authority. 'I will leave you now. After a few hours, when you are ready, we will start for Lahore.'

Before his guest could offer polite protest, the old gentleman got up from the bed and left the tent.

The servant boy reappeared, carrying a brass basin and a water vessel. Yusuf grunted his thanks while the boy poured a stream of water over his outstretched hands.

A little later, the boy backed through the door with a loaded tray.

The food was princely fare, not the simple meal of boiled lentils Yusuf had expected. A thick buttery round of bread hung over the edges of a straw plate, its centre laden with chunks of spiced meat. There was fruit. Oranges, guavas and pomegranates rolled on the tray beside the bread. There was even an earthen dish of yogurt. Sighing with anticipatory pleasure, Yusuf tore off a piece of bread and used it to pick up a bit of meat. He ate rapidly, using only his right hand to serve himself, picking dexterously at the food with his fingers. For all the simple poverty of Shafi Sahib's tent, the old man had resources.

When Yusuf could eat no more, he washed his hands again. Leaving his weapons with the boy, he carried the string bed outside. There he lay down gratefully, one arm shading his eyes.

The sounds of the camp flowed around him. His eyes closed beneath his protecting sleeve. He would forget the privations of his journey south, his failure to find Faqeer Azizuddin on the way, his long night of travelling towards the British camp, partly on foot, leading his horse by instinct in the near blackness. All that remained now was to ride north with Shafi Sahib to the Maharajah's camp. Inshallah, God willing, the chief minister would be there. If anyone could help them free the baby, it would be Shaikh Waliullah's childhood friend who was also, by all accounts, the Maharajah's closest adviser. Their duty done, they would then travel with all speed for Lahore.

Yusuf yawned. If this effort failed, he would do whatever was needed to restore Saboor to his father. If killing would bring Saboor back, he would kill. Why not? Danger was something to be enjoyed. Unlike Hassan, he was a fighter and a hunter. Hassan had never fought as he had with the Maharajah's irregular cavalry, or travelled to the hills to hunt white leopard. Hassan had never shot pigs in the forests near Chhangamanga.

Yusuf gave a short, barking laugh. Hassan, his clever, city-dwelling, silk-wearing friend, at a pig shoot? He would pay good money to see that.

Would Hassan kill for him? What did it matter? Hassan was

72

no soldier, but he was his friend. Hassan would certainly die for him.

Die for him – die for him. Yusuf floated over the Citadel, the child in his arms. Eunuchs on horses leapt into the air beneath him. Hassan appeared, a great sword in his hand, and spurred his horse through the air to guard them.

Two hours later, his hair still wet from a bath, Yusuf sat watching from a fresh horse as Yar Mohammad helped Shafi Sahib into his saddle. There could be no mistaking the groom's solicitous manner, or his choice of an ancient mare for the old gentleman. If the old man had ever ridden a horse, it had not been for years. What had possessed him to come on this journey where haste meant everything?

Good manners did not allow Yusuf to show his feelings. Keeping his face still, he watched Shafi Sahib climb creakily into the saddle, then sit gripping its pommel while Yar Mohammad gathered up the reins, mounted his own horse and led the mare with her elderly passenger towards the avenue.

When the two men had passed out of earshot, Yusuf allowed himself a snort of annoyance. Travelling with such an old, unfit companion meant losing all hope of speed. The journey as far as the Maharajah's camp would require frequent rests. Those twenty miles alone, accomplished by him in one night, would take them two days. From the camp to Lahore might require as much as four infuriating days more.

The clay track they followed was deeply rutted from past rains. The ground under their horses' hooves had cracked into a crazy pattern as it dried. Dust hung in the stillness, colouring distant villages with soft greys and browns. There was little vegetation, only an occasional spreading thorn tree. Here was a land good only for lizard hunters and cattle thieves.

73

Yar Mohammad rode beside Yusuf, leading Shafi Sahib's mare. Yusuf had noticed the small axe tied to his saddle. A heavy, curved Gurkha knife hung from his waist. At least the man would prove useful if they were attacked. Moving so slowly, they made a perfect target.

'How,' Shafi Sahib asked from behind them, 'did Saboor come to be the Maharajah's hostage? Is there some dispute between the Waliullah family and the court?'

'No, sir.' Yusuf slowed his horse, allowing Yar Mohammad to pull ahead. 'It has to do with the child himself.'

'Ah.' The old man nodded, swaying in his saddle.

Yusuf slapped at a fly. 'You may already know that Hassan is assistant to Faqeer Azizuddin, the chief minister. He was appointed to the post because of the friendship between the Faqeer and Shaikh Waliullah.'

'Yes,' replied Shafi Sahib. 'I knew of that.'

'After Saboor was born,' Yusuf continued, 'Hassan went, as a courtesy, to show his son to the Maharajah. Unfortunately, the Maharajah fell in love with Saboor at first glance.' He sighed. 'Since that day, he has not been allowed to leave the Maharajah's side.'

Shafi Sahib said no more, and Yusuf drew level with Yar Mohammad once again. The groom stared ahead, his face intent. Behind them, Shafi Sahib rode with his eyes closed.

Two hours later, they were less than halfway to the Sutlej. Shafi Sahib had not spoken. Yusuf hunched his shoulders. The time had come to decide on a plan of action.

'When we have crossed the river, shall we go straight to the Maharajah's camp?' he asked, turning politely in his saddle.

Shafi Sahib did not reply.

Yusuf tried again. 'Once we cross the river,' he said, more

74

loudly, 'we can inform Faqeer Azizuddin of the tragedy, and ask him to help us free Waliullah Sahib's grandson.'

Again there was silence. Had the old gentleman gone deaf?

He had not, but when he spoke it was in a tone that put an end to any further conversation. 'We shall see,' he replied, without inflection, as if to himself.

Yusuf looked over his shoulder again. Shafi Sahib sat, leaning forward on his mare, his knuckles pale on the pommel of his saddle, his lips moving.

So be it. Shafi Sahib was dear to Shaikh Waliullah. That and his age made him the senior member of the party, the person whose wishes must be respected. But what had he meant by 'we shall see'? Was it possible that he would refuse to let them stop at the Maharajah's camp? No, that was out of the question. The poor old man must be desperate to reach a tent and a cooking fire; he could hardly sit straight on his horse.

Yusuf squinted into the northern distance, hoping for some sign of the green belt of trees that followed the riverbank, but saw only an empty plain dotted with mud villages. They should probably travel for another hour before resting and offering their prayers. He glanced backward again at a sudden noisy fit of coughing from Yar Mohammad to see the groom gesture with his eyes at Shafi Sahib. The old gentleman was swaying, grey-faced, in his saddle.

When had they last had water? What a careless fool he was!

Hastily, Yusuf pulled up in the shade of a tangle of thorn bushes whose branches swept the ground. It was not the old man's fault that he could hardly ride. He was poor. Poor men did not own horses, or even ride horses. Poor men walked. Yusuf tugged at the water skin while Yar Mohammad helped Shafi Sahib to the ground.

75

A while later, lying on Yar Mohammad's coarse shawl, his head propped on one of the saddles, Shafi Sahib had begun to revive.

'Do not apologize,' he said in a faint voice, flicking long fingers in Yusuf's direction. 'I should have said something.' Drops of water clung to the stubble of his beard and spotted his snowy shirt.

Before Yusuf could reply, a noisy thrashing erupted from the bush nearest to Shafi Sahib's makeshift bed. The dusty branches parted as if by themselves, and a ragged figure of a man lurched into the sunlight, brandishing a wooden staff. The man turned his head rapidly from side to side as if looking for someone, then, his staff high, moved jerkily to where Shafi Sahib lay full length on the ground.

Praying that Yar Mohammad knew how to handle his knife, Yusuf reached for his tulwar, his eyes moving rapidly from the attacker to the tangle of bushes. Where was the rest of the gang? How many were there?

'You are the one,' the intruder cried, his voice a dark, rasping sound, 'who can tell the foreign lady, who can tell her—'

'Stop!' Yusuf shouted to the man's back, drawing his heavy, curved sword from its scabbard. 'Do not move!'

Ignoring him, the stranger took another step towards Shafi Sahib.

As Yusuf swung his sword arm, preparing to slice the intruder in half, fingers gripped his wrist.

'Wait,' said Yar Mohammad into his ear. 'Look at Shafi Sahib.'

The old gentleman had made no move to shield himself. Instead he peered interestedly at the tattered figure standing over him. 'Speak,' he commanded.

76

The stranger's staff fell to the ground as he raised his arms over his head. 'You must tell the foreign lady,' he said, 'whose horse bears the five lucky signs, that the path she takes will bring her peace.'

'Which foreign lady?' Shafi Sahib raised himself on one elbow.

The madman ignored him. 'Tell her to be careful.' His voice sounded like stones rolling down a hill. 'Tell her, *khabardar*, *khabardar* . . .'

Without finishing what he had begun to say, he reached for his rod and strode to the bush. Ignoring the long, cruel thorns, he parted its branches with his bare hands, turned, and stepped backwards into the thicket. The branches quivered, then closed upon him.

With Yar Mohammad beside him, Yusuf peered into the silent bush. Seeing nothing, he turned away, shaking his head, to find Shafi Sahib on his feet.

'We must go now,' the old man said. His face, ashen when they had stopped, was now fresh and animated.

Yusuf stared.

'We must start for Lahore at once,' Shafi Sahib insisted, in the voice of one accustomed to command.

'But we are going to the Maharajah's camp, are we not?' Yusuf protested. 'We must find the Faqeer and—'

'No,' the old gentleman said firmly. 'We have no need of Faqeer Azizuddin. Come, there is no time to be lost.'

Once again Yar Mohammad helped him onto his old mare. He waved an arm towards the north. 'Lahore,' he said. 'We must ride for Lahore!'

Yusuf kept his face averted to hide his rage. Why, oh why did Shafi Sahib insist on bypassing the Maharajah's camp? Yusuf let a lungful of air out through tight lips. He had done his best to explain their urgent need to contact Faqeer Azizuddin, but his efforts had come to nothing. Ah, if Allah in His wisdom had given him a golden tongue, he could have made the old gentleman see reason. But his skills, useless in this case, lay in the steady hand and tight-clinging knee of a cavalryman. He leaned and spat into the dust. Surely this change in their plans was not because of a stick-waving madman? Surely Shafi Sahib did not believe in that nonsense?

Two days later they were within sight of the tents of the Maharajah camp. Yusuf steered his horse impatiently round a groaning bullock cart piled high with firewood, which was crawling towards the camp, the same camp that they were to leave, unvisited, behind them. Had it been safe to do so, Yusuf would gladly have galloped alone towards the line of tents. Once there, he would have begged the Maharajah's chief minister for his help in freeing little Saboor, then hastened back to rejoin his companions. But Yar Mohammad was not a professional man-at-arms, and Allah knew the road was not safe. Among the many merchants and travellers between Lahore and the Maharajah's camp, there were certain to be cutthroats and thieves. Left to themselves, Shafi Sahib and the groom could be robbed and killed ten times over before he returned.

No, the facts could not be changed. There was no hope of carrying out the instructions he had been given. Hassan's poor little son would have to be rescued by someone else.

Yusuf skirted a deep rut in the road, glancing behind him to make sure Yar Mohammad had seen it. All this had happened because, by some ill fortune, Shafi Sahib, the Shaikh's trusted friend, had gone mad. Tears stung Yusuf's eyes. How could he face Hassan, his most loved friend, with this news?

Shafi Sahib had begun to speak. Was it to him? Yusuf turned to look behind him.

'Yusuf Sahib.' The old gentleman's tired voice held a teasing note. 'Why do you try to do all the work yourself? Do you not remember Allah, the All-Powerful? If it is His will that the child is to be rescued, then no one can keep him at the Citadel. If it is not His will to spare the child, then no power on earth can save him. Is that not so?'

Yusuf nodded numbly. His saddle creaked.

The old man cleared his throat. 'In any case, oh kind and honest soldier,' he said, smiling serenely, 'there is no need to worry. Your prayers have already been answered.'

Chapter Five

A troop of Bengal Lancers trotted past Mariana on the avenue, their black moustaches bristling. Artillery shots boomed in the distance. She slowed her mare, her eyes following the lancers. Her father would enjoy as much as she did all the preparations for the campaign into Afghanistan. She imagined him bent over a map at her writing table, working out the various roles of the British and Sikh forces in the assault. She saw him speak, his gentle face alight, of the difficulty of moving the heavy British guns over the mountain passes into Afghanistan, and of the likelihood of Afghan resistance to the British-leaning monarch who would replace their present king.

The Governor-General, together with his political secretary and everyone else, was looking forward to the moment when Shah Shuja, their hand-picked Afghan prince, would enter Kabul at the head of the triumphant Sikh and British armies, to be installed upon the throne of the most strategically valuable country in Central Asia.

What would be the result, Mariana wondered, of this exciting invasion whose preparations had taken two years? British supremacy in Afghanistan would of course squash for ever the Tsar of Russia's ambition to control Central Asia,

80

but surely there would be other changes. Surely there would emerge a new, almost British Afghanistan, with English officers in the streets, and English horse races being held in its far-away cities with wonderful names: Kandahar, Jalalabad, Kabul . . .

One day, she would see Afghanistan for herself, eat its fabled fruit, read its poetry, and breathe its air.

Ahead of her, a British officer rode towards the red gate. Mariana watched the sentries stiffen to attention as he passed through. If Papa were here, he would understand her passion for languages, as she understood his passion for war. He would appreciate Munshi Sahib.

She nodded to the sentries as she rode through the entrance. It had been days since her last lesson. What if Munshi were ill? He had not looked well since the day he had come to her in the rain. She must talk Major Byrne into giving her a second chair. The poor old man should not be made to stand all the way through their lessons.

People had begun to gather in the doorway of the dining tent. She was late. It was lunchtime already, and she was still wearing her riding clothes!

A man in a blue uniform stood talking to the White Rabbit. Was it Harry Fitzgerald? She strained to look, leaning awkwardly in the side-saddle, and saw that it was Fitzgerald just as her mare stumbled, wrenching her from her seat, and knocking her foot from the stirrup. Unable to stop herself, Mariana plunged, head first, to the ground.

Someone approached. She sat up, gasping at a sharp pain in her shoulder. Her skirts had now settled modestly about her, but her legs had flown into the air in front of every-one. She must get away at once. Where was her riding hat?

'It's lucky her foot came out of the stirrup,' said a man's

81

voice. 'She might have been dragged. Look at these sharp stones. She may be hurt. Call the doctor.'

'No,' Mariana tried to say, over the sound of someone running off.

She forced herself dizzily to her feet, crying out when a hand gripped her by her injured arm. It was the White Rabbit. He peered at her, his chinless face full of concern. 'We must get you to the shade, Miss Givens. Allow me to help you into the dining tent.'

To be stared at by everyone in camp? Absolutely not. She pulled away, shaking her head. 'No, thank you, Lieutenant Sotheby,' she said hastily. 'Please help me remount my horse.'

'Your horse has been taken away, Miss Givens.'

Mariana looked behind her. It was true. Her mare was gone. So was Fitzgerald. 'Well then, Lieutenant Sotheby,' she said, smiling, holding out her good arm, her teeth clenched against a sudden desire to weep, 'you must walk me to my tent.'

'Of course, Miss Givens,' said the White Rabbit, who pretended, all the way to her tent, not to see the tears of shock she could not hide.

'Memsahib, Memsahib!' Dittoo's voice pierced Mariana's sleep. She sat up, still wearing her riding habit. Her mouth tasted sour. Her head ached from her fall. What time was it?

'The ladies are calling you. They want you to join them outside their tents before dinner.'

Injured or not, Mariana could not refuse. She stood and began to undo her buttons. The last thing she wanted to do was face them all now. Wincing, she pulled her injured arm from a tight sleeve. She could not bear to think what had come into view when her legs had gone over her head.

82

She took her second best gown from her trunk, and pulled it on. She had thought of asking Miss Emily to seat her with Fitzgerald at dinner tomorrow or the next day, but would he wish to sit beside someone who could not button her clothes properly or stay on a horse?

'I did not mean to hurt his feelings, poor little rajah.' Miss Fanny adjusted her shawls as Mariana arrived at the square of ground between the residence tents. 'But as none of us can endure the smell—'

'Ah, there you are, Miss Givens.' His jowls wobbling, Lord Auckland rose from a basket chair and towered above Mariana.

'I am sure Mariana will agree with me, Fanny,' Miss Emily said from her own folding chair. 'You should not have sent those camels back.' A corner of her long mouth turned up. 'You do not have a sufficient number of animals in your tent. A pair of camels would do nicely if your spotted deer should die, although of course we would need a larger sofa if they wanted to lie down.'

It was nearly sunset. Mariana lowered herself into a chair and accepted a glass of sherry as a pair of Miss Fanny's peacocks picked their way past her tent, their iridescent tails dragging behind them.

Miss Fanny bent forward. 'Marianna, we heard of your accident this afternoon. Are you hurt? Ah, here is Dr Drummond, the very person we need.' She nodded as the doctor bowed formally to the little group, his heels together.

The doctor sat down with a groan and put his cane on the ground beside him. 'Are you all right now, Miss Givens?' he enquired, removing his spectacles and frowning at Mariana. 'I tried to see you earlier but your servant told me you were sleeping.'

She touched her sore shoulder. 'I am quite well, thank you, doctor.'

'That is a great relief.' He nodded several times, then turned. 'Well, Miss Emily,' he said heartily, 'no rain today!'

Mariana's ears buzzed as the conversation drifted from the weather to lepidopteran collecting. As soon as the doctor had gone, she would ask Miss Emily about Fitzgerald. If only the doctor would go away . . .

'Is that not true, Miss Givens?'

Mariana returned to the conversation to find the doctor looking expectantly at her across the dusty space between their chairs. He raised his eyebrows.

What had he said? Was it about butterflies? 'Yes, of course, doctor,' she agreed, smiling.

'I do not find this a smiling matter.' Miss Fanny's eardrops shook gently. 'I, for one, am disgusted by the natives. I cannot abide their peculiar habits and their grinning idols. One even hears of human sacrifices . . .' Her voice trailed off.

What had she agreed with? Mariana sat up. 'I do not believe,' she heard herself say, 'that one ought to feel disgust at the natives unless they are mad or diseased. Of course,' she added, thinking back, 'if they are, one might be able to help them.'

Miss Fanny gasped. Dr Drummond laughed aloud. 'My dear young woman, what a preposterous remark!'

As heat rose to Mariana's face, Lord Auckland, who had not appeared to be listening, sat forward in his chair. 'Let me give you some advice, Miss Givens.' He spoke slowly and clearly, as if addressing a halfwit. 'As long as you are in this country, you must make every effort to avoid the natives. Do *not* speak to them unless absolutely necessary. They are an uneducated, heathen people, and must be treated as such.'

84

'But Lord Auckland, I myself am being educated by a native. Munshi Sahib comes every—'

'Munshi *Sahib*?' Dr Drummond made a snorting sound. 'You address a native in a manner reserved for Europeans?' He turned to Miss Emily. 'Miss Givens, I must say, is a most *extraordinary* young person.'

Mariana abruptly and with some force put her sherry glass down on the tray.

'My dear girl,' Miss Emily said after the doctor had departed, turning a sharp blue eye on Mariana, 'I have rarely seen anything as transparent as your temper just now. What did you mean by banging down your sherry glass?'

A hand to her throbbing head, Mariana looked up, but she did not answer.

Miss Fanny sniffed. 'I cannot imagine what the poor doctor could have done to offend you. He has made a point of studying the natives, and he knows much more about them than we do. You made a silly remark, and he had every right to correct you.'

'I certainly hope you will behave properly at dinner,' said Miss Emily, changing the subject before Mariana could reply. 'I have had a request from someone who wishes to be seated beside you tonight.'

Richard Sotheby, of course, thought Mariana. She must be grateful. One could do worse than sit beside a kindly rabbit.

'He is the younger of two brothers who came out here within a few years of each other. Major Byrne describes him as a promising young horse gunner, which I take to mean he is in the Horse Artillery. His name is Fitzgerald.' Miss Emily picked up her parasol and got out of her chair with a rustling of skirts, leaving Mariana free to flush with excitement behind her back. 'Let us go in. They are all waiting.'

85

It was only by chance that Mariana had made a real effort to arrange her hair, although, possessing only a small handglass, she could not tell how she really looked. A few loose curls had already fallen to her shoulders. Oh, please, let her hair, for once, not come out of its pins . . .

Lieutenant Fitzgerald stepped forward, even handsomer by candlelight than he had been in the rain. His braid and buttons shone; his white doeskin breeches fitted him to perfection. Mariana took the arm he offered her and steadied herself, willing away her increasing dizziness.

Beside her at the table, a spidery stranger bowed elaborately. She inclined her head to him, aware that on her other side, Fitzgerald had pulled his chair so near to hers that their knees met. She turned from the stranger and opened her mouth to speak, but found herself about to address a blue-clad shoulder.

'Ah, Peter,' Fitzgerald was saying to someone across the table, his animated baritone carrying so far that Miss Fanny caught Miss Emily's eye, 'I have been looking for you all day. I shall not let you get away until we have settled our argument.'

Peter, a round-faced man with black curls, bunched a fist on the table. 'You are wrong, my boy. The French artillery would never have won the day. The whole battle was decided by our infantry squares against their cavalry. We exhausted them into defeat.'

'Nonsense.' Lieutenant Fitzgerald waved a hand over his soup. 'They had us outgunned nearly three to two. If they had defended their forward guns properly—'

The Battle of Waterloo!

'We should have lost,' Mariana put in, more loudly than she had planned.

Four seats away, his spoon in mid-air, Dr Drummond gazed at her as if she were a talking parrot. Someone nearby clicked his spoon against his teeth. In the silence, Fitzgerald turned to Mariana.

'I beg your pardon?'

'I agree with you.' She nodded seriously. 'If the French had resisted the charge of Ponsonby's Union Brigade and saved the seventy-four guns we took early in the battle, we should have lost.'

Fitzgerald lowered his soup spoon.

'Of course Marshall Grouchy's failure to join the battle was also important . . .' Her voice faded under his stare. Could he tell how much she liked him? What should she do now?

Around them, conversations started up again. Mariana clearly heard her name murmured up and down the table. She looked at her plate, feeling her stays bite uncomfortably into her ribs.

Fitzgerald's napkin was at his mouth. He seemed to be choking.

She cleared her throat. 'My father,' she said, answering a question he had not asked, 'is interested in military history. I've read all his books.'

Why was Fitzgerald laughing?

He lowered his napkin. 'Forgive me,' he said. 'I am glad to have you and your father on my side when it comes to Waterloo. I hope you will forgive my rudeness just now. It's just that we shall all be leaving for Afghanistan soon. I am not myself. I can't seem to think of anything but the army.'

'Oh.' Mariana looked away.

'What an inconsiderate fool I am!' He leaned towards her. 'I should have asked if you are recovered from your fall. I went to fetch the doctor, but when we returned you had gone to your tent. We went there, but your servant turned us away. Are you all right?'

'Yes, thank you.' She dropped her eyes. Those running feet had been his, but what had he seen as she fell?

'I also want to say,' he added, 'that I was very sorry to leave you with the elephant the other day. I missed a great opportunity. You could have translated my questions.'

'You like elephants?'

'I like everything here, but I have not learned much, except about the army. I've wanted to ask you, how do you come to be on this journey with all of us?'

Mariana watched as he buttered a piece of bread. His hands were square and competent-looking. The other eligible men never asked questions. They tried only to impress or please her. 'It was my Uncle Adrian's idea,' she replied. 'We were at Simla, and I had begun learning Urdu and Persian from his old munshi. Lord Auckland and all of you were about to come down from the hills and begin travelling again when the real lady translator fell ill. When we got the news, my uncle dragged me to the political secretary's cottage in the middle of dinner to offer my services. He thought the post would give me a chance to see more of India.'

'The *real* lady translator?' Fitzgerald gave her a crooked smile. 'But what did Macnaghten say when you appeared at his door with your dinner napkin still under your chin?'

She lowered her voice. 'He stared as if we were mad, but my Uncle Adrian is such a darling, no one can refuse him, so Macnaghten let us in. Then, very stiffly, as if he were doing my uncle the most *enormous* favour, he asked me to describe, in Urdu, the scene outside his window, which wasn't exactly fair because it was pitch-dark outside. I said something about the scent of roses under the window and distant mountains, and he gave me the post.' She spread her hands. 'He had no choice, really. There was no lady for a thousand miles who spoke Urdu or Persian or anything.'

Fitzgerald nodded seriously. 'You are new to translating, and this is my first campaign. Everything is new, isn't it?' He sighed. 'I do not know when I shall be getting my next leave. It might be a long time.'

The table was turning. With an apologetic smile to the bewhiskered general on her left, Miss Emily turned brightly to the sharp-faced general on her right. At the other end of the table, Lord Auckland nodded to his political secretary, then turned, smiling wearily, to a small, energetic-looking foreigner on his other side. Up and down the table, bodies turned in unison. Fresh conversations began.

Harry Fitzgerald's face reddened suddenly as he nodded to Mariana, taking his leave. Suddenly wanting to touch him, she tried, while turning, to brush against his shoulder, but without success.

'Well, Miss Givens, how great a pleasure it is to sit beside you on this lovely evening.' The Spider's warm smile revealed several missing teeth.

Later, as Mariana undressed for bed, the stiffness in her shoulder made every movement painful, but she did not mind. Fitzgerald had somehow intercepted the Spider and seen her to her tent after dinner. When they reached her door he had bowed politely, then looked hard, not at her face, but at her mouth. His eyes had swept the front of her gown, not as they had before when her buttons were crooked, but as if he were looking at what lay beneath the silk of her bodice.

She reached to undo her gown, thinking of the feeling that had swept over her at that moment, a feeling that reminded her of another time in a little rowboat on a river, when a young man's eyes had met hers.

This, however, was real. The Eden ladies approved of Fitzgerald. Major Byrne had called him 'able'. This time there would be no closed study door, no promises extracted from her to avoid the person she liked best.

She pulled her gown over her head. *Do not marry the first man who asks you*, Mama had said, as the gardener carried the trunks to the carriage. But no one *had* asked her yet, except seventy-year-old Colonel Davenport in Calcutta, who asked everyone. Until now, Mariana had not cared. Since her arrival, she had been too captivated by India and too concerned about her letters to her father to think of marriage. In spite of a hundred warnings, she'd given no thought to her own future happiness.

She suddenly became still. As soon as Lord Auckland and the Maharajah signed the treaty, Fitzgerald would march for Afghanistan, and she would begin the long return journey to Calcutta. When would that be? Had Macnaghten really said three weeks? *Three weeks?*

Why had she not met Fitzgerald earlier? She dropped onto her bed and reached to unbutton her boots, remembering that only days ago she had bristled with impatience to reach Firozpur. How wrong she had been. The journey must last as long as possible. Let there be a disaster of some kind, a month-long downpour or, if necessary, a plague among the camels or the bullocks. Yes, a plague would be acceptable, as long as there was no danger to the elephants.

Would there be time enough for courtship, even marriage, before it was too late? Her head whirling with possibilities, Mariana dropped her second boot, lay down, and pulled the covers to her chin.

Chapter Six

A blacksmith's son recognized Yusuf Bhatti and raced off, a small barefoot figure in filthy clothes, to bring the news of their arrival to the Shaikh's house. As he ran, his treble shouts pierced the din of the crowded streets so successfully that by the time the three men reached the haveli, the tall carved doors had already been thrown open.

Handed down from his mare, Shafi Sahib shuffled wearily towards the inner courtyard, waving away solicitous strangers. 'Yar Mohammad will help me,' he told them, his impatient voice echoing behind him in the vaulted entranceway. 'Someone else can look after the horses.'

Yar Mohammad's heart filled. He looked upward at the carved balconies overlooking the main courtyard, and the arabesques painted high on the courtyard walls. He had come here only once, long ago, but he had never forgotten this house. Now, as he brought Shafi Sahib through the seated crowd, Yar Mohammad could see that, like his house, Shaikh Waliullah was unchanged. He still wore his tall, starched headdress, and his expression was still as deceptively calm as a banked fire.

The seated men fell silent as the Shaikh and Shafi Sahib embraced. Weak-kneed from excitement, Yar Mohammad

91

took his place against a wall. The Shaikh had not recognized him.

A young man also embraced Shafi Sahib. Yar Mohammad nudged his neighbour. 'Who is that?' he asked.

'That is Hassan Ali Khan,' the man replied, 'husband of the dead lady, and father of the baby Saboor.'

Hassan was tall and lean like his father but his face told a different story. While the Shaikh was as dark and wrinkled as a raisin, his face all liveliness and sharp points, Hassan was fair and smooth-faced above his beard. As they sat together, the son on a straw stool beside his father's platform, the Shaikh's gaze moved slowly through the crowd, fixing on one man at a time, while Hassan's eyes darted from face to face, gathering nods of recognition and half-smiles of greeting.

Yusuf Bhatti pushed his way to Hassan's side. Yar Mohammad watched the Shaikh's son stand and wrap his arms about his friend. For all his grace, Hassan looked ill. His lips were cracked, his hair was dull and dry, his fingers looked sore. He seemed like a man who had more than one tragedy to bear.

Your prayers have already been answered, Shafi Sahib had told Yusuf as they rode for Lahore. If prayers for the child's safety had been answered, Yar Mohammad thought, the child's father had not yet been told. Moments later, when Yar Mohammad caught Hassan's red-eyed gaze, he thought he felt something leap from Hassan's heart into his own. Before he could guess what it was, the Shaikh put his feet over the side of his platform and felt for his slippers.

'If I am not mistaken,' he said, addressing the crowd as he stood up, 'the call to prayer is about to sound. Come, my friend.' He held out a hand to Shafi Sahib. 'You and I will offer our prayers in my room.'

As he strode off, with Shafi Sahib staggering a little beside

92

him, Shaikh Waliullah's voice carried across the courtyard. 'Speak, Shafi,' Yar Mohammad heard him say. 'Tell me what knowledge has come to you. Teach me that which I do not know.'

Shafi Sahib's voice floated behind them as the two men began to climb a flight of stairs. 'I have no knowledge, Wali. I am as ignorant as the buffalo that turns the water wheel on the roof of this house. But I have brought with me a groom whose name is Yar Mohammad . . .'

'*Allah-hu-Akbar, Allah-hu-Akbar*, God is great, God is great,' cried the muezzin, leaning from a high minaret of Wazir Khan's Mosque, cupping his hands over his mouth to be heard in the streets below. 'Come to prayer, come to prayer!'

Yar Mohammad closed his eyes and was immediately transported to an empty plain far from the busy courtyard. Shaikh Waliullah stood in front of him, his gaze a silent question. In the palm of his hand, Yar Mohammad could feel the smooth weight of a small ceramic vial, the same vial that he had received years before, in his first vision. He opened his eyes and looked out at the scene before him. There were the high, frescoed walls of the Shaikh's house, the carved balconies, the eddying crowd. He opened his hand and found it empty. That was the reality. But what was the vision? He closed his eyes again and found himself standing once more in that same barren place. The Shaikh's eyes did not leave his face as Yar Mohammad began to open the small, flat bottle.

What had he been given? Was it a gift he could offer to others, even those as elevated as Shaikh Waliullah? The thought of actually helping the great man caused sweat to form on Yar Mohammad's forehead. He reached behind him for the tail of his turban and wiped his face. But perhaps the

Shaikh did need help. For all his strength, how could he not weep for his daughter-in-law? How could he not fear for his tiny grandson?

The crowd in the courtyard had begun to funnel slowly through the gate towards the mosque. Near Yar Mohammad, Yusuf Bhatti raised his voice over the muezzin's cry. 'Surely they will have found someone to look after Saboor.'

Hassan smiled wanly at his friend. 'Those courtiers care nothing for my son,' he replied. 'And now, God help us, the Maharajah has fallen ill at his camp. All this must be causing trouble among the women here at the Citadel.'

'Trouble?' Yusuf raised his eyebrows.

'Who knows which queens will die on the Maharajah's pyre? The choice of suttees is the prerogative of the senior queen. Some will want to die. Others will not. All will be trying to please her. No one will think of my son.' Hassan shook his head. 'The pushing, the lying, the cruelty between people at court is beyond our imagining.' He kicked at a pebble on the tiles. 'We may be sure that the Maharajah will now send for Saboor to cure him of his latest illness.'

Yusuf snorted. 'What madness this is! How can the poor child cure anyone?' He rested a thick hand on Hassan's embroidered sleeve. 'Do not worry, my friend. We will find a way to get Saboor away from the Maharajah. We will do it during the confusion of the durbar. If you and I and others are there, and we work together—'

'But, Yusuf,' Hassan interrupted, his eyes alight, pushing away Yusuf's protecting arm, 'how could I have forgotten your journey? Tell me of your visit to the Maharajah's camp. Surely you have some good news for me?'

Yar Mohammad had time to see Yusuf's face tighten grimly before his attention was caught by one of the Shaikh's servants who had edged up beside him, a man whose henna-dyed hair was a flaming red.

'You are to go to Shaikh Sahib's rooms as soon as you have offered your prayers,' the red-haired man said. 'When you are ready, I will show you the way.'

After climbing a flight of stairs, Yar Mohammad found himself outside a curtained doorway. As he scuffed off his sandals, he heard a light voice coming from inside.

'Well, my dear Shafi,' the voice was saying, 'I must confess that what you suggest seems unlikely. After all, the Maharajah and his people style themselves as lions. Why should the rescuer be English and not one of their Sikh women? But it is you, not I, who are the interpreter of dreams.'

The red-headed servant gestured impatiently towards the doorway. Yar Mohammad stepped nervously into the room.

When the room's two occupants looked up, Yar Mohammad noticed that the Shaikh had exchanged his tall, embroidered headdress for a fitted cap. Without the headdress he seemed sharper and more forceful than ever. Although he and the old man were the same height, he seemed to tower over Shafi Sahib. His eyes struck Yar Mohammad with contained force.

How should he greet his true murshid, his spiritual teacher? Should he touch the man's knees, his feet? He started forward, but something in the narrow face caused him to stop and salute in the usual way, his head bowed, his cupped hand to the centre of his forehead.

'*As-Salaam-o-Alaikum*, Shaikh Sahib,' Yar Mohammad said to the floor.

'*Wa'alaikum Salaam*, and upon you, peace.' The Shaikh pointed downwards. His heart pounding, Yar Mohammad sat down a little distance from the Persian carpet where the other two men sat, their backs to the wall.

'Tell us,' ordered the Shaikh, 'the five lucky signs of a horse.'

The question was so unexpected that Yar Mohammad did not grasp it at first.

The Shaikh frowned at him. 'You do not know the signs?'

So, Shaikh Waliullah and Shafi Sahib wanted only to understand the ravings of the madman who had jumped from the thorn bush. Yar Mohammad was disappointed, but then he chided himself. Had he really expected to be remembered after so many years?

'I do, Huzoor,' he said, recovering his voice. He would not have these great men believe him ignorant. 'The five lucky signs are these: four white stockings to the knee, and a white muzzle rising to a blaze on the forehead.'

The men on the carpet exchanged glances. 'And is there such an animal at the horse lines of the British camp?' the Shaikh asked.

Yar Mohammad nodded. 'There are two such horses.'

'And are either of these horses ridden by the ladies?'

'No, Huzoor.' Forgetting his nerves, Yar Mohammad grew fluent. 'One is a stallion, very wild, unsuitable for women. Even his owner, a captain in the British army, is afraid of him. Each day he comes with a new reason why he cannot ride the horse.'

'And the other?' The Shaikh's eyebrows lifted under his embroidered cap.

'The other is an old mare, weak in her legs. She was included in a lot of animals we bought when the hot weather killed some of our riding mares. The ladies ride the better animals. I expect that this mare will be killed soon. She is not worth her feed.'

'Ah.' The Shaikh turned to his companion. 'And there are three ladies attached to the British camp?'

'Yes, three.' Shafi Sahib helped himself to a handful of pomegranate seeds from a servant who had appeared silently through a curtained doorway. 'The youngest I have already described. The other two are sisters of the Governor-General.'

The Shaikh nodded, waiting.

Shafi Sahib poked through the seeds in his hand, ruby-red juice staining his fingers. 'What can one say about these foreigners? They have strange habits, to be sure, and an odd manner of dressing. They wear tight clothes, even in hot weather. But I believe both sisters are kind-hearted. One of them,' he added, looking up from his seeds, 'keeps a pair of spotted deer and several other animals in her tent.'

Yar Mohammad looked from the startled Shaikh to Shafi Sahib. Where had Shafi Sahib learned this? Surely the old man did not frequent the cooking fires?

Shaikh Waliullah did not respond, but turned and stared at the wall, his face softening. For a moment, hunger and sadness seemed to pour out of him. Yar Mohammad dropped his eyes. Clearly the Shaikh suffered like other men.

Shafi Sahib leaned towards Yar Mohammad. 'I have told Shaikh Sahib of your vision of a lioness. Tell us, are you a practitioner like us, a follower of the Path?'

Yar Mohammad took a long breath. 'I am, Huzoor.'

'And you perform the necessary spiritual exercises?'

'Yes, Sahib.' At last they were to talk of spiritual matters. Yar Mohammad could not keep his voice from shaking with excitement. 'To the best of my ability, I try to be honest and charitable. I offer five daily prayers, and also one optional prayer. I perform Zikr, the repetition of the name of God. I invoke Allah's blessings on the Prophet Mohammad both night and day.'

'And what is the name of your Brotherhood?' The Shaikh had turned his sharp gaze on Yar Mohammad. 'And your murshid – who gives you spiritual guidance?'

How could he meet his teacher's eyes? 'I belong to this Brotherhood, to the Karakoyia, Huzoor.' Yar Mohammad stared down at his hands. Rough and callused, they were not the hands of a mystic. 'It is you who are my true murshid. I came to that knowledge many years ago after I met you for the first time.'

The Shaikh pushed a long finger under his embroidered cap. His eyes narrowed. 'Tell us of your first visit to me.'

Yar Mohammad cleared his throat. If he did not say it now, he might never have another chance.' 'I came to you once, in the company of my cousin. We had travelled from our village to tell you of an event concerning me that had recently occurred.'

Shafi Sahib sat straighter. The Shaikh leaned forward on the Persian carpet.

'I had seen a vision of our Prophet,' Yar Mohammad went on, 'upon whom be Allah's blessings and peace. In that vision, he had given into my hand a small ceramic vial which I took to be a container of perfume or of scented oil. Perhaps you do not remember.'

For a long moment, Shaikh Sahib and Shafi Sahib stared wordlessly at each other. Disappointed, imagining his interview finished, Yar Mohammad moved to stand.

'*You* are the man who received the vial? *You?*'

The Shaikh's voice struck him like a blow. Yar Mohammad froze.

'You fool!' The Shaikh's voice rose. 'If you are the same man who was given the vial, why did you not tell this to Shafi Sahib when you first went to him?'

Yar Mohammad felt each word as if it were a dagger.

The Shaikh pointed at him. 'What was wrong with you that you withheld this information?'

His bowels churning, Yar Mohammad stared at the tiled floor in front of him, unable to reply.

'Shafi and I had assumed that the lioness dream was your first important vision. Now you tell me that it was you who received the ceramic vial. You should have told Shafi Sahib of this.' The Shaikh tugged a bolster towards him and leaned against it with an impatient sigh.

Yar Mohammad sat under the Shaikh's accusing gaze, tears of shame leaking from his eyes. There must have been a mistake. The vial must have been meant for another man, one who would know what to do, who would not make error after error in the telling of the story.

A small, comforting noise came from Shafi Sahib. Yar Mohammad looked up to find Shaikh Waliullah peering at him in surprise.

'Did I frighten you?' The Shaikh's voice had returned to normal. 'I should not have spoken so harshly, but you do not know how long we have searched for you.'

Searched? Yar Mohammad's brain emptied.

'You had received an important vision. I wanted to know who you were and where you lived. It never occurred to me that day that your cousin was not still attached to this household. When I discovered that he had returned with you to an unknown village in the north, I sent people to look for you, but they failed to find you. Since then we have waited for your return, hoping that another vision would bring you back to seek my advice.' He sighed again. 'Eleven years have passed since that time. But do not worry,' he added, speaking directly to Yar Mohammad's fear, 'there has been no mistake. It is Allah Most Gracious who sends visions. Unlike us, He is perfect.'

Yar Mohammad, who had known only the simple tutelage of his cousin, took a deep breath.

The Shaikh's gaze seemed far away. 'I have often thought of your vision,' he said absently. 'I have wondered if my interpretation was correct.' His eyes shifting suddenly to the present, he waved an impatient hand. 'And stop worrying about everything, Yar Mohammad. You still have much to learn. Remember that too much humility is a bad thing.'

Yar Mohammad buried his face in his sleeve. Air escaped him, hissing into his clothes.

'Shafi Sahib here,' the Shaikh said, laying a hand on Shafi Sahib's knee, 'is the foremost interpreter of dreams and visions among the five Brotherhoods.' His light voice was almost tender. 'Teach us, Shafi. Tell us the meaning of Yar Mohammad's dream of the vial.'

Us. Yar Mohammad's heart rose in his chest.

Shafi Sahib coughed delicately. 'The vision of the vial,' he began, 'means only one thing: that the recipient has been chosen to do a particular work, and that he has received all that he needs in order to accomplish it. This work, most assuredly, is of great importance and concerns the lives of many people.'

Yar Mohammad blinked. Was he dreaming?

'That is not my exact interpretation, but it is near enough.' The Shaikh sounded pleased. 'Go on, Shafi.'

Shafi Sahib took another handful of pomegranate seeds and studied them, his mild face drawn in thought, as if the answer could be discovered in the palm of his hand. 'The lioness vision

100

shows an important rescue in which you, Yar Mohammad, will play a major part.'

'And the baby?' the Shaikh asked softly.

Shafi Sahib closed his eyes. 'In a vision,' he said, 'a baby signifies the future of the Brotherhood. I believe that Yar Mohammad's dream tells us two things: that Saboor is to be rescued, and that he is to be the next Shaikh of the Karakoyia Brotherhood.' He looked up and turned his fingers over to indicate that he was finished.

The Shaikh let out a long breath.

Yar Mohammad could not move. His heart seemed to have stopped beating.

After a moment the Shaikh turned to Yar Mohammad. 'Now do you understand the importance of your visions? You are an uneducated man and the goal is still very far distant, but you have travelled much further than you realize on your journey towards God.' He raised an admonitory finger. 'Remember, each vision, no matter how small or how insignificant it may seem, must be reported immediately to me, your murshid.'

Your murshid. Yar Mohammad wanted to weep with relief, but there was more to be told. 'Shaikh Sahib,' he said, fidgeting where he sat, 'I have seen something else.' He forced the words out quickly, afraid of another mistake. 'Just now I saw myself standing in a barren place, the ceramic vial from my first vision in my hand. You, Shaikh Sahib, stood before me, watching as I reached to pull the cork from the vial.'

'Is that all?' The Shaikh's voice seemed to tremble.

'Huzoor, that was all.'

'So,' Shafi Sahib put in quietly, 'your work is about to begin.'

Yar Mohammad's head suddenly felt as heavy as a cannonball. He clenched his teeth against a yawn he could not stop.

The Shaikh shifted on the carpet. 'Although I am your murshid, you must understand that the gift you have received and the work you will do are yours alone. It is you, and no one else, who will know when the time has come to act. We can only offer you our advice.'

Our advice. So he was to have Shafi Sahib as well. Yar Mohammad's hands opened with joy.

Shaikh Waliullah sat in silence for a time, then turned towards the door. 'Tariq,' he called.

A servant boy pushed back the curtain.

'Call Allahyar.' He looked at Yar Mohammad. 'You will have your food downstairs,' he said briskly, as the same fiery-headed servant who had shown Yar Mohammad upstairs appeared in the doorway. 'Allahyar here will show you where to sleep. Tomorrow, after your observances, you will take your horse and Shafi Sahib's, and return to the British camp. It is fortunate that the camp is now far closer to Lahore than it was when you set out on your journey to this house.'

But what of—

The Shaikh held up his hand, reading the question before it was formed. 'Shafi Sahib has done enough horseriding. He will travel to your British camp in one of our palanquins. You have done good work already. I expect that very soon you will find there is more to do. In the meantime, follow the instructions of the madman on the road. Two horses at the British camp bear the five lucky signs you have described. One of these will, Inshallah, be given to a memsahib to ride. When that happens, relay the message to her and stay in touch with Shafi Sahib. Godspeed.'

The red-haired servant stole a curious glance at Yar Mohammad as they descended the stone stairs towards the kitchens. 'Shaikh Sahib usually gives no more than a few moments to any of his followers,' he said as they reached the kitchen door where thick rounds of bread had been stacked high, fresh from the baker.

Yar Mohammad blinked. How long had he been in that room? Oh, how his head hurt!

'Well,' he said politely, 'due to unusual circumstances, I have not seen Shaikh Sahib for more than ten years. It took some time for me to tell him all that has happened.'

Allahyar nodded dubiously. 'I see.'

Chapter Seven

At her writing table, pen in hand, Mariana stared out through her doorway, watching camp servants as they hurried back and forth between the tents. A flock of sheep passed by on its way to the back of the compound, each animal marked with great splotches of orange dye.

On the table lay a half-written letter to her father:

We have reached Firozpur at last. As only two days remain before the great procession that will begin the durbar, the camp is in a frenzy of activity, practising intricate drills on the parade ground, beating the carpets, building places to sit. All the preparations seem to require shouting, and as many of them are carried out at night by torchlight, no one has slept properly for days. To think we used to complain about the servants' nightly coughing!

The state visit will last about seventeen days, with marches past, trick riding, dancing girls and hundreds of wonderful elephants, all taking place in a spirit of vigorous competition to see whether we or the Sikhs are richer and grander.

A lizard clung to her tent pole, watching her. Where was

Fitzgerald? Why had he let two precious days go by without coming to see her?

Apparently even the handsomest of our men will be no competition for the Sikhs. They are said to be extraordinarily good-looking and marvellously well dressed in exquisite shawls and Moghul jewellery. The only one of them who is neither handsome nor elaborately dressed is the Maharajah himself, a tiny little man who has only one eye, having lost the other one in battle. He apparently wears only the simplest of clothes and very little jewellery, unless you count his enormous diamond, the Koh-i-Noor, or Mountain of Light. He is said to be a magnificent horseman who commands the absolute loyalty of his people. His army, after ours, is the best fighting force in India.

Speaking of someone who is no competition for the Sikhs, fat Major Byrne has become frantic about the Maharajah's tents. We hear they are made of silk and cashmere, while our camp, after all its travels, is a sea of dilapidated, mud-covered canvas. Major Byrne was so nervous at lunch yesterday that he honked in front of everyone! But he says our gifts, at least, will be more dazzling than Ranjit Singh's.

Since Ranjit has a passion for horses, the Major has ordered all the best ones to be kept aside to be preened and polished for the durbar. We are to ride only the ones that remain. As I am very far down the list, I am sure mine will be a hundred years old.

She put down her pen. Papa must wait. Since Fitzgerald had not come to her, she decided, she must go to him.

'Dittoo,' she called. 'I wish to ride.'

Yesterday's ride had been an ordeal of nerves. Still feeling the effects of the madman's sudden appearance in front of her the day before, she had brought her grooms with her and taken a different path, this one away from the army camp. But neither stratagem had worked. Certain that she was being observed, she had hurried through her ride, starting at every sound, peering into each thorn bush. After returning to the safety of the compound, she had been so unwilling to fall again that she had walked her horse all the way to her tent. Worst of all, Harry Fitzgerald had appeared at neither lunch nor dinner.

She put away her half-written letter and closed her writing box. Everyone who rode a horse fell occasionally, even Lord Auckland, who had broken several ribs two months ago. As for native fortune-tellers, what could they know of her future, of her feelings?

Remember who you are, Uncle Adrian had said. What would Papa say?

Of course, if the adventure with the lunatic had happened to someone else, she would have been panting to know every detail of the encounter, down to the ragged clothes he had been wearing when he lurched out of the thorn bush. It would seem exciting rather than unnerving, exotic rather than unsavoury. It had, after all, been a very *Indian* experience. But the effect was quite different, she decided, when the adventure happened to oneself.

Half an hour later, hearing a clopping sound outside, Mariana tied on her riding hat and stepped into the sunlight, then stared in surprise. Instead of the usual half-grown boy, her favourite senior groom waited at her doorway, the reins of a little mare in his hand, his bony face intent beneath a roughly tied turban.

He bent to greet her, a hand over his heart. 'Peace,' he said in a resonant voice.

The mare he held was old and her ribs jutted from her sides, but she had spirit. She pawed the ground with a frail

106

white stockinged foot when the groom handed Mariana the reins, and nudged his shoulder with a muzzle from which a white blaze rose and flared between her eyes.

'Patience, my friend,' the groom murmured.

As she arranged herself in the side-saddle, Mariana felt the tall groom fix his attention on her. 'There is a message for you, Memsahib,' he said, glancing at her, then away. He shifted his weight as if reluctant to speak, his hands moving aimlessly in and out of invisible pockets in his clothes.

'The path you will take,' he continued, 'leads to peace. You must be careful, very careful.'

She froze in the saddle.

'My name is Yar Mohammad,' the groom added. 'I will send two men to accompany you on your ride.'

Without seeming to hurry, he moved away before she had found her voice.

Mariana willed her hands to stop their trembling. She clucked to the mare and started for the gate. Whatever happened, she must not show fear.

Later, as she crossed the open stretch of ground between the government and army camps, she glanced over her shoulder. Who was sending her these messages? Were they watching her now?

At the army camp she avoided the stares of the British soldiers who sat outside their tents, waiting to be called for afternoon drill, and rode cautiously towards the newly cleared parade ground, her pair of grooms trotting behind her.

With no idea how to find Fitzgerald in the huge, busy camp, she followed the margin of the ground, uncertain what to do next.

Fifty yards from her, native infantrymen marched up and down to shouted orders, their shabby red coats buttoned tightly over their chests, their faces sweating in the sun. A pair of elephants crossed the ground, each carrying half a dozen men. In a veterinary tent at the far end, an Englishman in high boots swabbed the back of a handsome bay horse.

Mariana began to perspire. Perhaps Fitzgerald had not liked her as much as she had thought. Perhaps she had said something tactless at dinner that had driven him away, something she could not remember. Perhaps he was even now avoiding her, laughing with his friends, waiting until she had gone. She patted the little mare's neck with an absent hand. Mama and Aunt Rachel had warned her endlessly against tactlessness.

A British army captain passed her, riding the other way. She returned his greeting with a stiff little nod. If anyone asked, she would say she had simply come to see the preparations for the campaign.

Someone was about to overtake her on the path. She turned in her saddle and saw Fitzgerald thundering towards her on a grey horse. Barely avoiding her grooms, he pulled up beside her, red-faced. 'Forgive me, Miss Givens,' he said, breathing hard, 'I've only just learned that you are here.'

He seemed genuinely upset. In her lap, Mariana's damp hands loosened on the reins. She beamed beneath her veil.

They rode side by side, his grey dwarfing her little mare. 'I have hoped since dinner that your ride would bring you here,' he said. 'I've been too desperately busy with my men to call on you. I cannot even come to meals.'

They turned from the path and started across open country. One of his hands held the reins, the other rested on his thigh. His legs were long and muscular. 'It's the drilling that takes so much time,' he added, then turned to meet her eyes. 'I hope you will come again.'

Mariana pushed a curl under her riding hat. 'Only if

you promise to describe all your preparations for the campaign.'

He smiled. 'I promise to shower you with every tedious detail.'

Her dreams fulfilled, Mariana sighed.

'War lasts longer than we think,' he said abruptly. 'Look.' He twisted in his saddle and pointed to the horizon. 'This country was reduced to emptiness by pillage long before Ranjit Singh came to power. It has never recovered. I believe violence can soak into the soil and become part of a place. I feel it here.'

'You feel violence here?' Mariana looked towards the placid scene where he pointed, with its distant mud villages and a single ragged man leading a black buffalo. Her soothsayers had not mentioned violence, but they had mentioned courage. Of what future calamity had they tried to warn her?

They had reached a stand of feathery trees. Fitzgerald reined in his horse. 'Shall we stop for a moment in the shade? I do not believe,' he added, seeing her hesitate, 'that anyone knows we are here. Besides, it's only for a little while.'

Before she could make up her mind, he called to her grooms. 'Leave us,' he told them. 'Return to the horse lines.'

They watched her escort trot away towards the government camp. 'I am not sure you should ride alone with native menservants,' he said seriously. 'Men like those may not be safe.'

She dismounted. 'Are those poor underfed things your idea of a pillaging horde?' She sat down on an upturned stone and swept a spider from her skirts. 'It would be worse to ride out with no escort at all,' she added, thinking of the mad fortune-teller. 'Besides, a senior groom chose them for me.'

'Still,' Fitzgerald said softly, as he came and sat beside her,

109

'they *are* native men. You should be careful.' His face had tightened. His voice sounded hoarse, as if he suddenly needed something to drink.

His face was close to hers. 'I wished to speak to you alone,' he said, dropping his eyes, 'because I must know . . .' Her hands lay together in her lap. Reaching out swiftly, he took them, his square fingers brushing her legs through the wool of her riding habit. 'I should not say this, Miss Givens,' he murmured, turning her hands over in his, 'but since dinner, I have thought of nothing but you.' As he spoke his eyes roamed over her face and the front of her body as they had after dinner. Unable to stop herself, she leaned towards him, her eyelids lowered.

In an instant, he dropped her hands and raised the veil from her face. Taking hold of her shoulders, he pressed his mouth on hers.

He smelled of horses. The weight of his hands on her shoulders and the moist pressure of his mouth carried her away from everything she knew. As she pressed towards him, one of his hands, then the other, slid behind her back. Heat rose from the centre of her body and spread to her face.

'Oh, Mariana.' His cheek to hers, he rocked from side to side, breathing rapidly, as if he had run up a flight of stairs.

He had called her by her name. She wanted to reach up and touch his lips with her fingers.

An artillery shot crashed in the distance. Shouts from closer by signalled that someone was approaching.

She started backward. What had she done? They would be seen coming out from the trees alone, without even her grooms for propriety! Pushing him away, she jumped to her feet.

He, too, stood up. 'It's all right,' he said as he moved to

untie the horses. 'We can go out by the other way. No one will see us.'

Afterwards they hardly spoke, but as they parted, he looked at her again, his eyes luminous in his square face.

'Mariana,' was all he said before he left her.

Later, still rosy and breathless, she stood over her basin, splashing water on her cheeks, remembering the exact moment when Fitzgerald's lips had met hers. Behind her, on the floor, her riding habit lay in a black heap where she had dropped it when she changed into a fresh gown.

'Memsahib!' Dittoo cried, rushing inside, shattering her reverie. 'Your clothes! If they lie on the floor, a snake or a scorpion might get inside!'

What did she care for snakes and scorpions? Mariana groped blindly for her towel as Dittoo began to shake out her riding coat, thickening the air with dust.

'A snake, even a small one, can kill you with one bite, Memsahib,' he went on, now shaking her skirt. 'It can come into this tent through the tiniest hole. As for a scorpion, its sting can make the strongest man scream. That is why the other memsahib did not come with us to translate for the Governor Sahib's ladies. She was bitten by a scorpion that got inside her clothes.'

Was she not to be allowed a moment's peace? Mariana flung her towel onto the chair and pointed to the door. 'Take those clothes outside, Dittoo!' she snapped.

Unperturbed, Dittoo gathered up her habit, then waved a careless hand. 'You should be getting ready, Memsahib,' he told her. 'Your Munshi Sahib is coming this way.'

Munshi Sahib had recovered. Her lesson! How could she have forgotten the poem he had given her, so full of feelings that mirrored her own? Mariana turned a softer eye on Dittoo.

111

'Ask him to wait a moment, until I am ready to receive him,' she said.

She returned to her table, opened her writing box and took out the paper on which he had written the poem in Persian, and the larger piece on which she had copied her translation. She smoothed them carefully out on the table.

'Are you quite well, now, Munshi Sahib?' she enquired moments later, taking her seat and searching her teacher's face, noticing that he looked a little wan but reasonably well. Careful of the formality between them, she did not mention his new lamb's wool hat.

'I am quite well, Bibi,' he replied, nodding gravely. 'And now, let us see how you have translated our poem.'

Mariana had worked on the poem until late the previous night, her lamp flickering beside her, dreaming of Harry Fitzgerald as she chose her words. Now he had kissed her. Her voice trembling a little, she began to read:

> I, the candle, burn myself away
> For thee, the blazing morn, my heart's desire.
> Consumed by heat of longing for thy face,
> At thy first glance I perish in thy fire.
> Far distant yet close by, I die for thee,
> Whose radiant being lights my funeral pyre.

She waited, blushing.

For a time her munshi rocked silently on his heels, his eyes moving over the walls of her tent.

'Bibi,' he said at last, poking a long finger at the paper in her hand, 'you have taken words from the page I gave you and written your own poem. You have not translated *that* poem.' He gestured towards the paper on the table.

112

Mariana picked up the page decorated with his delicate Persian writing. 'But Munshi Sahib,' she said, pointing to the first line, 'I *have* translated it. There it is — *Main shama jan gudazan—*'

'No, Bibi.' He shook his head firmly. 'The poem I gave you is about a candle and about the morning light, that is true, but it does not contain the sentiments you have expressed.'

'Sentiments? But Munshi Sahib—'

'Moreover, fire does not appear in the original poem, and there is most assuredly no mention of a funeral or a funeral pyre. I regret having given you this poem when you were not in a frame of mind to do a proper translation. It is my mistake. Do not concern yourself. We will not mention your poem again.'

Her poem. *Her* frame of mind. Suddenly hot, she looked away. What had she revealed? What had he guessed?

'I will now give you a better translation,' he went on in a businesslike tone. 'This one is not in poetic form but it is, nonetheless, better.'

His hands clasped behind him, he recited in his curiously accented English:

I am the self-consuming candle.
Thou art the brilliant morn that draws the heart.
I burn with desire to see thee,
Yet I perish before thy glory.
I am both close to thee and immeasurably far away.
Separation from thee is like dying,
Yet in thy presence I cannot survive.

Hardly hearing him, Mariana stared at her hands. He knew. He read her so easily. He was worse than Miss Emily. 'Oh, Munshi Sahib,' she said, 'I do not think I—'

'This,' her teacher interrupted solemnly, his eyes holding hers, 'is not a simple poem. It does not concern itself with fires and burning. It concerns itself with the pain of separation. Its subject is the striving of the soul to reach God.'

'Oh.' If only the lesson would end . . .

'Yes,' the munshi continued, 'this poem describes the pain of longing. It says that the soul is a candle burning in the darkness, longing for the morning. But when the sun appears, the candle's light diminishes to nothing. Like a candle in sunlight, the soul becomes nothing in the presence of God. That is why the candle and the soul both fear that which they long for most. And that,' he said, his old eyes on Mariana's face, 'is what you are to learn from translating this poem.'

Her munshi had a curious ability to hold Mariana's attention. Against her will, his words reached her and dominated her thoughts, temporarily driving away Fitzgerald's kiss.

She nodded. 'The candle and the soul,' she repeated, 'both fear what they long for. That is sad but lovely, Munshi Sahib. But,' she asked, suddenly needing to know, 'to what religion do you belong, Munshi Sahib? Are you Hindu?'

Her teacher raised his hands. 'No, Bibi, I am not Hindu, although there are many noble and God-fearing Hindus in India. In fact, there are noble men of all religions in India. But I myself am Muslim.' He smiled. 'That much you may know of me.'

When he had gone, Mariana read her own poem once more, then crossed out its original title, 'Love's Candle', and replaced it with 'To H.F.' After folding it carefully, she slipped it beneath the papers at the bottom of her writing box.

She shivered. So much had happened today, but for all the

beauty of Munshi's poem, for all the excitement of Fitzgerald's kiss, she had not forgotten Yar Mohammad's eerie message. A groom, a madman, even Fitzgerald, had warned her to be careful. But of what?

Chapter Eight

Wednesday, 27 November

Quiet had settled over the Lahore Citadel. The usual jostling crowd of nobles, traders, soldiers and servants was missing from the outer courts, having gone to wait upon the Maharajah at his distant camp, leaving the fountains to play to an audience of sweepers who stood knee-deep in the water, their garments tied high, scrubbing slime from the waterways.

Only the Jasmine Tower, home to the Maharajah's queens, was as busy as usual. Throughout the afternoon, maidservants had covered and re-covered the distance from the kitchens to the tower, carrying the ladies' meal – twenty-one dishes of goat, fish from the Ravi River, quail, venison, duck, wild mushrooms, rice dishes cooked with saffron and scattered with almonds, rounds of bread, mountains of fruit. The eunuch guards lazed, waiting in the marble court, while servant children, their clothes the colour of dust, watched from the shade of nearby porticos.

In the long room with the delicately fretted window at its end, the meal had now finished. The silk squares still lay in a line on the carpet, but the dishes and platters that had covered them were gone. Still sitting, the queens waited, greasy fingers held away from their clothes, for slave women to come and pour a stream of rosewater over each pair of royal hands.

For the remainder of the afternoon, the ladies would rest. They dried their fingers, then still chatting, moved to the cool walls to arrange themselves on bolsters and let the servants cover them with satin quilts. The ladies stretched, curled and sighed, their bangles clashing sweetly in the perfumed air.

While the queens dozed, those servants who had not stayed to fan away the flies snatched their own sleep on reed mats thrown onto the bare tiles of the women's servant quarters. There they would lie until the sonorous voice of the court caller summoned them back to serve their queens. They, too, had eaten. The eunuch guards, as always, had pounced on the leftover delicacies from the tower, leaving only a few morsels for the most senior women servants, and nothing for the others but rice and boiled lentil mush.

After swallowing her last bit of dry bread, Reshma had found a mat in the larger of the two women's quarters. She liked to sleep in a corner but, being young and unimportant, she rarely had her wish. Today, she was crowded into the middle of the room with a pair of feet inches from her face.

The afternoon was bright and not too hot for rest, and the morning's work had been easy. Preoccupied, Saat Kaur had not pestered Reshma to bring her this, no, bring her that, no, take it all away. But Reshma had worries more serious than cracked looking glasses and misplaced lengths of brocade. Without moving her eyes, she reached out with cautious fingers and felt for the small body that shared her mat. Saboor was there. When she dared a hasty glance, she saw that his eyes were open, fixed on the cobwebs that hung from the rafters overhead.

He, who used to chatter to his mother every waking

117

moment, had not spoken since excited voices from the ladies' tower had called them from their hiding place in the garden. The running servants had been too breathless to explain, but Reshma had not needed to be told of the horror that had occurred. Surrounded by panting women, she had carried Saboor down the narrow stairway to the crowded room where his mother lay dead, and from that moment he had lapsed into a heavy, unbroken silence. His slight body in its starched cotton pyjamas had also changed, its bright energy replaced by sodden weight. Her arms had ached as she dragged him away from the sight of his dead mother.

The lady had seemed asleep. Only the liquid that trickled from the corner of her mouth onto the scarlet bed-covering had hinted that something was amiss, that she would not at any moment sit up, put her head on one side and reach for her tortoiseshell comb with the pearls set into its frame. The silver cup, fallen from her fingers, had rolled away across the room. It was the cup that had betrayed the source of the poison.

Reshma raised her head and looked cautiously about her before she rolled onto her back and, like Saboor beside her, stared at the rafters. There never seemed to be a moment when she was not watched.

Since his mother's death, Saboor had suffered. His starched clothes had become limp and unclean; his head, shaved to thicken his curls, was scabby. He ate little, only the mouthfuls that Reshma saved from her own poor meals and fed him hastily, looking over her shoulder, afraid to be seen. He had endured blows. Worst, in all that time no one had embraced him. Before his mother's death, he had never been more than an arm's length from someone who loved him, and now he had only Reshma to carry him here and there, and she did not dare to embrace him with love. How could she, when all eyes were upon her, when Saat Kaur, murderess that she was, had now offered a pair of ruby earrings to the first servant to see him dead?

All this was because the Maharajah was old and ailing. Some of the queens wanted to burn alive on his pyre after he died, but not Saat Kaur. Terrified for her life, she had tried to gain importance through her sickly little princeling, but it had been Saboor, not her baby, who had won the Maharajah's love. For this, she had ordered Reshma to poison Saboor.

Saboor sighed. Reshma heard him, but did not move. Children were said to forget quickly. He should have forgotten his mother by now, but she knew with certainty that he had not. She knew that, since his mother's death, there had been no moment when he did not long to hear her voice, to feel her arms about him. Reshma squeezed her eyes shut against the panic that threatened her every waking moment. *What had she done?*

She wished he would look at her. It would lighten her burden to feel he understood her efforts to help him, but even when she fed him, he looked into the distance, as if dreaming of some far-off place. When he swallowed the water she brought, he looked away from her, refusing to meet her sorrowful gaze. Was he thinking of the sweet sherbets his mother used to stir into his drinks?

Only one thing seemed to interest him: the queens of the Jasmine Tower. Whenever he came near them, he looked ceaselessly from face to face, lapsing after each search into a dark, disappointed sadness. He sat day after day, alone in the shadow of a portico, watching the ladies in the garden. Every day he grew weaker.

Reshma sat up on her mat. 'Come,' she said loudly, keeping

her voice careless. 'You must come to the latrine before you soil yourself or me.'

She stood and dragged the little boy to her hip. Her hands shook. She should call the sweeperess, who sat against the wall outside, to do this, but the woman's hands stank, and she, who needed the earrings most, was the cruellest of all.

Avoiding the gaze of the other servants, Reshma carried Saboor away to the noisome cupboard behind a rotting wall.

They had returned to their mat when a eunuch appeared in the doorway. He was no ordinary eunuch, but a functionary of the court. His tall, pear-shaped form was clothed in silk, not cotton. His turban was elaborately tied, and he wore a gold bangle on one wrist. He stood, his arms dangling at his sides, his eyes half closed.

'The Maharajah,' he announced languidly,' has called for the child Saboor to be sent to him at once. His best clothes are to be sent as well, the ones he wears at state functions.'

The women servants stared.

The corners of the eunuch's mouth turned down. 'Do not gape like a herd of camels. Go and fetch the child. He is to leave without delay. The Maharajah's own palanquin is waiting by the door. You,' he added, pointing to one of the senior servants, 'are to tell the senior queen of these instructions. And tell her the child's mother is to remain here until Saboor returns.'

A murmur ran through the group of women. Their eyes fixed on Reshma as a hollow voice echoed from the courtyard outside, 'Reshma, Reshma, go to Rani Saat Kaur.'

God help her, it was the caller. The little queen was awake.

Reshma seized Saboor, pushed through the crowd, and ran for the ladies' tower.

She carried him up the stone stairs to the dusty storeroom at

120

the top of the tower, high above the room where the queens lay sleeping. There, breathing hard, she put him down and began to throw aside boxes of all sizes as she searched for the little basket where his mother had stored his embroidered court clothes.

'We must hurry, Saboor,' she panted. 'We must get you away before Saat Kaur learns you are going to the Maharajah.' She shook her head. 'Poor Saboor. Your light, if you have it, has brought you no luck.'

Reshma's hands trembled as she worked. She imagined the young queen, her face twisted with rage, appearing at the head of the stairs, snatching up the little boy and hurling him from a tower window.

'How little our lives matter, Saboor,' Reshma said as she turned over tin trunks and leather boxes. 'We are nothing to these important people. Your mother was nothing. If we hurry, we can save you from Rani Saat Kaur. Now you will go to the Maharajah who will give you the best food. He will protect you from harm. This will be better, you will see. This will be better.'

She glanced towards the door. Too weak to stand for long, Saboor had sat down, silent and dirt-smeared, at the top of the stairs, his hands open at his sides.

As Reshma found his basket and snatched it up, the caller's distant voice found its way up the stone stairs.

'Reshma, oh, Reshma.'

Saboor on her hip, Reshma clutched the basket with one thin arm and took the stone stairs two at a time down to the doorway. Before she carried him out into the sunlight, the child turned his head and looked solemnly into her face for the first time since his mother's death. Her eyes filling, Reshma stopped in the doorway and met his gaze.

In the marble courtyard by the Queens' Garden, a magnificent carved palanquin stood with its curtains closed, the long carrying poles protruding front and back from a curved roof. Twelve bearers in the scarlet uniform of the Maharajah's service stood ready, while a group of mounted guards waited on impatient horses, the blades of their ceremonial spears flashing in the sunlight. The eunuch leaned, picking his teeth with his thumbnail, against a second, plainer palanquin. A little distance away, another group of bearers sat, watching silently.

Reshma bundled Saboor into the grand palanquin and pushed the basket of clothes in after him.

'Wait, stupid woman, daughter of an owl.' The eunuch was beside her, his mouth twisting. 'What is this nonsense? What filthy brat are you passing off for the child Saboor? You will be punished for this.'

'Reshma!' The caller's hollow voice had grown impatient. 'You must go at once to Rani Saat Kaur.'

Reshma's eyes jerked from the eunuch to the doorway of the ladies' tower. She stepped back from the palanquin. 'That *is* the child Saboor,' she said.

He stared, his mouth open. 'Are you sure?' he asked, his dusky voice high and startled.

'Please.' She cleared her throat. 'His mother died ten days ago. Please take him away quickly.'

The eunuch's eyes widened. 'The mother is dead?' Recovering himself, he glanced at the sky. 'Never mind. This is no time to be concerning ourselves with details.' He flapped his fingers towards the palanquin. 'We must hurry.' He glanced at Reshma. 'Women,' he said, and spat on the marble paving.

With a ceremonial groan, four of the bearers hoisted the Maharajah's palanquin to their shoulders. The head bearer gave a command, and all twelve men began to trot. In seconds, the palanquin with its relief bearers and mounted guards rounded the corner of the courtyard leading to the elephant stairs. Following closely, the eunuch's palanquin with its own complement of bearers and guards passed out of Reshma's sight.

'May God forgive me for my crime,' she whispered when they had gone, 'and grant my Saboor a safe journey.'

Turning away, she ran as fast as she could to Rani Saat Kaur's room.

Saat Kaur's child was coughing when Reshma entered, a weak, unpleasant sound.

'Where have you been?' Saat Kaur asked irritably from her bed. 'Where is the brat Saboor?'

'He has gone, Bibi.' Reshma's throat was dry. When she closed her mouth, grit from the storeroom cracked between her teeth. 'The Maharajah sent for him. He has gone in the Maharajah's own palki to the royal camp.'

Saat Kaur sat up, her eyes stretched wide. 'In the Maharajah's own palki?'

When Saat Kaur rose from the bed, Reshma stood motionless, although her heart beat painfully. Where was there to run in this enclosed tower? An instant later, her head snapped sideways as Saat's open hand took her full in the face, leaving a fiery imprint on her cheek.

This time one slap would not suffice. Panting, Saat Kaur reached for her shoe.

Reshma sought to save herself from the next blow, but she was not quick enough. It fell, sickeningly, on her ear. She covered her head with her arms and hunched her shoulders against the blows that followed.

'For this,' Saat Kaur gasped, out of breath from the work

123

of beating her servant, 'my father brought me at the age of eleven to run beside the Maharajah's palanquin so he would notice me? For this I enticed the Maharajah to take me as his youngest wife?'

Reshma waited, whimpering, for Saat Kaur's arm to tire. Her own arms ached and burned. The blows to her body echoed in the small room. When at last they weakened, she ran for the doorway, but sharp-nailed fingers grasped her braid and yanked her back.

'People will tell the Maharajah what I have done! What will become of me now?' The Rani's eyes were swollen. The little queen had been weeping even before she heard the news. On the bed, her son began to wail fretfully.

'No, Princess,' Reshma cried out, stepping back painfully. 'He will not know, he—'

'Liar!' A sour smell rose from Saat Kaur's pretty body. She shook Reshma by her bruised shoulders. 'He will see the brat's condition. The others will tell him of the poison. They have guessed. I can feel it. *Why did you not wash the cup?*' She let go of Reshma and clutched at her face. 'What will save me from the pyre now? They would not burn the mother of a beloved son, but the Maharajah cares only for the brat Saboor. It should be my son, *my son* in that palki! This is your doing. I will kill you for this. I will kill you!'

She flung herself onto the bed beside her wailing son. Reshma crawled to a corner and huddled there, her arms wrapped round her body. Helpless tears ran down her nose and dripped onto the front of her long, worn shirt.

From the bed, Saat Kaur sighed, breaking the silence. 'Come here, Reshma,' she ordered, rolling onto her stomach. 'I want you to press my back.'

Her battered body still shook with shock and fright, but Reshma did as she was ordered. She bent over the bed, and pressed her hands rhythmically up and down the length of the little queen's back until she fell asleep.

Chapter Nine

The two palanquins made good time along the road to the Maharajah's camp. In three hours they covered a little over twelve miles. The Maharajah's personal head bearer called a halt, and the running men and their escort left the road.

They set the palanquins down and squatted beside them while the armed guards tethered their horses. The relief team would come soon. With luck, they would do eleven more miles before dark.

The bearers stretched. Since they had started their journey, there had been no sound from within the royal palanquin.

'We might as well be carrying an empty palki,' remarked one man. He yawned. 'I wish we had such small passengers every time.'

'His condition is bad,' said another. 'I'll be surprised if he lives to finish the journey.'

'The child's condition is no concern of yours.' The eunuch pushed his way past the men who now sat grouped around the silent box. 'Your only concern should be getting him to his destination by the day after tomorrow morning. Show him to me.'

A bearer held a tasselled curtain aside. The eunuch put his head inside and withdrew it instantly. 'He stinks,' he cried, his face puckering. 'He cannot have been bathed for days.'

The bearers and the guardsmen peered into the palanquin. Saboor's stained shirt had lifted as he slept, exposing protruding ribs. His body and clothes smelled. He looked at the men with lightless eyes.

'This evil is the work of women,' said one of the guards, shaking his head. 'Who but a jealous woman would harm a lovely child such as this?'

Two days later, breathing the harsh 'hah, hah, hah' rhythm that is the way of bearers, the final team was only five miles from the Maharajah's camp. They would arrive with time to spare.

The palanquins skirted a dead jackal on the road, scattering a flock of carrion crows. Neeloo, the head bearer, turned to the man trotting beside him. 'The child is too quiet. I am worried about his condition. He came with no food or drink for his journey. The previous bearers have fed him from their own meals, but he has not eaten since this morning.'

'Where is his food?' asked Neeloo's companion. 'Why is he travelling in the royal palanquin with nothing to eat or drink?'

'Perhaps he is dying,' said another man.

Neeloo did not reply.

Small muffled sounds came from behind the closed curtains. Neeloo signalled for a stop, then squatted beside the royal palanquin and pulled apart the curtains. Saboor lay whimpering on the satin sheets, his hands opening and closing at his sides.

'What is this? Why have we stopped?' The eunuch climbed from his palki.

A hand on his tiny passenger, Neeloo looked up. 'The child needs food.'

'Food? Now? Don't be stupid. Move on.'

Neeloo looked from the eunuch's retreating back to the baby, then pointed to a village near the road. 'Gupta,' he said to a young bearer, 'fetch some dung from there. We must make a fire and cook for the child.'

The other bearers stared. They were Kahars from Farrukhabad. Hereditary palanquin bearers did not fetch dung from villages, and they never cooked or ate food during the day.

'What? Cook for the child? The eunuch swung round. 'Are you mad?'

Neeloo spread his hands. 'The child is valuable to the Maharajah,' he said. 'He must be delivered to the camp alive.'

The eunuch paced, muttering to himself, while they made a small fire and stirred a pot of lentils. He fumed aloud, watching the child open his mouth like a baby bird's to receive his food.

'He is very hungry,' said a bearer.

'These things happen over deaths and marriages,' agreed a guard, shaking his head as Neeloo tore off a child-size morsel of half-dry bread and scooped up a little of the yellow mush.

But it seemed that food and drink alone would not satisfy Saboor. As soon as they started off, wailing arose from inside the curtained box. On and on it went, wavering a little with the bouncing of the palki, pausing as the child breathed, only to begin again. The running bearers shouted encouragement. When the cries did not stop, Neeloo and the unburdened bearers opened the palanquin's curtains and trotted alongside, arguing with the little boy's tears.

'Come, child, do not weep,' they called, putting their hands inside to pat his dirty little body. 'Look, there are so many things to see. We will open the curtain on the other side also.

128

There is not far to go. You will have so many things to eat at the Maharajah's camp!'

But Saboor went on wailing, his eyes squeezed shut, his mouth stretched wide.

'You are making us late!' shouted the eunuch as Neeloo stopped again and lifted the child once more from the Maharajah's satin sheets. 'I order you to move!'

Neeloo did not look up. He folded Saboor onto his lap as he had done for his own children when they, too, had wept from want and misery. 'We will wait until he has ceased crying,' he declared as he wiped Saboor's wet face with a callused hand. 'No child should be left to weep alone.'

The other men nodded their agreement.

The eunuch raged, but for all his authority he was only one and there were twenty-four bearers and twelve armed guards. Their backs to the eunuch, all waited by the beautiful carved palanquin until, cradled in Neeloo's arms, Saboor had sobbed himself to sleep.

Chapter Ten

Thursday, 28 November

Miss Fanny rocked a little on the narrow seat as she, Miss Emily and Mariana returned on an elephant from the camp parade ground. 'I must say, our troops made a stirring show this morning,' she remarked.

Miss Emily, who sat hunched over with fever beside her sister, pulled her shawls closer about her in the morning heat. 'Did you enjoy the practise review, my dear?' she enquired, peering out at Mariana from the shade of a large purple silk bonnet.

'Oh, yes,' Mariana cried, 'it was marvellous! How do you suppose they persuaded the baggage elephants to behave so well on parade?'

For her, the best part of the show had been the horse artillery, especially Lieutenant Fitzgerald on his tall grey gelding, his brass dragoon helmet flashing as he led a team pulling a twenty-pound gun.

'I hope they do as well at the real review.' Miss Fanny sighed. 'I always think I have become used to seeing our British soldiers in India, but when the Queen's Buffs marched past this morning . . .' Her voice quavered.

'Yes indeed, Fanny,' said Miss Emily, speaking through

gently chattering teeth. 'You always weep at the sight of the Buffs. For my part, a bagpipe always fills me with excitement. At the first hint of a drone I long to snatch up a weapon and attack someone.'

Miss Fanny tugged her bonnet lower over her eyes. 'And whom would you attack? I can only imagine myself attacking rampaging natives.'

The two ladies subsided into silence, their eyes on the horizon. Opposite them, Mariana fidgeted on her seat.

'Miss Fanny,' she asked after a moment, 'do you really dislike the natives?'

'In a way I do, Mariana,' replied Miss Fanny, as she took out her handkerchief. 'There is something far too foreign about them, something mysterious and upsetting.' She pointed down at a group of dark-skinned men walking beside the elephants, wearing only dirty-looking loincloths, their hair tangled and uncombed. 'Look at those men. How can one not feel distaste?' She sniffed, her handkerchief to her nose.

'But not all of them are like that.' The elephant shifted its weight, causing the wooden box where the ladies sat to lurch sideways, pushing Mariana against the railing. 'Surely some of the natives are worthy of respect. My munshi says there are noble and God-fearing men of all religions in India, and—'

'Their worthiness, or lack of it, is not the point, Mariana,' Miss Emily put in from her corner. 'The point is that you show far too much interest in their affairs. You have been seen poking about with elephants and mahouts. You speak of helping diseased natives. I worry about that munshi of yours. I fear he has filled your head with unsuitable ideas. The only way to behave with natives,' she added, tightening her shawls, 'is to ignore them. Do not like them, do not hate them, do not fear them. Those who do, pay a heavy price. Our previous

131

lady translator, silly woman, developed a horror of natives. I am told she barricades her bedroom door at night, for fear one of them will get in while she is sleeping.'

Miss Fanny put a hand to her bonnet. 'Something happened to her, you see. People are saying she will never be the same again.'

Mariana sat up.

'The lady,' said Miss Emily, 'was awakening from sleep one morning when her serving man came in with her coffee. As he put down the tray, he noticed a scorpion on the bedclothes. It was, if I am correct, crawling up the lady's person, on its way to her face.' She turned to Mariana. 'Hill scorpions, as you know, are large, black and very fierce.'

Mariana remembered Dittoo holding up her riding habit. 'The sting of a scorpion,' he had said, 'can make the strongest man scream.'

Miss Emily pointed into the air with a gloved hand. 'The servant tore open the mosquito curtains, reached out with his bare hand and swept the scorpion to the floor, where he killed it. At once the lady began to shriek at the top of her voice. People rushed to her room to find her fainting with terror, but not,' she added, closing her eyes as the howdah rolled, creakingly, to one side, 'from fear of scorpions.'

Mariana smiled to herself. Dittoo had, as usual, got the story all wrong, but it was perfect for her next letter to Papa. 'So why did she faint?'

Miss Emily pressed her lips together. 'She fainted because a native man had touched her. The servant was dismissed, and the lady, since then, has been unable to be left alone for five minutes.'

Mariana stared from one Eden sister to the other. 'What a fool the woman must be!'

132

'Yes, she is a fool because she gave in to fear.' Miss Emily frowned. 'You must do as we say, Mariana. Natives are very different from us, although most of the time I would not go so far as to call them savages as some of our Englishmen do.'

Savages? Her dear old Munshi Sahib? Her irritating, clumsy, harmless Dittoo? Mariana opened her mouth to protest, then closed it.

'And now, my dear,' Miss Emily continued, fixing her gaze on Mariana's face, 'I understand you have taken an interest in Lieutenant Fitzgerald.'

Mariana smiled nervously. By now, everyone must know.

Yesterday, on the way to their grove of trees, she and Fitzgerald had talked animatedly of the intricacies of artillery drills, of the Afghan Campaign, and of his uncle's estate in Sussex, not ten miles from her own village. Alone together, they had kissed again. This time he had laid a hand on her breast. She flushed, remembering the heat of it, and the longing it had aroused in her.

'I am sorry to say that we have had a bad report of him.' Miss Emily pronounced her words with care.

On the elephant ahead of them, Mr Macnaghten, the political secretary, laughed loudly.

A bad report? Mariana smiled uncomprehendingly. 'Miss Emily?'

'It seems Lieutenant Fitzgerald jilted a young lady in Calcutta a year ago. He and the girl had been engaged for months when he broke it off with no explanation, leaving her to return, unmarried, to England.' Miss Emily sighed. 'He has very much blackened his name in Calcutta.' She folded her hands. 'I am sorry, Mariana. I wish we had known this earlier.'

The howdah shook. Mariana clutched at the railing. 'But

133

Miss Emily, there must be some explanation. I cannot believe he would do such a cruel thing.'

'It seems that he did it after meeting a second young lady with a greater fortune. She had the sense to refuse him. Since then, he has not been received in proper society. It was his good fortune that his regiment, where he was still popular, left Calcutta soon afterwards to join this camp.'

Miss Fanny nodded from her corner. 'Of course it will not be long before the entire camp learns of this.'

Mariana reached out a hand. 'But Miss Emily, Miss Fanny, we *must* hear his side of the story.' Her voice sounded high and strange.

'No, Mariana.' Miss Emily peered at Mariana's reddening face from the depths of her bonnet. 'It is too late for explanations. Your connection with Fitzgerald must be severed. I am sure this is painful for you now but in time you will be grateful.'

In her mind's eye Mariana saw her father's grave face as he told her she was not to see her friend Jeremy again. How could this happen a second time? How could she be forbidden the only person she wanted, the only one whose presence gave her joy?

Miss Emily leaned forward. 'You will not need to break off the friendship yourself,' she added briskly. 'I shall have a word with General Cotton. Fitzgerald's commanding officer will speak to him tomorrow morning. After that, he will not approach you again, you may be sure.' She smiled kindly. 'Do not worry, my dear. There are several suitable men in this camp with spotless reputations. I am sure one of them will make you very happy.'

Miss Fanny reached over and patted Mariana's knee. 'My sister is right. Good looks are all very well, but they do not last. A kind heart and a sufficient income are what make a good husband.'

Mariana's chest ached fiercely. 'Miss Emily,' she said as firmly as she was able, 'I cannot sever my connection with the Lieutenant until I have spoken to him myself.'

'You may *not* speak to him.' Miss Emily drew herself up in her seat. 'Believe me, my dear, men like Fitzgerald are great charmers, capable of getting young women like you into all sorts of trouble.'

Mariana's thoughts flew to the grove of feathery trees, and Fitzgerald's hand on her breast. She could not bear the unfairness of this.

Miss Emily pursed her lips. 'And now, let us cease this unpleasant conversation. We have no need to speak of the young man again.'

After lunch, the sky through Mariana's doorway was drained of colour. In Sussex, it would be cool and rainy. If she were wearing her blue striped gown there, she would need a hood for her cape when she and Fitzgerald drove to his uncle's house to be received as husband and wife.

She dipped her pen into her inkpot with a little stabbing gesture.

As for me, she wrote to her mother, *I look constantly into my boxes to make sure nothing awful has happened to my gowns. Several of them are borrowed from ladies in Simla whom I hardly know, and I am terrified of losing or ruining one of them.*

She wiped her pen. She could write no more of this drivel. Having saved her news about Fitzgerald until she was certain of him, she now had only her hurt and fury to report, and they were too painful to put on paper.

She pushed herself out of her chair and paced to her bed, then

135

flung herself about and paced back to her desk. Hesitating no more, she jerked open her trunk and pulled out her riding habit. 'Dittoo,' she called out, 'get me a mare and two grooms.'

The little mare was brought to her by a silent stranger. That meant she was spared any further messages from Yar Mohammad, which was a good thing. She did not think she could stand any more advice from soothsayers.

At the army camp, she rode towards the parade ground, aware that people were looking, that someone might report her to General Cotton. She did not care. Who was General Cotton anyhow but a fussy old man with a scarlet face and bushy side whiskers, who sat next to Miss Emily at dinner? Activity surrounded her as she rode past rows of tents. Soldiers, both native and European, were busy polishing weapons and repairing uniforms. A team of bullocks hauled a gun carriage out of the way. English officers inclined their heads as she rode by.

She had circled the parade ground only twice when Fitzgerald emerged, waving, from between two tents. At the sight of him riding towards her, she began to perspire.

When he arrived at her side, smiling happily, she tried to smile in return but could not.

'Is something wrong?' He studied her face.

'Yes,' she forced out, knowing she was about to ruin everything for ever. 'Miss Emily spoke to me this morning. There has been a bad report of you from Calcutta.'

Afraid to watch his expression change, she bent her head and played with her reins. When she looked up, his face was tight.

'What did she say?' His voice was level, but his knee jogged up and down on his saddle. 'Did she say I had jilted someone, that I had ruined the girl's chance at marriage?'

Someone had lit a campfire nearby. The smell of burning

charcoal reached them. Mariana pinched her lips together. 'Did you do it?'

'Yes. No.' Fitzgerald looked away, then into her face. 'I did not jilt her. I refused to marry her when I learned what she was. That is all.'

Birds chattered in a nearby tree. Under her veil, Mariana's hair stuck to her forehead. 'You can tell me more than that,' she said.

He shook his head. 'What good would it do? The girl is ruined, and so am I. Why add to it?' He stared past Mariana, into the distance. 'I never thought her lies would reach all the way to the Punjab. Has Miss Emily told you not to see me again?'

Mariana took a shaky breath. 'Your commanding officer will speak to you tomorrow morning.'

Horses approached. Collecting herself, she nodded to two officers as they rode past, then turned back to Fitzgerald.

He looked so forlorn, his face averted, his shoulders sagging, that she stretched out a gloved hand. 'I am sure there was a reason for what you did. You don't need to tell me now,' she added, when he did not respond. 'I mean, we can meet tomorrow when nobody is—'

'I am an officer in the Bengal Native Artillery,' he cut in harshly. 'I cannot disobey orders.' He dropped his face into his hands. 'Oh, God, why does my commanding officer have to be brought into it?'

She must return to camp before they guessed where she had gone. 'Were you,' she asked, needing to know, her face tight against his answer, 'I mean, would you have married me?' Waiting, she twisted the reins in her fingers.

'Of course, Mariana.' He kicked his horse. 'Whatever did you think?' he said over his shoulder as he rode away.

*   *   *

She would not break her connection to Fitzgerald. She did not care what anyone said. As Mariana dismounted angrily by her tent, a forceful, irritated voice came from beyond the red wall.

'I do not care in the slightest what the carpenters think,' the voice said. 'The stairs will be erected *there*, and they will be erected *now*.'

It sounded like Major Byrne.

'And,' the voice continued, as flat as a file, 'you will find the stair carpeting and you will have it nailed onto the stairs.'

It was Major Byrne. Mariana took off her riding hat and shook out her hair. Must he shout so, when her emotions were in such turmoil?

'And Sotheby, you are to make absolutely certain that the gifts are presented in their proper order. Repeat your instructions to me now, please.'

Unable to resist earesdropping, Mariana crossed to the red wall and looked through a hole in the canvas.

Major Byrne stood planted on the avenue, his back to her, addressing the White Rabbit, who stood at rigid attention. Across the avenue, a group of native workmen gestured at a stack of wooden boards.

'Yes, Major.' The White Rabbit's scarlet coat was stained with perspiration. When nervous, he tended to shout. He had talked so loudly when he sat beside Mariana at dinner that Miss Fanny had kept her napkin to her mouth for most of the soup course.

Her eyes to the hole, Mariana shook her head. How could the Eden sisters ever have imagined her marrying the White Rabbit?

'The portrait of Her Majesty,' Sotheby yelled, 'is to be given first, arrayed upon a velvet cushion—'

'Has the goldsmith returned the frame yet?' the Major interrupted, tapping an impatient boot.

'The gold—'

'I certainly hope you told Johnston not to take his eyes off the jeweller while he set the diamonds into the picture frame.' In order to interrupt Sotheby a second time, Major Byrne was obliged to raise his voice to a bellow. The carpenters stared. 'They all steal, you know. They must be watched every moment of the time.'

'Sir, the frame is ready,' Sotheby yelled, his eyes starting out of his chinless face.

'Yes, yes. Go on, man, repeat your instructions.' The Major took out his watch. 'I don't have all day.'

At the sound of Dittoo's voice behind her, Mariana flapped a hand for silence.

'Following the presentation of the smaller gifts, the two guns will be brought forward, and—'

'By God, Sotheby,' the Major bellowed, 'I particularly told you that those howitzers are to be *in place* for presentation by the time the two elephant processions have met at the midpoint of the avenue, there.'

Howitzers! Here was something Papa would enjoy: short-barrelled cannon made especially for firing shells at a high angle of elevation. He had never seen one close up . . .

Papa. If he were here, he would see that she was right about Fitzgerald, who loved her, who loved India as much as she did. This time he would not close the door and make her promise to give up her only friend, the only person who understood her. He would see that Fitzgerald must have left his bride-to-be for a reason.

Major Byrne was still shouting. 'I have also told you at least twice that you are to have them moved by coolies, not

139

by animals. The ground near the tent will have been swept, and I will *not* allow pack animals to tear it up. And you must not forget that the ammunition is to be arranged *close by* for the Maharajah's inspection. I want two hundred shells over there, and they must be stacked properly. If I find they have been thrown carelessly onto the ground, you shall be called to account. Do you understand me?'

Mariana sniffed. She should go inside and get a handkerchief.

The Major pointed at Sotheby's chest. 'And make sure the groom Yar Mohammad comes himself. He is not to send that fool Gulab Din with the horses. And mind that the grooms leading the animals for presentation are in *clean clothes*. We made a poor showing last time. I should not have to remind you that it is not the business of the British East India Company to be outdone on these occasions by native princes, whatever their pretensions may be. Remember that, my boy.' Smiling suddenly, he clapped Sotheby on the shoulder. 'Cheer up, lad,' he said. 'We'll show Ranjit Singh a thing or two. You'll see!'

He turned on his heel and strode across the dusty avenue, a barely discernible honk hanging in the air behind him. A moment later the sentries at the entrance came to clanking, stamping attention.

Five miles away, two horsemen rode across the broad parade ground at the Maharajah's camp.

'Since I do not have a quarter of your eloquence,' Yusuf Bhatti was saying, 'I am glad we are doing this together.'

'Eloquence?' Hassan made an exasperated gesture. 'In this case, eloquence has no value. There it is,' he announced, pointing to a yellow shawl tent set up near a spreading tree at the edge of the ground.

'No one is here but the guards.' Yusuf frowned as they approached the silent tent.

Hassan shook his head. 'A saddled horse is tethered outside. That means the Maharajah is here. Even when he is ill, his horse is kept ready for him. He is very weak, I am told. We need only wait there.' He pointed to a group of reed stools set out in the sun not far from the tent. 'If Uncle Azizuddin is not with him now, he will be here soon. He rarely leaves the Maharajah's side.'

A short while later, a stooping, bearded figure emerged from the tent's doorway. Yusuf and Hassan got to their feet.

'Ah, my dear boy,' cried Faqeer Azizuddin, the chief minister, as he reached for Hassan. 'I am so sorry to have missed you at Lahore. You had just left when I arrived there. I am heartbroken at the terrible news of your wife.'

Hassan offered the Faqeer a brief embrace, but did not reply.

'Please, let us sit. We do not wish to disturb the Maharajah.'

Yusuf studied the chief minister as he lowered himself onto a stool. His long woollen coat was creased, his beard untrimmed. The man looked as if he had not slept for days. The Maharajah must indeed be ill.

The Faqeer waved away a servant offering tumblers of water and turned to Hassan. 'You have come,' he said, 'to ask for Saboor's return.'

Hassan nodded. Beneath his elegant turban, his face was as still as stone.

'I cannot lie to you, my boy.' Faqeer Azizuddin took a crumpled handkerchief from the folds of his coat and wiped his face. 'The Maharajah needs your son. I know it does not seem reasonable, especially at this sad time, but he does.' He glanced towards the yellow tent. 'When Saboor is beside him, the Maharajah feels hope. He comes alive. He is able to rule. Without Saboor, he is weak. He falls victim to illness, to fits of paralysis and despair. Who can explain such things?' He returned his handkerchief to its hiding place in his clothes. 'As to your son's whereabouts, I can tell you this much – he left the Citadel yesterday. He will, God willing, arrive here tomorrow morning, in time for the beginning of the durbar. After he arrives, he will remain with the Maharajah until the close of the durbar.'

Hassan stiffened. Beside him, Yusuf flexed his shoulders, his weapons clashing against one another.

The Faqeer looked briefly at Yusuf. 'Do not worry,' he continued, turning back to Hassan. 'I have arranged for a reliable servant to look after Saboor. I promise you that after the state visit is concluded, you may take your son home to Qamar Haveli.'

'Faqeer Sahib, I *must* see Saboor before then.'

'Of course you will, son.' Faqeer waved an airy hand. 'Of course you will. And now, Hassan, we all know that the business of the Maharajah does not stop for durbars.' He tapped a finger on his knee. 'The leaders of Kasur have again refused to pay the Maharajah's tribute money. You must go there and get it from them. It will take no more than a few days. After that, you will see Saboor.' He nodded towards Yusuf. 'Take your friend with you. At this painful time, you should have your friends.' The Faqeer's voice softened to velvet as his eyes moved from Yusuf's weapons to his face. 'I am sure,' he said smoothly, 'that there will be no attempt to take Saboor away before the close of the durbar in fifteen days' time. You should know that anyone who tries to do so will be risking his life.'

Yusuf did not look at Hassan. Both men got to their feet as

the chief minister, responding to the beckoning of the armed guard, stood and took his leave.

As they walked to their horses, Yusuf spat on the ground. 'So even now you must wait fifteen days to embrace your son while the Faqeer caters to the Maharajah's whims!' He tugged angrily at his horse's reins. 'How can the Faqeer not take your side? Is it for the sake of the villages the Maharajah gives him? How can the Shaikh bear to be his friend? I myself would willingly kill him for his greed.'

Hassan sighed wearily. 'Cruel as he seems, the Faqeer is not to be hated. My father and I know what you do not. The Maharajah is dying, and has not yet chosen his heir. Faqeer Azizuddin is only trying to keep him alive until he names his successor, for if he dies without choosing, who knows what evil will befall us all. The Faqeer humours the Maharajah for the sake of the Punjab, not for himself. How can I refuse him when so many lives are at stake?' He shook his head. 'No, it is the Maharajah whom I cannot love. And now we must do his work, but we will be back soon. At least here my son will be safe from the queens.'

Chapter Eleven

'At all times of the day,' Mariana's munshi had told her one afternoon as they stood outside her tent, 'there are vultures overhead. They look like black spots circling in the sky.' He waved a wiry arm. 'Can you see them?'

Her hand over her eyes, Mariana peered upward.

'They are searching,' the munshi explained, 'for dead and dying creatures on the ground below. Some people believe that they have not always been here. They say that when the Moghul King Babur first entered India, he was shocked to find the carcasses of animals lying where they had fallen, with only ants and crows to carry away their rotting flesh. "Has India no vultures?" he asked. When he was told that it did not, he sent for several pairs to be caught and brought back to him from his homeland in Central Asia.' The munshi nodded. 'According to the story, they have remained here ever since. Whenever you look up, you will see them making their slow circles in the sky.'

Right now they were making their appointed rounds high above the River Sutlej, looking down on two camp cities that had arisen there in the space of only a few days.

South of the river's east-west course stood a large, orderly camp divided into two parts. In one, soldiers in red coats and white cross-belts marched to shouted orders on a newly cleared parade ground, while rows of heavy, wheeled guns waited, their barrels pointing to the north. The other part boasted a grand avenue with a red-walled compound and spacious tents. From the avenue, smaller streets spread out in all directions. Thousands of tents stood clustered around fires whose smoke joined together to send a horizontal cloud over the camp. A great crowd of men and boys tended long lines of horses, elephants, camels and bullocks. At three separate bazaars, each a small city in itself, men, women and children busied themselves at various tasks – cooking, stitching, throwing pottery, hammering brass, cleaning ears, shaving hair. At the midpoint of the camp's avenue, between a red wall and a grand tent with dancing pennants, a dozen decorated elephants knelt on the ground, their velvet housings trailing in the dust. At the avenue's far end, four troops of cavalry in dress uniform waited on gleaming horses.

Across the river stood another camp city. This was similar to the first but more fanciful in style, with an expanse of garden blooming at its centre and a sea of silk, Kashmir shawl, and striped canvas tents reaching in gay profusion into the distance. Here, a different body of infantry in native costume practised intricate drills on their new parade ground. Howitzers boomed practise shots into stands of distant trees. Brightly dressed cavalry charged imaginary enemies.

Heading south from this camp towards a newly constructed bridge of boats across the River Sutlej, painted elephants marched behind a detachment of troops in yellow silk and chain-mail along a newly cut road towards the river's bank. Beside and behind them, horses danced impatiently in the morning light, their riders aglitter. Bare-chested men in loincloths and loose, waist-length hair followed on foot. Drummers beat a steady tattoo as the procession prepared to cross the bridge on its way to the great camp on the other side.

As the first elephant stepped onto the bridge, a cluster of running men carrying two palanquins approached the Maharajah's camp from the north, a dozen armed horsemen riding in their wake.

Groaning with fatigue, the palanquin bearers made their way towards the camp's centre, passing at last under a carved wooden archway into a great crowded square where broad pathways led between masses of potted chrysanthemums. The mounted guard shouted, pushing aside excited children and men carrying cloth-covered trays.

The palanquins were set down by a silk tent, the largest of those fronting the square. The scent of musk and amber came from the tent, joining other smells – jasmine, orange blossom, cooking spices, horse and elephant.

There was only one elephant to be seen. It knelt twenty yards away, its gold-dipped tusks catching the light while a group of courtiers climbed, one by one, up a ladder to its howdah. More men on elegantly caparisoned horses rode off towards an archway in the distance. Of a royal procession, there was no sign.

The eunuch stretched his legs out of the smaller palanquin and extended a flapping hand until one of the guards pulled him to his feet. He peered about him. 'Where is the Maharajah's procession?' he choked out. Perspiration ran down his face. 'We are too late!' His silks flapping, he rushed towards the squatting bearers. 'This is your doing, Neeloo. It is you who are to blame!' As he swung his open hand at the head bearer's face, a white-haired man with a full silver beard appeared in the entrance of the silk tent.

146

'Stop,' he said.

The eunuch's hand, arrested in mid-air, fell to his side. Faqeer Nuruddin, manager of the Maharajah's vast household, strode towards the palanquins. 'The Maharajah waited half the morning for you to bring the child,' he snapped. 'Did I not tell you to have Saboor here before noon?'

The eunuch gave a high squeak, but the silver-bearded man waved dismissive fingers. 'I have no time for your lies, Gurbashan. Where is the child?'

Neeloo pointed to the carved palanquin, where a small foot protruded from beneath a curtain.

Gurbashan the eunuch bent himself nearly double. 'Most Respected—'

'The boy's servant is there,' Nuruddin interrupted, pointing to a small man with a sparse beard who squatted in the shade of a nearby tent. 'His name is Ahmad. He is to dress the child and take him to the Maharajah.' He smiled grimly. 'You are fortunate that one of the elephants was kept back.'

Nuruddin moved off, leaving the eunuch to dart towards the waiting servant.

'The boy is very important to the Maharajah,' Gurbashan informed the servant, gesturing grandly as he hurried back to the palanquin. The small, bearded man followed, walking with a long, rolling stride. 'He is the son of Hassan Ali Khan of the Maharajah's court, and the grandson of Shaikh Waliullah of Lahore City.'

At the sound of these names, the little servant's eyes widened briefly.

When they reached the palanquin, Gurbashan flung back the curtains, covered his nose and bent down, only to pull back almost immediately, his face puckering in disgust as the sweetish smell of unwashed human skin escaped from the palki.

147

'I do not care what you do with him,' he told Ahmad, 'only do it quickly. I have had enough of this child.'

'He is hungry,' the head bearer offered as the servant squatted down and looked inside. 'We last fed him at—'

'Quiet! What have you to do with this?' The eunuch pointed at Neeloo. 'You will be punished for making us late. Do not think you will evade my wrath. And you, Ahmad,' he said, turning to the servant, 'dress the boy in his court clothes and be quick about it. And do not forget his necklace of emeralds and pearls, his gift from the Maharajah.' He watched Ahmad lift the baby from the palki. 'We are fortunate. He is most likely too ill to cry. Let us hope,' he added briskly, 'that he does not die before the end of the day. But if he does,' he raised his hands, palms outward, 'it will not be my work.'

Neeloo and the other bearers did not speak as they trotted away to find water, food, and a place to rest.

'Do you think, as I do,' asked the oldest bearer finally, 'that the child in the palki is different from other children?'

Neeloo nodded. 'Yes,' he replied firmly, 'he is different.'

Saboor sat unmoving on the ground while the bearded servant studied him carefully, examining bruised skin and frail limbs.

'Look at this small one, grandson of Shaikh Waliullah,' Ahmad said aloud. 'What does he need?' He poked through Saboor's things. 'He needs his clothes and he needs his necklace. But as to his state, it is very bad.' He shook his head worriedly, looking about him at the people eddying to and fro on the paths of the Maharajah's potted garden. Among them, a water carrier swung his goatskin, spraying the path with droplets of water to keep down the dust. Ahmad stood up and beckoned to him. 'Bhisti, come here!'

'What do you need?' the man asked with the good nature of

all water carriers. The full goatskin on his back dragged one of his shoulders downward. He was small and wiry, but he walked with the wide, heavy gait characteristic of the water carrier. He looked at the child. 'Ah,' he said, 'the boy needs a bath.'

He readied his skin as Ahmad pulled off Saboor's shirt and pyjamas, then poured water over the child's head until his hair ceased to be matted and his skin no longer stank of neglect. With his fingers, Ahmad wiped the crust from Saboor's nose and the tear stains from his cheeks, then dressed him in a pair of fine satin pyjamas and an embroidered satin tunic with gold buttons. The bhisti looked on interestedly, his now empty goatskin slung over his shoulder, while Ahmad set Saboor's round embroidered cap on his wet curls and hung the rope of emeralds and pearls about his neck.

'What bruises he has,' remarked the water carrier. 'May whoever has hurt this beautiful child endure ten times his pain in retribution.'

'God is great,' replied Ahmad. He drew Saboor to him and got to his feet.

A man passed carrying a heavy tray of sweetmeats. 'Stop,' Ahmad called, and ran after him, the child bouncing in his arms.

Moments later, holding Saboor against his shoulder with one hand and a sweet in the other, Ahmad the servant climbed up the elephant ladder and into the crowded howdah. There he broke the sugary square into small pieces and put them, one by one, into the baby's mouth.

Chapter Twelve

'Memsahib, Memsahib, you must hurry!' Dittoo cried, hoarse from excitement. 'Maharajah Ranjit Singh has come. He is at the end of the avenue with all his nobles, readying himself for the procession!'

Mariana stabbed a last pin into her hair, snatched up her bonnet and rushed towards the main entrance.

Miss Emily and Miss Fanny sat in front of the great tent, in the first of a double row of occupied chairs. As Mariana crossed the avenue past Major Byrne's staircase, Miss Fanny beckoned her to hurry, pointing to the lone empty seat beside her.

Behind the chairs, an expanse of white cloth covered the reception-tent floor. Someone had arranged chests of drawers, tables and chairs along the walls in an effort to imitate an English drawing room. Beyond, in another, smaller tent, Miss Emily's sofa and the least travel-damaged of the dining-room chairs had been arranged in a half-circle.

Miss Emily turned and surveyed the arrangements. 'I am sorry for poor George,' she sighed. 'I can see his bedside table by the doorway. They might at least have left him somewhere to put his book.'

'I'm pleased they have not taken my bed,' returned Miss Fanny in a stage whisper.

A large crowd had gathered along the avenue. Mariana stirred in her seat. Where was *he*? The red coats across the avenue belonged to the infantry. The blue-coated artillery, Fitzgerald among them, must be somewhere else.

Miss Fanny leaned confidentially towards her. 'Poor Emily has had dreadful spasms all morning. I do not know whether she will be able to last out the durbar.'

On Miss Fanny's other side, Miss Emily sniffed. 'I most assuredly *will* last out this durbar. If necessary, I shall have my bed carried to every review and every dinner. I have not come all this way to—'

The crowd's voice rose with excitement. Children ran out of sight around the side of the tent, then reappeared, dancing excitedly, as Lord Auckland rounded the corner on a large elephant, alone save for his mahout.

'Ah', breathed Miss Fanny, 'have you ever seen the like of George's elephant? What artists these natives are!'

The elephant's state housings of ruby-red velvet, heavily worked in gold, fell below its knees. Its face, above gold-painted tusks, was a mask of indigo and carnelian. A fringed canopy of gold brocade on four gold posts shaded the curved, golden howdah.

Miss Emily pursed her lips. 'A charming effect, like that of a fairy tale. I have never seen George dressed entirely in gold tissue and brocade. What a pity,' she added as her brother looked down and offered her a private, lopsided smile. 'I don't think he likes being a fairy prince.'

European and native soldiers now lined the avenue, craning expectantly in both directions. Children of shopkeepers and camp servants ran, shouting with excitement, among the crowd. Behind the troops, servants stood on boxes, grinning and pushing one another.

Where *was* Fitzgerald? Mariana peered up and down for several breathless minutes, until a British officer galloped past at full tilt, waving his hat over his head, signalling that the Maharajah's party had begun its advance. Orders echoed up and down the avenue. The rows of troops jerked to attention and presented arms.

The Maharajah rode alone in his gem-encrusted howdah, his tall elephant dwarfing the horses of his mounted guard. Behind him, among a group of dignitaries, his only legitimate adult son, Kharrak Singh, gnawed his fingernails and stared down vacantly at the pageantry, while in a corner a servant gripped a frail baby with one hand and the howdah's railing with the other.

The Maharajah's most senior ministers and advisers followed on other elephants, also surrounded by a swirling throng of men and horses. Riders danced their horses in the Maharajah's train, while behind each horse, grasping its tail as he ran, flew a half-naked man, his long hair streaming out behind him. Village children darted in and out of the line of elephants, risking death for the sake of the coins the Maharajah showered onto the crowd from a basket at his feet.

At a command, the Maharajah's wiry little mahout leaned over and spoke to his charge. As the elephant, responding, began to trot, the Maharajah tossed the last of the coins over the side of the howdah and reached, smiling, for a handhold. Little boys broke from the fighting crowd and raced beside the lumbering procession, coughing in the clouds of dust that rose from under the elephant's feet.

On the second elephant, the servant Ahmad began to pray soundlessly, his eyes closed in fright, while the baby drooped in his arms.

As the Maharajah's train came swaying into view, Lord

Auckland's mahout urged his own elephant to a lumbering trot. Behind him, the decorated elephants of the other officials followed suit. Peacock-feather fans, tasselled standards and crook-shaped silver sticks bobbed beside the lead animal, their bearers now sprinting to stay abreast of the elephants.

Alone in front, Lord Auckland jounced on his flimsy golden seat, his face pale with nerves. 'Slow *down*, slow *down*, I say!' he shouted, one hand holding his golden tricorn on his head.

The mahout, who understood no English, took Lord Auckland's shouts for cries of encouragement, and urged his elephant to run faster.

Bagpipes began to wail. Mariana searched the avenue with her eyes. Miss Fanny reached for Miss Emily with one hand, and for her handkerchief with the other.

'Oh, Emily,' she quavered, 'I am so very proud of George, and of England!'

The music grew louder. Cheers erupted from the troops along the avenue as the two parties advanced towards each other, each one heralded by a great storm of dust.

'Something is wrong,' declared Miss Fanny as two British cavalry officers rode, shouting, into the avenue, waving their swords. 'I think they're coming too fast.'

'Look!' Miss Emily pointed to their right as the first of the Maharajah's elephants appeared, as if from a dusty dream, two hundred yards away.

It came at surprising speed, its lone passenger shielded from the sun by a great tasselled parasol. More elephants and a swirling throng of outriders and standard bearers followed. Chain-mail flashed in the sun.

A moment later, Lord Auckland burst out of a swiftly moving dust cloud to their left, leading his own running elephants and

153

four companies of Bengal Lancers straight at the Maharajah's procession.

'They can never stop now,' breathed Miss Fanny.

Mariana held her breath and looked from side to side at the two processions. How were they to escape? She looked behind her and found Dr Drummond, the vicar, and an elderly visiting scholar wedged together in the second row of chairs.

As the two processions closed rapidly on one another, the lead mahouts stood on their elephants' necks, iron prods waving, their shouted words lost in the martial din of the bands. Runners and outriders dropped their tasselled standards and peacock feathers and raced for the margins of the avenue, scattering soldiers and onlookers as they ran.

'Get up, run for your life!' cried Dr Drummond. As one, the three men behind Mariana lurched to their feet and began to climb over their chairs. Miss Fanny and Miss Emily sat rigidly upright in their bright silks, neither moving nor speaking. Mariana half stood, then realized that she could not get over her own chair wearing her blue-striped gown. She had waited too long to run onto the avenue. She bent double on her seat, making herself as small as possible.

Abandoning language at last, the mahouts signalled wildly with their arms. The Maharajah's elephant veered left and crashed with a great tearing sound past Lord Auckland's elephant, carrying with it a dozen yards of velvet housing and a corner of the British state howdah.

'Ah-h-h!' Abandoned by the doctor and the vicar, the old scholar let out a terrified scream.

Dust filled Mariana's nose and mouth. Chaos washed over her as the remaining animals, still advancing at speed, sought a way out of certain disaster, their frightened trumpeting accompanied by the staccato shouting of excited natives and the clamour of competing bands. Some were able to turn aside but others collided in slow motion while their mahouts clutched the harnesses for balance and the occupants of the howdahs were flung about like rag dolls.

Had anyone been thrown out? If so, they had certainly been killed. Mariana gripped Miss Fanny's hand as Lord Auckland's elephant, trembling with fright, its damaged howdah apparently empty, stumbled towards their row of chairs.

'*Shabash,* well done!' its mahout shouted happily, slapping away at his elephant's head as Lord Auckland reappeared suddenly, upright on his seat, knocking dents from his tricorn hat. 'Well done!'

Beside Mariana, Miss Fanny sat immobile, her eyes straight ahead, a statue in dusty silk and ribbons.

The mahouts manoeuvred the two lead elephants until the animals were side by side. Many hands dragged the Maharajah's small red-clad figure head first into the Governor-General's howdah. A swarm of grooms led Lord Auckland's nervous elephant to the specially constructed stairway where Lord Auckland and Ranjit Singh, one tall and pale, the other tiny and dark-skinned, offered one another their embraces – the Maharajah with enthusiasm, Lord Auckland with solemnity.

Only then did Miss Fanny turn, her face alight, to Mariana. 'Is this not marvellous, my dear?' she cried. 'Is this not a wonderful spectacle?' She pressed her hands together. 'One can only wonder what will happen next!'

Chapter Thirteen

The child Saboor still in his arms, Ahmad the servant looked down from the kneeling elephant. The clash at the meeting had thrown them to the howdah's floor, but the child was unhurt.

They were alone on the elephant. When the confusion waned, their fellow passengers had all scrambled down the elephant ladder to the ground and followed the Maharajah into the durbar tent. Even the elephant's mahout had gone.

Men surged along the avenue, soldiers and onlookers stepping around the row of kneeling elephants. Ahmad rubbed his swelling wrist while the baby lay silent on his shoulder. 'Baba is not well,' he said aloud, his eyes on the durbar tent. 'He should not be taken into that crowd.' He wiped his forehead with his good hand. 'Baba must have his food. Who knows when this meeting will finish.'

Holding Saboor, he climbed gingerly down the elephant ladder, then stood still, searching the stream of soldiers and onlookers for someone useful.

'Cook,' he called to a man whose clothes smelled of wood smoke and spices, 'will you make me food for this child?'

The cook, a round-faced man, came near. He peered at the baby who lay unmoving on Ahmad's shoulder. 'I am a poor

156

man,' he said seriously, 'and this child is of rich birth. Will you pay for what I give him?'

When Ahmad did not answer, the man poked a thick finger at Saboor's fine clothes. 'Give me a gold button from this baba's suit and I will make you both a dinner fit for the Maharajah himself.'

Mariana let herself be swept with everyone else towards the durbar tent. Dark-skinned men wearing silk turbans, earrings and necklaces, with luxuriant beards and moustaches, seemed to be everywhere. Behind her, a horde of British officers pushed aside sentries and aides-de-camp in their rush to gain admittance to the tent.

Inside, the crowd surged forward, carrying Mariana through the main tent and towards the inner tent with its sofa and dining chairs. Someone barked an order and, with a rush of canvas, the main door flap rolled to the ground, throwing the packed tents into near-perfect darkness. The small tent's outer doorway had also been closed, cutting off air circulation. Murmuring arose around Mariana as she groped her way to the half-circle of dining chairs and seated herself. She waited for her eyes to adjust to the darkness, then blinked with relief when she made out Miss Fanny beside her, struggling to get out of her shawls in the sudden, stifling heat, and Miss Emily fanning herself on one end of the sofa.

Her chair rocked as someone pressed against it from behind. Where was the Maharajah? As Mariana strained to see, Lord Auckland appeared, one hand gripping the red silk elbow of a tiny, silver-bearded native, the other arm straight out before him as he felt his way towards the sofa. Arriving, he pushed the old Maharajah down without ceremony next to Miss Emily, then sat down on his other side.

The hot air thickened. An English voice shouted an order and the crowd edged back as the blackness of the inner tent turned to grey. 'Someone has opened the main entrance again, thank goodness,' murmured Miss Fanny. 'But whatever is wrong with George?'

Turning to look, Mariana saw Lord Auckland sitting perfectly still at the Maharajah's side, his eyes starting from his head.

No – something was wrong with the little Maharajah. His red-turbaned head had fallen forward onto his chest; his silver beard rested against the row of pearls at his waist. He seemed unconscious of the handsome youth draped in emeralds who had appeared at his feet and now sat kneading his legs and gazing anxiously into his face.

The perspiring throng shifted. A group of Sikhs forced their way towards the sofa, their eyes on their stricken king, their hands on the dagger handles protruding from their sashes. Near Mariana, a pair of unarmed British officials watched nervously. Major Byrne caught hold of a young officer of the Thirteenth Foot, whispered to him, then pushed him towards the doorway.

A trickle of perspiration began at the crease in Mariana's knee and ran down the back of her calf. An unpleasant feeling invaded her head as the Sikhs muttered to each other. Every one of them carried at least two weapons. Lord Auckland edged away from the Maharajah and perched, his jowls quivering, on the edge of the sofa.

At last the air began to move. The outside door of the small tent was open.

The Maharajah raised his head and looked straight at Mariana. Ignoring her headache, she gazed back at him, memorizing his appearance: his long, pointed silver beard, his closed

158

blind eye, his luminous, intelligent seeing eye, the humour in his face.

As a wave of collective relief blew through the tent, a shrewd-looking man with a thick black beard and a coarse woollen robe sat down at the Maharajah's knee, greeted Lord Auckland, and began, without irony, to deliver a series of elaborate compliments involving perfumed gardens and the song of nightingales, while Mr Macnaghten, the political secretary, translated rapidly from his chair beside the sofa.

The man on the floor speaking with such ease, turning his hands for emphasis, must be Faqeer Azizuddin, the Maharajah's chief minister, thought Mariana. His title of Faqeer, Munshi Sahib had told her, denoted humility, although seed pearls gleamed on the loose shirt he wore under his cheap-looking robe. Mariana mopped her face. It was astonishing that anyone could talk of gardens in this stifling, noisy place.

As the crowd parted to allow an officer to carry in the Queen's portrait upon its plump, velvet cushion, a new unpleasant feeling in Mariana's stomach joined the one in her head. She closed her eyes, measuring her discomfort. This was too unfair. It was Miss Emily who had suffered all morning from spasms. And yet now she sat, smiling composedly, on her end of the sofa, apparently as fit as a fiddle. Mariana, who had waited months for this moment, realized that if she did not immediately leave the tent, she would either fall from her chair in a dead faint or be sick on the carpet, or both.

As the Maharajah reached for the portrait, a deafening noise erupted outside, eclipsing the voices around Mariana. The pain sharpened in her head. She pushed herself to her feet, a hand to her mouth.

'I hope they are firing that salute away from the horses,' she heard a British voice say as she clawed her way towards the doorway. Ahead of her, a tall bearded native was also leaving the tent, helping her unknowingly, opening a way for her, his long embroidered coat acting as a beacon, guiding her through the half-dark. After reaching the entrance, he paused for a moment, as if searching for someone, then hurried away.

Yar Mohammad's eyes roamed the avenue as he waited by the durbar tent with Major Byrne's gift horses. When Shafi Sahib had instructed him to locate the Shaikh's grandson among the members of the Maharajah's court, he had thought his task would be easy, but there was no sign of a small male child. Perhaps Saboor Baba, unseen in the crowd, had already been taken into the tent.

Beside Yar Mohammad, a young groom smacked dust from his new clothes. 'What riches, what jewels we have seen!' he marvelled.

Yar Mohammad nodded. Qamar Haveli, the most important house he had ever visited, did not compare in wealth to this. For all his fame, Shaikh Waliullah did not own an animal like the draped and painted elephants that stood tethered across the avenue, or even the horses whose bridles they now held.

A sudden movement caught his eye. A familiar-looking man erupted from the durbar tent, looked about him, then ran across the avenue towards the elephants. Behind him, someone else staggered into the sunlight, a hand to her head. It was the young memsahib.

Yar Mohammad turned back to the avenue in time to see Hassan reach the tethered elephants and begin speaking, his hands moving, to someone squatting in the shade.

Hassan Ali Khan was still breathing hard when Yar Mohammad arrived at his side. He looked less ill than he had at his father's house, but shadows still marked his eyes.

Hassan glowered at the squatting man, who got to his feet. 'You are saying that the child came here on your elephant, but now he is gone?'

'As I have told you, Huzoor,' replied the mahout, 'the servant must have taken the child with him. I did not see which direction he took. If I had known . . .' He shrugged.

Hassan glanced at Yar Mohammad without recognition, then turned back to the mahout. 'Describe the servant,' he ordered.

'He walks with long strides,' said the man, 'and he stands like this.' He bent his shoulders forward to hollow his chest. 'His name,' he added helpfully, 'is Ahmad.'

Yar Mohammad shifted his feet. 'Peace, Sahib,' he offered.

Hassan turned. At close quarters he was nearly as tall as Yar Mohammad himself. 'Speak,' he ordered carelessly, his impatient gaze wandering past Yar Mohammad's shoulder to the men on the avenue.

Yar Mohammad pointed to where the gift elephant and horses stood waiting. 'If what this man says is true, Saboor Baba was not carried past the horses. If he had been, I would have seen him.'

Before Yar Mohammad could add anything more, Yusuf Bhatti strode up, red-faced from hurrying, and took hold of Hassan's arm.

'I have waited by the guns since the processions arrived,' he said without preamble. 'I have not seen Saboor. He must not have come with the procession.'

'He came.' Hassan waved irritably at the kneeling animal whose ladder still stood against its side. 'He was on this elephant, and now he has gone, no one knows where.'

Yusuf Bhatti blinked. 'What is to be done now?'

'Saboor is not lost.'

161

All four men turned toward the gentle voice beside them. Shafi Sahib, friend of Shaikh Waliullah and interpreter of dreams, gestured towards the guarded entrance in the red canvas wall. 'I, too, waited,' he said. 'Although he is not to be seen, I can assure you that Saboor is not lost. Have patience, my dear Hassan. God is kind.'

'Shafi Sahib,' Hassan said opening his hands, 'I must return to Kasur this afternoon. If I do not see Saboor now, when will I see him?' He closed his eyes. 'Pray, Shafi Sahib, that I will see my son alive.'

Poor man. Yar Mohammad thought of Nusrat, his solemn little daughter, the light of his eyes, who waited for him in his mountain village. How would he endure it if she went missing?

Shafi Sahib nodded. 'Your father and everyone at Qamar Haveli are praying for you. Inshallah, if God wills, we will all see Saboor soon.'

'Look.' Yusuf pointed across the avenue.

At one side of the durbar tent, a score of coolies with ropes over their shoulders dragged a pair of howitzers towards a large pyramid of gunpowder shells. Sikh nobles and British officers poured from the durbar tent and headed the same way.

As Yar Mohammad made his way back to the horses, he caught a glimpse of Hassan crossing the avenue behind him.

'Are you quite well, Mariana?' The sharp voice startled Mariana as she sat, pushing loose hair into her bonnet, in one of the visitor's chairs. 'I am astonished at your behaviour,' Miss Emily admonished as Mariana got unsteadily to her feet. 'Why did you rush out of the tent just when we were presenting the Queen's picture? Everyone saw you do it.'

'I suddenly felt very unwell. I'm sorry, Miss Emily, Miss

162

Fanny.' Mariana patted her upper lip with her crumpled handkerchief.

Miss Emily sniffed. 'I do not care how you felt. You must never behave that way again.' She held out an armful of shawls. 'And take these. I cannot carry them a moment longer.'

The air had done Mariana some good. Clutching the shawls, she followed Miss Emily and Miss Fanny to the side of the tent, where they watched the presentation of the animals. But it was the guns she really wanted to see, brand new and gleaming, each barrel emblazoned with the Maharajah's crest. It was often the heavy guns that decided a battle. She could name several important—

She gasped. In front of her, at attention before the two howitzers, stood a double row of men in the dress uniform of the Bengal Horse Artillery. At one end of the first row, his sabre at his side, was Lieutenant Harry Fitzgerald, his eyes fixed on the air above her head.

'Oh dear,' murmured Miss Fanny.

'There is *no* need for us to notice the honour guard.' Miss Emily gripped Mariana firmly above the elbow and marched her towards the pile of artillery shells. 'The view is perfectly good from here,' she declared as she stopped. 'Look, here come my brother and the Maharajah.'

A sound beside Mariana caused her to turn her head. The tall bearded courtier who had preceded her from the tent was standing beside her, raking the crowd with tired eyes, as if searching for something he had lost. Sadness seemed to pour from him. When he moved, his beautiful coat brushed against her sleeve. He gave off the scent of sandalwood.

Munshi Sahib had once brought her vials of scented oil: rose, amber, musk. Her favourite had been the warm, inviting, complicated scent of sandalwood. Fitzgerald might have worn sandalwood, if she had asked him to.

The crowd shifted to let Lord Auckland and the Maharajah approach the waiting howitzers. Both men looked exhausted after so much ceremony, Lord Auckland clammy-faced in his wilted finery, the little Maharajah tottering weakly beside him.

Major Byrne, looking hot and smug, had appeared, with Sotheby in tow, and both men had stationed themselves behind the pyramid of shells. Sotheby blinked anxiously.

As the Maharajah approached to inspect the guns, the crowd pushed forward. A voice shouted a warning as someone knocked into the carefully arranged pyramid of shells. While Mariana watched, still holding Miss Emily's shawls, the top shell slowly disengaged itself from the others and rolled down one side of the pyramid into the Maharajah's path.

He saw it too late. Gaining speed, it caught his ankles, knocking him off balance. Before anyone could catch him, Ranjit Singh, Maharajah of the Punjab, lay flat in the dust before the British guns.

Miss Emily's hand closed on Mariana's wrist as the Sikh bodyguards reached for their weapons. The unhappy man beside Mariana launched himself forward, his fine coat flapping, but before he could reach the Maharajah, Major Byrne and the White Rabbit had dragged the old man to his feet, while Lord Auckland stared into the distance, pretending not to have seen.

'A bad omen, very bad,' someone muttered in Punjabi. 'These British will bring nothing but evil to this country.'

Mariana looked to see who had spoken but could only make out the back of the clever-looking chief minister's coarse robe as he led his Maharajah away.

Chapter Fourteen

Sunday, 1 December

'We need not have worried so about Ranjit Singh's camp,' Miss Fanny remarked two evenings later over the drumming of the Maharajah's musicians, as she studied the embroidered canopy above their heads. 'His tents are very fine, to be sure, but they are quite as dusty as ours. And have you noticed the plants? No one can have watered them for days.'

Hundreds of small oil lamps lit the outdoor enclosure where they sat wrapped against the evening chill, the Maharajah with his feet under him on his golden, bowl-shaped throne, the egg-sized Koh-i-Noor diamond refracting light from a heavy bracelet on his upper arm.

Behind Lord Auckland's silver chair, Harry Fitzgerald looked over Mariana's head, unbearably handsome in gold braid. A little while ago he had caught her eye and given her the faintest of nods.

The Maharajah was talking to Lord Auckland through his black-bearded chief minister, his hands rising and falling. Earlier in the evening the Maharajah, too, had caught Mariana's eye, but his look had held no warmth, only appraisal. Now she felt his single eye on her again, and saw to her discomfort that it had fastened upon her bare chest and shoulders, both exposed by the pretty neckline of her borrowed gown. Before she could look away, he had treated her to a blatant leer.

'If consulted,' said Miss Emily in an undertone as the seated musicians began to play faster, 'I should say we have had a sufficient number of dancing girls for one evening. I believe I have seen all the undulating and stamping I can endure. Look, here is a fresh one, just when I had hoped it was all over. And Mariana,' she added, raising her eyebrows, 'why have you wrapped yourself like a mummy in that shawl? I thought you looked quite nice in your blue and white.'

A girl with a dozen gold bangles on each arm stepped forward to stand before Lord Auckland. While he gazed over her head, she took a deep breath and, accompanied by the twanging of the instruments, began a delicate, soaring song. Her voice was fine and supple and so filled with longing that Mariana felt the hair rise on her arms.

> In pursuit of your image
> My distract thought
> Has wandered everywhere,
> Like a pauper's lamp.

Miss Emily turned to Mariana. 'What is that fat girl shrieking about? She seems to have fallen in love with George at first sight.'

Mariana sighed. Did this song, too, describe the soul's longing for God, or was she allowed to give it her own meaning?

She spoke into Miss Emily's ear. 'She says her thoughts have wandered everywhere in pursuit of her beloved. It is a poem.'

Miss Emily sniffed. 'How they do exaggerate. It would have been quite enough to say she was pleased to see him.'

How well Mariana understood those plaintive words! For all his nearness, Fitzgerald might have been a thousand miles from her.

I am both close to thee, her own poem had read, *and immeasurably far away* . . .

'Ah,' Miss Emily said a little later, nodding with satisfaction towards the dancing girls and their musicians, 'that must have been the last song. See, they are all going away. We shall leave soon, thank heaven.'

As the last of the entertainers drifted away, a small servant appeared at the Maharajah's side, carrying a baby boy. Mariana stared. How curious these people were, letting such a tiny child stay up until nearly midnight. Why would the Maharajah want to have a baby with him now? The child's eyes drooped with exhaustion but, strangely, he turned his head, searching the crowd as if he were looking for something.

'I have invited Lieutenant Marks to dinner, Mariana,' Miss Emily announced the following evening, smoothing her blonde satin skirts with her palm, 'in hopes that he will show his hand. There is not much time left before we sign the treaty and the army leaves for Afghanistan.'

Mariana felt her toes curling inside her boots. 'Show his hand, Miss Emily?'

Miss Emily opened her fan with a little snap. 'If he is interested, he should say so. And since a little competition might concentrate his mind, you are to have Peter Edwardes on your other side. Edwardes has been pestering me about it for days.'

The breeze from Miss Emily's fan carried a hint of violet water. Mariana bit her lip. Colin Marks, Peter Edwardes, the White Rabbit, they were all the same to her. Let Miss Emily marry them herself.

'The girl needs to be pushed,' Miss Emily whispered loudly a while later, as she and Miss Fanny walked towards the dining tent with Mariana close behind. 'Marks is the most suitable of them. I know his uncle. There is no point in her waiting, now that Fitzgerald has been disqualified. She should choose *someone* before they all leave for Afghanistan. A number of them are quite eager . . .'

As they entered the tent, several young officers stopped talking and bowed in their direction.

'There you are, my dear.' Her skirts rustling, Miss Emily turned. 'You remember Lieutenant Colin Marks of the Queen's Buffs.' She nodded towards the little man who was bowing elaborately beside her. 'I have put him on your left this evening.'

Marks' ears were not only large, they were hairy. Behind him, also bowing, was Harry Fitzgerald's curly-haired friend from the Waterloo dinner.

Fifteen minutes later, as conversations rose and fell around the table, Marks bent toward her, his soup spoon in his hand. 'I fear, Miss Givens,' he said, favouring her with a patronizing smile, 'that I sit here under false pretences.'

'False pretences, Lieutenant Marks?' This was agony. Mariana stole a glance towards Peter Edwardes on her right. He was Fitzgerald's friend. How much did he know of the past?

'Yes.' Marks lowered his voice. 'My name is not Colin, it is actually *Bartholomew* Colin.' He wrinkled his nose. 'I wish you to know *everything* about me.'

The hair sprouting from his ears appeared thicker than ever. His shin was within reach of her booted foot. She crossed her ankles decisively under the table.

It was another full hour before the table turned. At last, her face stiff from trying to smile, she turned to her right in time to see Lieutenant Edwardes tip back his head and swallow half a glass of wine in one gulp.

'Good evening.' He inclined his head. 'Glad to sit beside a woman who knows military strategy. Heard you talking about Waterloo some time back. You agreed with Fitzgerald. Good man, Fitzgerald.' He nodded several times.

Mariana pushed bits of vegetable around her plate. Her appetite had long since vanished. 'Have you and Lieutenant Fitzgerald known each other long?' she asked cautiously.

'Since I came out here. It must be three years now.' Edwardes pronounced his words with care. 'We are the best of friends,' he added, nodding significantly.

Mariana put down her knife. 'And were you in Calcutta a year ago?'

'I was.'

'Then you must know what happened with the young lady, his fiancée.' She held her breath. This was madness. The man had clearly had too much to drink.

He swayed towards her, red-eyed in the candlelight. 'You have heard ill of him,' he said in a stage whisper, 'and you want the truth.' His head bobbed up and down. 'Thought you would ask.'

Under the table she wiped damp palms on her knees.

'I'll tell you about it, Miss Givens, but you must keep it to yourself.' Edwardes wagged a finger in her direction. 'People know you are fond of Fitzgerald. If you repeat this story, they will, if you will excuse me, think you are stupid with love.'

Stupid with love! Mariana snatched up her knife and fork and attacked her roast venison.

'Two years ago,' Edwardes began, ignoring Mariana's scowl, 'a young lady came out from England. Very pretty, she was. Miss Owen was her name. Several men took a liking to her,

Fitzgerald among them. I was not in Calcutta then, so I missed his marriage proposal.' Edwardes glanced at her. 'Are you all right, Miss Givens?'

'Yes,' she snapped, so loudly that the White Rabbit glanced up from across the table.

'Harry and Miss Owen became engaged,' Edwardes went on. 'Not officially, as they had not yet had permission from his commanding officer or her guardian. Only one or two of us knew.' He took another gulp of burgundy, then wiped his mouth, trailing his napkin in the gravy on his plate as he did so. 'By the time I returned to Calcutta and met Harry and Miss Owen at the usual dinners and balls, she had begun paying attention to another man. This man, you see, was to inherit a little money, while Harry has no hopes of that sort. When Harry found them together, he understood her game, and broke the engagement.'

'Game?' Mariana repeated.

'Miss Owen had been using Harry as cover while she pursued the other man.' Edwardes waved a hand over his plate. 'She returned, husbandless, to England, of course.' He snorted. 'Served her right.'

A pair of finely wrought silver peacocks stood opposite Mariana in the centre of the table. She stared past them at the tent's open doorway. The woman had been an adventuress! How could Fitzgerald have been taken in?

The White Rabbit giggled at someone's joke. Edwardes yawned behind his stained napkin. 'Later, to save her face, Miss Owen told people that Harry had jilted her for someone with a better income.'

Mariana picked up her wine glass, then put it down again.

Edwardes shrugged. 'Harry took it well, good man, and never revealed the truth, but life in Calcutta was difficult for him afterwards. The Afghan Campaign was a godsend for him. Got him out of there. But now, of course, everyone here knows, so it's all the same.'

'Does everyone in Calcutta know?'

'Oh yes. *Her* version.' He sighed. 'Poor Harry.'

Mariana pushed away her uneaten food. In her mind's eye, Fitzgerald rode his grey horse, stood guard at the howitzers, kissed her. 'Why doesn't he tell the real story now?'

'Who would believe him? It's too late.'

Half an hour later, the fruit had been taken away. The men rose from the table as the Eden sisters and Mariana stood and made their way out of the dining tent's back entrance, leaving the gentlemen to their brandy.

'Well, Mariana,' began Miss Emily as she subsided into a basket chair between the tents, 'I observed you deep in conversation with Lieutenant Marks over the fish.'

Over the fish, Marks had given Mariana a scrupulously detailed account of trout fishing in Galway with his rich uncle.

'Colin Marks is well suited to you, my dear,' said Miss Fanny warmly. 'According to everyone, he is an able young officer, and he stands to inherit property. It is thought he will go far in the army.'

Miss Emily shook out her skirts. 'Now we shall see whether he offers to see you to your tent.'

Unable to contain herself, Mariana let out a great, noisy sigh.

An hour later, the men's brandy-drinking had finished. Sounds faded inside the dining tent as the dinner guests began to leave by the main doorway. Servants shouted to each other across the compound. Jimmund, the servant of Miss Emily's dog, came out of Miss Emily's tent with Chance under his arm. The Eden ladies rustled quietly.

'Ah, here comes someone,' said Miss Emily with satisfaction.

A figure emerged from the dining tent's back door.

'May I have the honour of seeing Miss Givens to her tent?' enquired a swaying Peter Edwardes.

Mariana made no effort to contain her broad, delighted smile.

As she and Edwardes started away, she looked over her shoulder to see the Eden sisters gazing after them in the semi-darkness.

'Sorry I took so long,' Edwardes muttered. 'Had to outflank that fool Marks.' When they had rounded a corner of the tent, he stopped. 'I have a surprise for you, Miss Givens.'

Waiting in the shadow of the dining tent, a finger to his lips, stood Harry Fitzgerald.

'Are you surprised?' he asked quietly as they watched Edwardes weave his way back towards the main entrance.

Mariana took her hands from her mouth. 'Yes,' she whispered. She looked over her shoulder, her heart thumping. 'You have taken such a risk!'

'It doesn't matter,' he said. He looked strained, but his hand felt warm when he squeezed her fingers. 'I could bear it no longer. Yesterday evening you were not seven feet from me and I could scarcely look at you for fear Miss Emily would see. And Marks has been puffed up for days.'

'I *hate* Colin Marks,' she whispered.

Fitzgerald's uniform was unbuttoned at the neck. Mariana drank in his profile as he walked beside her. 'What has Peter told you?' he asked.

'I think he has told me everything.'

172

Her heart was still racing as they reached her tent. She stopped, anticipating Fitzgerald's embrace, but before she could close her eyes he grasped her roughly by the shoulders and kissed her awkwardly, his teeth banging hers. 'Oh, Mariana,' he muttered, breathing heavily as he fumbled at the front of her gown.

'Stop! What are you doing?' She took a step back and glared at him. 'I do not like that at *all*.'

Still breathing hard, Fitzgerald peered at her in the half-dark. 'I'm a clumsy fool,' he muttered. He dropped his hands. 'Forgive me, Mariana. I've been so unhappy without you.'

His brass buttons gleamed in the starlight. He *was* clumsy, and he had been fooled by Miss Owen in Calcutta, but he had not jilted her, and Peter Edwardes had called him a good man. Best of all, he had been unhappy without her.

'Well,' she offered, 'other people can be clumsy too. I fell off my horse in front of everyone.'

He returned her smile, then wrapped his arms about her and gave her the kiss she wanted.

Chapter Fifteen

Monday, 9 December

'Nine days, Macnaghten.' Lord Auckland stopped partway up his elephant ladder to look balefully down at his political secretary. 'Nine days and nights of drinking, dancing girls, bawdy jokes, fireworks, lavish costumes and potted plants. Nine days of gifts given and received, and not one hour of negotiation. Not one moment's discussion of the Afghan Campaign. We *must* get Ranjit Singh to come to terms over the campaign and sign this treaty.'

He climbed into the howdah, sat down on the narrow satin-covered seat and rested a hand gingerly on his waistcoat. 'I did not sleep at all last night after his dinner party. Never mind the poisonous food – whoever drew up the regulations on durbars and native princes should have been warned about the man's wine. Englishmen should be expressly forbidden to drink the stuff.' He sighed. 'I had at least three glasses of it. I was forced to keep one foot on the floor all night to stop my bed from turning somersaults. I suppose, Macnaghten,' he added, as his political secretary climbed up, puffing, and took his seat, 'that as you were sitting on the Maharajah's blind side, you were able to pour your wine onto the ground.'

'I was, my lord, yes,' replied Macnaghten apologetically. 'I poured it away all evening.'

Lord Auckland stared down at the honour guard below. 'The old goat did not take his eyes from my cup. Someone told me his wine is made from raisins and ground pearls. Tell me, Macnaghten, when you poured it away, did it burn a hole in the carpet?'

The political secretary would have preferred to ride, as he usually did, with his dear friend Major Byrne, but this time there was no escaping the Governor-General. 'My lord,' he said, gripping the howdah's railing with unnecessary tightness, 'I have tried every possible stratagem to get the Maharajah to come to terms. I have exhausted my store of compliments. At today's meeting I had just started off with some nonsense about the sun shining down a hundred years from now on the glories of both England and the Punjab when the old man actually interrupted me to say in that irritating way of his that the two nations, hand in hand, would conquer Afghanistan, that it would be a "great show".'

Lord Auckland gave a wan smile. 'A great show. What a waste of time this is!'

The next day's meeting had already consumed two hours. Outside the Maharajah's grand reception tent, the sun had shifted. It now gleamed down nearly vertically on the rows of potted crotons and chrysanthemums along the pathways, shrinking the shadows of passing men and horses.

From his seat beside Lord Auckland, the little Maharajah spoke animatedly in a combination of Urdu and Punjabi, his eyes on Lord Auckland's expressionless face. Behind his throne, Sikh grandees, three deep, murmured their approval.

'I see,' William Macnaghten translated without inflection.

'The colours of the silks are meant to show the identities of the owners. Wah, wah, how clever!'

Lord Auckland smiled politely at the Maharajah, then turned to his political secretary. 'Macnaghten, this must stop. I will *not* discuss horse racing.'

The baby on the Maharajah's knee watched them with shadowed eyes. On the carpet before the Maharajah's feet, Chief Minister Azizuddin smiled knowingly.

Catching the man's expression, Lord Auckland blinked and straightened. 'Ask the Maharajah,' he said sharply, 'how long it will be before his army starts for Afghanistan.'

The Maharajah replied to Macnaghten's question in a soft, rapid-fire voice, waving his small hands.

The political secretary folded his own hands over his dove-coloured waistcoat. 'He says that it will be soon, but that when they go, they will cross rivers. He, of course, will have bridges of boats built for the crossings. He wishes to know how many stone bridges England has, and how they are constructed.'

'I do not know!' Lord Auckland's jowls shook. 'Tell him anything. I cannot bear any more of this. I have never been so suffocatingly bored in all my life. What is the old fool saying now?'

'He wants to know,' Macnaghten replied dully, 'the difference between a Sikh temple and a Christian church.'

'Macnaghten, you must ask him how many of his troops he intends to commit to the campaign,' Lord Auckland said a few minutes later, taking advantage of a lengthy conversation between the Maharajah and his chief minister. 'And find out when he intends to send them.' He shifted irritably in his seat. 'It must been soon. He cannot mean to send an army to Kabul in deep winter, when the mountain passes are full of snow. None of our troops except the Gurkhas are used to the cold. And tomorrow we will discuss laying our supply lines and moving our troops across his territories.'

The frail baby had fallen asleep face down on the Maharajah's lap. 'That child looks even feebler than the Maharajah,' murmured Macnaghten.

'Why are they all in such bad health?' asked Lord Auckland querulously. 'The Maharajah pretends to be in the peak of condition, but anyone can see the man's as weak as a cat. And as for that child . . .' he made a face while pretending to cough. 'How unpleasant it is to deal with such poor-looking people. And the chief minister,' he added, his eyes on Faqeer Azizuddin, 'now there is a man not to be trusted.'

Outside the tent, people moved to and fro. On the Maharajah's lap the child lay motionless. Resting one hand on the tiny back, the Maharajah beckoned with the other to one of his courtiers.

'Please,' murmured Lord Auckland, as the Maharajah spoke animatedly to the thin, dark-skinned man who stood before him, a hand over his heart, 'let the old man not be sending for wine!'

After the man had gone, the Maharajah reached out and poked a small brown finger into Lord Auckland's uniformed side, jerking Lord Auckland to startled attention, 'Governor Sahib, I have great news!' Sitting back in his throne he threw out an expansive arm. 'Tomorrow,' he announced, as Macnaghten translated, 'we will all go to Amritsar. I wish to show you and your party the Golden Temple, the seat of our Sikh religion, before we travel on to Lahore to enjoy further entertainments.'

Lord Auckland sat up. 'Is this a good sign?' he whispered to Macnaghten.

'Yes, my lord,' replied Macnaghten, 'I believe it is.'

177

'Yes, yes, we will have a great show.' The Maharajah beamed, his one good eye alight. 'After we have seen the Golden Temple, we will go to my treasury and armoury at Gobindgarh.'

A silken rustle ran through the crowd of Sikhs. Two tall men standing close by nudged one another.

'The English are our dear brothers,' the Maharajah added in his reedy voice, leaning forward to peer into Lord Auckland's face, 'from whom we must never be parted. It is therefore our duty to share with them the innermost secrets of our kingdom. They must see Gobindgarh, and look with their own eyes upon my fort, my riches, and my weaponry.' He laughed aloud and suddenly clapped his hands, waking the baby on his lap.

'My lord, he keeps all his artillery at Gobindgarh,' Macnaghten said animatedly. 'We will see not only Ranjit Singh's treasure, but also his guns. He must have brought only a small part of his artillery to the durbar. What a grand opportunity for the generals. This must mean something, my lord, it must!'

Lord Auckland smiled crookedly. 'Now then, Macnaghten,' he murmured, 'you must flail your imagination back to life and compose a suitably splashy answer. Perhaps all this wasted time here at the Sutlej has been some mysterious native preliminary to the real talks. Perhaps the real negotiations were never meant to take place until after we reached Amritsar.'

'You will, of course, leave your army at Firozpur,' Ranjit Singh was saying, 'and bring the ladies, and an escort of your soldiers.' He waved a hand in the direction of Lahore. 'When you cross my bridge of boats with your party and enter my territories, it will be a great show, a great show!'

The rustling among the sirdars had been replaced by murmuring. A hundred dark eyes moved from Ranjit Singh to Macnaghten and Lord Auckland.

Macnaghten cleared his throat. 'There is,' he pronounced, gesturing at the bright sky outside, 'a canopy of stars covering our two nations, now bound together for evermore in loving brotherhood.'

'Wah, wah,' returned the Maharajah, clapping his hands. 'Excellent. And they are never to be parted.'

'There is a saying,' Macnaghten remarked later to Lord Auckland as the Maharajah and his chief minister escorted them to their elephant, 'that if no heir is chosen, whoever holds Gobindgarh after Ranjit Singh's death will rule the Punjab. His treasure and his guns are the cornerstone of his power.'

'Indeed, Macnaghten,' Lord Auckland replied, smiling with satisfaction as he began to mount the elephant ladder. 'Indeed.'

The little servant stood inside the entrance of the elaborate reception tent, his bare toes pushed into the thick carpet. 'Mahraj,' he said, interrupting the Maharajah's conversation with Faqeer Azizuddin, 'Baba must have his food.' He pointed to Saboor.

The Maharajah looked up from the child on his lap, his expression blank. 'Now?' He stroked the baby's face. 'My little Saboor,' he crooned, 'my pearl of pearls! How dear he is to me!'

Ahmad did not budge from his post. 'Mahraj, it is time for his food. I must take him now.'

'Yes, yes, all right.' The Maharajah lifted his hands. 'You may take him to the kitchens,' he said as Ahmad crossed the tent and took hold of Saboor, 'but I must have him back as soon as he has eaten.'

From his place at the Maharajah's feet, Faqeer Azizuddin spoke softly. 'Mahraj, do you remember that we decided to send Saboor back to his family after fifteen days?'

'Of course I remember.' The Maharajah waved dismissive fingers. 'But we are not going to Lahore now; we are going to Amritsar. He can go to his family later.'

'Why,' the servant muttered as he carried Saboor towards the kitchen tents, 'does Mahraj not see how unhealthy Baba has become?' He patted Saboor's back with his free hand, his face creasing with worry. 'How has Mahraj become so slow in his thinking, so weak?'

At the royal kitchens, he stood outside the door of the first tent, watching a row of cooks slicing onions and crushing garlic, ginger and spices on a great stone surface.

A tall, shaven-headed cook looked up and saw Ahmad and the child. 'Ah, there you are,' he said. He wiped his forehead with his sleeve and bent to smile into Saboor's solemn face. 'We are ready for you, Baba,' he said. 'We have baked a quail for you today. Come, see what you will eat.' His eyes met Ahmad's. 'Has he smiled yet?'

'No, Avindra. He only stares, as if he is waiting for something. Perhaps he is waiting to die. Every day he grows weaker. He cares for nothing.'

'He is missing his family.' A second cook with a jutting belly had joined them. 'He grieves for his own people.'

'When will Baba see his father, his grandfather?' asked Ahmad as he squatted down in the shade, Saboor on his lap. 'When will he see the ladies of the Shaikh's family? The Maharajah wants Baba beside him all the time. He has promised to return him soon but I do not think he will keep his promise.'

The tall cook strode off, then returned, balancing a round of bread and a tiny baked bird on a leaf plate. 'Do not give him the quail yet,' he cautioned, 'it is still too hot.'

As Ahmad tore off a piece of bread for the child, the second

180

cook eased himself down with the others by the sheltering wall of the kitchen tent. 'Can we not take him away ourselves and send him to his family?' He pushed greased hair from his eyes. 'So many merchants are going back and forth from here to Lahore. Surely there is one good-hearted man among them.'

The tall cook shrugged. 'Who can tell a good heart from a bad one, Rana? Besides, who would take the chance of being caught with one of the Maharajah's hostages?'

'But what of the foreigners who have come to meet the Maharajah? He wouldn't kill his guests, even if they were found with the child. I am told there is a woman among them who speaks Urdu. If we ask her, she might take Saboor Baba to his family.'

'She might treat him badly.' Ahmad put a bit of the quail's breast into Saboor's mouth. 'She might sell him.'

'She will not sell Baba,' put in the tall cook. 'These English do not traffic in children. As for kindness, who knows?' He shrugged.

'She is a woman.' The fat cook yawned. 'She will know what to do with a child. Any life is better than the life he has now. The Maharajah loves Baba but does not see his misery. If Baba remains here much longer, he will die.'

Saboor refused to have yogurt, but he drank water from the battered tin cup they offered him. The tall cook shook his head. 'Poor little thing. You should watch for an opportunity to give him to the Englishwoman. When you have done it, we will find a way to send a message to his family, telling them where Baba can be found. He won't have to stay with her for long.'

After a moment, Ahmad nodded.

Chapter Sixteen

Sunday, 15 December

The journey of the Governor-General's much-reduced camp from Firozpur to Amritsar took six days. Ranjit Singh's bright and noisy camp departed first, followed by the Governor-General's party, the most senior British officers, an honour guard and a cavalry escort. At each halt, the British reviewed the Maharajah's troops and watched trick riding and artillery displays. In the evenings, they sat under his canopy and watched his entertainments.

On the sixth day, they were five miles from Amritsar, the city most holy to the Sikhs. At just after ten o'clock, breakfast was nearly over at the British camp.

William Macnaghten sat at one end of the dining table, stirring a rapidly cooling cup of coffee. He looked mournfully at his companion.

'Did you achieve anything last night?' asked Major Byrne.

'Nothing.' Macnaghten drew a pattern on the tablecloth with one finger. 'Everything is exactly as it has been. The Maharajah talks of infantry manoeuvres, or God, or steeplechasing, any subject but the Afghan Campaign.'

Major Byrne's nose looked even redder than usual. He sniffed and fumbled for a handkerchief. 'It is odd to have the preliminary courtesies extend this long, but cheer up, William. His offer to take us to Gobindgarh must mean something. God knows how much he is spending to feed us, never mind the bags of rupees for our escort and all those greasy sweetmeats. Why would he do all this if he didn't intend to sign the treaty? Why would he show us his treasure and his guns?'

Macnaghten's frock coat was unbrushed. His fingers trembled a little on the handle of his cup. He glanced over his shoulder and bent closer to Major Byrne. 'I fear something is wrong, Byrne,' he whispered. 'I fear that we have blundered, that for all the Maharajah's courtesies, he is making fools of us. We have brought a ten-thousand-strong army all the way from Calcutta, believing that within days of our arrival our army and Ranjit's would be on their way to Afghanistan, but Ranjit Singh shows no interest in the campaign. He laughs when we try to discuss the treaty. Lord Auckland is beginning to blame *me* for the Maharajah's behaviour.' He squeezed his eyes shut.

Major Byrne blew his nose vigorously. 'True enough, but we have the upper hand. The old boy knows a real army when he sees one. His troops look smart enough on parade, but I'll wager they'd run away in a real fight. We have Europeans, the cream of our native infantry, and the best horse and foot artillery in India. Ranjit Singh will never cross the Army of the Indus.'

Macnaghten sighed as a servant took away his coffee cup. 'Have you considered the possibility of a trap?'

Major Byrne frowned. 'What are you saying, man?'

Macnaghten spread his hands on the tablecloth. 'Our party, including three ladies, is now sixty miles inside the Maharajah's territory. We have only an honour guard and a cavalry escort. We are surrounded by the Maharajah's huge army, as he reminds us daily with his endless reviews and artillery displays.

183

The rest of our army and all our heavy guns are out of reach at Firozpur. If it came to a fight, Major, what chance do you think we would have?'

The post-breakfast elephant procession to the Golden Temple was to be informal, allowing the Governor-General to travel with his political secretary.

His eyes half closed against the sun, Lord Auckland winced as their elephant shifted his weight, rocking the howdah. Beside him, Macnaghten tugged at his collar. 'My lord,' he said, his eyes moving from Lord Auckland's hollow gaze to the mahout riding on the elephant's neck, 'I have one or two suggestions regarding our afternoon conversation with the Maharajah.' He hunched his shoulders. 'If, at this afternoon's meeting, the Maharajah still refuses to discuss committing his troops to the campaign, I think we must assume that he does not intend to do so. In that case, sir, I suggest we proceed into Afghanistan without him.'

Lord Auckland looked silently down on his cavalry escort as they waited for the Maharajah's elephants to join the march. 'I agree. We mustn't wait any longer for the old man.' A sigh shook his large frame. 'All this is most disappointing. I shall be very sorry to lose the Maharajah's army, although our own force is certainly strong enough to take Kabul without him. But we must get written assurance of a right of way up to the Khyber Pass. We must have a signed treaty before another week goes by.'

Macnaghten wiped his face. 'I believe we will, my lord.'

'Then get it for us.' Lord Auckland tugged his brocade coat over his midriff. 'The Honourable East India Company cannot be held hostage by a petty Maharajah.'

Macnaghten swallowed. 'No, my lord, of course not.'

Three elephants behind Lord Auckland, the two Eden ladies perched on their seats like a pair of bonneted birds. Across from them, Mariana leaned forward, looking for a sight of Fitzgerald riding ahead with the honour guard. She had not seen much of him in the evenings recently, as the ladies had been excluded from Ranjit Singh's nightly drinking parties – orgies by all accounts, most unsuitable for gentlewomen. That exclusion had been a relief. The Maharajah's leering glances at her had been unnerving enough in the daytime when he was sober. Heaven only knew how he would behave when tipsy.

As if he had read her thoughts, Ranjit Singh and his elephants materialized like a mirage on the plain, heralded by a great cloud of dust.

'Miss Emily,' Mariana ventured, ignoring the advancing native train, 'I am sure there is an explanation for Lieutenant Fitzgerald's broken engagement. Can we not ask him what happened? Perhaps the story has been exaggerated by gossip.'

If only they would speak to Peter Edwardes.

Miss Emily turned a stern blue eye on Mariana. 'My dear child, we would all like to think well of the young man but I do not believe in smoke without fire. While I agree that some details of the story may have been exaggerated, I cannot allow you to risk your future on someone with his reputation. Deserving or not, Lieutenant Fitzgerald has been *disqualified*.'

The Maharajah's procession was drawing closer. The discordant sounds produced by his musicians, the bellowing of his men, the thud of his nobles' horses all reached them through the dust before the party itself came into focus. Mariana bit her lip. This should be one of the great moments of her life. She would never see a durbar like this one again. She turned her bonneted head away from the ladies and wiped away tears of frustration with the back of her hand.

185

India was ruined for her.

Villagers squabbled over the Maharajah's shower of coins. Petitioners ran, shouting and gesturing, beside his elephant. His band played 'God Save the Queen', leaving out several parts of the melody. Slowly, the Sikh and British elephants merged into one procession.

'Poor dear,' sighed Miss Emily as they watched Lord Auckland climb into the royal howdah and embrace Ranjit Singh. 'I do believe he could almost bear this durbar if he did not have to keep hugging the Maharajah.'

The march to the Golden Temple began at last. Peacock-feather fans, yak tails, and silk standards were raised. At a signal, the official drummers began their steady pulse and the band took up the marching song. One by one the elephants shifted their weight and the ponderous, gaudy, noisy procession began to move.

As they set off towards the city and the temple whose dome gleamed in the distance, Mariana caught sight of one of the honour guard riding ahead of the elephants. He wore the blue dress uniform of the Bengal Native Artillery and a shiny dragoon helmet whose red horsehair plume rippled in the sun. He looked back briefly, a hand shading his eyes, then turned and rode on.

Ten miles behind the marching elephants, a small caravan of horsemen and loaded camels followed the road to Amritsar.

Yusuf Bhatti turned to Hassan, his saddle creaking. 'If we do not stop for food, we should reach Amritsar by early evening. In that case, we may see the Maharajah tonight.'

'No, Yusuf, we must eat,' said Hassan beside him. 'God willing, my Saboor will be waiting for me whenever we arrive.'

Yusuf nodded silently. He did not have Hassan's patience.

Even in his agony, Hassan had done his duty. Days and nights spent arguing with the leaders of Kasur had gained him half the tribute money he had been ordered to bring. Now, with a line of laden camels roped together behind them, they both had hope. Saboor's fifteen days had now passed. Surely the Maharajah would keep his word and return the child, especially when he saw the camel-loads of treasure they had brought him. But, Yusuf asked himself, if all were well, why had Hassan's father sent that mysterious letter, delivered three days ago to their camp at Kasur by an exhausted courier from Lahore?

My son, the Shaikh had written, *I have not told you this before, but according to Shafi Sahib, Saboor is to be rescued by an outsider whose identity is yet to be determined. As Shafi Sahib is rarely wrong, I believe you may comfort yourself with this news.*

Yusuf had seen the letter himself. He knew that it lay, grimy with dust, in the pocket over Hassan's heart.

Rescue. The Shaikh used no word lightly. He must mean that the Maharajah would refuse to return Saboor. He might also mean, although Yusuf had not said this aloud, that Saboor's condition was worse than they had imagined. Who, then, would intervene and return the child, alive, to his family?

'Hassan,' Yusuf said carefully, 'if, God forbid, all does not go as planned, there is the letter.'

The air had grown cold.

'Yes,' Hassan said, as he drew his shawl about his shoulders. 'There is the letter.'

Chapter Seventeen

The interior of the Golden Temple was airy and cool, but it lacked chairs. The three Englishwomen lowered themselves as decorously as they could onto the expanse of carpet covering the floor.

Mariana crossed her legs under her skirts and looked over at the men who sat facing each other at the centre of the space. Lord Auckland seemed most uncomfortable on his cushion. Fitzgerald must be there, but she could not see him.

'I do not know how much longer I can bear sitting like this,' Miss Fanny murmured, wincing as she shifted her limbs beneath rose-figured skirts. 'My knees are aching horribly.'

Miss Emily, her face set into grim lines, said nothing.

'I see a lovely, comfortable-looking wall,' added Miss Fanny mournfully, 'but it's miles from here.'

Above their heads, perfumed smoke from hundreds of incense sticks hung in the air, catching the light from the temple's high windows. From the direction of the altar, stringed instruments took up a melody in a minor key, joined by nasal voices. Along the walls, the Maharajah's turbaned chiefs stood in elegant, whispering groups.

Mariana felt herself relax as she absorbed the scene. The Eden ladies had ruined her happiness with Fitzgerald but, she realized, they had not spoiled India for her after all. India, with all its peculiarities, would always belong to her, and she would always share it with her father. That much, at least, they could not take from her.

On his own cushion, the Maharajah talked steadily, weaving pictures with his hands. Facing him, Lord Auckland, his face a mask of strained politeness, nodded at intervals while Mr Macnaghten translated, his brow knit in concentration. From time to time, Lord Auckland detached his gaze from the Maharajah and stared towards the entrance.

'He looks,' whispered Miss Fanny, 'as if he hopes someone will come through the door and rescue him.'

'Sh-h,' replied Miss Emily without moving her face.

The Maharajah turned on his cushion and noticed the Eden ladies' pained expressions. 'The ladies are becoming bored,' he announced, and caught the eye of a white-bearded priest. 'Let them see the Granth Sahib,' he ordered, then turned his attention back to Lord Auckland.

On the marble altar, beneath a golden canopy supported by silver poles, the holy book of the Sikhs lay under its many fine coverings. The priest motioned for the ladies to approach.

Miss Emily and Miss Fanny rose gratefully and, supporting each other, rustled unsteadily towards the altar and its row of elderly priests, with Mariana trailing in their wake.

As she passed a shadowed corner, a small, bearded man stepped suddenly from the shadows to stand in her way. On his shoulder lay a baby in a round, stiffly embroidered cap, whose mouth hung open as he slept. She gasped.

The man addressed her softly. 'Memsahib,' he said, his eyes moving as he spoke, not meeting hers, looking at the ground, at the ceiling, over her shoulder, 'Memsahib, you speak our language.'

189

The baby had drooled, leaving a stain on the man's shirt. He shook the child gently against him. 'This little one is a hostage of the Maharajah. His condition is bad.'

This was the exhausted child she had seen with the Maharajah that night. 'Hostage?' she asked, frowning.

'Yes. To be sure of the loyalty of his courtiers, the Maharajah sometimes keeps their children in his Citadel. Baba has spent much of his life there with his mother. Now his mother has died, and poor Baba is all alone with the Maharajah. He cannot see his father or his grandfather, or any of those who love him.'

The Eden sisters had reached the altar. They leaned over it, cooing in mannerly appreciation. The priest spoke beside them, his voice a deep rumble. They turned, uncomprehending, looking for Mariana.

'There are those at the Citadel who are jealous of the favour the Maharajah bestows on Baba.' The servant pushed up the child's scarlet sleeve. In the half-light of the temple, Mariana could see fading bruises on the small forearm. She felt her heart contract.

'Where is his family?' Her sharp whisper echoed back from the stone walls.

'They are in Lahore, except for his father who has been sent away.'

What a peculiar, cruel country this was, but what could she do? She spread her hands. 'I am sorry.'

The ladies beckoned. Mariana moved to pass, but the servant stepped sideways, blocking her way. 'The Maharajah loves him,' he went on, his voice trembling, 'but he knows nothing of children. He does not see how sad Baba is, how much Baba longs for his dead mother, and for his father who loves him. Baba never smiles. I fear he will die of grief.'

190

Music, tender and insistent, rose from the altar, surrounding Mariana. She put a hand to her throat.

'What can I do,' the man murmured, 'I who am only a servant? How can I save him?'

The first covering of the Granth Sahib, a fringe of enormous pearls and emeralds, hissed and clicked as the eldest of the priests lifted it from the book. The ladies beckoned again.

The servant blinked and raised his eyes to the ceiling. 'The cooks make him the best food, others make him playthings, but all he wants is his family.' He fingered the rope of precious stones round the child's neck. 'The Maharajah gives him jewels, but what does poor Baba care for such gifts?' His gaze was urgent. 'His grandfather, Shaikh Waliullah, is a noble man, Memsahib. He once saved my brother's life. Take the child from this place before he dies. Carry him with you when you leave here, Memsahib. Send him to Shaikh Waliullah in Lahore. It is his only hope.'

There are noble men of all religions in India, her munshi had said. She would like to meet this Shaikh. But how many children in India were lost, how many were beaten? Was this baby not one of a hundred thousand small victims of India's odd customs?

The baby's eyes were tightly shut. He stirred on the servant's shoulder. Mariana dragged her eyes from him. She should never have shown interest. 'I am very sorry,' she whispered firmly, 'but I cannot help you. How can I steal a child from Maharajah Ranjit Singh?' She gathered her skirts. 'Stand aside, and let me pass.'

She stepped round the servant and child and started towards the altar. The priest had begun to read from the book, his voice a high, hypnotic singsong. The Eden sisters motioned for her to hurry.

The man's voice followed her. 'Allah will aid you. Allah Most Gracious will aid you.'

She looked back to see him wipe his eyes with a brown finger. On his shoulder, the child still slept. She paused briefly, her lips pressed together, then moved on towards the altar.

The visit to the temple eventually came to an end. The ladies returned, smiling, from the altar. The gentlemen rose from their seats on the carpeted floor.

The Maharajah unfolded himself from his cushion and, taking the Governor-General's hand, helped him to rise. 'It is getting dark,' he announced, still holding Lord Auckland's hand. 'We will have a firework display.' He looked about him, his single eye alight. 'Where's my baba?'

Standing behind the others, Mariana shivered and looked away as the bearded servant stepped forward and gave the sleeping baby into the Maharajah's hands.

Wrapping themselves against the chill, the Maharajah and his guests filed out of the inlaid doorway. At the far end of the causeway they climbed a narrow stair to a group of balconies, where they looked back at the temple in its square lake. The dying sun had left only a faint glow in the western sky over the city of Amritsar. From where she stood, Mariana could see torches moving below her. Lamplight glowed in the windows of adjacent houses.

The first explosion startled everyone. It rocked the air before them and rang in their ears as a great spray of sparks lit up the golden dome of the temple, its decorated outer walls, and the waters of the great tank in which it stood. As rocket after rocket went off, the temple became a fairy palace, now blindingly bright, now bathed in shadow, lit from every angle by sudden flares and showers of sparks.

192

'Look, my pearl,' an old man's voice said between explosions, 'you can see the fish swimming in the lake.'

Mariana turned. The Maharajah stood among his bejewelled chiefs on the next balcony, enjoying the show as if he had never seen fireworks before, the baby from the temple twisting in his arms. The child, his face puckered around the thumb in his mouth, looked as if he were trying to burrow his way into the Maharajah's chest. There was no sign of the servant. The Maharajah laughed, throwing his head back. Against the old man's chest, the child turned and looked directly into Mariana's face.

His body stilled. His eyes wide, he stared at her, unblinking, his gaze heavy, full of expectation.

She looked away. When she looked again, the baby still stared, oblivious of the deafening sounds and the cascades of light around them, drinking in her face, his mouth working round his thumb. Baby Freddie sucked his thumb too; but Freddie had been round and pink when she last saw him, with fair hair that stood out in a halo about his head, not at all like this brown baby in his strange, shiny clothes. Baby Freddie had never looked at her as this tiny stranger did now, as if she were the most important person in all the world.

His eyes locked on hers, the child rested his head on the Maharajah's shoulder. Weighed down by his stare, she lowered her gaze.

'Are you all right, my dear?' Miss Emily enquired. 'What are you looking at?'

Mariana shivered. 'Nothing, Miss Emily.'

The child had been asleep when his odd little servant had stepped out of the shadows and begged for her help. Why, then, did the baby look at her now with such keen recognition?

It was too late to save him now. Rescue, difficult enough

in the temple, was impossible here. She could not reach across the space between her balcony and the Maharajah's and snatch the baby from the old man's grasp. She kept her eyes on the shimmering waters of the tank, knowing the child had not taken his eyes from her. She reached for a hopeful thought. Even if keeping the baby for himself was selfish of the Maharajah, he was clearly fond of the poor thing. Surely he would see to it that someone kissed the baby tonight, that someone kept him warm in the cold night air. She wrapped a shawl tightly about her. That expectant little face, she feared, would haunt her for the rest of her days.

With one last explosion of light, the fireworks ended. As the crowd began to shuffle down the staircase, Mariana lost sight of the Maharajah. She turned to descend the stairs, relieved to be free of the baby's stare; but a high, despairing wail rose from the direction of the city gate, and she knew instinctively that it came from him. She followed the Eden ladies helplessly down the stairway as the child's cry lifted over the noise of the crowd and filled her ears.

They moved slowly by torchlight towards the rows of waiting palanquins. In front of Mariana, Mr Macnaghten spoke in a low tone to Major Byrne.

'. . . tomorrow morning,' he was saying. 'I cannot persuade him to meet the Maharajah more than once a day, but he *must* do so. We cannot be certain of the Maharajah's continued good health.' His voice dropped to an indecipherable hiss.

Major Byrne patted Macnaghten's shoulder. 'Of course, William,' he replied, then strode off to hail a junior officer, while Macnaghten's fingers knotted and twisted behind his back.

Alongside Mariana, two British officers helped a third, who staggered between them, his head drooping as if he were about to faint. She quickened her steps. There was her palanquin, waiting on the ground, her bearers, anonymous in their shawls, crouched beside it.

As she prepared to swing her legs into the curtained box, a small bearded man dashed towards her through the crowd, his head turning as if he were searching for someone, a child in his arms. The servant's labouring breath was visible in the cold air, his neatly wrapped turban lay askew on his head. The baby rode his servant like a king on his way into battle, his fists pounding the man's shoulder, urging him on.

Child, servant and young woman saw each another in the same moment.

Mariana's mouth fell open. The running man turned and came straight for her, his lips moving as if he were talking to himself, but before he reached Mariana's side, the baby in his arms lunged dangerously towards her. Without thinking, she reached up to prevent the child from falling to the ground, then gathered him onto her lap and looked up, ready to scold the servant for his presumption. But where the little man had stood, there was only empty space.

Still holding the baby, she stood up and searched about her, but found no trace of the servant among the throng of British officers and Sikh sirdars. His work accomplished, the concave man with the sparse beard had vanished into the crowd.

The child in her arms smelled faintly sour. Wrinkling her nose, she held him away from her. In his outlandish clothes, with black powder ringing his eyes, he seemed unpleasantly foreign. Moments ago, she had wanted a second chance to rescue him, but now that the chance had come, she did not want it, or him. Foreign or not, he relaxed his dirty little body in her arms and raised solemn, expectant eyes to hers over the thumb in his mouth.

Her arms tightened round him. 'You need a bath,' she said.

He needed a bath, and he needed to get warm. Beneath his rich satins, the baby's skin felt cold to Mariana's fingers; his curled feet were icy. Why was there no woolly shawl for him? Why had his comfort been forgotten when evening was closing in? And what was it in those round, tired eyes, Mariana wondered, as she tugged her shawl about them both, that seemed to promise her joy, that made her feel powerful and good?

Men moved past them in groups. Palanquins edged through the crowd, their bearers shouting to clear the way. A spear-carrying Sikh, a precious Kashmir shawl tied carelessly about his waist, pushed by on a nervous horse, too close for safety, his gold-studded bridle gleaming in the torchlight.

Anyone she asked would say it was her duty to stop a British officer or one of the Sikh courtiers and hand the baby over, explaining that she had no right to him, that he belonged to the Maharajah. It was wrong, they would say, to take someone else's child.

The White Rabbit and two other aides-de-camp passed close by, talking among themselves. Debating no longer, Mariana ducked her head and bundled the child into her palanquin, praying that they would not see, but they did not seem even to notice her. Without looking in her direction, they passed, still talking, out of her sight. Even Mariana's own bearers appeared not to have seen anything unusual. As she climbed into the box after the baby, they glanced at her as incuriously as ever, before getting languidly to their feet.

Everyone was leaving. Lord Auckland's elegant palki had already passed. A troop of horsemen now trotted away into the dark, followed by a crowd of servants on foot carrying banners and fans on long sticks. Only one palanquin, a tall one of coloured glass, remained fifty yards away surrounded by gesticulating natives.

'Go, Munnoo,' Mariana ordered as she wrapped the baby up to his eyes in her best blue shawl.

Who, exactly, was this child? She had not paid proper attention to the name his servant had given her in the temple, the name of the child's grandfather. But even if she had bothered to listen, what was the likelihood of finding the man? The walled city must house ten thousand grandfathers with names like Wali Mohammad, or Wasif or Waheed.

'I have saved you from the Maharajah,' she whispered as she tucked the child into the crook of her arm, 'but I don't even know your name.'

If he understood her words, he did not seem to care. He lay beside her, his eyes still on her face beneath the circular cap that had, by some miracle, remained on his head during the confusion.

She must get him home. She banged on the roof, urging the bearers to hurry.

The journey seemed to take for ever. For an hour, as they covered the distance to the English camp, Mariana lay on one elbow, her free hand inches from the baby's face, ready to clap it over his mouth if he should cry out and betray them. Torchbearers galloped beside her, their flames throwing an eerie, wavering light against her curtains. Harsh, rhythmic breathing told her another palanquin was close by. She hoped it did not contain Major Byrne. Only yesterday, she had heard him savage one of his subordinates over a brass uniform button. She tried not to imagine what he would say if he found her with the Maharajah's baby hostage.

The child snuggled closer. Had anyone seen her take him?

197

It must be a serious crime to steal one of the Maharajah's hostages. What would happen if she were caught? Needles of fear pricked unpleasantly at her hands and feet.

She moved stiffly in the cramped space. Very well. If she were caught, unnerving as that would be, she would not apologize. In fact, she would insist on keeping the child. If he did not belong to her, he did not belong to the Maharajah either. He belonged to his family. The Maharajah had not cared for him properly. She touched a small cheek with one finger. How was if possible that, in all that seething camp, only one servant had thought of his welfare, or noticed his misery?

The familiar sounds of the avenue at night reached her through the curtains. Minutes later, her bearers slowed their pace. When they set the palanquin down, Mariana struggled awkwardly out of the box in the darkness, the swaddled child in her arms. Bent double so her bearers would not see, she dashed into her tent, letting out her breath as the reed door curtain flapped safely shut behind her.

Dittoo had left an oil lamp on the bedside table. She carried the baby to the bed, put him down, and was reaching to pick up the lamp when she thought of something.

She ran back to the door and pushed the covering aside. 'Munnoo,' she called.

In the starlight, a figure detached itself from the group of retreating bearers and turned back. 'Go and find Dittoo,' she ordered. 'I need him at once.'

She returned inside and, holding the lamp aloft, bent over the child on the bed. The lamp threw great shadows on the tent walls and gleamed on the tawny satin of her gown and on the baby's broad, tender face. His skin was the shade of her milky morning coffee, but with a touch of gold. Curving

198

lashes shadowed broad cheeks that should have been plumper than they were.

She had seen native children rushing about naked in the villages the camp had passed, but she realized as she studied her tiny guest that she knew nothing about a native child's life. What did he do all day? What toys did he have? Did he wear leading strings when he was taken out into the garden? One thing was certain. As soon as the bath water came, she would wipe away the black powder that encircled his eyes.

She pulled off her straw bonnet and shook out her hair until it fell from its pins and lay tangled on her shoulders, then sat down beside him on the bed.

'Well, you odd little thing,' she said tenderly, a hand on the baby's body, 'what should we do now?'

Still wrapped in her shawl, he sighed, his eyelids fluttering.

When had he last eaten? 'You need your supper,' she said, frowning. 'Where is that silly Dittoo?'

There was nothing to eat in the tent, but her jug of water stood on the bedside table. She poured some into her tumbler, and, holding the baby carefully upright, put the tumbler to his mouth. Suddenly animated, he leaned forward eagerly, his eyes wide, and took it in great panting gulps. They hadn't given him anything to drink! Her hand holding the glass shook with anger.

When he would drink no more, she put the glass down. What if he were really ill? She pushed away the memory of another helpless native creature and another water glass.

She tucked his arms into the shawl and got to her feet, leaving him on the bed. At the doorway, she lifted the blind aside and looked out. All she could see in the starlight was the familiar expanse of clay stretching from her tent to the red compound wall, and the distant tents of Lord Auckland and his sisters.

199

Where was Dittoo? He was an irritating servant – he talked on and on, dusting her tiny bedside table when she wanted most to be left alone, fussing over things that did not matter and forgetting those that did, but he was warm-hearted. Alone with her stolen baby, Mariana could scarcely wait to hear his shuffling footsteps rounding the side of her tent.

The child lay still, his face framed by blue fringe. As she watched, he tried to free his arms but could not, for the shawl was wrapped too tightly about his body. Whimpering, he fought with the entrapping fabric, his eyes filling with tears. As Mariana flew towards him, his embroidered cap came loose and rolled away, exposing his head. It was bald, save for a fine, newly sprouting crop of black hair.

At the sight of that round, shaven head, Mariana felt herself transported to another time and place. In his illness, his own head shaved, Ambrose, too, had whimpered helplessly; Ambrose who had adored her, whom she had loved more than anyone in the world.

She lifted the baby onto her lap and tore away the shawl. 'There, there,' she whispered, rocking him, her face against his, as she had rocked Ambrose when he was a baby. 'Don't cry, my darling, my lambkin.'

She had feared he would give the same high-pitched wail that had carried to her over the crowd earlier that evening, but instead he hiccuped and put his thumb in his mouth.

'Oh,' she cried, relieved, 'you only wanted to suck your thumb!'

Like dew, tears filled his lashes and lay on his cheeks. She touched his face. When he was better, would he flap his hands when he laughed, as Ambrose had done? Would he run to her, shrieking with pleasure, when she held out her arms? Would he die?

200

As her own past sorrows welled up and spilled from her eyes, bumbling sounds came from outside her door. Help, if only in the form of Dittoo, had come at last. Bent over the baby, Mariana began to weep in earnest.

Chapter Eighteen

In the mysterious way that news travels, word of the baby's disappearance had reached the English camp even before the young lady translator's palanquin had passed by the saluting sentry and into the Governor-General's compound. Within half an hour it had made its appearance at cooking fires in all quarters of the camp.

When a water carrier arrived at the row of fires along the back wall of the Governor-General's compound, Dittoo and three friends had already finished their evening meal. The youngest of the four men was on his feet before the fire, a slim silhouette in motion, his feet stamping, his arms over his head. He sang as he danced, a light melody full of trills and catches. The bhisti watched, nodding.

'Look, Sonu,' said Guggan, the eldest of the three, by way of greeting, pointing to a comfortable place by the fire, 'Mohan thinks that's the way a dancing girl moves her arms.' He gestured, palm up, at the swaying figure before them. 'Look at him. Dittoo here says no real *nach* girl would—'

'Of course this is right.' Mohan went on dancing, his fingers extended to resemble lotus buds. 'Who was it that stood with his eye to a crack in the durbar tent while a whole troop of them entertained the Governor-General and the Maharajah?

202

You wouldn't know, Guggan,' he added, lowering his arms, 'you were too lazy to leave the fire.'

Sonu put his head on one side. 'I can tell you one thing, Mohan,' he offered, 'you may know how to sing, but you cannot dance. But I have not come to your fire to talk of dancing girls. I have come to tell you some big news. The Maharajah's favourite hostage has disappeared.' He bent closer to the fire. 'The hostage is a baby boy with magical powers.'

Mohan's song stopped. All four servants fixed their eyes on the water carrier.

'The child's grandfather is Shaikh Waliullah of Lahore, a man of great powers. That is how the child came by his abilities. He is said to bring good fortune wherever he goes. That is why the Maharajah keeps him.' Sonu found a stick and poked the fire. 'In fact, the Maharajah never lets him out of his sight. He calls the child his pearl of pearls.'

His audience exchanged glances.

'This evening, the Maharajah made a great display of fireworks to entertain the British sahibs. Afterwards, when it was time to return to camp in his palanquin of coloured glass, he sent for his little hostage to accompany him. The servant came, bringing the child. He had almost reached the palanquin when suddenly, just like that, the baby vanished from his arms and into the air.' Sonu paused, his eyes on the flames. 'Everyone saw it happen.' He stirred the embers. 'Now, with the child disappeared, everyone fears some calamity will befall the kingdom. That is why the Maharajah is offering a great reward for news of the baby's whereabouts.' His stick had caught fire. He brought its end up and blew it out. 'No one knows why the child disappeared. He was given everything, jewels, everything.'

As the friends considered this point, the voice of the sirdar bearer came from the direction of the tents with an unwelcome message. 'Dittoo, Memsahib is calling you.'

Four faces grimaced.

'The boy has powers,' Sita said thoughtfully. He picked at his teeth with a twig.

'Perhaps, for a child so small, this is too great a feat,' Sonu offered. 'In that case, it was his grandfather who caused the child to disappear.'

All four servants nodded.

Munnoo appeared from the shadows and stood impatiently over the fire. 'What are you doing, Dittoo? Memsahib is calling.'

'In any case, it is said that every person in the city, down to the humblest sweeper, is searching for the child,' Sonu concluded as Dittoo gathered himself and stood. 'He will be known by his clothing, for it is red satin, embroidered with silver thread. He wears an embroidered cap, and a string of emeralds and pearls about his neck that reaches to his waist.'

The men's speculations followed Dittoo as he stumbled away towards the cold English tents.

As much as he liked to keep his distance from the Europeans he served, Dittoo made a point of talking to his memsahib.

He had made the decision to share his wisdom on his first meeting with her. Recruited at the last moment from his lowly post at Government House to serve a young memsahib on the journey to Lahore, he had put on his cleanest clothes and followed a lofty serving man of the Governor-General to a neat cottage on one of the better roads in Simla.

On their arrival, the serving man had left him standing, not on the porch but under a tree, in heavy rain. There he waited, shouted at by monkeys, the rain soaking his clothes, until an

Englishwoman emerged from the house, an umbrella over her head, and approached him. The Englishwoman looked him up and down in a pointed, catlike way from beneath the rim of her umbrella, then, to his surprise, greeted him properly in his own language. At that moment, it had come to Dittoo that, unlike other foreigners, this person might be able to learn something about real life.

From the first days of his service, he talked whenever he was in Memsahib's presence, giving advice, imparting knowledge. Soon after they left Simla, he told her that there would be no orange ice at lunch because no one had covered the shallow earthen dishes in which ice was made overnight, leaving the ice to be licked, or worse, by dogs or other animals. Another morning, he warned her that breakfast would be cold because one of the under-cooks had stabbed another with a bread knife, demonstrating the perils of borrowing money. His memsahib showed no interest in his stories. Sometimes, he suspected, she pretended sleep in order to avoid him, but he went on talking, sure of his mission.

Now he must leave his friends and Sonu's exciting story, but at least he would have the satisfaction of teaching Memsahib something. Confident of her interest in his news, he crossed the compound and approached her tent. 'Memsahib,' he began before he had even finished scuffing off his shoes outside the door, 'a most strange thing has happened!'

There was no reply. The door hanging fell back into place with a slap as he entered. She was there, sitting silently on the edge of her bed, her back to him, bent over as if in pain. The lamp threw a long trembling shadow across the bed.

Was she ill?

She sniffed convulsively. He blinked. Perhaps she had summoned him to help her bear some tragedy. He crossed the

205

floor with his uneven gait, the woollen socks she had given him silent on the striped rug. Reaching the end of the bed, he leaned cautiously forward.

She sat bent over a bundle on her lap, rocking it as if it were a child. He blinked. It *was* a child, wrapped in her shawl, its small brown hand resting on her bosom, among strands of blue fringe. How had Memsahib come to have a native baby in her tent? Babies and talk of babies seemed to be everywhere.

'Ji, Memsahib?' It was better to pretend he had not seen. He tore his eyes from the bundle on her lap.

She tucked a loose curl behind one ear and looked up at him through her tears. 'You must help me, Dittoo. This little one needs food, and warm water for his bath, and plain, ordinary clothes. He cannot be seen in these.' She pulled the shawl aside. Under it was a fair-skinned boy child, just old enough to be walking. His red satin costume was stiff with silver embroidery; a rope of pearls and emeralds lay heavily on his chest. The child, too, had been weeping.

Dittoo's own chest rose and fell under his thin shawl as if he had run all the way from the cooking fire. He glanced towards the doorway.

Memsahib raised her voice. 'Bring him food, your sort of food, from one of the native fires. I doubt if he has ever eaten European food. And hurry. He is very hungry.' Her voice wavered as she spoke, but she did not seem to care. Perhaps it was too late to pretend she was not crying.

'*Zaroor*, most certainly.' Dittoo nodded as if he were dreaming.

'And,' she continued, startling him with the sudden fierceness in her voice, 'if you speak one word of this, I shall dismiss you from my service and you will find yourself walking all the way from here to Simla. Do you understand me, Dittoo?'

206

'Ji, Memsahib.' He backed out of the tent and set off towards the red wall, tapping his head once or twice to make sure he was not dreaming that he had just seen his own memsahib in her tent with the Maharajah's vanished hostage in her arms.

Dittoo hurried past the large tent of the Governor Sahib's chef and the greasy cooking tents, his mind in turmoil. How great was the reward? Was it enough to allow him to return to his village and build a proper house for his family?

He thought of Memsahib's sharp words. Once she discovered he had betrayed her secret, she would dismiss him instantly from her service; but how could he miss this opportunity to gain a princely reward? How, for that matter, could he keep such thrilling news from his friends? The baby, the very hostage whose story they had just heard, was *in his memsahib's tent*! He could scarcely believe it himself. Not only was this a good story, it was one in which he actually had a part!

Over the past month, the four men at the fire had become like brothers. He hurried on, imagining their reaction to his story. Should he tell them yet, or should he savour his news?

He arrived out of breath. 'Is the food finished?' he asked quickly. His story crouched in his throat, ready to spring out. He swallowed.

His friends regarded him with surprise.

'Yes,' said Mohan, 'it is finished.' He raised his chin. 'Why do you want more food?'

'Someone has asked for it. It does not matter. I will be back soon.' There was no time to stop. He must find food for the child, then get warm water. Then, his work done, he would return to the fire and at his ease tell them his news in each delicious detail. He hurried away, feeling his friends' eyes on his back.

The other fires in the Governor-General's compound were

also cold. Clutching his arms against the chill, Dittoo tramped out onto the avenue, looking for a fire where men were still eating. He grunted with irritation as he stepped out of a misshapen shoe in the darkness. It was late. Wherever he went, men sat talking of the vanished child; but for the child himself, there was no food.

He was a long distance from the red-walled compound when he found what he sought, a group of Muslim men still eating, talking carelessly among themselves. He lifted his chin. He must not give his secret away. It would not do for another man to report the child's whereabouts and gain all the credit and the reward.

He went straight to the man whom he took to be the senior person at the fire.

'I have need,' he said, after exchanging greetings, 'of food.'

'Food?' A tall hill-man, whom Dittoo remembered to be a senior groom, looked up, interested, from where he squatted, chewing.

Dittoo looked away. 'Yes,' he replied, refusing to elaborate.

As the man studied him, Dittoo shifted nervously under the weight of his secret. His fingers twitched. He thrust his hands behind his back.

'Are you not the serving man of the young memsahib?' The man held a piece of bread partway to his mouth as if arrested in mid-thought.

Dittoo's hands clutched at each other behind his back. 'I must hurry,' he said, hunching his shoulders. 'If you have food, please give it to me.'

The groom stretched his long body and stood. He bent and rummaged among the pots until he found the circular lid to one

208

of them, and began without comment to scrape the leavings of the evening meal onto its flat surface. He laid a folded chapatti over the small mounds of rice and lentils, then nodded and handed the lid to Dittoo.

After hurrying from the fire, Dittoo paused to look back. The groom still squatted there, staring pensively into the fire. Dittoo walked on, relieved. The man did not suspect.

Were Dittoo a first-class serving man, his shoes would fit properly. His livery would be spotless, unlike the semi-clean dhoti and shirt he wore, for his sahib would buy him many uniforms. A first-class man would have himself shaved every day, and his turban would be starched like those of the Governor Sahib's servants, not limp like his own. But Dittoo had been born a second-class servant, attending to junior people like his memsahib, and he and his two surviving sons would for ever remain second-class servants. He passed a group of soldiers on their way to their tents from their evening meal. They were Brahmins, high-caste men from Oudh or Bihar who looked down on him and his friends. He kicked a stone out of his way, careful not to spill the food.

He thought of his family. His wife had given birth to eleven children. Of the eleven, eight had died, most of them lost to want and illness in times when crop failures had wiped out the food supply in his small village. For Dittoo, it was not difficult to recognize need on a child's face.

He turned into the avenue. The richly dressed child in his memsahib's tent had certainly been ill-fed. There was more to this story than the water carrier had told.

His step quickened. That the boy had vanished from his servant's arms in front of witnesses did not surprise him. He had heard of such things before. What he found difficult to believe was that the child had been transported by magic

209

to the tent of his own memsahib. She, an ignorant foreigner, had taken part in a great supernatural feat. Her powers must be enormous to have been recognized by the child's magician grandfather who was miles away in the city of Lahore.

As he passed the uniformed sentry at the entrance, he forced his mind back over the previous months but could remember no event that even hinted at her being a sorceress. One never knew to whom such powers might be granted, but to one of *them*? Even odder, to one of their *women*?

The English were ugly, with their odd clothes and odder hair. They were often abrupt, demanding, difficult to fathom, and furious when misunderstood. They had yellowing skin and dirty habits and their music was agony to the senses. Once, when he served at Government House, hearing loud noises and rhythmic thumping coming from the main salon, he had stolen across the garden and peeped inside through a window. There, to his open-mouthed astonishment, he had seen Europeans, men and women, dancing together in clumsy groups, running into one another as they moved, clapping and laughing loudly, heads thrown back, when their horrible music stopped.

They controlled most of India, these foreigners; yet for all their great power, most of them knew as little about life as they did about dancing. Once when Memsahib had been ill and Dittoo had served her for hours with no time for his midday meal, she had actually offered him her uneaten supper – meat, possibly even the flesh of a cow, covered with brown liquid, and other things, vegetables, equally repulsive. Had she not known what pollution she offered him?

Memsahib spent her day rushing from place to place, fearing to be late, her toilet incomplete, her curly hair escaping its pins. She seemed to have time only for the munshi who had taught her many languages, but who was not Hindu like himself and was therefore as ignorant as the rest of them.

She waited for him now in her small, pointed tent, whose walls glowed faintly with the light of her lamp. If she *were* a sorceress and he were to tell his friends, report the child's whereabouts and collect the reward, she would know it at once. He would then lose both his position and an opportunity to observe this curious being, a foreign female magician, at close quarters.

He frowned. Her weeping over the child had been unexpected. Being a sorceress, she must have known the baby's condition before he arrived in her tent. Why then had she been so pained at his misery? Perhaps her tears, like the offer of her uneaten food, were signs of a generous heart. It was certainly unusual to see an Englishwoman cradling a child of India as if he were her own.

Perhaps the instinct that had led him to talk instructively to her had been correct. Perhaps it had been her heart that he had recognized on that rainy morning in Simla.

At her door, he shuffled out of his shoes. It was difficult to trust the English, very difficult indeed, but who knew? Perhaps, reward or no reward, he could do worse than to serve this curious person and keep her secrets. Perhaps, Englishwoman or no, she deserved the finest gift he could offer, his loyalty.

He sat on the floor, the baby's legs dangling across his lap, squeezing rice and boiled lentils into bite-sized balls with his fingers. The little fellow's head was dirty and scabby. When had he last been bathed?

'Good boy,' he said, thinking of his youngest son as he pushed a ball of food into the baby's open mouth.

There was something strong about this child. Even in his

weak condition, he gave off a light that drew Dittoo, making him think of shrines and offerings. Had not Krishna-Ji himself appeared as a baby, a powerful force for good, able to perform magic? Perhaps it was this same sweet power that gave the child such value in the Maharajah's eyes.

'Dittoo,' Memsahib said from the chair, 'there is no sign of rain, and so I will not be travelling in my palanquin tomorrow. I certainly cannot take this baba in the carriage with the Governor-General Sahib and his ladies. You must bring him with you on the march. Pretend he is your nephew, or your own child.'

He sat still. How little she knew of things! How could he suddenly produce a baby and make the absurd claim that the child was his relation? And what if he were discovered? At the very least, he would be sent away with no pay. He might even be subjected to some horrible torture at the hands of the Maharajah's men. Why did she not simply perform some feat of sorcery?

'It will be difficult for me to bring him with the baggage,' he replied, using the begging singsong he reserved for refusal. He grinned, hunching his shoulders. 'Everyone in camp is looking for him. Everyone knows his story.'

The baby pushed Dittoo's hand away. His curled fingers lay on Dittoo's knee. Dittoo wiped the small mouth with a rag. Regarding him gravely, the baby reached up and patted his face, then turned away, his thumb in his mouth.

Memsahib stared. 'Story, what story?'

Dittoo avoided her gaze. 'His story – that he is a lucky talisman for Maharajah Ranjit Singh, that he has disappeared into the air from the arms of his servant in front of everyone.' He looked at her out of the corner of his eye. 'All the camp knows that his disappearance is the work of his grandfather who is a famous magician of Lahore, and that an enormous reward has been offered for his return.'

Her mouth fell open, then shut smartly. 'What nonsense.' She pushed back her hair and pointed to the child. 'He was . . .' She hesitated, then let out a little puff of air and raised her chin. 'Well,' she said, 'it does not matter how he came here, does it? In any case, I shall travel in the morning with the other English ladies. You will please bring the child. I do not care what you say to the others in camp. And now, it is getting late. Bring me hot water for his bath.'

Chapter Nineteen

Yar Mohammad squatted silently in the darkness beside the young memsahib's doorway, his head and upper body wrapped in a length of cotton, his nose protruding sharply from its folds. Memsahib's voice came from the tent, speaking softly and kindly. No one answered, no shadow moved on the wall. Yar Mohammad rubbed his eyes. Her servant must have gone out.

The man's appearance at his fire had mystified Yar Mohammad at first. Hindu dietary laws would never have allowed such a man to approach a Muslim cooking fire to feed himself. His memsahib could not have desired dal roti, the simple bread and lentils of the people. Only a stranger in need would be fed from a random cooking pot. Then it had come to him – there could be only one stranger at the camp whose need was great enough to send an Englishwoman's servant tramping about, searching for food like a beggar.

Yar Mohammad closed his eyes at the soothing sound of the woman's voice. Yes, Shaikh Waliullah's little grandson was here. *Al-Hamdulillah,* praise be to Allah.

At the fire, he had waited until the servant had taken the food away before making his way to Shafi Sahib's tent. The old man's beads had clicked quietly while Yar Mohammad told his

214

story. 'I believe you have guessed correctly, Yar Mohammad,' he agreed, nodding, when the groom finished speaking. 'Go now,' he added, 'and give Memsahib a message.'

Yar Mohammad had come directly from Shafi Sahib, entering the red compound through a narrow servants' entrance in the high back wall, saluting the uniformed Punjabi sentry in his own tongue as he passed, gaining the compound without difficulty. Leaving the entrance, he had skirted sleeping servants and banked fires, then crossed the open space towards the great tents of the Governor-General and his sisters. Moving quietly from shadow to shadow, he had approached the young memsahib's tent unobserved. His instructions were to deliver this new message at once, but he had not called out for fear of startling her. He pulled his shawl over his head and round his knees. He would wait.

He did not wait long. Footsteps approached, then her servant appeared at the side of the tent, his eyes on the ground, muttering to himself, a brass pail in each hand. Steam rose from one pail. A bath for the child.

The servant had not seen Yar Mohammad. Without looking up, he set one pail on the ground, and reached to lift the reed curtain covering the doorway. Lamplight streamed through the entrance and onto the dusty ground. In one silent motion, Yar Mohammad got to his feet and stepped from the shadows.

'Hai-ai-ai!' Startled, the servant shouted with sudden terror. The pail of hot water jerked in his hand, swinging sideways, splashing scalding water onto the ground.

Curiosity waxed in Yar Mohammad. While the servant grasped for the reed curtain, breathing hard, Yar Mohammad stepped forward and looked past him into the tent.

He drew in a long breath. The young memsahib sat facing the doorway, satin skirts the colour of a lion's coat spread

215

about her, pale brown curls framing her face as she crouched over a fair and broad-faced baby. Behind her, shadows leapt on the tent wall. For an instant, she returned Yar Mohammad's gaze, her eyes wide and fearless.

The servant forced the hanging shut and stepped hastily in front of it, his buckets before him on the ground. 'Why have you come?' he croaked.

'I have a message for Memsahib.'

'It's too late to be bringing messages.' The man was trying to sound forceful. Through the curtain Yar Mohammad could hear a rustling sound. Perhaps Memsahib was trying to conceal the baby.

'This message is important.' Yar Mohammad's own voice was tight with excitement. 'It is to be delivered at once. Tell her that I, Yar Mohammed, wish to deliver this message in person.'

He could see that the man wanted to chase him away with shouts and curses but was afraid to raise his voice again, fearing, most likely, that interested people might come from the servants' quarters and ask questions. Yar Mohammad did not move. He stood still, towering over the servant, and waited.

The servant looked as if he were about to weep. He raised a shaking hand and pushed aside the door hanging, then, clearing his throat, entered the tent. 'A man named Yar Mohammad is outside,' he said, his choked voice muffled by the closed hanging. 'He says he has a message for you.'

There was more rustling. Memsahib put her head round the entrance, then emerged and stood in front of Yar Mohammad, her face ivory pale in the moonlight.

'Yes, what is it?' White fingers gripping the doorway, she shifted her weight to block his view of the interior.

'Peace be upon you, Memsahib,' Yar Mohammad began. 'I

bring a message. It is this. You have done well. Tell no one what you have done. Wait for your instructions.'

She stood motionless, her skin glistening, then gave a high little laugh and wiped her hand on her skirt. 'Thank you, Yar Mohammad, although I have no idea what your message means.'

'Wait.' Yar Mohammad put up a hand as she moved to withdraw. 'I have something for you.'

Whimpering came from inside. Memsahib glanced over her shoulder, then back to Yar Mohammad. 'Go away,' she hissed, her eyes wide. 'Go away.'

Without answering, he squatted down and took out the muslin-wrapped packet of coarse brown sugar that he always carried for his horses. As she watched him, her body erect, he took out his small, crooked knife and cut off a square of muslin, wrapped two lumps of the raw sugar in it and held it out to her.

'Children like to eat this,' he said, as she took it with trembling fingers. 'The horses will not miss it.'

As he strode away, he considered how afraid the young woman had been when he handed her his gift. And yet, he had seen clearly that, for all her fear, if he had tried to force his way into the tent, it would have been her, not the old servant, who would have fought him.

He looked back over his shoulder at the small tent. What had the two old men said to him at Shaikh Waliullah's haveli?

Your work is about to begin, Shafi Sahib had told him.

Only you will know when the time has come to act, the Shaikh had said.

Mariana let down the flap and turned back to the tent, the little cotton packet dangling from her fingers. 'You told

Yar Mohammad,' she said accusingly. 'Dittoo, what have you done?'

Dittoo stood still in the centre of the floor, the baby in his arms. When Mariana looked at him, her face drained of colour, he bent double over the baby. 'I swear,' he burbled, tears in his eyes, 'I swear I did not tell. The groom is an odd man. I do not know how he could have guessed. Oh, I beg of you, Memsahib, I am telling the truth! Please, oh please, Memsahib, do not send me away!'

Her shoulders drooped. 'What does this mean, Dittoo? Does everyone in camp know the baby is here in my tent? Does the Maharajah know?'

The baby reached for her. She took him and sat down at the table. 'I thought we were safe, but we are not.' She untied the packet, then broke off a piece of the sugar and put it into the baby's open mouth.

'And do stop weeping, Dittoo. Of course you must stay.' She sighed loudly as he mopped his eyes with his rag. 'I cannot be left all alone with a native baby.'

'The groom brought a message, did he not?' Dittoo asked. 'What was his message?'

'It was nothing, Dittoo,' she replied. 'His message was nothing.'

It was not nothing. She feared it, this third message. No longer vague and dismissible, it proved that someone was watching her. 'Tell no one,' Yar Mohammad had said. 'Wait for your instructions.' She wrapped the baby in her arms and held him to her. She must not give in to fear. Yar Mohammad had also brought a gift. However afraid she was of his message, he had not threatened her.

'Dittoo,' she said, reaching out a calming hand, 'if Yar Mohammad had meant to betray us, he would not have given

Baba the sugar. He would have told us what he knew, and then he would have tried to snatch Baba away. I think no one knows but Yar Mohammad, and perhaps one or two others. But I do not think they mean us harm.' Calm rushed over her. 'Did you not fear, when he came, that he would take Baba away from us? Did you not think at first that Yar Mohammad was bent upon carrying away our baby and claiming the Maharajah's reward?'

She patted the baby's face, and laughed, and then Dittoo laughed, and seeing them, the baby brightened and he smiled, his eyes becoming two half-moons in his broad face, and she got up and spun him in a circle, her tawny skirts swinging about her, in the middle of the floor.

Chapter Twenty

The moon sent a faint silver light onto the Maharajah's yellow shawl tent and the tall palanquin of coloured glass that stood empty before its entrance. Guards spoke quietly among themselves as Faqeer Azizuddin walked Maharajah Ranjit Singh up and down outside the tent, an arm about the old man's shoulders.

Yusuf glanced at Hassan as their camel caravan approached the yellow tent. Something was indeed very wrong. It must be true, the frightening news they had heard upon reaching the Maharajah's camp.

Hassan's voice sounded flat, as if all his feeling had been lost.

'But why, Yusuf?' Who would steal my son from the Maharajah?'

'Do not fear, Hassan.' Yusuf reached out a steadying hand as they halted under a tree. With news this bad, he must think for them both. 'Saboor will be found. Remember your father's letter.'

'Where is Saboor?' Seeing them dismount, the Maharajah pushed his chief minister aside. 'Where is my little pearl?' he cried as he hurried towards Hassan. 'What have you done with him, you and your magician father?'

Before Hassan could reply, the Faqeer seized the old man by the elbow and guided him into the yellow tent. 'Come, Mahraj,' he soothed, throwing Hassan and Yusuf a warning glance. 'Speak to Hassan inside. You must rest now.'

Inside the tent, Yusuf watched Hassan approach the Maharajah's bedside. 'Mahraj,' Hassan began, standing beside his king, his eyes on the carpet, 'I arrived from Kasur only this evening, while you were at the Golden Temple. I came to bring you the first part of—'

'What do I care for gold and riches?' The old voice trembled. 'All that matters to me is my Saboor.'

Yusuf sweated at his post near the door. At least the guard had not disarmed them; they were not under arrest. But all those days and nights in Kasur, the discussions, the warnings, the flattery, all Hassan's patient efforts to win the Maharajah's tax money, his prayers that the Maharajah would allow him to take Saboor home at last, his quiet anxiety on the journey here – all were lost. Or were they? Had someone already rescued Saboor? If so, which stranger had risked death to save him? Where had he taken the child?

'Mahraj,' said the Faqeer caressingly, 'Hassan cannot have had a hand in this terrible business. He has been at Kasur on your behalf. He has come from there only this evening, carrying news and part of the tribute money. He is not to blame.'

The Maharajah signalled for his quilt. 'Bring me my Saboor,' he said simply, reaching for the Faqeer's hand as a servant pulled the red satin quilt round his shoulders.

A faint motion of Faqeer Azizuddin's head told Hassan and Yusuf to leave. As the two men backed from the yellow tent, Yusuf saw tears on his king's face.

*   *   *

221

It was still dark when Mariana was startled awake by the sound of hoarse, urgent whispering.

'Memsahib, Memsahib,' Dittoo was saying. 'I must take Baba outside.'

Baba, who was Baba? Must Dittoo talk even at night? Groaning, she began to turn over, then found herself jerked into wakefulness by a small stirring at her side.

The stolen baby!

'But Dittoo,' she whispered into the blackness, a hand on the little body beside her, 'it's still the middle of the night!'

'No, Memsahib, it is nearly morning. He must come outside and do soo-soo.'

'Soo-soo?'

'Pishab.'

Pishab? What important words had her munshi neglected to teach her?

'He will wet your bed,' Dittoo hissed, arriving by her side and groping for the baby. 'Babies must do their soo-soo at the proper time,' he insisted, his voice fading as he pushed open the blind, the child in his arms.

Mariana rolled over onto the warm place left by the sleeping baby and listened to Dittoo's muffled wheedling through her tent wall. Lahore was still four marches away. However would she conceal a baby on a four-day march?

She thrust her covers aside and, without bothering to light the lamp, felt for her boots. There was no time to find fresh clothes; she would wear the same ones she had worn the evening before.

She had dreamed again of the ship. As she fumbled with hooks and buttons she tried to recapture her dream but was able to conjure up only a vague image of taut rigging above

222

her head and wind-carried spray stinging her face. The dream reminded her of part of yesterday's poem.

> Grieve not, oh heart,
> For Noah shall be thy guide:
> Thy pilot-master of the deluge.

She reached to light her lamp. If only Noah were indeed guiding her. Believing that, she could endure anything. But perhaps she had been guided to steal the Maharajah's hostage. What other explanation could there be? The baby had wanted her to steal him, of that she had no doubt. It was he who had reached out to her from his servant's arms, he who had worn that expectant look on his little face. But why?

You have done well, Yar Mohammad had told her last night.

Yar Mohammad. He was no simple groom, to be bringing her these mysterious messages. He denied it but he, too, must be a soothsayer, like the madman on the road and the creature in the garden. Soothsayers seemed to be everywhere, giving her advice about courage and about the path she was said to have chosen . . .

At least Dittoo was no soothsayer, she thought, as he returned with the baby.

'It's far too cold,' she said worriedly a little while later, from where she sat on the bed. 'How can you take him outside without any clothes? He will become ill.'

His round eyes fixed on Mariana, the baby stood shivering in the lamplight before Dittoo's squatting figure, one small arm in a firm brown grip as Dittoo smeared cold mud onto his naked body. Miserable sounds came from round the thumb in his mouth.

'Why must you dirty him after his nice bath?' Mariana asked.

223

'They are searching for a rich child,' Dittoo explained as he worked. 'If he is naked and dirty I can say I found him on the road. These things happen all the time.'

'I suppose you're right.' Mariana crossed to her dress trunk and dragged out her ruined tartan gown. She found the torn place, then with a grand gesture, ripped the skirt apart. She held it out. 'Wrap him in this. Tell them I saw the baby and took pity,'

Moments later, the tartan-wrapped baby struggling under his arm, Dittoo tramped away towards the red wall while Mariana watched from the doorway, her heart thudding anxiously.

It was cold, even at the fire. From Dittoo's lap, the child looked steadily from face to face, returning the curious gazes of Dittoo's three friends, while one tiny foot, free of the torn dress, swung rhythmically back and forth.

'How could I leave him alone on the road for the jackals and hyenas?' Dittoo demanded, pushing a wad of bread into the baby's open mouth with a practised hand.

'Of course you could have left him there. Why is he any concern of yours?' asked Sita from where he sat drawing circles in the dust with a stick of kindling wood. 'And what of his caste? For all you know, you have an untouchable child on your lap and are putting your fingers into his mouth.'

With an apologetic grunt, young Mohan edged away, leaving a meaningful space between himself and the baby.

Guggan chewed thoughtfully on a neem twig. 'The children one finds here and there on the roads are nothing but trouble. Of course,' he added, changing his tone, 'if he were the Maharajah's hostage—'

'I know he will be trouble,' Dittoo interrupted hastily, wiping the baby's mouth. 'But what could I do?' His fingers

224

shook as he wrapped the baby more securely in his tartan rag.

'You are too soft-hearted, Dittoo.' Sita reached over his head to scratch his back with his stick. 'Of course you can always sell him. You might get a good price from Sirosh the tailor or what's-his name, the blacksmith.'

'No, don't do that.' Guggan peered into the baby's attentive face. 'He is here now. We can look after him. A blacksmith — pah! Who can entrust a child to a blacksmith? He's different, you know,' he added thoughtfully. 'He's not like most babies.' He spat a bit of bark into the fire. 'He should have clothes.' He poked a pudgy finger at the tartan rag. 'A man from my village does tailoring for the army. I'll ask him.'

Nodding, Dittoo held a cup of milk to the child's lips. As he did so, the baby's body went rigid. Then, in one startling motion, he reached a small hand up and dashed the cup from Dittoo's fingers. The four men watched as it fell to the ground and rolled away, spilling a pool of milk into the hissing fire.

'Good gracious, Mariana, it is the second time you've asked,' Miss Emily remarked after breakfast, shading her eyes with a gloved hand. 'It's never any use wondering where our things are. I, for one, expect to be reunited with my parasol precisely at sunset. But I must say, I never saw anybody so feverish for the sight of a muddy tent and an incompetent servant.'

'I quite understand,' put in Miss Fanny kindly. She shifted in her folding chair. 'I like to know where all my things are after every march, especially the spotted deer. I always worry until everything is just as it should be.'

'Not that in India anything is ever as it should be,'

commented Lord Auckland. He yawned as he consulted his watch. 'Thank goodness we need not entertain a single native until four o'clock.' He leaned back in his basket chair.

'Why not go out for a nice ride later, my dear?' said Miss Emily, studying Mariana. 'It will do you good to exercise. You are probably a little overdone from all the excitement of yesterday.'

Excitement. Mariana felt her throat go dry.

'It was exciting, was it not?' Miss Fanny said animatedly. 'I thought the fireworks made the temple and water tank seem like a fairy palace!'

Miss Emily's eyes were still on Mariana. 'You really do look pale, child. I shall arrange for you to ride one of the nicer horses. I've seen the poor little nag they've given you. No wonder you've not been riding.'

Hot in her tawny silks, Mariana stood an hour later before her collapsed tent, watching a group of coolies lay out ropes and tent pegs. Where in the chaos of the rising camp was her small guest?

As soon as her tent was standing and its furniture arranged, she rushed inside and stood tingling in the centre of the striped floor, anticipating the familiar and now thrilling sound of Dittoo blundering into her tent.

At last he stood before her, his face creased in a smile, the child wriggling under his arm.

'Oh, thank goodness you've returned,' she breathed, burying her face in the baby's neck. She laid him on the bed and cooed delightedly at his slow, lovely smile. 'He should have another bath. Were you seen?'

'No, Memsahib.' Mud streaked the grey stubble on Dittoo's chin, making him look even shabbier than usual. 'We were—'

They were interrupted by the sound of two men talking outside accompanied by the clopping of a horse's hooves. Her grooms had arrived with one of Miss Emily's horses.

'Go,' she urged Dittoo, waving a hand towards the entrance, 'and send them away. Tell them I do not wish to ride.'

As Dittoo put his head out through the entrance, she let the baby down and watched as he trotted across the floor. He stopped, balancing carefully, then squatted down, reaching out with delicate fingers to pick something up from the floor.

'No, darling, not Mariana's hairpin,' she whispered, snatching him up and opening his small fist.

The receding sound of hooves was replaced almost at once by the sound of someone clearing his throat outside. Dittoo and Mariana stared at one another. They had forgotten the munshi!

She handed Dittoo the baby and pulled open a canvas curtain on the inside wall of her tent, but as she motioned Dittoo to step into her tiny bathing space, a clanking of pails from outside told her that the sweeper was about to enter from the outside. Swiftly, she secured the curtain, shutting the sweeper out, then turned back, her finger to her lips, searching desperately for another hiding place.

Outside the entrance, a second throat-clearing held mild impatience.

'What can I say to make Munshi Sahib leave?' she whispered to Dittoo.

Her servant shrugged, the baby in his arms.

It was too late to hide the baby now. Mariana held out her arms for the child. 'Come in,' she called.

Her teacher stepped carefully inside, stooping as usual, blinking in the dusky light. At the sight of the baby in Mariana's arms, he took a step back.

227

Before he could speak, she crossed the floor to him. 'Munshi Sahib,' she whispered, as the sweeper banged pails behind the curtain, 'this child is the son of a great man from the walled city of Lahore. No one is to know he is here.'

'Ah,' replied the munshi.

One arm curled round Mariana's neck, the baby gazed bright-eyed at their visitor.

She drew herself up. 'I have stolen him from the Maharajah. People had been unkind to him. Look.' She pushed up the red satin shirt. 'He's been hurt.' Without thinking, she took the baby's hand and held it against her cheek.

'How did you come to steal him?' asked the old man, his expression unreadable.

'His servant came to me in the Golden Temple and showed me all his poor little ribs and his bruises. I could not help him then.' She sighed, remembering. 'But at the end of the evening, the same man rushed up and simply handed him to me. I put him into my palanquin and brought him here.'

'Did anyone see you?' The munshi's face was grave.

'No. It was quite curious,' she answered slowly. 'I felt oddly invisible. Everyone walked past as if I wasn't there. No one, not even the Indians, looked my way.' She stroked the baby's head. 'It was all so simple and happened so quickly – I could have stolen several children and no one would have cared.'

'There you are mistaken, Bibi.' Putting his hands behind him, the munshi straightened his back. 'Very much mistaken. There are those who care very much about this child. To help anyone to escape the Maharajah's household, especially if that person is one of the Maharajah's hostages, is a serious crime. Had your action been discovered, the alliance between your people and the Maharajah would have been most severely tested. The child would have been returned to the Maharajah and you might very well have been sent back to Calcutta in disgrace.'

She tightened her grip on the baby.

At that, his face softened. 'But you were *not* seen.' Approaching, he bent and peered into the baby's face. 'What is your name, son?'

The baby took a breath and spoke his first word in Mariana's hearing. 'Thaboor,' he said, wriggling in her arms.

The old man smiled. 'Saboor, is it? Well, well.'

'What should I do now, Munshi Sahib?' Mariana asked. Tingles of fear ran down her spine.

'It is clear that to save an ill-treated child is a good and charitable act. It is also clear that what has happened thus far has been the work of Allah Most Gracious, who inspired the servant to give you the child, and who protected you from discovery once you had taken him. You ask me what to do. I suggest that you pray.'

'Pray?' Mariana watched Saboor run unsteadily to where Dittoo held out his arms.

'You offer your prayers to God the All-Powerful, do you not, Bibi?' the munshi asked mildly.

'Yes,' she returned, 'but surely there is—'

'I must have time to think,' her teacher interrupted, raising an admonitory finger. 'And you, Bibi, must now put this whole affair into the hands of Allah Most Merciful.'

At Mariana's forlorn sigh, Munshi Sahib made an indefinable gesture, indicating the subject was closed.

'As to our lesson,' he went on, smiling at Saboor, 'this is a most unusual day, not the proper day for a lesson. Today shall be a holiday.' He looked towards the tent door. 'If I may have your permission, Memsahib, I will leave you. If you should need my help, Dittoo knows where to find me.'

229

Without looking back, he stepped from the tent. Mariana sat down on the edge of her bed, a little giddy, a hand to her breast.

In the munshi's wake, faint wisps of fog seemed to hang in the air. In the first moments they had spent together, the baby Saboor had taken hold of her heart. He was hers, and she was his. No one could tell her otherwise. Perhaps, in taking him, she had chosen a path of some kind, as the soothsayer had predicted. But whether or not she had taken a path, she would be careful. Yes, she would most certainly be very careful.

Chapter Twenty-one

Tuesday, 17 December

Early the next morning, half awake under her covers, Mariana listened as rain began to fall on the canvas above her head.

'But Memsahib, he must sleep with *me*,' Dittoo had insisted the previous evening as the baby in his arms reached out to her with urgent cries. 'The other servants will be expecting him. They will ask questions if he is not with me.'

He was right. How could they pretend Saboor was abandoned if he disappeared at night to someone else's bed? Unable to argue, she had waved Dittoo and Saboor away, then slept badly, certain that Dittoo had not wrapped the child well enough against the cold.

Only Dittoo, Munshi and Yar Mohammad knew about Saboor, and none of them seemed inclined to give him away. The English were not even aware of his existence. If they were, they would never imagine that one of their own people had stolen him.

Someone else knew. Mariana pushed away the pillow and opened her eyes. How could she have forgotten Yar Mohammad's message to wait for instructions? No, she must not think of that. She must think about how to keep darling little Saboor safe and fatten him up and make him happy.

Footsteps approached. 'Memsahib, I have brought Baba,' Dittoo whispered. 'Rain has begun, and so you will be travelling to the next camp by palki. I have told my friends that I have sent Baba to travel in a covered cart with a barber's family.'

'*Shabash*, Dittoo, well done,' she said, smiling her wide smile as she rose to greet them. 'Well done indeed.'

'Matthew, Mark and Luke and John,' she sang softly an hour later, her voice echoing inside the closed palanquin, 'bless the bed that I lie on . . .'

A gusting wind threw spatters of rain against her palki's thin walls. Outside, the steady 'hah, hah, hah' of her bearers told her all was well.

'How kind of the weather to let us travel together,' she whispered. 'Wasn't Dittoo clever to knock over the coffee things and distract our bearers while I bundled you inside!'

The shaven-headed child in the crook of Mariana's arm did not have her brother's rosy skin, and his eyes were brown, not blue, but his small weight against her eased her old sense of loss. His eyelids dropped, and he made little effort to sit up, but he seemed content in her company. He gazed into her face, letting her nuzzle and stroke him as much as she liked. She sat up, stuffed the pillows behind her back and pulled him onto her lap.

'There,' she said softly, as Saboor rested against her breast and closed his eyes.

She was glad that he did not fidget. The space inside the palki was long enough, extending past her feet, but it was barely wide enough for her to move, and each time she sat up, the roof grazed her head.

'Listen to the rain on the roof,' Mariana whispered. 'Today we love the rain, do we not, my little treasure?' She rubbed her nose against Saboor's cheek. 'You see,' she whispered, as he reached with delicate fingers for the locket she wore on a gold chain round her neck, 'you and I are quite safe and happy together.'

She could not, of course, tell her family about him yet; it would be unwise to write a letter that might be read by someone else. She imagined her mother's response to the news. 'How like Mariana to make off with a native infant,' she would say. 'I hope she gives it straight back. Think of the diseases it might have.'

But what of Mariana's dear, soft-hearted papa? He *had* made her give up Jeremy Harfield, but surely he would understand her protective feelings and Saboor's misery. Surely, this time, he would know she was right.

Due to the rain, the march took longer than usual. Breakfast, usually served as soon as everyone arrived at the new site, was late and crowded. Officers and staff members who would otherwise have taken their breakfast outdoors had elected to join the Governor-General and his party under cover. The dining tent was filled to capacity. Unable to sit at the table, the younger men ate standing in groups, juggling crockery and cutlery.

A servant pulled out a chair for Mariana beside Miss Fanny. Mariana sat down and arranged her skirts, surveying the laden breakfast table. Turning Saboor over to Dittoo at the end of the march had been tricky but successful, and now she was free to enjoy her breakfast. She took a brioche and reached for a butter knife.

Harry Fitzgerald had appeared in the crowd. She glanced up, wishing she could edge over and tell him all about the baby while no one was looking.

233

Lieutenant Marks who, thanks to Miss Emily, was also in the honour guard, stood by Miss Fanny, eating a plate of eggs and trying to catch Mariana's eye. He was invited for a glass of wine tomorrow, and Miss Emily expected her to attend *and* be civil, although she had twice been very clear about her feelings. The second time, she had even mentioned Marks' ears.

'His ears,' Miss Emily had replied, 'are of no consequence. In time, you will cease to notice them.'

Mariana would *never* cease to notice them. They symbolized all her feelings about being pushed into a marriage of convenience. This morning, as Marks smirked at her over his fork, she imagined them growing longer and longer until they reached his shoulders.

Beyond the simpering Marks, Fitzgerald balanced his cup on a plate, his fine profile turned to Mariana. His hair looked ruffled, as though he had not slept well. She would run away with him tomorrow if there were anywhere to run in the Maharajah's territories, if he were not leaving any day to march for Afghanistan.

She turned deliberately, avoiding Marks' eyes, and stared with pretended fascination at a servant balancing a tray of dirty plates. All she could do now was travel back to Calcutta with Lord Auckland and his party, praying all the way that Fitzgerald would finish his tour of duty in Afghanistan and return to her. Sooner or later his real story would reach Miss Emily. Sooner or later, everything would be all right.

'Where is Major Byrne?' Miss Fanny's voice broke into Mariana's thoughts.

'He has gone to arrange for sheep,' offered Lieutenant Marks.

'Sheep?' Miss Emily stopped slicing a lamb kidney. 'What do we want with sheep?'

'We're having them for lunch tomorrow, Miss Emily.' Marks nodded seriously.

Miss Emily's eyebrows lifted. 'What sort of sheep are we expecting for lunch? I hope no one has invited the vulgar ones with orange splotches.'

Marks gaped in confusion. At the table's end, Lord Auckland folded his napkin. 'If I were you, Emily,' he suggested, a corner of his mouth turning up, 'I should not wear wool at tomorrow's lunch.'

Miss Fanny bent confidentially towards Mariana. 'Sheep is one of my sister's favourite words.'

'And now, dear Mariana,' said Miss Emily, changing the subject, 'you must hear the latest excitement from the Maharajah's court.' She set down her porcelain coffee cup. 'We have just learned that while we were at the Golden Temple two evenings ago watching the firework display, someone performed an interesting feat of magic.'

Mariana caught her breath.

'Yes indeed,' Miss Fanny put in. 'It is such a pity we missed seeing it happen. The story has all the romance of an Oriental Tale.'

Miss Emily patted her mouth with her napkin. 'You must have seen the sickly looking baby that the Maharajah keeps beside him all the time. The child is a hostage, kept to ensure the loyalty of his father, a young man who assists the mysterious Faqeer Azizuddin, the Maharajah's chief minister. The little hostage,' Miss Emily went on, waving her knife over the butter dish as the standing crowd quieted to listen, 'was present at the fireworks that evening. You may have noticed him, Mariana, when the Maharajah held him up to see the display.'

Mariana nodded mutely.

'Apparently, the child vanished immediately afterwards, in spite of every precaution having been taken to ensure his security.'

Miss Fanny leaned forward. 'According to the natives, he evaporated into the air from his servant's arms as he was being carried to the Maharajah's palanquin. Since that moment, no trace of him has been found. The Maharajah is said to be quite desolate at the loss of the child who, he believes, brings him luck.'

Mariana noticed Fitzgerald watching her speculatively from across the tent.

Miss Emily's eyes shone bright blue. 'As if that were not enough, we are told that the child's grandfather is a well-known magician. The natives believe it was he who spirited the boy away, but this theory suffers from the fact that, at the time of the baby's disappearance, the grandfather was not at Amritsar with all of us but forty miles away in Lahore.'

A burst of amusement came from the young officers. Behind Lord Auckland's chair, Colin Marks exchanged a whispered remark with another man, who threw back his head in suppressed laughter.

Miss Emily lowered her cup onto its saucer, her smiling mouth making her look very like her brother. 'Of course, that explanation is ridiculous, but I enjoy picturing the old man muttering spells in his room after supper, while miles away the Maharajah's hostage vanishes into the air.'

Mariana tried to smile along with the others.

Two seats away from her, Dr Drumond cleared his throat. 'Considering the carelessness of the natives,' he intoned, 'it is only surprising the child has not been lost before. He was probably stolen right in front of them while they were all looking the other way.'

236

A wave of mirth circled the table. Mariana felt the colour drain from her face.

'Are you all right, my dear?' Miss Emily frowned. 'Take a piece of fruit.'

'Oh no, thank you very much.' A lovely guava was within Mariana's reach but she could not trust her shaking hands with the fruit knife.

'An enormous reward has been offered for the baby's return,' Miss Fanny said, threading her napkin into its silver ring. 'Is that not so, Mr Macnaghten?'

The political secretary sat back in his chair and waved away a servant bearing a coffee pot. 'Let us hope,' he said, glancing towards the head of the table, 'that the child is returned before anything happens to the Maharajah's health. Any illness he suffers now may be blamed on the child's absence. If it is serious, the illness might affect the treaty.'

Lord Auckland had stopped smiling. 'Do you really think,' he asked sharply, 'that the Maharajah might actually refuse to sign our agreement over the Afghan Campaign because of the disappearance of a *child*?'

'There are two possibilities, my lord,' Macnaghten replied. 'One is that the Maharajah may fall ill, delaying the signing of the treaty. The second is far graver.'

The crowd around the table shifted. Mariana twisted her handkerchief in her lap.

'The natives are a treacherous lot, as we all know,' Macnaghten continued, lifting his heavy brows. 'It is possible that someone opposed to the treaty may have taken the child and planted him in this camp.'

'Planted him *here*?' Miss Emily stared, her cup poised halfway to her mouth.

Macnaghten nodded. 'If that were the case and the child

237

were to be discovered here, the Maharajah would certainly believe we had stolen him.'

'*Stolen* him? Why should we do such a thing?' Miss Fanny's voice rose in astonishment.

At the end of the table, Lord Auckland twirled his butter knife. Macnaghten made a steeple of his fingers. 'Because, Miss Fanny,' he replied, 'the Maharajah believes this particular hostage to be responsible for all his present good fortune. In fact, it is said that next to the great Koh-i-Noor diamond, the baby is Ranjit Singh's finest possession. He calls the child his pearl of pearls. He would naturally assume that we had abducted the child in order to procure his luck for ourselves. He might not, under such circumstances, sign our treaty. We might be forced to abandon the Afghan Campaign.'

Prickles of panic raced up Mariana's arms and legs. She suppressed an urge to run from the tent.

Lord Auckland scowled. He picked up his knife and made little stabbing motions at the tablecloth. 'Are you certain of this, Macnaghten?'

Macnaghten did not look well. 'My lord,' he said, 'we must be mindful of the extraordinary power of native superstitions. The natives attach enormous importance to the oddest of things.' He spread his hands. 'Since the possibility exists that the child is here, I would urge everyone in camp to look for him.'

Mariana concentrated on breathing in and out, in and out.

'You are quite right.' Lord Auckland nodded. 'We must make sure that this business of the baby does not interfere with our plans.' He raised his voice and surveyed the crowded tent. 'As we all know, there is no time to be lost in signing the treaty. I recognize how unlikely this is, but if any of you should learn anything at all of this child's whereabouts, you are to report such information immediately to Mr Macnaghten. Is that understood?'

Everyone nodded. The standing aides-de-camp, junior officers and Harry Fitzgerald all murmured their agreement.

Mariana could bear it no longer. Her hands on the tablecloth, she pushed herself to her feet. 'I beg your pardon, Lord Auckland, Miss Emily, Miss Fanny, but I have just remembered that my teacher is coming early today.'

A male voice followed Mariana as she fled the dining tent. 'Aren't these natives extraordinary?' Lieutenant Marks was saying. 'Imagine making such a fuss over a little black baby!'

Mariana sat on the edge of her bed, her knuckles to her mouth. With everyone looking for Saboor, how long would it be before he was found and handed over like a lost parcel to the Maharajah – to die of grief and neglect while she stood helplessly by?

But she would not be standing helplessly by, she would be on her way to Calcutta in disgrace. And if the scandal meant that the British were forced to abandon their plans for Afghanistan and lost all chance of controlling Central Asia, everyone would blame her.

She dropped her face into her hands and let out a little howl of terror.

Who would betray them? Who knew of Saboor's presence in her tent? Did the sweeper know? Had he heard Saboor's voice while he was emptying her chamber pot? Had he overheard her talking to Dittoo? What of her palanquin bearers? They had already had the chance to see Saboor on three occasions. What of Dittoo's friends at his cooking fire? Had they guessed the identity of the child Dittoo slept with at night? And what of those mysterious people who also knew but had not revealed themselves?

She stood up and began to walk the floor. She must not allow herself to panic. There must be something she could do to keep Saboor's presence in the camp a secret. Dittoo had certainly been correct to disguise him as a lost village child. That disguise could work. It *must* work.

Scuffling outside interrupted her whirling thoughts, and there was Saboor, rolled in his torn tartan gown and tucked under Dittoo's arm, chirping with delight as the blind dropped shut behind them, wriggling to get down, already reaching for her.

'What has happened, Memsahib?' Dittoo asked, suddenly still, his face turning from warm brown to dusky grey.

'The English sahibs have guessed,' she said as Saboor wrapped his arms about her neck. 'They have guessed that Saboor is here in camp. Everyone is to search for him.'

Dittoo put his tongue out in dismay, then smiled. 'But Memsahib,' he rejoined happily, 'you have only to perform your magic and all will be well, is that not so?'

'No, Dittoo, it is *not* so,' she snapped over Saboor's head. 'Don't be idiotic.'

'And so, Munshi Sahib,' she said a little later, staring down at the ruined handkerchief between her fingers, 'it seems that Saboor is in grave danger of being discovered.'

Her teacher stood where he had stopped as she began telling him her story. When she finished speaking, he turned and gazed out through the open doorway to the dusty compound with its drooping canvas wall.

'You and Saboor, God willing, will soon be safe, Bibi,' he said, nodding gravely.

'Safe? Both of us?' Mariana gazed doubtfully at him, then at

240

Saboor, who bounced, watching them, in Dittoo's lap. 'But how, Munshi Sahib?'

'When Saboor came into your hands at Amritsar,' the munshi said, his eyes on the child, 'we were forty miles from Lahore. We have made two marches since that day. Lahore is now only twenty miles away.' He folded his hands before him. 'By tomorrow, having marched another ten miles, we will be close enough to the walled city for you to return Saboor to his grandfather's house there. You can do this at night, while everyone is sleeping.'

Mariana jumped from her chair and began to pace the floor. 'Of course! We will hide him until tomorrow night, and then I shall spirit him from camp after dinner and hand him back to his family. No one will ever know.' She clapped her hands. 'What an adventure that will be! And by the next morning the camp will have arrived in Lahore and I shall simply slip into my tent, and no one will be the wiser. Oh, Munshi Sahib, I am so relieved!'

Her teacher nodded. 'Exactly so, Bibi.'

Her face fell. 'But how am I to find the Shaikh's house?'

The munshi made a sweeping gesture, including himself, her and Dittoo. 'There is one other person besides the three of us who knows that Saboor is with you, am I correct?'

'The groom, Yar Mohammad, knows.' Mariana hesitated. 'Also some mysterious people who have sent me messages, but I do not know who they are.'

Munshi Sahib gave a small, dismissive wave of his fingers. 'Then it is Yar Mohammad who will find the grandfather and arrange your journey.'

After two days in Mariana's and Dittoo's care, Saboor had begun to play. While Mariana brooded over her interview with her teacher, Saboor sat on the floor beside her, sorting her hairbrushes and thumping them on the floor.

After her meeting with Munshi, Mariana's relief had been replaced by a pain that had wrapped itself around her heart and moved up to weigh upon her shoulders. Tomorrow night she was to give Saboor back to his own people, to grow into a man and live a native life. She would never see him again, never, never, never.

She bent and patted his back. 'Good boy,' she said tenderly. When she was an old lady in a lace cap she would remember Saboor's luminous presence, his slow, beautiful smile, the happy sigh he gave when she picked him up, the dear pressure of his arms about her neck.

His sweet company had consoled her since she had been cut off from Fitzgerald. Now she must endure the months of travel back to Calcutta without Saboor, without Fitzgerald, and with only the dimmest hope of a happy future.

The baby pushed himself to his feet and clung, hiccuping, to Mariana's knee. She cupped his soft chin in her hand. 'Must I return you to your family tomorrow?' she asked him.

He was getting better, and he loved her so. Surely Dittoo could hide him for one more day among the English tents. After all, they had hidden him successfully for three days already. Two days from now they would reach Lahore. Why not wait until then – at least until then? Surely they could keep him hidden if they were clever . . .

Munshi Sahib would not approve of her keeping Saboor any longer, but Munshi Sahib did not understand how much she needed her tiny companion.

A little while after the sun had begun its decline, the muezzin of Sohani Kot arrived at his mosque. He climbed the narrow stair of its single minaret slowly, pausing on the way to catch his breath. Arriving at the parapet, he wiped his face before leaning out, his hands cupping his mouth, to chant the azan as he had chanted it five times a day for twenty years, reminding all those within the sound of his voice to offer their prayers. His voice was still melodious and strong. It carried past the wall of the little town to the horse lines of the British camp where Yar Mohammad sat deep in thought, polishing a harness.

The groom raised his head, then set down his work, got to his feet, and strode towards the mosque. Inside the courtyard, he rolled up his sleeves and plunged his arms into the cool water of the mosque's fountain. He worked quickly, his lips moving in recitation as he washed for his prayers.

As he finished, he felt a hand on his shoulder. He did not turn to see who was there, but waited, without speaking. Beside him, Shafi Sahib made himself ready for his prayers.

Together, they studied the arriving men as they, too, washed and formed rows facing towards Mecca. Yar Mohammad pointed towards a stocky man who stood nearby, his feet apart, his eyes closed, his hands clasped before him. Shafi Sahib shook his head. Yar Mohammad pointed out a second man. This time Shafi Sahib nodded.

Shaking their hands dry, Shafi Sahib and Yar Mohammad joined the worshippers as they rocked up and down with the rhythm of their prayers.

By the time they left the mosque, they had chosen twenty-four men.

Chapter Twenty-two

'We have no information yet.' Faqeer Azizuddin motioned his assistant towards a pair of reed stools that waited in the shade. 'If I knew your son's whereabouts, I would already have sent someone to bring him here.' He tipped his head to the Maharajah's silent yellow shawl tent, twenty yards away, the saddled horse tethered beside it.

'You would have sent someone to bring him *here*?' Hassan sat down wearily. 'Why, Faqeer Sahib? Saboor is ill. He must be allowed to come home to us.'

The Faqeer drew his robe over his knees. 'I know, my boy, I know your son should be with you. I have tried many times to persuade the Maharajah to send him home, but this is not the time to do it.' He patted Hassan's knee. 'Do not fear. We will find Saboor, we will look after him, and we will return him after the durbar. That I have promised you.'

Hassan's eyes did not leave the Faqeer's face. 'People say he was too weak to stand when he arrived at this camp.'

The Faqeer dropped his eyes. 'Saboor was weak when he came, yes,' he agreed, 'but he has recently become stronger. He has a reliable servant. The cooks have been ordered to make fresh food for him.' He leaned forward. 'Hassan, you know how I love you and your father. I am desperate at your pain and at Saboor's loneliness, but the Maharajah, too, deserves our affection. Who else has his energy, his curiosity, his courage? Who else could have forged the Punjab, beaten and impoverished after a hundred years of plunder and destruction, into this great kingdom?' He opened his hands. 'Like all men, he has failings. He drinks too much wine, he eats and sleeps too little. These failings are killing him. There are times when he cannot move his limbs, when he cannot speak. He will not take his medicine of ground pearls. All he wants is Saboor. I know it is madness and not reason that leads him to believe in Saboor's power to save him, but I cannot stand by and see my king die without trying to give him what he wants. If, at this moment, I could bring Saboor to him, I would do it.'

'Will the Maharajah die because he is without my Saboor, or will Saboor die because he is with the Maharajah?' Hassan asked. His tone was soft, but his face was hard.

Faqeer Azizuddin did not answer. Both men turned as a servant boy stepped from the parade ground and approached them. 'Are you, sir, the Maharajah's chief minister?' the boy asked in a clear voice, after planting himself in front of the Faqeer.

'I am,' replied the Faqeer.

'Then this letter is for you.' The child held out a folded paper.

As the boy departed, Faqeer Azizuddin turned the letter over. 'My old friend Shafiuddin,' he said warmly. 'How well I remember his hand! I was so sorry to have missed him when he was at your father's house.' He smiled at Hassan, the letter between his fingers. 'Our friendship is as old as our childhood. Shafi was the best at kite flying. How daring he was then, leaning far out from the rooftops to swoop his kite with its coloured, glass-embedded string, cutting

245

the other kites from the air! Ah, those were wonderful days, running on the rooftops of Lahore with Shafi and Waliullah!'

He unfolded the paper, read it, then looked up and gave Hassan an appraising look. 'Do you know,' he asked, 'the contents of this letter?'

Hassan shook his head. 'Sir, I do not.'

'Then I will read it to you. "Waliullah's grandson is at the British camp. You should know that we intend to return him to Qamar Haveli tomorrow evening. If you can arrange for him to remain there undisturbed, we will be most grateful."' The Faqeer held the letter out to Hassan. 'Who are "we"?' he asked, his voice silken. 'Who joins in Shafi's request besides you and my friend Waliullah?'

Hassan's face had changed. He did not reply.

The Faqeer stared into the distance. 'So,' he said at last, 'I find myself alone with my king. My two oldest friends have taken the side of your son. Poor Saboor, poor Maharajah.' He shook his head. 'Keep it,' he said brusquely, as Hassan offered the letter back.

Hassan, his eyes shining, slipped the folded paper into the pocket over his heart where it rustled against another, older letter.

Someone else had come. Outside the yellow tent, a showily dressed eunuch attended by a trio of servants had begun to argue in a loud whisper with an armed guard. The guard signalled to the Faqeer with a raised arm.

Faqeer Azizuddin sighed. 'What does that fool want? How I dislike these household eunuchs!'

The eunuch performed an elaborate salute as the two men approached. 'My name is Gurbashan,' he said grandly. 'I have come to tell you that I know the whereabouts of the child

246

Saboor.' He beamed at the Faqeer, who blinked, but did not respond. Beside the Faqeer, Hassan stared at the man, his shoulders tensing.

'I would know the boy anywhere,' the eunuch added, waving an arm. 'It was I who escorted him to—'

'Indeed,' the Faqeer interrupted smoothly. 'And how did you find him?'

The eunuch's smile broadened, displaying yellow teeth. 'Faqeer Sahib, it is kind of you to ask but, if you will forgive me, I have come to give this news only to the Maharajah himself.'

The Maharajah's guards had heard. Two of them hurried into the tent, talking as they went. A high, cracked voice issued at once from inside.

'Come in,' it commanded. 'Come here, Aziz!'

A servant held the door hanging aside and gestured for them all to enter.

The air was cold inside the little tent. The Faqeer pulled his cloak about his shoulders as he lowered himself to the carpet beside the Maharajah's pillow. The eunuch edged up to stand beside the bed. Hassan watched from the shadows.

The wadded satin quilt had been thrown aside, leaving the Maharajah's fully clothed body to sweat on the thin mattress. Uncut since his birth, his hair was twisted into a tight, iron-grey knot on his crown. His beard lay unfurled and tangled on his chest. His seeing eye was open and bright with fever. A figured cup stood on a carved table behind his head.

'Yes, yes, of course I remember Gurbashan,' he croaked, as the Faqeer began his introduction. He turned to the eunuch. 'Speak, man, speak.'

The eunuch gave another elaborate salute. 'The baby is

247

at the English camp, Mahraj,' he said in his dusky voice. 'When I was visiting one of my friends there, I saw him myself.'

'And how did you recognize him?' The Faqeer laced his fingers together.

'It was I, Faqeer Sahib, who escorted the child to this very camp from the Citadel. I would know him anywhere.'

'Yes, yes, I know.' The old Maharajah glared up from his pillow. 'You are the one who made us wait all morning for Saboor before the procession. Go on,' he waved impatiently, 'tell us which Englishman is keeping my Saboor.' Colour was already returning to his face. 'Hah, Aziz,' he added, turning his head, 'and you were telling me only this morning that there was no news!'

'The child is in the red compound where the British governor and his ladies are quartered.'

The Maharajah's sharp intake of breath induced such a fit of coughing that two servants were obliged to step forward, sit him up and pound him on the back.

When the Maharajah was quiet again, the eunuch pulled a small silver knife from his cummerbund. Bending over beside the bed he drew a large rectangle in the pile of the carpet with the point of his blade.

'This,' he said, pointing to its centre, 'is the compound where the governor and the ladies keep their tents. It is surrounded by a high red wall and has three entrances.'

The Maharajah propped himself on one elbow and studied the marks on the carpet, breathing noisily. 'Hassan,' he cried, 'your son has been found!'

The eunuch showed his teeth again. 'A man from the Citadel has recently been hired as one of the Governor-General's cooks.'

248

The Faqeer shifted on the floor. 'We know, Gurbashan,' he said a little wearily.

'The guarded main entrance is here, on the avenue.' The eunuch stabbed the middle of one long side of his rectangle. 'And the two service entrances are here, and here.' He pointed to the ends of the other long side. He then drew three rectangles in the centre of the space. 'The tents of Lord Auckland and his ladies are arranged so, so, and so, and here is their dining tent.' With a flourish he drew a fourth rectangle to form a square.

The Maharajah pointed eagerly to the carpet. 'And my little Saboor is in one of these tents?'

'No, Mahraj.' Bending again, the eunuch put a finger on the left corner fronting the avenue. 'The child is here, in the tent of a young woman who translates for the Governor-General's sisters.'

Hassan drew an audible breath.

The eunuch stood straight, his silks rustling. 'My friend said he had seen the same child being carried to and from that tent three times in the past two days.'

'How could Saboor be in the Governor-General's compound?' the Maharajah demanded shrilly. 'Has he been stolen by the British?'

The eunuch shrugged. 'I do not know, Mahraj, but I can tell you this much.' He drew a line of crosses along the back wall. 'The child has been seen here, among the servants' cooking fires, and here, entering the translator's tent.' He pointed, once more, to the corner.

'The girl? He was stolen by the *girl*? The girl they brought . . .' Gasping, the Maharajah lay back on his pillows. 'Aziz, tell me what this means!'

Hassan retreated further into the shadows, a hand to the pocket over his heart.

Faqeer Azizuddin cleared his throat. 'Whatever may be the truth of this matter,' the minister said slowly, 'we must think carefully before proceeding.'

'Think carefully?' the Maharajah cried from his pillow. 'Why think carefully? I must have the boy in my arms by nightfall!'

'That can easily be done,' the eunuch said, waving a manicured hand. 'There are men in the city skilled in the stealing of children.' Faqeer Azizuddin stiffened. 'We will pay one of them to do it. I will go now and—'

'A child stealer!' Hassan lunged from the shadows and caught the eunuch by his shirt. He grasped a handful of satin at the man's neck. 'Snake,' he hissed, twisting the shiny fabric, his face distorted. 'Son of shame!'

The eunuch squeaked with fright and clawed at his throat. The Maharajah, his eye wide, wheezed on his bed. The Faqeer reached out, grasped the hem of Hassan's coat, and gave it a sharp tug.

'Mahraj,' he said smoothly, letting go of the embroidered cloth as Hassan dropped his hands, 'Gurbashan has been most clever to discover the whereabouts of young Saboor, but I must counsel against any plan to steal him back.'

'But why, Aziz, when stealing him is so simple?' The Maharajah attempted to raise himself again, but could not. He lay back on the pillow, his breathing strained. Pockmarks stood out against his greying skin.

The Faqeer rested an arm on the mattress. 'It is my duty, Mahraj,' he said softly, 'to remind you of the British, of their greed and their cleverness, and of our need to be most wary of them and their intentions. If they have indeed stolen the child, they have taken an unusual and uncharacteristic step. Consequently, we must expect a trap.'

Hassan made a small sound.

The eunuch opened his mouth, but the Maharajah lifted a silencing hand. 'Speak, Aziz,' he said.

'It is possible,' continued the Faqeer, 'that by taking Saboor, the British hope to provoke us into doing what Gurbashan has suggested – sending thieves into their camp. If we do so, they will be waiting, and the thieves will be quickly discovered. Then the British will have an excuse to break off the treaty negotiations, thus saving themselves from their mad attack on Afghanistan.'

The Maharajah blinked.

The Faqeer tilted his head. 'Without a treaty, their great army will not go to Afghanistan. It will instead remain on our border, aimed at us. After all, which is the greater prize, barren Afghanistan, with only dry fruit and camels, or this fertile plain with all its riches, including your priceless Koh-i-Noor diamond?'

The eunuch fairly danced up and down in his place by the bed. 'But Mahraj, I—'

The Faqeer raised his voice over the eunuch's. 'As much as I dread the prospect, it is my duty to ride to the British camp with senior members of our court and request an open search of the red-walled compound.'

'An open search?' The eunuch's voice cracked. 'If the child has been stolen, he will never be found in a search! Tents have nooks and crannies. A baby as small as that one could survive for hours, drugged and hidden in a trunk or carried in a sack.'

A rustling outside the tent told them the guards had moved closer to the door.

'Very well,' replied the Faqeer equably, 'in that case we can arrange a surprise visit to the compound, and an ordeal of some sort to identify the child thief. The rice test, perhaps.'

'Give me my medicine, Aziz.' The Maharajah took the

figured cup from the Faqeer's hand, drained it noisily, then wiped his mouth and lay back against the pillows.

Gurbashan's face was dotted with perspiration. 'But why should the rice test—'

Without looking in the eunuch's direction, the Maharajah pointed to the door. A servant rose and held open the hanging.

'The rice test,' the Maharajah said thoughtfully, as the eunuch, his shoulders sagging, backed out of the tent. 'How will you do it?'

'I will approach one of the senior British officers,' replied the Faqeer promptly. 'If they have indeed stolen Saboor, they will return him at once by some subterfuge, fearing the test. If they have not stolen him, they will protest but will submit to the test to prove their innocence. They will also work to find the child, in order to prove their good faith to us. In either case, we will win.'

The Maharajah nodded. 'Yes,' he said, smiling at the yellow ceiling as Hassan and the Faqeer prepared to leave him. 'We will do it tonight.'

'Tomorrow night, Mahraj, at midnight,' the Faqeer said gently from the doorway. 'It is too late for me to speak to the British today. See,' he added as the servant raised the door hanging, revealing a rapidly darkening sky, 'it is already evening. Sleep, Mahraj. We will have the test tomorrow night.'

As Hassan and the Faqeer crossed the Maharajah's parade ground together, Hassan cleared his throat. 'Faqeer Sahib,' he began, 'I am sorry that I was so—'

'Do not speak, Hassan.' The Faqeer put a finger to his lips as they left the yellow tent behind them. 'Walk me to my tent, but do not speak.'

They walked in silence all the way to the main camp, the

252

Faqeer striding purposefully along, his hands clasped behind his back, Hassan moving silently beside him, his eyes on the ground.

At his tent door, the Faqeer raised his arms to allow two of his servant to remove his coarse brown coat. 'There is much for me to do,' he said. 'You will not see me for some time. Meanwhile, you would be wise to burn Shafi's letter.'

Chapter Twenty-three

Wednesday, 18 December

'The rice test,' Faqeer Azizuddin repeated the next morning from his basket chair at the British camp. He nodded gravely to his two companions, then glanced past them to the political secretary's spacious tent whose doorway stood propped open with bamboo poles. A bullock cart creaked by on the wide avenue, unnoticed.

'The Maharajah does not require that I conduct the test myself,' added the Faqeer. He returned his gaze to William Macnaghten's face and crinkled his eyes. 'The Maharajah's other ministers and I will only observe.'

Beside Macnaghten, Major Byrne frowned with incomprehension. Macnaghten turned to him. 'They think someone has brought that wretched little hostage here,' he murmured. 'They wish to perform some sort of test to identify the culprit.'

Macnaghten breathed in, challenging the buttons of his frock coat, and shifted from English to Urdu. 'And when, Faqeer Sahib, do you propose we perform this test?'

Faqeer Azizuddin smiled encouragingly. 'At midnight tonight. The rice test is only successful if it comes as a surprise to those who are to be tested.'

The sun had not yet reached its full height. It shone,

colourless and painful to the eye, on the curving rise of the tent roof, and glanced upon the red wall whose left front corner, thirty feet away, abutted Macnaghten's allotted space.

'I knew they would try something like this,' Macnaghten muttered to Byrne. 'I was sure they would accuse us of taking the child.'

Major Byrne gave a short honk, only partially disguised as a cough. 'Do you suppose, William,' he said behind his hand, 'that the old man is doing this deliberately, to delay the treaty signing? He knows the passes will freeze soon. Is he trying to make us fail in our campaign?'

Macnaghten's foot, not quite hidden beneath his chair, began to vibrate. 'Faqueer Sahib, how, if I may ask, have you come to believe the child was brought here?'

The Faqeer bent forward conspiratorially. 'Ah,' he replied, beaming, 'this is just the place to have brought him. Whoever stole the child would have asked himself two questions. Question one is: which of the two camps is a safer hiding place for the little hostage? The answer is obvious. This is the safer camp, for here people would be less likely to recognize the child. Furthermore,' he added, waving a hand towards the red wall, 'what better hiding place could there be within this camp than the Governor-General's own compound?'

Macnaghten's fingers tightened on the arms of his chair.

'Question two,' the Faqeer went on, 'is: what would happen if the child were discovered?' He lifted his shoulders, his hands turning. 'Clearly, if the child were found in this camp, the actual child thief would not be blamed. No indeed. If the baby were found in this camp, his disappearance would be blamed on the supreme government of India, the British government!' Putting back his head, he smiled, his eyes closed, signalling perfect happiness. 'And so, we come at

255

midnight to catch this child thief. After that, there will be nothing at all to prevent our immediately signing the treaty.' His speech delivered, he opened his eyes and sat back in his chair as the political secretary, smiling at last, fumbled for the appropriate compliments.

After many politenesses, Faqeer Azizuddin departed down the avenue on his elephant, surrounded by his escort. Once out of sight of Macnaghten's tent, however, he called a halt and signalled to his mounted escort until one of them, an ox of a man from Mianwali, detached himself from the group and rode up.

The Faqeer leaned from his howdah. 'You are to take a message, Mirza,' he said, 'to a man called Shafiuddin. I am told his tent is in that direction.' He pointed to the end of the avenue and the British horse lines. The man nodded. 'The message is this: "There is to be a rice test in the red compound tonight, at midnight." You must say this message comes from me. Do you understand, Mirza?'

The man nodded again, kicked his horse and rode away.

They had found a thorn bush half a mile from camp and dismounted behind it. While Mariana watched, Fitzgerald took off his coat and spread it on the ground. 'Mariana,' he said as she sat down, impatient to hear why he had arranged this daring meeting. 'There is something I must say to you.'

She flushed. He was about to ask her to wait for him in Calcutta. 'And I have something to tell you, too,' she offered conspiratorially, imagining his response when she told him the Maharajah's baby hostage was in her tent.

Fitzgerald's back was to the afternoon sun. It was only after he sat beside her that she saw the expression on his face. 'What is it?' she breathed, as an unpleasant feeling formed in her stomach.

The square, freckled hands that had gripped her shoulders lay on his knees. He made no move to touch her. 'I cannot see you again, Mariana,' he said.

'But Harry,' she stammered, 'we—'

He shook his head and offered her his clear green gaze. 'I have thought about it ever since I walked you home from dinner. After we arrive at Lahore, Lord Auckland will sign the treaty. I will leave immediately afterwards. If I am not killed fighting in Afghanistan, I will be sent to an army post somewhere in Bengal Presidency. I doubt we will meet again.'

'But why?' She bent towards him, her shoulders aching, willing him to look at her, to fight for them both, to ask her to marry him. 'I shall wait for you in Calcutta. You can send for me after you return. *Why* should we not meet again?'

He shifted his body, moving away from her. 'Please, Mariana, this is so difficult.' He sighed. 'I will never get permission to marry you, after the horrible things people have said. If I did, I could never make you happy. You must find someone else.'

'Harry, I can't bear this. You did nothing wrong. I would do anything—'

Before she could touch him, he stood. 'You will find yourself a nice husband before your year is over.' He gave her his crooked smile. 'It doesn't have to be Marks, you know.'

Shading her eyes from the setting sun, Mariana looked from face to face among the small group sitting in front of Miss Emily's tent.

Why must she be civil to Lieutenant Marks when she

wanted so desperately to be alone? How could she plan her campaign to win Fitzgerald back if she must attend to this simpering fool?

'I quite agree, Lieutenant Marks,' Miss Emily was saying. 'One must never forget the chasm that lies between our two races.'

Miss Fanny reached for her wine glass. 'Why should an Englishwoman ever spend more than a few moments with a native anyhow? The only ones we see, after all, are the servants.'

'But Miss Fanny,' Mariana offered, covering her impatience, 'surely you have met the wives of Maharajahs. Did you not like them?' She kept her gaze on Miss Fanny, aware that Marks was trying to catch her eye.

Miss Emily opened her fan with a snap. 'Fanny and I,' she countered, 'have seen a dozen Maharanis, and have found them hopelessly ignorant. Of course they are shut away all the time, poor things, with no one to talk to, but still, I cannot imagine spending more than a few moments with such people.'

'I agree entirely,' purred Lieutenant Marks from his folding chair. A recent haircut made his ears more pronounced even than usual. 'In my opinion an Englishwoman should not show interest in any native, not even a native queen.'

'But if we take no interest in them,' Mariana asked tightly, 'how can we learn anything about India?'

Marks' face creased into a lofty smile. 'Ah, but Miss Givens, one cannot take an interest in the natives without becoming entangled in their affairs. It is uncanny,' he added, nodding to Miss Emily. 'Each time someone I know has shown the slightest concern for a native, the native in question has instantly overstepped the bounds of propriety and become unpleasantly

258

familiar, even intimate.' He fluttered a damp-looking hand. 'One feels quite disgusted.'

'And do you know of many such stories?' Loathing had crept into Mariana's voice.

Miss Emily glared across at her and closed her fan with another snap. 'Of course, Lieutenant,' she interposed, 'no one in his right mind would—'

'Good gracious!' exclaimed Miss Fanny. 'Whatever is the matter with Mr Macnaghten?'

Bent over in apparent pain, Macnaghten approached from the direction of the dining tent, one hand pressed to his midriff. His face was ghastly.

'Lieutenant,' breathed Miss Emily.

Marks sprang to his feet, took the secretary's arm and guided him to a folding chair.

'My dear Mr Macnaghten,' said Miss Emily, leaning from her seat, a hand outstretched, 'may I call Dr Drummond?'

Macnaghten, now slumped in the chair, took a ragged breath. 'No, thank you very much, Miss Emily. It is only dyspepsia. I shall be perfectly well by the evening. Meeting Faqeer Azizuddin often has this effect on me.'

Lieutenant Marks bowed to the ladies and to Macnaghten. 'I beg your pardon for a hasty departure, but I must return to my men.' He bowed to Mariana. 'May I see you to your tent, Miss Givens?'

Mariana set her face. 'No, thank you very much, Lieutenant. I shall stay here for now.'

An hour later, not wishing to argue with her teacher, she spoke firmly. 'I have asked you to see me at this unusual time, Munshi Sahib, because I have decided not to take Saboor to Lahore tonight.'

Her teacher stood beside her, the sunlight casting his shadow past the chair where she sat. In her lap, the baby flapped his arms as if trying to fly.

'I see no reason,' Mariana continued, 'why Saboor cannot remain with me until we reach Lahore. After all, we will be there tomorrow. Once the camp is settled, I can return him easily to his family since they live in the walled city.' She nodded decisively to indicate that the subject was closed. How could she give Saboor up today, of all days, when everything was going so badly?

But her munshi did not let the subject drop. 'Yesterday afternoon, Bibi,' he said evenly, 'you seemed delighted to learn that Yar Mohammad had arranged for you to take Saboor to his grandfather tonight. As I remember, you were very much afraid of his being discovered in your tent.'

'I may have been frightened then,' she countered firmly, while Saboor bounced excitedly up and down on her knees, 'but I now see that I cannot travel all that distance alone at night without an escort.'

Saboor climbed down from her lap, smartly dressed in a tiny regimental uniform of white pyjamas and a red coat with cross-belts. He tottered for a moment on his feet, smiling broadly at the munshi, then sat down on the floor with a thump.

'And how can I take instructions from Yar Mohammad?' Mariana added. 'I am an Englishwoman. He is a native groom.'

'A native groom,' her teacher said gently, 'who is willing to risk his life to escort you and Saboor to safety.'

'Besides, Munshi Sahib,' she went on, a little too loudly, 'no one will recognize Saboor now that Dittoo's friend has made him new clothes.'

The munshi did not reply.

260

It was silly and dangerous to go all the way to Lahore with only Yar Mohammad to guard her. Hunching her shoulders stubbornly, Mariana looked at the ground, wishing her teacher would say something. Saboor got up and hurried unsteadily towards Dittoo.

At last, her heart aching, she told him the truth. 'Munshi Sahib, I do not want to give him back.'

Her teacher's face became grave. Ignoring Mariana's filling eyes, he offered her his reply, emphasizing every word. 'It is one thing, Bibi, to rescue a little child from harm. It is something else to keep that child from his family, knowing that they love him and are longing to see him.' He straightened. 'If you will permit me, I will tell you a story.' Without waiting for her consent, he clasped his hands behind his back, and began. 'A man,' he said in a singsong, his eyes fixed on the wall of her tent, 'dreamed all his life of finding the Path to Paradise. Driven by his dream, he asked every person he met where the path lay. One day, he met a wise man who pointed to an ordinary gate leading to an ordinary road. "That," the wise man said, "is the path you seek."'

Mariana sniffed and wiped her eyes. How could she listen to fairy tales when all she wanted was to be left alone to nurse her losses and her sadness?

'Following the path,' the munshi went on, 'the man came to a well. He pulled on its rope, hoping for water to drink, but when the bucket came up, he saw to his astonishment that it held not water but jewels — diamonds and rubies, emeralds and pearls. Shaking his head, he lowered the bucket back into the well. "What a foolish place to hide a treasure," he said.'

With a piercing shriek Saboor danced across the floor towards Mariana who swept him onto her lap and kissed the top of his head. 'Quiet, Saboor,' she murmured.

'As the man walked on,' the munshi continued, 'he saw a large, silken umbrella with a golden handle and golden fringes lying beside the path. "This umbrella," he said as he passed by, "must belong to the same fool who has hidden his jewels in the well, for there could only be one man in this world foolish enough to leave such a valuable item in plain sight." After a time, the path began to climb up the side of a mountain, winding its way to the top with many sharp turns.'

A fly banged obstinately into the tent pole. 'Munshi Sahib,' Mariana interjected, forcing a smile, 'you seem a little tired. Why do we not hear the rest of your lovely story another time?'

'No indeed, Bibi.'

Her munshi had changed in the past few days. Why was he giving her orders: to pray, to return Saboor? Why was he suddenly so fond of the sound of his own voice?

'The path was steep, and slippery at the corners,' he went on a little sternly, 'but the man was determined to follow it. He climbed all afternoon until he arrived, exhausted, at a wide ledge. There, on a great rock, sat a giant. The giant wept, his head in his hands. 'What ails you?' asked the man. '"All my life," wept the giant, "I have searched for the Path to Paradise. Finding it gave me joy; but alas, as I travelled, I saw a well full of jewels. Giving in to temptation, I put a small ruby into my pocket."'

A small ruby – her arms round Saboor, Mariana felt a stab of remorse.

The munshi rocked slightly on his feet as he went on. '"As I climbed this mountain," the giant continued, "the ruby began to grow heavy. It grew heavier and heavier until now, as strong as I am, I am too weary to continue, and I can never reach Paradise." Leaving the giant behind, the man climbed on until, after turning a steep corner, he was met by a sudden powerful blast of wind. Terrified of falling, he clung to the side of the mountain until the wind died as quickly as it had sprung up. When the wind died, the man noticed a small person sitting alone beside the path. Like the giant, he, too, was weeping.'

Mariana let Saboor down, bracing herself for another illustration of her faults.

'"As I travelled along this path," said the small man, "I saw a beautiful umbrella lying on the ground. I only borrowed it, to shade my head, and to make others believe I was a prince, since the umbrella symbolizes royalty. I meant no harm."'

Make others believe I was a prince. If only she could take back those thoughtless words about Yar Mohammad . . .

'"But a wind came up and blew the umbrella away. In my fight to save it, I exhausted myself. I am now too weak to go any further, and I will never see Paradise." Sobbing, the small person buried his face in his hands.'

The sun had shifted. The munshi smiled. 'Leaving the small person weeping behind him, the man climbed until he could climb no more. His eyes misted over with weariness and he could not see what lay ahead. Abandoning his quest, he crawled with his last strength to the edge of the path, and looked down. Spread below him was a green and glorious valley with sparkling brooks and gardens of fruit trees. Rising from the valley, a breeze carried with it the faintest hint of jasmine and roses. It was the Garden of Paradise.'

His story was finished, but her teacher went on smiling, his eyes on Mariana's face.

She sighed. 'All right, Munshi Sahib,' she said quietly, 'I will go to Lahore tonight.'

Chapter Twenty-four

'I told them I have sold Baba to Sirosh the tailor,' Dittoo replied to Mariana's question as he handed her the sleeping baby two hours after dinner.

'Sold him? To a *tailor*?' She still wore her rose dinner gown and shawls, although it was long past her bedtime. Her breath was visible in the tent.

Dittoo nodded his head decisively. 'Yes, Memsahib. My friends think I have sold him to Sirosh for eight annas. They were only surprised I had not waited until Baba was fatter. They think I have made a bad bargain.'

When Dittoo had departed, Mariana tucked Saboor into her quilts and sat down beside him, still wrapped in her shawls. It would not be long before Yar Mohammad came to take them away.

The oil lamp threw shadows on the tent wall. She stroked Saboor's sleeping face. 'I wish you and I were in Sussex, my love,' she whispered. 'It's nearly Christmas, you know. What a lovely time we would have – you in a coat with a little fur collar, with dozens of jam tarts all to yourself, and no one to sell you as if you were a Christmas turkey!'

But it was not to be. Nothing was to be. Saboor was to leave her. Fitzgerald had kissed her only twice, lovely, hasty, stolen kisses. Those kisses were all she would have when she returned, childless and husbandless, to England. But she had cried enough. She lay down beside Saboor, pulled up the quilts, and closed her eyes.

'Memsahib, Memsahib, it is midnight.' The resonant whisper roused her from heavy sleep. 'We must be quick.'

Shivering, she groped through the darkness to the doorway and pushed the hanging aside. A palanquin with woven-cane side panels stood before her in the starlight. Around it waited a dozen men, their breath coming in white clouds. Four would carry the palanquin, eight would trot alongside, awaiting their turn. Behind her, the baby sighed in his sleep.

Yar Mohammad appeared beside her. 'These men,' he said quietly, 'will carry you through the back entrance and onto the road to Lahore. After three miles, you will change to another palki. The second one will be from the house of Shaikh Waliullah, the baba's grandfather. Do you understand, Memsahib?'

She nodded, her heart quickening. *A groom who is willing to risk his life* . . . Was she, too, risking her life to take Saboor to safety? It was too late, now, to ask that question.

'I will not carry the palki but I will be with you.' Yar Mohammad's urgent whisper followed her as she reached for Saboor in the darkness. 'Hurry, Memsahib, hurry!'

Someone was talking loudly on the avenue as Mariana pulled her skirts into the strange palki and held up her arms for Saboor. Distant torchlight flickered through the holes in the red canvas wall. The voice sounded like Major Byrne's, but why would the Major be giving orders out there in the middle of the night? She tucked Saboor beside her, slid the palanquin's side panels closed and laid her head on a thin pillow that smelled of hair oil. The activities in the camp no longer concerned her. What mattered was that she had been unable to find her bonnet in the dark. What would Shaikh Waliullah think of her, she wondered, arriving at his house without a bonnet?

The palanquin started off jerkily. Voices, pained and breathless, came from outside.

'I said the left foot first, Javed.'

'Lift your pole higher, Saleem.'

She opened her eyes. The men standing by the palki had not been wearing dhotis. The wrapped dhoti of the Hindu palanquin bearer exposed a man's bare legs as he moved. These men had not worn dhotis but shalwars, the gathered, full-length trousers of the Muslim. She wedged Saboor's sleeping body more securely against her side, and reached for a handhold as the palki lurched sideways. Whoever these men were, it was plain that none of them had carried a palanquin before. How were they ever to travel three long miles like this?

They had stopped moving. Someone spoke nervously. '*Band hai*. It's closed.'

She sat up, slid aside the cane panels and looked out.

To her right, the row of servants' campfires glowed, their flames spent. Near them, wrapped forms lay motionless. Somewhere among them was Dittoo. To her left rose the deserted kitchen tent. Holding on tightly, she craned her head cautiously out of the palki to look ahead. Before her, where the cook's entrance should have been, there was only blank red canvas. Where was the yawning entrance, wide enough to admit a bullock cart of food?

They knew. Someone had discovered Saboor's whereabouts and laid a trap. That had been the reason for Yar Mohammad's haste. That *had* been Major Byrne's voice on the avenue!

'Yar Mohammad,' she whispered as loudly as she dared, and saw him separate himself from the knot of bearers and approach a group of sleepy-looking coolies standing by the gate. She could not hear what was said, but over the murmuring of voices came the chink of coin on coin, then the palki moved forward again. As it moved, she heard the scraping of canvas along its sides.

'Have no fear, Memsahib,' came his quiet voice beside her after they had cleared the gate. 'You and Saboor Baba will soon be far from here.'

Her heart thudded. She *was* risking her life, as were Yar Mohammad and the other men. This must be like being in battle, except, of course, that she was unarmed. Curiously enough, she felt no fear.

If only Papa were beside her now.

'*Uto*. Get up.' A soldier, his white cross-belts gleaming in the starlight, nudged his foot for a second time into Dittoo's ribs.

Dittoo opened his eyes. All around him and down the line of cold fires, men were sitting up, untangling themselves from shawls and sheets. Soldiers stood by, their weapons ready.

Beside him, Guggan grumbled, 'All right, all right. I'm coming.' Sita Ram cursed as he pushed his feet into his shoes.

Exchanging uneasy glances, the men stood. Prodded by the soldiers, they joined the servants straggling towards the front entrance of the compound, past the great tents of the English governor and his sisters. Looking behind him, Dittoo saw guards arrive and stand at attention beside the closed kitchen entrance.

The groom Yar Mohammad had insisted that Memsahib and Baba leave tonight. He must have anticipated this exercise, whatever it was. Dittoo yawned. Well, it did not matter.

267

Even with an army to help them find Baba, the British were too late. Yes indeed. He knew because he had forced himself to stay awake long enough to see the kitchen entrance closed, then re-opened just enough to allow a palki carried by amateur bearers to slide through.

Following Guggan, he joined the file of servants.

'The rice test. It is the rice test.' The word, carried back from the front of the line, caused Dittoo to stumble. He knew of the test, of its infallibility, of the panic of the guilty party, waiting to be discovered, trying desperately to bring saliva to his mouth.

Was the rice test to do with Saboor Baba? Were they looking for those who had stolen him? He shuddered. Perhaps not. Perhaps it was something else, some diamonds missing from the English ladies' jewel boxes. His body relaxed, then stiffened. No, it must be Baba. Memsahib had been certain his where-abouts would be discovered. She had been so frightened.

'They are looking for the Maharajah's hostage,' said a voice behind him.

They would ask if he had seen the baba. His head jerking, he searched for a way to evade notice. There was none; they had seen to that. All along the column, red-coated Brahmin soldiers prodded the camp servants into line as if they were so many cattle.

There would be a terrible price to be paid for stealing the boy. The water carrier had told him that, merely for holding Saboor Baba at the moment when he disappeared, Baba's servant had paid with his nose. How much more had he himself done, hiding the child, feeding and clothing him, sleeping with him, rubbing him with mud to guard him from discovery?

He imagined the heavy blow of the sword as it severed

his nose from his face. He tried to walk normally, although his arms and legs felt as if they belonged to another man. He looked among the others in the line, hoping to distract himself with familiar faces. There was old Sirosh the tailor, bent double as always, helped along by his son-in-law. Ahead of them marched Jimmund, the servant of Miss Emily's little black dog, straight-backed, as tall as ever, as if even now he was walking a few paces behind Miss Emily, his canine charge under his arm. The fat dog boy, whose duties were less elegant, trailed miserably behind him.

'Keep moving,' grunted a soldier.

Would he be put to death? Would they cut off his hands, his feet? Whip him in public?

'What is the matter with you?' whispered Mohan at his elbow. 'You are walking like an Englishman.'

The line of servants pushed its way through the folded front entrance and onto the avenue. There, by the light of dozens of torches, more soldiers waited, standing shoulder to shoulder, an impenetrable barrier to escape.

Dittoo kept his eyes down. If he were to look up and meet the eyes of the black-coated Englishmen who stood beside the wall, or those of the unfamiliar, turbaned courtiers beside him, there would be no need for the test.

They might torture him first, or question him first; or they might do both at once. What would he tell them about his memsahib? He had forgotten to wrap himself in his cotton sheet before joining the other servants, but there was no need. Sweat ran down his back and into the folds of his dhoti.

Why had not she protected him from this horror? Why had she run away, abandoned him, performed no magic to save him? Tears joined the sweat on his face and trickled into the stubble on his chin.

A soldier separated him from Guggan and Sita, motioning him to squat in the dust beside a boy who grinned happily as if they were playing a game. Alongside him, prodded and cursed by the soldiers, others folded themselves down, forming themselves into five parallel rows.

The fat, red-faced Major Byrne Sahib clapped his hands and coughed noisily. The murmuring along the rows instantly quieted. Beside him, his friend Macnaghten Sahib, the man with a moustache for eyebrows, also cleared his throat. They conferred for a moment.

'We are here,' announced Macnaghten, 'because we believe that, in the past few days, someone in this compound has committed a very serious crime. This crime is so serious,' he continued, stepping forward and pacing, hands clasped behind his back, up and down between the first two rows, 'that it has been deemed necessary to perform the rice test in order to discover the identity of the criminal.'

Behind him, the two elegant strangers, one wearing a coarse woollen robe, moved eagerly forward, scanning the faces of the squatting men.

The men near Dittoo began to talk among themselves. 'Those men are from the Maharajah's household,' declared one. 'They have come to take the child thief away.'

The soldiers shouted for silence.

'Each of you is to be given a small handful of rice,' Macnaghten went on, glaring at the rows of men as if each one of them were guilty. 'I will then ask all of you a question. The question is simple. It requires only a yes or no in reply. When I have asked the question, I will come to each one of you to hear your answer. After giving your answer, you will put the rice into your mouth and chew it, then spit it into your hand and show it to me. Is that clear?'

He motioned to the soldiers, who began to move up and down the rows, carrying trays on which rice lay in pale heaps.

Dittoo was too terrified to pray. He waited, frozen, as a soldier approached down the row, giving out handfuls of rice. Against the flaring torches, the man's tall shako and tight-fitting uniform gave him the look of a creature from a nightmare.

'Hold out your hand.' The man's voice was nasal and superior. Dittoo held out both his hands, willing them not to tremble. With a flourish, the soldier scooped up a small amount of rice and poured it into Dittoo's palms.

The giving out of the rice seemed to last all night. When at last it was done and the soldiers were shouting again for silence, Dittoo regretted his failure to enjoy those moments. Now it was too late for him. Macnaghten had begun to speak once more.

'Now,' he began, 'when I ask the question, you will all listen carefully and be ready with your answer when I come to you.' He raised a hand. 'Many of you already know of this test. For those of you who do not, I can tell you this: it is a test of truthfulness. Whether you answer yes or no to my question, if you are lying, I shall know it at once. A man who tells the truth will have water in his mouth. His chewed rice will be wet. But,' he added over the murmuring of the crowd, 'a man who lies will have a dry mouth. His rice, when he spits, will be powder. Therefore, do not lie. I repeat, *do not lie*. Any man who lies will be most severely punished. Is that clear? And now to the question. *Silence*, do you hear? I require *absolute silence!*'

Soldiers moved among the men, threatening them with raised fists.

The two courtiers had come to stand beside Macnaghten

and Major Byrne, peering into the faces of the servants nearest them. The crowd subsided.

'Do you, or do you not,' thundered Macnaghten, 'know the whereabouts of the child Saboor, the infant hostage of Maharajah Ranjit Singh? Once again, *do you know the whereabouts of the child Saboor?*'

How could this be happening? Paralysed, Dittoo squatted, the rice unnoticed in his hands. Leaning forward from another row, Guggan looked at him, his eyes wide. When Dittoo tried to shrug, Guggan turned quickly away. Ditto's eyes flooded. Even his friends must forsake him now. If they guessed at the real identity of his 'foundling', they, too, would pay. How could he have been so reckless? How could he have trusted Memsahib?

Macnaghten, with Major Byrne close behind him, stepped up to the first row. He moved deliberately, listening to each man's answer, watching him chew, then spit. Soldiers held torches aloft, illuminating each servant as he was questioned.

They arrived at Dittoo's row and approached at a measured pace, the courtiers behind them, a soldier on either side, ready to seize the liar, the criminal, Dittoo himself. Dittoo tried to lick his lips, but his tongue had become as parched as old leather.

What was the question? Did he, Dittoo, know the whereabouts of the child Saboor? Of course he knew Baba's whereabouts, for was the child not at this very moment on the road between this camp and Lahore City in the company of Mariana Memsahib?

If he were to answer yes, he would not be punished for lying, but he would certainly be punished for the part he had played in hiding the baba inside the red compound. And what of the oath he had made to himself? What would his loyalty, even his

272

soul, be worth if he were to betray Memsahib and Saboor Baba? Perhaps it did not matter. Was she not, after all, a sorceress, capable of escaping any trap, of disappearing, if need be, into the air? Yes indeed, and it was he, Dittoo, a normal man, who had been left to face this terrible ordeal. Sniffling, he wiped his eyes, then licked his fingers. All the water he needed inside his mouth was streaming down his face.

Beside him the boy replied in the negative, chewed his rice rapidly, then, making a face, spat a slimy white blob into the dust.

It was Dittoo's turn.

He took a shallow breath. Yes, he knew the answer, but then again, perhaps he did not, for exactly where Memsahib and Saboor Baba were on the road to Lahore, he could not say. In fact, as he himself had never taken the road from Amritsar to Lahore, he did not have the smallest idea where they were.

'Well?' asked Macnaghten.

'Well?' repeated Major Byrne.

A perfumed breeze seemed to pass by, carrying away Dittoo's terror, drying his tears and the sweat on his face, allowing him to breathe deeply again as saliva rushed into his mouth and lay in a sweet pool under his tongue.

'No, Sahib,' he replied firmly, 'I do not know the where-abouts of the child Saboor.'

The rice he chewed and spat out in a great glorious wet gob was filled with dust and other things, perhaps the bodies of dead insects, but never in all his life had Dittoo tasted anything as delicious as that little handful of grains.

Chapter Twenty-five

Thursday, 19 December

The palanquin's lurching progress along the dark road to Lahore seemed to go on forever. Inside, fighting nausea and unable to shut out the groans, cries and occasional curses punctuating each sway and jolt of the box, Mariana held Saboor against her and clung to what handholds she could find, grateful that the child, at least, was managing to sleep through their ordeal.

Surely this nightmare journey would soon end. She could not guess how far her amateur bearers had carried her, but they must by now have covered most of the three miles to their meeting point with Saboor's family palanquin. Reaching cautiously past Saboor, she slid open a side panel.

From inside, it had seemed that they were racing along the road. Now she saw that they were scarcely moving forward. The bearers seemed to be putting all their energy into moving the box sideways and bouncing it up and down. It would do no good to scold them – they seemed miserable themselves – but she was exhausted and her head throbbed so much that she felt it would burst, and she was about to lose Saboor for ever. She slid the door shut and, without caring whether the men outside heard or not, she wept with great, noisy, gulping sobs.

At last, with a great chorus of groans, the men dropped

her palanquin to the ground. Looking dizzily out, Mariana saw another palanquin standing beside the road with a group of efficient-looking men in real bearers' clothing waiting beside it. As she started towards the second palki, she caught Yar Mohammad's eye and acknowledged his apologetic salute with a tired wave of her hand.

She pushed Saboor into the new palanquin, and crawled in after him. Within minutes, soothed by the rocking of Shaikh Waliullah's commodious old palki, Mariana fell into exhausted sleep.

Sleeping, she missed hearing the lies the Shaikh's sirdar bearer told the guards at the Delhi Gate and the sound of the iron-studded door as it creaked reluctantly open, letting the palanquin and its twelve-man team into the curving lanes of the walled city. She missed the groaning of the Shaikh's haveli doors as they swung wide to allow the palki inside, and the whispers of waiting servants as the palki was carried past two courtyards, past windows where lamplight gleamed and figures moved quietly behind latticed shutters.

She woke only when the palanquin stopped moving. Women's voices, hushed and excited, surrounded her as she pushed open a panel and looked out. The palki had been set down beside a shrouded doorway. Behind curtains, lamplight moved and flickered. A slim hand reached for hers and helped her to stand.

As soon as Mariana was on her feet, a dozen children darted past her skirts and flocked excitedly about the palanquin where Saboor still slept, thrusting their heads inside, talking at once.

'Shireen-Jan is the eldest. She should carry him.'

'But I am his re-e-eal cousin. I should do it.'

'Be quiet, you'll wake him!'

What were children doing up at such an hour? There was

no time to wonder, for she was being shown up a narrow flight of stone steps by two female servants with lamps. The young woman who had helped her up now led her by the hand, while other women crowded the stairway, pointing and whispering as she climbed away from the excited little voices at the foot of the stairs.

The stair opened into a passageway. To the right, a heap of shoes lay beside a curtained doorway. The girl scuffed off a pair of embroidered slippers and looked meaningfully at Mariana's feet. Remembering that Munshi Sahib never wore shoes indoors, Mariana removed her boots and found herself drawn though the doorway and into a room full of women.

Oil lamps set into niches in the walls cast a golden light over the faces of a score of women who sat like nesting birds on a white-sheeted floor. Long shirts and fine, soft-looking shawls shrouded their bodies and hair. Toes peeped from beneath the hems of their loose trousers. Twenty pairs of eyes fastened on Mariana's gown with its tightly fitted bodice, billowing sleeves, and its six yards of wide, gathered skirts, so different from their own loose clothing.

The only native women Mariana had seen before had been dancing girls or peasants, their faces either painted and worldly or seamed with hardship. These were different. Shaikh Waliullah's family women were instantly recognizable as ladies of quality. While most had large features, a few of the faces turned to Mariana with open-eyed curiosity were delicate and fair. Some reminded her of people she had known in her childhood.

Mariana's young woman guide let go of her hand and hastened away to sit among a group of girls her own age. All stared at Mariana before leaning together, their heads touching, to whisper among themselves. Loose veiling on some of the ladies' heads revealed hair parted smoothly in the centre and gathered in a single plait. Why were they all awake at such a late hour? A hand to her own hair, Mariana realized she had lost a great many pins. Loose strands swept across her face and brushed the back of her neck. Twenty pairs of brown eyes watched her over bent knees, past shoulders. What must she look like?

Across the room, a stout woman in white signalled to Mariana. 'Peace,' she said in a baritone voice. She waved a hand, indicating the roomful of ladies. 'We have been waiting for you.' She pointed to an empty place on the floor beside her. 'I am Safiya Sultana, the sister of Shaikh Waliullah.'

Mariana lowered herself to the floor, blushing as the woman studied her. Safiya Sultana's face could have belonged to a man. 'So you are Mariam,' the woman said.

Mariam?

'*Hai*, the poor thing,' said a sympathetic voice, 'travelling alone in the night.'

Mariana arranged herself as best she could at Safiya's side, crossing her legs, feeling the bite of her stays against her ribs.

Safiya Sultana glanced towards the door at the sound of the children coming upstairs. 'And you have brought my brother's grandchild, Saboor?'

There was no time for Mariana to reply, for at that moment the door curtain was jerked aside and a fat girl entered triumphantly, puffing with exertion, Saboor in her arms. He was still sleeping. His creased face lay on a plump shoulder, his legs dangled below her knees. The other children crowded about, touching him, still arguing in whispers, while the roomful of ladies sighed and swayed in their places on the floor.

'Ah, my Saboor has come, he has come!' Burying her

277

face in her shawl, one of the women began to weep loudly.

Her Saboor? Mariana looked away from the woman.

'That is his grandmother,' Safiya Sultana rumbled, nodding with approval. 'She has waited a long time for his return.'

The ladies' silent attention returned to Mariana, who gazed back at them, memorizing each face, and each fold of their clothing. Few European women had visited a house like this. There was so much to see besides the ladies: the beamed ceiling of the room, the carpeted floor covered in white cotton sheeting. What did they keep in that painted cupboard in the corner?

By the window, someone gasped aloud. A birdlike woman pointed through filigreed shutters towards the courtyard below. 'Someone has come, someone has come!'

Had they been followed from the English camp? Mariana barely breathed while the women around her fluttered, their eyes on Saboor who now sprawled, still asleep, in the fat girl's lap.

Safiya Sultana raised a hand for calm. 'We'll see what it is,' she said, pushing herself to her feet.

Mariana stood and followed her to the window. She stiffened as other women crowded her, hemming her in, bracing their hands on her shoulders, trying to see what was happening in the courtyard. At first Mariana shrank from the crowding bodies; but then, unable to avoid them, she tried to relax. An old, gap-toothed lady in the crowd smiled and patted her arm.

A crowd had gathered in the courtyard below. Servants stood about, the flames from their torches illuminating the haveli's frescoed walls. At a shouted order, someone opened a low gate between the courtyards and a group of armed men entered on foot, followed by a horse carrying two riders.

278

As soon as the horse was inside the small gate, the guards reached up and lowered one of the riders from the saddle. As they stretched him out in the dust, Mariana saw a gleam of salmon-coloured satin in the torchlight. Elsewhere in the courtyard, men rushed to and fro. A man carrying a string bed ran out of a doorway and set the bed down opposite the ladies' window. In the shadow of a portico beside the string bed, an unoccupied platform waited.

From what Mariana could see, the haveli was not a single house but a three-storeyed building surrounding both this small busy courtyard and another, perhaps larger one, beyond the low gate. Several doors opened onto the small courtyard. Was all this part of the Shaikh's house? Were they really inside the walled city? She craned to see upward. Men had gathered on a roof opposite her window. They bent over the parapet, watching the scene in the courtyard from above.

'Ah,' said Safiya Sultana, patting Mariana's arm, 'it is only a case of snake bite. It has nothing to do with Saboor or with you, my dear.' With a satisfied sound, she turned away from the window.

'Snake bite?' Mariana had heard of the horrible effects of snake bite – the agony, the swelling, the bleeding mouth, the inevitable death. Could the man collapsed on the ground really have been bitten by a snake? She stared, unable to look away as two of the armed escort lifted the man by his arms. Bent double with effort, they carried him across the courtyard, his feet dragging like a condemned prisoner's, and laid him, kicking, onto the string bed.

After a moment's hesitation, Safiya Sultana motioned with her head towards another window. 'If you want to see, come over here,' she said, and led Mariana through the press of ladies.

This window had a better view of the padded platform and the string bed with its twitching occupant. No longer empty, the platform now held a dark-skinned man with jutting ears who wore billowing white clothes and a high cylindrical headdress. Other white-clad men clustered nearby. The bejewelled second rider, now dismounted, stood wringing his hands over his ill companion while the armed men milled about. Everyone except the man on the platform seemed to be talking at once.

'Is that Shaikh Waliullah?' Mariana whispered.

Safiya Sultana inclined her head in assent.

So this was the great magician Miss Emily had been talking about. He certainly looked like one, with his tall snowy headdress.

Mariana held her breath.

The torch-lit scene, eerie already, was made more so by the sudden silence that came over it as soon as the Shaikh raised a bony hand.

Although the charpai, the string bed, could have been no more than a foot from the platform, the Shaikh made no move to touch the patient. Instead, he sat motionless, his back straight, his gaze fixed on the salmon-coloured figure. For some minutes, the only movements in the courtyard were the convulsions of the man on the bed. Mariana narrowed her eyes, trying to see, wishing her window were closer to the platform. Was that a trick of the light or was sweat beginning to gleam on the Shaikh's face?

'Is he saying something?' she whispered into Safiya Sultana's ear. Even at this distance, it seemed wrong to make a sound.

'Yes,' Safiya Sultana answered, then pressed her lips firmly into a straight line.

Mesmerized, Mariana looked down again.

A powerful connection seemed to have formed between the magician and his patient. It seemed almost as if another snake – a good, healing, invisible snake – had linked them together and was now at work undoing the virulent effects of the poison. But there was no cure for poisonous snake bite. From her first day in India, Mariana had been warned never to walk outdoors, even on the streets of Calcutta, without laced boots. In camp, Major Byrne had instructed her to wear her boots all the time, even in her tent. Since then, she had heard stories of servants and even soldiers being killed by cobras, vipers or other snakes. Only recently, Dr Drummond had recounted the story of a subaltern at the army camp who liked to walk about in a pair of bedroom slippers. 'I warned him several times,' the doctor had said, shaking his head, 'but once he had been bitten, it was too late. What a terrible sight the man was – his leg was monstrous and livid. The poor fellow was in agony. "Doctor," he told me, before he lost consciousness, "I should not be dying now if I had listened to your advice."'

Murmuring rose from below. The body on the charpai had stopped twitching. Mariana watched it move, then sit up, no longer a terrible, suffering thing, but a showily dressed man with a full curly beard who rubbed his face, then smiled.

Mariana stared, too fascinated to move.

With a grunt, Safiya Sultana took her arm and led her firmly from the window. 'Well, that's done,' she said briskly. 'And now, Mariam, my brother has asked to see you; but first you must sit for another moment. It will be a little time before all those men have left.'

The ladies had seated themselves once more as if they expected to sit in those same places for ever. What time was it?

'More men are coming. Look!' A girl of about fifteen, whose

long reddish plait hung down to her knees, pressed her face to the shutter.

Safiya Sultana sighed heavily as she lowered herself to the carpet beside Mariana. 'Tell me what you see, Mehereen.'

'Three men are riding into the courtyard – ooh, they are so beautifully dressed, Bhaji. They have swords and one has a big feather in his—'

Safiya Sultana waved a hand. 'Only tell me what they are doing, Mehereen,' she instructed, shifting a little, making room for Mariana in the crowd.

'They have brought servants carrying covered trays. They are uncovering them and oh, there are shawls, so many shawls, although I cannot see how good they are, and they are leading in a horse, and one of the trays is heaped with gold jewellery. Lala-Ji must have saved someone very important, someone very rich!' Her eyes alight, she turned from the window. 'What does it mean, Bhaji? Are these gifts for us?'

'It means nothing, you will see.' Safiya Sultana shook her head. 'Nothing at all.'

But the girl was looking out again. 'Why doesn't Lala-Ji look at the gifts? Why does he not show gratitude? The men look so disappointed, and now they are going away. They are taking their gifts and going away. Why, Bhaji?'

The bright young voice was suddenly so sad that Mariana wanted to comfort the girl. Safiya Sultana patted the carpet on her other side. 'My darling, we all know that Lala-Ji never accepts payment for this work. Come and sit beside me, Mehereen-Jani,' she rumbled. She looked at Mariana. 'The children call my brother Lala-Ji.'

'But what if those gifts were from the Maharajah? Won't his feelings be hurt? What if he becomes—'

'Mehereen, you must not ask questions. And now that those

men have gone, it is time for Mariam to go down and meet my brother, and for all of us to go to bed.' She turned to Mariana. 'It is unusual for him to meet a woman. Indeed he has never met a foreigner, but it is his express wish to meet you before you return to your camp. His servant Allahyar is waiting now at the foot of the stairs to show you the way.' Safiya Sultana braced herself on young Mehereen's shoulder and pushed herself to her feet. 'Now, goodnight, and may God keep you, my child. In rescuing Saboor you have performed a great service for our family.' Leaning on Mehereen, she moved towards a curtained doorway at the end of the room and was gone.

Without Safiya Sultana, the room seemed somehow colder. The other ladies followed and soon there was no one left but a few yawning servants.

Mariana rubbed her face, wondering what she and the Shaikh would speak about. Perhaps he would only greet her quickly and then send her back in his palanquin to the British camp. Hands braced on the wall, she forced her tired legs down the winding stair to where, at its foot, the promised servant waited.

His bush of hair was an arresting shade of red but, odd though the servant Allahyar appeared to her, she must have appeared odder still, for his eyes widened in astonishment as she approached. But what could they expect of someone who had been carried three miles in a palki by the clumsiest men in India, and then been woken in the middle of the night to sit up with a group of unknown women?

She lifted her arms to tuck her curls into a knot, but abandoned the effort, too tired to care what the Shaikh thought of her.

Except for a few torchbearers, the courtyard was deserted as the red-haired servant led her towards the painted portico where the Shaikh sat, still upright on his platform. Of the patient and his escort, there was no sign, nor did there remain a single shawl or trinket from the trays of gifts that had been offered there only moments before.

The time had come to use the native manners that Munshi Sahib had taught her. Mariana inclined her head and saluted the old man, the fingers of her right hand touching her forehead. '*As-Salaam-o-Alaikum*, Shaikh Sahib,' she said.

When she looked up he smiled, not seeming to notice her rumpled dress and unruly hair. 'And peace be upon you, daughter,' he replied. He patted his platform. 'Sit down.'

She smiled in return. Daughter. No one had ever called her that.

His voice was light and pleasing, which surprised her, since his elderly face was as dark and wrinkled as a prune. But his eyes held a force she had never felt before. She approached the platform, which turned out to be covered in another white sheet, and sat down primly on its edge.

'The first part of your journey must have been uncomfortable,' he said. 'The men who carried you were not palki bearers. They were barbers and grooms. One was a soldier out of uniform. But all were good, brave men.'

She nodded, unable to take her eyes from his. *Willing to risk their lives . . .*

'And now,' he went on, 'I would like to express our gratitude for your rescue of my grandson. It is clear to us all that in this emergency you have acted with courage and compassion, and with a kind of love that is very rare in this world.'

Before she had time to flush with pleasure, he raised a brown finger. 'And now, I would like to ask you three questions.' He did not wait for her assent. 'First, have you seen all that you wish to see of India?'

284

His eyes seemed to hold important secrets. What did he want her to say?

'No,' she replied carefully, 'not yet, but I still have the return journey to Calcutta before me. The journey is to take us four months, after we stop at Simla for—'

'It is nearly dawn,' he interrupted, his voice unchanged, 'and you must be very tired. Perhaps you would like to answer my question truthfully.'

She sat straighter, chastened. 'That is, yes – no,' she stammered, 'I have not seen all I wish to see of India.' Why had she tried to fool a magician? Under his gaze, in spite of her exhaustion, she felt her imagination catch fire. 'I have not yet seen the walled city, except for this house,' she added, her voice broadening with excitement. 'Until now I had never spoken to native ladies, or—'

'Thank you,' he interrupted again, more firmly. 'You have answered my first question. And now the second.' As he leaned towards her, his headdress seemed to reach up to the stars overhead. 'Have you met my son Hassan, Saboor's father?'

This was not a trick question. 'No,' she replied.

'Very well, and now to my final question.' He removed his headdress and stood it on the platform beside him. It was of starched white cotton, delicately embroidered. A tight, embroidered skullcap covered his head, emphasising his ears. He looked entirely different.

'Have you ever loved before as you now love my grandson Saboor?'

She looked across the dark courtyard, remembering the wave of feeling that had rushed over her when she had first taken Saboor into her arms, and her sudden agony when he had wept, caught in her shawl. The recognition and hope she had felt with Fitzgerald, sweet and compelling as it was, had been quite different. Her abiding, protective love for her father was different. Even her love for Ambrose, great as it had been, did not compare to this. 'No,' she said in a small voice.

'Very good,' the Shaikh said briskly. 'You have answered my three questions well.' He signalled towards the shadows. Allahyar, the red-haired servant, stepped out and stood waiting.

The Shaikh pointed through the low gate to where the second courtyard lay blanketed in darkness. 'One of our palanquins is waiting in the entryway,' he said to the servant. 'Escort this young lady there, and tell the men that she is to be taken to a point seven miles from here, along the Amritsar road. At the seven-mile mark, she will be met by another palanquin. That is all.'

Although she knew she had been dismissed, Mariana did not get up from the platform. Instead, a hand on the white sheet, she looked into the Shaikh's wrinkled face.

'Shaikh Sahib,' she began, 'what you did earlier, the snake bite cure—'

Again he interrupted her in his clear, light voice. 'What you saw here, my child, was a spiritual feat, a matter of faith and practice. We, whom some people call Sufis, occasionally perform cures and do other things of that nature.' He raised a hand before she could respond. 'But you should know that we are followers of the Path, not tricksters or magicians. Those of us who have permission to do so perform cures as a service to the people, but it is only a very small and unimportant part of our spiritual practice.' He peered into her face. 'You must not speak of this, do you understand? Those who are told of these matters often do not believe what they hear. One must never, even by mistake, increase another person's disbelief.'

Behind him, the sky had begun to lighten. He indicated by a slight movement that their interview had ended.

'Shaikh Sahib . . .'

His expression had become distant. 'You will meet Saboor again,' he said, answering her unspoken question without meeting her eyes, 'but not tonight.'

As Mariana followed Allahyar through the low gate, a cry from beyond the wall pierced the chill of the courtyard.

'*La Illaha Illa-Allah*. There is no god save God. *La Illaha Illa-Allah* . . .'

The tall doors of Qamar Haveli thudded shut behind her. Mariana closed her eyes. In an hour, the British train would begin its daily march. Travelling towards her at its usual snail's pace, it would reach Lahore by mid-morning. Munshi Sahib had been correct. Thank heaven for Dittoo, sender of palanquins and performer of many exacting tasks. Safe in her own palki, she would wait until the camp had arrived at its stopping place a few miles outside the city, then she would rejoin it, unnoticed among other travellers busy with the raising of tents and the unloading of mountains of baggage. She would be at breakfast in the dining tent with the Eden ladies, Lord Auckland and all the others by half past nine.

She yawned. What a strange night it had been. As she looked out at the brightening fields along the road, the torchlit scenes of the night before seemed more and more distant and unreal.

What was real, and tugged at her, spoiling all chance of pleasant rest, was the emptiness in the crook of her arm.

Chapter Twenty-six

'You were sleeping in your *palanquin*?' Miss Emily's eyebrows had risen until they were invisible inside her bonnet. Tilting her parasol, she studied Mariana carefully from the depths of her folding chair. 'I cannot imagine myself sleeping so soundly in a palanquin that I failed to notice dozens of people searching for me. Lieutenant Marks has been quite beside himself.'

Mariana tried to look innocent. 'I am sorry, Miss Emily. My bearers did not wish to wake me, so they left me sleeping inside while the coolies were putting up my tent. I am sorry to have missed breakfast.'

In fact, tired though she had been, she had not really slept. Dittoo had seen to that. As soon as she arrived he had rushed to her palanquin and, ignoring her closed eyes, had recounted every detail of his own midnight adventure.

'Memsahib,' he had informed her at least three times, his voice rising excitedly each time, '*aik dum*, all at once the water rushed into my mouth, and I was saved!'

Now, at eleven o'clock in the morning, she could scarcely keep her eyes open.

'She is exhausted, Emily.' Miss Fanny pursed her lips. 'The child looks as if she has been wearing that dress for days.

And look at her hair! Mariana, you really must go and lie down.'

'In any case,' Miss Emily continued, 'I find it most tactless of you to have fallen ill, Mariana. I shall now be forced to watch the elephant fight all alone.' She sniffed. 'My sister's attachment to the animal kingdom must outweigh her attachment to me, for she has refused to attend the fight this afternoon. She does not, she says, watch animals kill each other for sport.'

Miss Fanny raised her chin but said nothing.

'Be warned, Fanny,' added Miss Emily, shaking her parasol in her sister's direction, 'the next time we are invited to some horrid occasion, I shall make a particular point of abandoning you. And speaking of horrid occasions, Mariana, please be recovered by Monday evening. We have been invited to dine with the Maharajah at his Citadel. I shall be expected to converse with him and will need you to repeat to me every word he says.'

Mariana winced. Maharajah Ranjit Singh who had hurt her Saboor – she would rather converse with a snake.

'Have we really to dine with him?' Miss Fanny sighed. 'Oh, Emily, it is sure to be exactly like the dinners poor George has sat through – hours and hours of pointless conversation, dancing girls, red-hot food, awful wine . . .'

'I know, Fanny. But what are we to do?'

'Ah, so Miss Givens has been found!' Lord Auckland ducked his head as he emerged, smiling, from the reception tent. Nodding in Mariana's direction, he pulled up his favourite basket chair. 'What a relief for us all. I trust you are all right?'

'She is not,' replied Miss Fanny. 'She is so exhausted that she fell asleep in her palanquin until just now. You must,' she added, peering at Mariana, 'have been *very* unwell last night.'

Mariana looked at her hands. Would they please, *please* talk of something else?

'Perhaps, being ill, Miss Givens missed last night's excitement,' Lord Auckland said, responding to her silent plea in the worst possible fashion.

She bent her head to express polite curiosity. 'What happened, Lord Auckland?' she enquired.

'Exactly as Mr Macnaghten had predicted,' he answered with a satisfied little smile. 'The Maharajah came to believe we had stolen that baby hostage of his and were concealing it in our own compound.'

'After we had all gone to bed,' Miss Fanny took up the story, 'at about midnight, a delegation of the Maharajah's courtiers arrived from the Citadel. Major Byrne rounded up all our servants and brought them on to the avenue, where he held something called a rice test. They were all made to chew handfuls of rice, then spit them out onto the road.'

Lord Auckland winced. Miss Fanny put a hand on her brother's arm. 'Only dear George, Major Byrne and Mr Macnaghten knew it was to be done,' she said, her proud nod causing the rosettes on her bonnet to tremble. 'It was all kept a dark secret, for fear the culprits might get away. What a shock it must have been for the poor servants to be rousted from their sleep by soldiers in the middle of the night!'

'Of course, nothing came of it.' Lord Auckland brushed an ant from his sleeve. 'There was never any question of the baby's being here. Anyone fool enough to bring that child inside this compound would have been found out at once.'

'Do you know, George,' Miss Emily said slowly, 'Jimmund told me that last evening as he was taking Chance for his late walk, a palanquin passed him. It caught his attention, he said, because it bounced and swayed as if none of the bearers had ever carried a palanquin before. And he insisted that there was something quite wrong with the way the bearers looked although I did not grasp what it was.'

'How odd,' said Miss Fanny, nodding politely to Major Byrne as he passed by. 'A palanquin in the middle of the night. Did he tell you where he saw it?'

'He said it came from the direction of Mariana's tent and was on its way towards the back kitchen gate. He said it passed him not five minutes before all the servants were rounded up for the test.'

'What nonsense, my dears.' Lord Auckland smiled affectionately at his sisters as Mariana hastily laced her shaking hands together in her lap. He shook his head. 'I cannot fathom why you let your servants talk to you at all, far less regale you with these absurd stories. Nothing of the sort happened, did it, Miss Givens?' He folded his hands over his middle. 'Not that it matters now that the treaty is at last to be signed.'

'I saw no palanquin,' Mariana said solemnly as perspiration broke out all over her body. 'If such a palanquin passed my tent, I knew nothing about it.'

'I want to know,' said Maharajah Ranjit Singh, peering down from his golden chair at his chief minister, 'who caused the rice test to fail.' He tapped his fingers on the arm of his throne. 'Who evaded the rice test and returned my Saboor to Qamar Haveli last night? Was it the same people who stole Saboor from the Golden Temple?' He narrowed his eye. 'And, Aziz, how do you know Saboor is at his grandfather's house?'

The carpet on the marble tiles of the marble pavilion kept the chill from Faqeer Azizuddin's bones, but it did nothing to slow the fresh breeze blowing through the fretted windows behind him. He drew his robe closer about his shoulders. The

Maharajah had now recovered, but days and nights of tending him had given the Faqeer a fever.

'A goatherd saw Saboor in the Shaikh's courtyard this afternoon, Mahraj,' he said for the second time. 'That is how I know. A messenger came at all speed with the news. As to how his captors avoided the rice test, I do not know. Perhaps they had intended all along to leave for Lahore last evening, and only escaped the Governor-General's compound by chance.'

The Maharajah made a snorting sound. He drew up a stockinged foot and rested it on the seat of his throne. 'And you, Aziz,' he enquired, studying his chief minister's face, 'do not know who these captors are?'

An eloquent gesture, a tilt of the head, a rueful smile were all Faqeer Azizuddin would offer. 'Do not worry, Mahraj,' he said as he tucked his robe about his feet, 'whoever stole the boy is certain to be found.'

'I do not like it that they have evaded me twice.' The Maharajah turned to the young man who crouched on his right side. 'Who do you think they are, Heera?'

Heera Singh, court favourite, stopped stroking the old man's leg. His heavy emerald necklaces clicked as he raised his handsome head. 'I think it was Saboor's family, Mahraj,' he replied, peering near-sightedly at his king. 'Real child-thieves would never have returned Saboor to his own house. They would have kept him for themselves, for the reward. Had he disappeared entirely, I would have blamed criminals.' He shrugged.

A corner of the Maharajah's simple turban had become unwrapped. It poked out behind him as he bent towards the Faqeer again. 'Saboor was living in the red compound. The servants there must have seen him. They all knew of the

292

reward. Why did they not come forward for the money? And how did the rice test fail to reveal their identities?'

Azizuddin stifled a sneeze. 'The question was faulty, Mahraj,' he said, his eyes on the carpet. 'The English officer in charge asked the servants only if they knew Saboor's whereabouts. Since the child had already been taken from the compound, the question was useless. None of them could have known exactly where he was. Had Mr Macnaghten asked if anyone had seen the child, then we would have had *real* results.'

The Maharajah gave a dissatisfied grunt.

'We also know,' the Faqeer added, 'that Saboor was returned to Qamar Haveli last night *after* the city gates were closed. The only gate to be opened during the night was the Delhi Gate, which is of course the gate nearest to the Shaikh's house. It was opened twice, once to admit a palki said to be carrying a dying cousin of Shaikh Waliullah—'

'But it was no dying cousin, it was Saboor,' the Maharajah interrupted crossly. Scowling, he rested his chin on his knee.

The Faqeer put a hand to his forehead. 'And once, a little time later, to admit Rajah Suchayt Singh, who had made the error of relieving himself onto a coiled snake after an evening's entertainment outside the city.'

'Yes.' The Maharajah's voice sharpened. 'After hearing that your friend the Shaikh had cured Suchayt, I sent gifts at once, to show my respect.' He jabbed the air with a forefinger. 'Although it was the middle of the night I sent shawls, gold, even a horse. Your friend Waliullah returned them all.' His voice rose and cracked. 'I do not like such treatment, Aziz. What does he mean by refusing my gifts? Does he think he deserves better gifts than those I choose to send? My men said he did not even look at them.' He turned a burning eye on his chief minister. 'I tell you, Aziz, I do not like this business.

293

I should not be treated with such disrespect. The man is too sure of himself. I am convinced he is behind the stealing of my child. He must return my Saboor today. I want the boy. I need him.' The old voice had become plaintive.

The Faqeer shifted his aching limbs. 'Mahraj,' he said, altering his voice to a conciliatory whine, 'why not leave Saboor with his family for a short while? After that, you need only ask and he will be returned to you. Remember, Mahraj, how you sat up, fully recovered, upon hearing from the eunuch that Saboor was found?'

When the Maharajah looked away from him, the Faqeer pressed on. 'The child was becoming sickly from so much travelling and excitement. To be constantly in your presence is too great an honour for a child so small. A few days in his own house will do him good.'

It was not often that the Faqeer resorted to begging. When the Maharajah's expression changed, the Faqeer seized the advantage and changed the subject. 'And now, Mahraj,' he said, in a normal voice, smiling encouragingly, 'what of the British? What of their plan?'

The Maharajah's face lit up. 'Ah, Aziz, you know how to amuse me. These British are going to invade Afghanistan; they are going to put their own king on the throne there, thinking they will control all of Central Asia. How little they know, how little they understand!' His shoulders shook with silent laughter. 'What a gift they gave us when they arrived with their army, already late to make the journey north, with no treaty allowing them to cross my Punjab. They have conquered half of India and yet we have made fools of them, making them wait for my permission, making the Governor-General dance like a black bear on a chain. What a *tamasha*, what a show this has been!'

The Faqeer nodded. 'Mahraj, you are indeed a master of delay.'

The Maharajah smiled. 'Winter is tightening its grip on the passes, but why should we concern ourselves? Let the Governor-General's English soldiers and his Maharattas and his Bengalis suffer on the way to Kabul. Let their army grow weak.' His expression hardened. 'That weakness can only benefit us, who wait for the moment when the English will turn that same army against us. These English dream of conquering Central Asia, but one day they will see that my Punjab is the greater prize.'

The Faqeer laid a tender hand on the royal knee. 'Come, Mahraj,' he crooned. 'It is cold here. We will go to your room, where it is warmer, and talk more about the British.'

The old man rose obediently, took his chief minister's arm and began to shuffle, wheezing a little, in the direction of his private quarters. The Faqeer bent and spoke into his ear. 'The girl,' he said softly, 'let us plan what we will do about the British girl.'

The Maharajah straightened. 'Yes, Aziz,' he whispered back, clapping his hands, his face suddenly younger. 'Ah, yes, there is much to be planned.' He gripped the Faqeer's arm. 'What do you suppose the English will do when I make my announcement about the girl? I will let them think it is a condition for my signing the treaty. That will be a great show, yes, a very great show!'

As they rounded the corner into his private courtyard, the Maharajah nodded happily into his chief minister's face, the loose end of his turban fluttering behind him like a tiny battle flag.

Servants moved to and fro across Shaikh Waliullah's courtyard, careful not to disturb the Shaikh on his platform. In a

295

corner, a piebald cat sniffed at a bush. Distant clattering and the sound of children's voices echoed from other parts of the haveli.

The Shaikh smiled at Hassan. 'I am glad, my dear son, that you were able to come so quickly last night. It must have been delicious to hold Saboor in your arms again, Allah be praised.'

Sitting beside Hassan, Yusuf listened to the slow groan of the water wheel on the roof. With the Shaikh, he always felt like a bear at a wedding. This peaceful courtyard was not his place. The men who sat silently here, moving only their eyes, were not his people. How much happier he would be galloping with Hassan across the ground outside the city, shouting aloud, celebrating Saboor's return!

Hassan was, of course, in no hurry to leave his home. Moving from man to man, he had greeted each of his father's companions. Why not? He was Shaikh Waliullah's son, the grandson of the renowned Shaikh 'Abd Dhul Jalali Wal'Ikram. Descended from great men, he too would one day be great, for all his luxurious tastes. Yusuf was certain of that.

'Yusuf,' the Shaikh said in his pleasant voice, breaking into Yusuf's thoughts, 'wait a little. You will gallop your horse soon enough.'

Yusuf lowered his eyes.

'I have called you here, Hassan, to tell you something of great importance,' he said, then paused, his eyelids drooping.

Yusuf realized that he had never seen the Shaikh look so tired, or perhaps so sad. The old man's embroidered skullcap lay askew on his head. His back, usually as straight as a staff, curved forward as he studied his son.

'In my letter to you,' he continued carefully, 'I wrote that events pointed to Saboor's rescue by an unknown outsider.'

The other men's eyes flickered. Although the Shaikh had not addressed him, Yusuf nodded. How could he forget that well-thumbed letter? *As Shafi Sahib is rarely wrong, I believe you may comfort yourself with this news.*

'The first event occurred soon after Mumtaz Bano was poisoned,' the Shaikh continued. 'A man named Yar Mohammad came to us from the British camp, describing a vision he had seen in which a female lion rescued a small child from grave danger. We believed the child to be Saboor, but we were unable to identify his rescuer until Shafi Sahib received a message indicating that the lioness was an Englishwoman, a translator attached to the British Governor-General's camp. Even then, we could not tell when the rescue would take place.'

Visions, messages – Yusuf's knee began to jog impatiently.

'Yusuf,' said the Shaikh without looking at him, 'you should listen. You have much to learn.' He pushed his cap further aside and scratched his head. 'For many days, Hassan, we waited and prayed. We prayed when we heard the news that Saboor had disappeared from the Maharajah's camp. We prayed until last night when, as Yar Mohammad had foreseen and Shafi Sahib had predicted, the young English translator came, at much risk to herself, and delivered Saboor to us.'

An Englishwoman – Yusuf twitched on his reed stool. After so many hopes and expectations, how was it that he had not made this rescue?

'Now, my dear son,' the Shaikh continued, 'we are faced with a serious problem for which there is only one solution.'

No one moved. Perhaps it was the Shaikh's sombre tone that brought silence to the courtyard. Except for the rattle and hum of the city outside the haveli walls, not a sound came from anywhere. Even the cat had vanished.

The Shaikh surveyed his audience. 'Yar Mohammad's dream

did not end after the lioness rescued the baby. Having carried the child from danger, she waited, standing over him, and when a second danger loomed, she lifted him in her jaws and moved away, out of Yar Mohammad's sight. According to Shafi Sahib and others, this signifies that the guardian is to remain with Saboor to protect him, perhaps for a long time, until he is grown.'

The sky was white. Distant birds circled far above Yusuf's head. A *woman* to protect Saboor? Perhaps Shaikh Waliullah was so old and tired he had lost his reason. And why tell this long story? Why did he not come to the point, he who always told even the bitterest truth without hesitation?

'Hassan,' the Shaikh said, finally, 'I cannot know the depth of your grief over poor little Mumtaz Bano. But whatever your suffering, you must act to protect Saboor from further dangers. You must marry the foreign woman who has rescued him.'

Chapter Twenty-seven

Monday, 23 December

Mariana sat outside her tent, her back to the sun, her hair spread in a damp cascade over the back of her chair. Where, she wondered, was Saboor now?

Perhaps, at this moment, he was playing with his cousins in the upstairs room where she had spent the hours before yesterday's dawn, his high, chirping laugh echoing down into his grandfather's courtyard. Did he miss her? He must.

She fluffed out her hair. Newly washed and flyaway, it would never remain in a smooth knot this evening at the Maharajah's dinner.

The whole story of Saboor was a mystery. Why had he chosen her to rescue him? Why did she love him so? He was a native baby, after all, one of thousands and thousands of native babies, and yet when he curled his little feet, or peered at her over his thumb, she could barely keep herself from snatching him up and covering him with kisses.

As she reached for her hairbrush, Dittoo approached, a paper in his hand. 'Memsahib,' he said, 'a letter has been delivered to the main gate. It is for you.' He held out the folded paper. 'This letter,' he said, 'is not from an English sahib.'

He was right. The elegant script on the outside of the letter was not English. She took it, frowning. 'But who would write a letter to me in Urdu?'

The writing on the outside of the paper did not travel in neat lines across the page like an English letter, but in a curving diagonal that gave it a vaguely artistic appearance. She unfolded the letter and bent over it, holding her hair out of the way.

I pray that, God willing, your journey back to the British camp was safe and comfortable. Saboor's return has brought joy to us all, especially to his father and his maternal grandmother, who have suffered very much. You have shown a warm heart and great courage in undertaking Saboor's rescue, and we are most grateful.

How nice. It was a thank you letter from Shaikh Waliullah.

In consideration of the fact that you are in India without your own family, it becomes difficult to arrange matters of importance concerning your future. However, the proposal we wish to make can most probably be brought to the senior sister of your Governor-General.

We have seen the love you hold for Saboor, and we recognize that it is in his best interest to remain near you, but in order to ensure your continued, kind presence, we must observe the proper formalities.

Ladies of my family will therefore approach the elder of the Governor-General's sisters tomorrow, to propose your marriage to my son Hassan.

The letter floated from Mariana's fingers to the ground, its remaining lines unread.

Dittoo stared at it lying in the dust. 'What is wrong, Memsahib? Have you had bad news? Is Saboor Baba ill?'

Unable to reply, she got to her feet and walked past him into her tent, imagining the son, a younger version of the Shaikh, his ears jutting like his father's from under a tall headdress, while behind him a caricature of the Shaikh gave a suggestive wink.

Lieutenant Marks' words echoed in her head. *Each time someone has shown the slightest concern, the native in question has instantly overstepped the bounds of propriety and become unpleasantly familiar, even intimate . . .*

This was so damaging. What would everyone think when a troop of native ladies arrived to ask for her hand in marriage? What had she done?

A moment later, her teacher stepped into the tent, the Shaikh's folded letter in his hand. 'Bibi,' he said, after greeting her, 'I found this lying on the ground.'

She swallowed. 'Please read it, Munshi Sahib.'

While she watched, her heart thumping, he opened the letter unhurriedly and ran his eyes over the words on the paper, then put it down and waited.

She searched his face. Where was his sympathy? 'Munshi Sahib, what am I to do? Shaikh Waliullah wants me to marry his son! He wants to send his ladies to Miss Emily with the proposal.' She pressed her hands to her cheeks. 'I must stop him, Munshi Sahib. Please help me write a letter that will make him stop!'

The munshi was silent for a moment. When he replied, his voice was even, but something in his tone discomfited Mariana. 'If you wish, Bibi, I will help you answer the Shaikh's letter when I return tomorrow morning for our lesson.'

Before she could say anything more, he excused himself and departed.

*   *   *

'I must say,' Miss Fanny confided that evening, as their elephant turned, swaying, onto the road from Shalimar to the Citadel and the Maharajah's banquet, 'that I am very glad our elephant has a blue face.' She gripped the railing of the silver howdah with gloved fingers. 'Do you not agree, Emily, that blue is a becoming colour for an elephant?'

'I do indeed,' replied Miss Emily from the corner where she sat, half hidden under several shawls.

Ahead of them, preceded by the honour guard, the Governor-General, his officials and a native ambassador sent by the Maharajah rode on other decorated elephants, surrounded by a swarm of liveried minions and servants and the inevitable crowd of local children braving clouds of dust to see the spectacle.

In her corner of the howdah, Mariana prayed that the ladies would exclude her from their conversation. She needed to think about the past eight days, of all the things that had happened in that time.

Saboor had come to her and stolen her heart. Three days later, after reluctantly returning him to his grandfather's haveli in the walled city, she had seen a case of poisonous snake bite completely cured. She had met a great mystic Shaikh, and then, only this morning, had received a proposal of marriage from that same Shaikh for his son. Equally extraordinary, no English person knew about these events.

At least she was over her panic about the Shaikh's proposal. Tomorrow she and her munshi would write him a polite refusal, which would reach him by tomorrow afternoon. There would be no need to worry about native ladies calling upon Miss Emily.

She yawned. A few days ago she had tried to write to her father and also to Uncle Adrian and Aunt Claire in Calcutta, but her head had been bursting with events she could not disclose and she had been unable to think of anything to say. Dear Papa must wait, although her letters to him, when she did write them, would be sure to make up entirely for the gap in time.

'I'm sorry that Mr Macnaghten and Major Byrne have been made to ride that nasty sulphur yellow one,' Miss Fanny observed, nodding towards the elephant ahead of them, 'but since Major Byrne has told me that the treaty is to be signed at last, I doubt if they would mind riding a donkey.'

'I think,' said Miss Emily, frowning down at the dancing throng of village boys, 'that Macnaghten and Byrne would mind a donkey very much indeed.'

Mariana turned to gaze behind them towards their camp at the fabled gardens of Shalimar. At the sound of the call to prayer, whose last echoes still floated around them, the western sky had changed colour, flooding the lacy buildings of the gardens with rosy light, turning cascades and pools of water into the stuff of dreams.

Dreams. Fitzgerald was not a dream. She would find a way to persuade him not to give up.

'Emily,' Miss Fanny said suddenly, 'I had forgotten the elephant fight. Was it dreadful?'

'It was unspeakable.' Miss Emily shrank a little inside her wrappings and tucked a maroon shawl with orange swirls more closely about her. 'One of the mahouts was killed. He lay on the ground like a smashed doll, with his elephant standing over him, trumpeting. I believe the poor animal's heart was broken. I cannot bear to talk about it.'

A little while later Mariana peered ahead, searching among the bodyguard for a familiar uniformed back. What an irony it was that her much anticipated proposal of marriage had come, not from Fitzgerald, but from a native . . .

Miss Emily's voice broke into her thoughts. 'Mariana, since the treaty is to be signed, I am sure your Lieutenant Marks will declare himself quite soon.'

Mariana could think of no appropriate reply.

A brilliant mass of stars had appeared by the time the Governor-General's party arrived at the towering picture wall of the Citadel.

High on the wall, tile figures of animals, birds and warriors seemed to dance in the torchlight, while below, accompanied by a detachment of cavalry in chain mail and silks, a cluster of the Maharajah's dignitaries waited on elephant-back to receive them.

As Mr Macnaghten moved forward to meet Faqeer Azizuddin, whose own elephant wore a pair of enormous orange tassels, Miss Emily turned to Mariana.

'As you can see, my dear,' she said innocently, 'it will be just as we described it, a simple dinner with our Sikh friends.'

After the usual interval, during which elephants and horses milled about and Major Byrne and Mr Macnaghten exchanged effusive greetings with a smiling Faqeer Azizuddin, the elephants fell into line and the gleaming procession with Lord Auckland at its head made its way through a high, guarded passageway leading to the narrow, protected gate of the Citadel.

'Good gracious! Look!' Miss Emily reached for her sister's arm.

To their left, a broad stone staircase led upward, turning as it climbed, towards bright light and the distant rhythms of oriental music. Instead of stopping, the elephants made straight for the shallow stairway — Lord Auckland's animal first, followed by the ambassador's silver elephant, and then, its hindquarters swaying, the yellow elephant of Mr Macnaghten and Major Byrne.

Miss Emily's bonnet bobbed with alarm. 'You must assure me at once, Fanny,' she implored, 'that we are not about to climb a flight of stairs on a blue elephant.'

But they were to do just that. As their mahout guided the great animal towards the stairs, harsh, rhythmic music erupted in earnest from somewhere above the wall.

'Oh, but Emily, it's so exciting,' breathed Miss Fanny as they began their ascent, their silver howdah swaying and their elephant's state housings aglitter in the light of a hundred torches.

Maharajah Ranjit Singh sat under a canopy of Kashmir shawls in the heart of a lamplit sandstone courtyard, his chief minister on the carpet at his feet, his nobles standing before him. On the Maharajah's seeing side, a stiffly smiling Lord Auckland perched on a golden chair near Mr Macnaghten, who was to translate. The two men ignored the Maharajah's drawn-up feet and the pair of socks that lay discarded upon the rich carpet in front of his golden throne.

On the Maharajah's blind side, beyond the Misses Eden, Mariana smoothed her blue-and-white-striped skirt and listened to the murmuring of the crowd.

The Maharajah's chiefs were a wonderful sight. They looked even more romantic than the honour guard, who stood behind the British chairs, splendidly turned out in plumes and gold lace. Among them, a pale-looking Harry Fitzgerald, resplendent in a black dragoon helmet with a red horsehair plume, kept his face turned away from Mariana.

How long had Major Byrne and Mr Macnaghten been glaring

at her like that? She let out her breath. Those two must *never* learn of the Shaikh's proposal.

Rising from some distant courtyard, fireworks burst noisily above them. Drums grew insistent and rows of dancing girls appeared. As the music quickened, Mariana felt her heart take up the rhythm of the drums. She must enjoy this spectacle now, while it was still night. By daylight, the Citadel would surely prove to be a crumbling ruin, despoiled by the Sikhs after the glories of the Moghul Empire, full of filth, beggars and starving dogs. Perhaps everything in India was like Shaikh Waliullah – able to enchant only in the darkness.

Eventually the dancing girls drifted away and a liveried servant appeared at the Maharajah's side carrying a tray heaped with jewels. 'While we are at dinner, Mariana,' Miss Emily had cautioned the day before, 'please remember that we British never notice the gifts given to us by Oriental potentates.' Mariana duly tore her gaze away from the tray of glittering jewels and stared for several seconds without thinking at one of the Sikh sirdars, who smiled back delightedly.

While the English party studied the air, Ranjit Singh poked with brown fingers through the treasure on the tray. Out of the corner of her eye, Mariana saw him fish two diamond bracelets and a diamond ring from the pile, then reach for Miss Emily.

Mariana glanced quickly across and was rewarded by the sight of Miss Emily staring into space, the bracelets already clasped onto one bony wrist, while, as if in some bizarre wedding ceremony, the Maharajah pushed the ring onto her finger. Then he returned his attention to the tray and began again, his head tilted, to poke among the jewels.

At length, a rope of pearls in his hand, he got up and came to stand over Miss Fanny, apparently intending to put the necklace over her head. But it was clear that the mid-length rope would

306

not fit over Miss Fanny's large bonnet. Mariana risked another glance and caught the Maharajah's gleam of enjoyment as his small hands worked near Miss Fanny's impassive face, looping the pearls inextricably among silk peonies and velvet ribbons.

As soon as this ceremony had ended, a fresh tray arrived, carried in by a beautiful young boy. As he put the tray down in front of the Maharajah, a sigh passed like a gust of wind through the assembled British officers.

The Maharajah clapped his hands with pleasure. 'Wah, wah, Governor Sahib, the wine has come,' he said happily.

'Poor George,' said Miss Emily in a stage whisper. 'He looks as if he's been sentenced to transportation.'

A moment later, someone pressed a wine cup into Mariana's hand.

Pursing her lips on the cup's rim, she took an experimental sip. Bitter and blisteringly hot, the wine found its way to the inside of her lips, causing tears to rush into her eyes. Forced to swallow, she felt as if she had scalded her insides.

'We had this wine at Simla,' Miss Fanny was saying confidentially as she poured hers surreptitiously onto the carpet. 'It tastes like bitter fermented red peppers. Oh dear, I see you've already tried it.' She blinked into Mariana's burning face. 'Are you all right? Poor George was in bed all morning after the last of these parties. Aren't we fortunate to be sitting on the Maharajah's blind side! The officer behind the Major's chair is very ill. He has been on a strict diet of toast and water for days, but even he cannot avoid the wine.'

For the next two hours, while the British officers stirred and yawned, the Maharajah drank steadily, his hand ever holding the golden bottle, ready to pour again.

Fitzgerald, who stood in the Maharajah's line of vision, was also being forced to drink. He was swaying on his feet behind Lord Auckland's chair, his face puffy, his eyes closing.

The toast-and-water officer had already been carried away.

'Are my brother and Mr Macnaghten not brave?' whispered Miss Fanny, nodding towards the rigid-faced Macnaghten and Lord Auckland. 'They know they must not offend the Maharajah, now that the signing is so very close.'

At last, several servants brought in a golden table and set it before the Maharajah.

Miss Fanny nudged Mariana and pointed to her timepiece as servants carried in dishes of food and set them out on the table. It was midnight.

Too tired now for hunger, Mariana picked at her plate while, before and behind her, the British and Sikh parties ate standing up. What was she eating, wild boar? Duck? What were those odd-shaped vegetables? The yellow rice tasted wrong, as if the cook had mixed into it all the spices for a Christmas pudding. Everything was like that, perfumed with a queer mixture of familiar and unfamiliar tastes. Her nose ran from the red pepper. She put her handkerchief to her face and looked up to see the Maharajah bend down, his single eye fixed on her, and say something to the black-bearded chief minister at his feet.

Faqeer Azizuddin's glance was speculative. She looked down at her clothes. Had she torn her gown? What were they staring at?

'Fanny dear,' Miss Emily said quietly, 'I have eaten all I can bear to, and Ranjit will not stop feeding me. I have already deposited two quails, several balls of spiced meat and a round of bread under my chair, and I fear I have used every bit of available space. Might I hire the carpet under your chair for the rest of the evening? I must find a home for two pears and a large sweetmeat decorated with gold foil.'

'Of course you may, Emily,' replied Miss Fanny in a stage whisper. 'I do hope this evening does not go on much longer,' she added mournfully. 'The wine has soaked right through my slippers.'

The Maharajah, still talking, was eating his dinner, including his rice, with one hand, sucking his fingers noisily. Having talked for the better part of an hour to Lord Auckland and Mr Macnaghten, he turned at last to Miss Emily.

This was Mariana's moment.

'Does the Governor Sahib not like women?' the Maharajah asked. 'Is that why he has never married?' Beaming, he reached into a serving dish, scooped up a handful of pomegranate seeds and dropped them onto Miss Emily's plate. 'Perhaps he would like to choose one of my dancing girls for himself? Or possibly my cup-bearer?'

Mariana felt her face redden. How could she translate such an unsuitable question? Besides, he could not have meant *that* cup-bearer, for he was most definitely a young man.

She looked to Mr Macnaghten for help, but he was speaking, his head bent, to Lord Auckland.

'Ask her, Bibi,' prompted the Maharajah, nodding to Mariana.

Miss Emily raised her eyebrows. 'What is he saying, my dear?'

'He is asking whether Lord Auckland likes the dancing girls,' Mariana said firmly. 'Please, do not say yes.'

'The Governor-General,' said Miss Emily carefully, 'likes the dancing girls well enough, I should say.' She paused, pursing her lips. 'But not as much as all that.'

'Lady Sahib says that the Governor Sahib has enjoyed your

309

entertainments,' said Mariana stiffly, 'but he is extremely busy and cannot take the time to see them again.'

The Sikh sirdars greeted her answer with hoots of laughter. The Maharajah also laughed, his head thrown back, his eye tightly closed, while at his feet the Faqeer gave a sphinx-like smile.

'Your sister is a very formal lady,' said the Maharajah, turning back to Lord Auckland.

Hooting, the sirdars slapped one another.

The king held out his hands to be washed. 'As to the matter of ladies, it fills me with happiness to know that I am at last to have an English wife.'

An English wife? Mariana blinked. What game was the Maharajah playing now?

Beside the Maharajah, Mr Macnaghten and Lord Auckland exchanged a look of puzzlement. On Mr Macnaghten's far side, Major Byrne yawned into his handkerchief

The Faqeer turned to Lord Auckland. 'The Maharajah,' he said, his tone velvety, 'says he has entirely forgotten that three full years have passed since he wrote to your government requesting an English wife.' His smile broadened. 'Now that the lady has arrived, he understands that this delay was due not to lack of desire by the supreme government but rather to a lengthy and careful search for the proper candidate.'

Mariana swallowed. Why were all the sirdars staring at her?

'Women are necessary, are they not?' interrupted the Maharajah, looking brightly from Lord Auckland to the Eden sisters. 'Marriage between two families ensures love and friendship, does it not?' He shook drops of water from his fingers. 'Our two families will now be joined for ever, and the nightingales will never cease to sing in the gardens of our

310

friendship.' Leaning back in his throne, he opened his hands expansively.

Mr Macnaghten turned grey.

Beside Macnaghten, Lord Auckland blinked. 'What is the matter, William?' he rasped. 'What is the man saying?'

'Your duty,' the Maharajah put in, waving in Mariana's direction, 'was to bring this young lady to Lahore, and mine is to offer the proposal.'

Macnaghten closed his eyes.

Mariana's mouth dropped open. Not him, too! A second marriage proposal in two days, this one from an ancient, one-eyed Maharajah whose head came to her chin! Whatever was the matter with them all?

Miss Emily frowned. 'What are they saying, Mariana?'

Behind Lord Auckland's chair, a glassy-eyed Harry Fitzgerald nodded on his feet. Was he even listening? Major Byrne's chin had dropped to his chest. Where was the odious Lieutenant Marks? Was anyone sober enough to stop this madness?

Mariana turned to Miss Emily. 'The Maharajah has—'

'And there is good news,' the Maharajah went on, his reedy voice gaining speed. 'Auguries have determined that the correct day for the ceremonies is the twenty-fifth of December, only two days hence!'

The day after tomorrow? Christmas Day? Clutching her handkerchief, Mariana twisted in her seat, searching the faces of the British officers. Why did no one stop him?

The Maharajah beckoned to someone standing in the shadows. 'Therefore, Governor Sahib,' he announced, 'I will begin the formalities by showering coins over your head.'

Miss Emily leaned towards Mariana. 'What are they saying? What is the matter with Mr Macnaghten?'

Macnaghten's head swayed from side to side. Mariana stared

hard at him, willing him to speak. Respond, she begged silently. *Pull yourself together and respond!*

This was Macnaghten's fault. Who had asked the political secretary to promise the Maharajah eternal love and friendship? Mariana's thoughts raced. Everyone knew that days ago Lord Auckland had given up hope of Ranjit Singh's joining in the British plan for Afghanistan. For all his expansive talk, it was clear that the old man would give little support to the campaign and would send no armies to fight beside the British. But what was he doing now? Would he refuse to commit himself even to a reduced treaty guaranteeing stability in the region and a safe passage for the British through the Punjab? Was he simply playing with them, calling their bluff, enjoying himself? Did he really want an English wife?

Would he refuse to sign the treaty unless she married him?

Sirdars murmured. Macnaghten blinked and raised his hands, palms out. 'Mahraj,' he began shakily, 'one moment please. Governor Sahib—'

'No, no,' the Maharajah interrupted, waving a hand in Lord Auckland's direction while a servant stepped forward with a silver tray, 'there is no need to wait now, no need at all. You have made a good choice. She needs fattening, of course, but she has good teeth. I like nice white teeth.'

Miss Emily tapped Mariana's knee sharply with her fan. 'What is going on, Mariana? Why won't you tell me?'

Dragging his gaze from the Maharajah, Mr Macnaghten looked across at the three ladies. 'He is speaking, Miss Eden,' he said, his words a little slurred, avoiding Mariana's glare, 'of Miss Givens' teeth.' He closed his eyes, clearly wishing he was somewhere else. 'He likes them.'

Miss Fanny blinked. 'He likes Mariana's *teeth*? Her *teeth*?

Really, these people are most extraordinary.' She leaned across her sister. 'Good gracious, Mariana, I thought you were on the Maharajah's blind side!'

Lord Auckland, his face the colour of parchment, swayed in his chair as if already returning on his elephant to the British camp. He frowned as Mr Macnaghten turned to him.

Mariana strained to catch his words. '. . . If we refuse . . . might claim bad faith . . . supply route across the Punjab . . .'

Sensing trouble, the officers behind Mariana began to shift nervously.

The old Maharajah reached for the tray of coins and began to fumble with its covering cloth.

What in heaven's name was the matter with Harry Fitzgerald? Why did he not act? Did he not love her? Why did he stand nodding on his feet while this preposterous scene unfolded, without making a single move to rescue her? Mariana wanted to stand up and shout his name. What sort of fool had she wanted to marry?

'Are you all right, my dear?' Miss Fanny reached across to her.

Mariana's nose was still running from the pepper. With one hand she pressed her handkerchief to her nose, while with the other she gripped Miss Fanny's small, kind hand.

The Maharajah had lifted back a corner of the cloth.

The Sikh sirdars pressed closer, relishing the Maharajah's performance. A man in an emerald necklace laughed, his eyes on Mariana.

Why was Lord Auckland silent? Was he actually going let the Maharajah have her in order to gain the treaty?

'Yes, yes,' the Maharajah was saying, as if he was planning a picnic, while the bearded Faqeer at his feet nodded delightedly. 'We shall have a grand wedding, a grand wedding the day

313

after tomorrow, with more wine than ever, and many more entertainments.'

Lord Auckland whispered something to Mr Macnaghten, who looked desperately about him, then took a breath. 'Most Excellent Maharajah,' he began, 'it is most . . . most . . .' With a sigh and a heavy wave of his hand, he subsided into silence. Beside him, Major Byrne hunched over, his chin on his chest, snoring faintly.

The old fingers were busy now among the golden coins on the tray. A picture formed in Mariana's mind's eye of her table as it had looked yesterday, with the folded letter from the Shaikh on it. Had the Shaikh made his proposal to save her from this ordeal? Had he known of the Maharajah's plan and written to warn her, his letter worded so delicately that she had missed its meaning? *It becomes difficult*, the note had said, *to make arrangements concerning your future* . . .

The Maharajah leaned over and raised a fistful of gold coins over Lord Auckland's head.

Who could comprehend the native customs? If the old man dropped the coins, would that mean the engagement was sealed? Would it then be impossible to turn back?

Mariana could wait no longer. 'Stop!' she cried, then rose clumsily, overturning her chair. She crossed the carpet, her eyes on the Maharajah's raised arm, and stood stiffly before his throne.

The crowd, which had moved back, murmuring, to let her pass, now pressed forward avidly. The Maharajah's hand stopped in mid-air as she offered him a full, breathless curtsy, her shaking knees locked together under her gown. Her ears rang. She had no idea what to say.

Still in her low curtsy, she began to speak, quoting from a legend she had started to learn that morning. 'How shall I tell

314

thee of myself? I cannot tell what has befallen me. I grieve day and night. Hunger and thirst have left me altogether. No joy by day; no sleep to my eyes. Heavy is my anxiety.'

'What is she doing? What is she saying?' the Governor-General asked loudly.

'*Shabash!* You have taught her Punjabi!' Still holding the coins, the Maharajah gave a high, wheezing laugh. He had fixed his eyes on the décolletage of her low-cut gown.

She shot upright, a hand to her throat. The rest of the fable, and the point she was trying to make by reciting it, vanished from her mind, lost in a haze of fright and self-consciousness. Searching her memory for something else, she found a Persian quatrain and began to speak again, her eyes closed against the sight of the staring Governor-General and the suddenly attentive Harry Fitzgerald.

Last night at the tavern I called for the cup.
'What lover,' I cried, 'leaves the last of the wine?'
As I lay on the threshold afire with joy,
Life came bearing gifts, saw my drunken state, and fled.

She looked up fearfully and found the old king staring at her, his mouth agape. Beside him, Miss Emily frowned furiously, pointing with little flapping gestures at Mariana's overturned chair.

Miss Fanny gazed from one face to another as if she were at the theatre. Mr Macnaghten, forced to translate Mariana's speech for Lord Auckland, seemed to be having difficulty with the Persian poem.

'Speak plainly, Bibi,' ordered the Maharajah impatiently, shaking the coins in his hand. 'What do you want to say?'

'How can I tell you that I am betrothed to another man?'

315

murmured Mariana. She glanced nervously behind her as the crowd of Sikhs began to edge forward.

There, now she had said it. Whatever else happened, the Maharajah must now abandon his pursuit of her.

Behind Lord Auckland's chair, directly in her line of vision, Harry Fitzgerald swayed on his feet, his eyes bulging.

The Maharajah's beard twitched. 'What is this? To whom are you engaged? To whom is she engaged?' He turned to Lord Auckland and grasped him by the upper arm. Macnaghten translated rapidly.

Must she tell them? 'To Hassan, the son of Shaikh Waliullah of the city of Lahore,' she said simply, her eyes on her feet.

As Macnaghten translated, Fitzgerald started so abruptly he seemed to leave the ground. In the crowd behind Mr Macnaghten's chair, Mariana caught a glimpse of Lieutenant Marks' horrified face. She squeezed her eyes shut. Surely she would awaken soon to find this had been a bad dream.

At a sound behind her she glanced over her shoulder. To her surprise, the Sikhs had turned to stare, not at her but at someone behind them. She swallowed. Surely Shaikh Waliullah's son was not here?

In front of her Lord Auckland had begun to swell visibly. Colour, a dangerous red, was returning to his face.

'Emily, we *must* do something about George.' Miss Fanny's whisper carried easily to where Mariana stood.

'Governor Sahib,' the Maharajah said in a voice they had not heard before, 'you brought the girl for me and now you have accepted another proposal for her? Is this a joke?'

Lord Auckland put a hand to his brow and closed his eyes. Perspiration ran into his stiff collar. The British delegation stirred and murmured as comprehension filtered through their ranks.

316

Fear made Mariana reckless. She plunged on, just as Mr Macnaghten drew breath to speak. 'Mahraj, it was I who accepted the proposal, on my own behalf. I did not consult Governor Sahib.'

The Maharajah turned, open-mouthed, to Lord Auckland.

Mercifully, Mr Macnaghten had seen his opportunity. 'If,' he said, 'the lady has given her word, it is not within the power of our government to force her to break it. However, Mahraj,' he added, glaring at Mariana, 'you may be sure she will be suitably punished for this mistake.'

Mariana stiffened. The mistake of speaking up, of saving herself when no one else would do it, of taking the blame on herself for not marrying the Maharajah and saving all their faces?

She tried to catch Fitzgerald's eye, but he had turned away.

The Maharajah sat without speaking. At his feet, the bearded Faqeer fiddled with his cloak, his eyes darting this way and that.

Deprived of their translator, the Eden sisters gestured excitedly for Mariana to come back and sit down. After a final trembling curtsy, she made her way back, past the Sikhs, to her overturned seat.

'My dear girl, what do you mean by getting up and making a speech?' Miss Emily demanded, her eyes narrow. 'What were you saying? What in the name of heaven is going on? It is quite clear that you have upset everyone, especially my brother.'

Before Mariana could reply, the Maharajah broke the silence with a sudden, harsh laugh that turned at once into a fit of coughing. Reaching to his right, he slapped the Governor-General on the leg, and held out his hand, palm up.

When Lord Auckland ignored his hand, the old king wiped

his eye. 'What a joke,' he cried. 'What a joke on us all! I tell you, Governor Sahib, there is no accounting for women. I have very many wives, and I tell you, the more wives you have, the more trouble you endure. You cannot imagine how my women fight with me.' Hiccuping, he slapped his black-bearded minister in the shoulder. 'Perhaps you have been wise, Governor Sahib, to have no wives at all!

'Now,' he went on in a businesslike tone, overriding Mr Macnaghten who was attempting to speak, 'since we are all brothers, we will have a great show at the wedding. You haven't seen one of our weddings, have you, Governor Sahib? We will have a fine show, a very fine show!'

'Wedding, Mahraj?' Mr Macnaghten blinked.

'Of course,' replied the Maharajah, spreading his arms expansively. 'The girl and Hassan are already engaged. Why waste the wedding arrangements? We will celebrate the girl's marriage to Hassan here at the Citadel in two days. I know the boy,' he added, his face suddenly unreadable. 'We will have a fine show, a fine show.'

With a groan, a government secretary standing behind Miss Emily fainted dead away.

Chapter Twenty-eight

Mariana perched on the edge of her chair, her damp hands hidden in the folds of her skirts, as two officers carried Captain Wallace away from the crowd. As they left, Mr Macnaghten cleared his throat several times and then recounted her speech in English for the benefit of the ladies. He spoke flatly, turning her poetry into odd-sounding English prose, translating her announcement to the Maharajah in the same tone he might have used to read a list of battle casualties.

Beside her Miss Fanny drew in a tremulous, audible breath. The Maharajah, his eye moving from face to face, watched from his golden seat.

No one looked at Mariana, not even the Maharajah, who appeared to have lost interest in her. Lord Auckland stared glassily ahead, his lips pressed into a thin line, his face as brick-red as the pattern in the Maharajah's carpet. Mr Macnaghten sank into his chair after his translation and avoided her glance. Major Byrne, finally awake, gave an echoing honk, his eyes on the ground.

Coming from the political secretary's lips, her speech had sounded all wrong – intimate, suggestive of liberties offered and liberties taken. She must explain her behaviour before they thought ill of her, but her head still whirled and her thoughts would not order themselves.

'So,' the Maharajah said gaily, 'there is much to do, much to enjoy! But we have business to perform. Tomorrow we will sign your treaty. The day after tomorrow, we will celebrate the wedding.'

So, the treaty was to be signed before the wedding. Mariana's heart lifted. Lord Auckland and Mr Macnaghten exchanged glances. With the treaty out of the way, she could feign illness, even death, and avoid the wedding. In two days, the army would be on its way to victory in Kabul, and she would be having Christmas with the Governor-General's party as they travelled towards Calcutta, safe from further drunken evenings with the Maharajah. She had done it! Having taken the blame on herself, she had prevented the Maharajah using British faithlessness to back out of the treaty.

'Excellent, Mahraj.' Mr Macnaghten's voice wavered but his relief was plain. 'We will sign the treaty, as you say, tomorrow.' As he spoke, he seemed to savour every word.

She was a heroine, was she not?

Since her speech the Maharajah had not looked at Mariana, but she did not miss the speculative gaze of the bearded minister at his side. She did not mind. There was no need to pay attention to these particular natives any longer.

She must write to the Shaikh thanking him for his proposal, explaining why she had spoken out at the dinner. What a good, kind man he was to have offered her such an elegant way to evade the Maharajah's wicked trap!

The evening was at last over. Permission for the Maharajah's guests to leave his presence had been asked and granted. The ladies got to their feet.

'I must tell you, Miss Fanny,' Mariana murmured as they made their way forward to offer their goodbyes, 'what happened to me the other night at Amritsar as we were—'

Without meeting Mariana's eye, Miss Fanny made a small but definite gesture for silence. 'My dear,' she said, holding up a gloved finger, 'do not speak of this. Whatever you say will only make your situation worse.'

Worse? Beside her, Miss Emily moved forward, her sharp profile as still as if it were carved from ivory. There was no trace of colour in her face. A chill crawled down Mariana's spine. She gathered her skirts, preparing to climb the ladder into the howdah after Miss Fanny. Surely it would be all right. Surely, when they understood about Saboor and the Shaikh and the rice test—

'All I am able to do, Mariana,' declared Miss Emily as she seated herself, 'is to put your extraordinary behaviour this evening down to the unfortunate effect of the Maharajah's wine.' She gestured for silence as Mariana tried to speak. 'You have disgraced yourself and humiliated Lieutenant Marks. You have made us all look like fools.'

Lieutenant Marks! 'But Miss Emily,' Mariana said, her voice sounding odd in her own ears, 'I did it to save the treaty. Now that the treaty is to be signed, I can tell you what really happened at Amritsar after the firework display. One of the Maharajah's servants came running and handed me the baby, and I—'

'Baby?' Both ladies stared.

'Yes, the baby, the little hostage. I took him to my tent and kept him there until the night of the rice test.' She looked from one incredulous face to the other. 'He is not yet two years old,' she added.

'But my dear Mariana,' exclaimed Miss Fanny, 'this is madness! We were there all the time! How could we not have seen you carrying a great two-year-old child from the Golden Temple? You must give up this preposterous story.

321

What can the Maharajah's hostage have to do with your being secretly engaged to a native while you were encouraging Lieutenant Marks?'

'Encouraging Marks?' Mariana's mouth hung open. 'But Miss Fanny, I—'

'Be quiet, Mariana! You have said quite enough.' Miss Emily's tone brooked no argument.

The remainder of the journey to the British camp took place in deep silence, with the Eden ladies staring fixedly into the distance, their chins held high. Miss Emily did not speak again until they had reached the entrance to the red compound.

'Mariana,' she said finally, after their blue elephant had dropped joltingly to his knees at the mounting steps, 'your behaviour has put us all into a most distressing and awkward position. You are fortunate that my brother is a kind man. Whatever he may think of you, I am certain he will find a way to spare you the horror of actual marriage to a native. I shall be very surprised if, by tomorrow afternoon, you are not already on your way back to Calcutta. But we shall say no more of this sad business now. Good night.'

Without another word, she swept off in her best blonde silk, leaving Mariana and Miss Fanny to climb down from the silver howdah in silence.

'What is wrong, Memsahib?' Dittoo was wringing his hands. 'What has happened?'

Looking up from where she lay face down on her bed, Mariana pushed hair and tears from her eyes. 'Oh, Dittoo, it's horrible. They want to send me away to Calcutta, and all because of what I did to save their treaty!'

'Send you away, Memsahib?' Dittoo's chin began to wobble.

'No one will listen to me. I cannot get them to understand.'
She struck her pillow with a balled fist. 'If they are so clever,
why did they not speak out when the Maharajah tried to betroth
himself to me? Why did Fitzgerald do nothing?'

'The Maharajah *betrothed* himself to you?' Dittoo's eyes
widened until white appeared all the way round their brown
centres.

'No, but he very nearly did. *I* was the one who thought of
a good excuse, so he would not be insulted and cancel the
treaty. Now they all despise me.' She sat up and wiped her
face with her sleeve.

'I know one thing,' she went on as Dittoo rummaged through
the clothes in her trunk, searching for a fresh handkerchief, 'the
Shaikh is a great man. He understood the danger and sent his
own proposal to be used as my excuse.' She took a clean square
of linen from Dittoo's fingers and blew her nose. 'Of course
he does not mean for me to marry his son.'

'Marry his son?' Ditto's expression was now a caricature of
bewilderment. 'The *Shaikh* wants you to marry his *son*?'

She glared at him. 'Of course not. His daughter-in-law has
just died. You told me so yourself. The Shaikh expects me
to break the engagement on some pretext. The Shaikh is a
marvellous, special native,' she said as she rose to splash water
on her face at her washbasin. 'I should never have doubted him.'
Her towel in her hand, she moved to the open doorway. 'Oh,
Dittoo,' she said, her eyes on the stars hanging in a bright web
over the camp, 'why am I not in Sussex, having Christmas with
Papa and Mama?'

'So, the young lady is to marry your assistant.' The Maharajah
held back his arms for a servant to take off his vest.

'So it seems, Mahraj.' Faqeer Azizuddin nodded solemnly.

323

The servant lifted the Maharajah's beard aside and began to remove the gold buttons from his silk tunic.

'Is this your doing, Aziz?' Ignoring the man working on his clothes, the Maharajah peered up at the Faqeer. 'If it is, I will give you many villages.' His buttons removed, he flung his arms upward as the servant pulled his shirt over his head. 'I never expected that foolish proposal to bear such sweet fruit!' Naked to the waist, the old king sat down on the edge of his bed. 'Ah, Aziz,' he added, happily, 'it is so easy to tease the British. It gives me such pleasure. Did you see Macnaghten's face tonight? What a *tamasha*! I had expected to confuse the British, but the lady's speech confused even me! But then I saw what she had done; saw the benefit to me from this engagement to Hassan.'

The Faqeer's face stilled. The Maharajah smiled broadly as he received a starched cotton tunic.

'These English are children! Do you not see, Aziz, the gift she has offered me? After the wedding, I will send for my Saboor. When he comes, some relative of his must accompany him of course, to see to his needs, now that his mother is dead. That relative will be the Englishwoman, his new stepmother.' He raised his chin, allowing the servant to lift his beard out of the starched tunic. 'Your friend Waliullah may think he is getting the English girl for his women's quarters, but he is wrong. It is I who will have her for my Jasmine Tower!'

'We must remember, Mahraj,' the Faqeer put in smoothly, 'that the British will do all they can to extricate the lady from this marriage.'

'After she herself has announced her betrothal before a hundred witnesses? Have no fear, Aziz,' the Maharajah yawned as he stretched himself out on the bed, 'the English may think themselves clever, but I also am clever.'

'Indeed you are, Mahraj,' Aziz agreed solemnly, as the servant carried in the Maharajah's satin quilt. 'Indeed you are.'

Ill and light-headed, Lord Auckland and the other male members of the British party sat huddled in the dining tent of the British camp. It was past two o'clock in the morning.

'There's no way out of it now,' Major Byrne declared. He pulled up the collar of his frock coat. 'She must marry the fellow, whoever he is. I am sorry for her, but she has done this to herself.'

'Marry a native?' Lord Auckland brought his hand down heavily on the dining table. 'Are you mad? Has everyone gone mad?' His face gleamed in the candlelight.

Side by side, Major Byrne and William Macnaghten wiped their foreheads, but said nothing.

'There shall be no marriage.' Lord Auckland's jowls shook. 'I shall not be party to such a disgusting scene.' He stared from face to face. 'Miss Givens,' he said, emphasizing each word, 'however low her actions, is a Christian and an Englishwoman. While it is true that she has behaved abominably, it is our duty to protect what remains of her honour.'

Byrne bent towards Macnaghten. 'She certainly did not look like the sort of girl who would throw herself at native men,' he said under his breath, 'but she must have been doing it all along. What an astounding thing, to announce to all of us and a hundred natives that she had secretly agreed to marry one of them!'

'To allow this marriage to go forward would be indecency of the most virulent sort.' Lord Auckland looked about him with reddened eyes. 'And the worst of it was how helpless she left us after that brazen speech.' He sighed bleakly. 'That dirty, winking old Maharajah has invited us to the ceremony.

325

Think how he will enjoy our discomfiture as we see her off to the consummation of her marriage.'

Byrne mopped his brow again. 'She has laid herself open to this,' he insisted.

Lord Auckland breathed deeply. 'Yes,' he said, 'and Ranjit Singh intends to celebrate the ruin of an Englishwoman while we stand uselessly by.'

Gathering himself, Macnaghten spoke soothingly. 'This whole display has been in shocking taste. Of course it must go no further, my lord.' Someone hiccuped. Macnaghten frowned. 'The girl's behaviour has been unfortunate. Now we know her for what she is and she will pay for what she has done. But there is a way out. We will play for time. Tomorrow morning, I shall send word to Ranjit Singh that the girl has been taken ill in the night, and that the wedding must be put off until she has recovered. As soon as the treaty has been signed, we shall simply break the engagement and send her back to Calcutta. After all,' he concluded, 'the old man hasn't long to live. When he dies, all of this will be forgotten.'

'And what,' Lord Auckland enquired, glaring at the men around the table, 'was that business about a letter? The Maharajah said he had sent us a letter three years ago, asking for a wife. No one told me anything about it. What happened to the letter?' His voice rose peevishy. 'Why wasn't I told?'

Macnaghten shook his head. 'I saw no such letter, my lord. Perhaps it never existed.'

'Never existed? What do you mean, William? It is just the sort of thing that wretched old goat would do. Can't you see the opening we gave him? We might have lost everything over this business of an English wife. It is incompetence of this sort that causes the worst kind of trouble.'

'If such a letter did come three years ago, whoever read it

probably believed it was a joke,' said a secretary thickly, 'and threw it into the wastepaper basket.'

In a corner of the tent, someone had doubled over.

'For God's sake, Fitzgerald,' the Governor-General bellowed, turning in his seat, 'get out of the dining tent if you're going to be sick. Think of breakfast, man.'

'I can't think of breakfast, my lord,' was all Harry Fitzgerald could manage before he stumbled away through the opening.

Lord Auckland sighed. 'It is time,' he announced, 'for us all to go to bed.'

He rose from his seat and marched through the door, past the vomiting Fitzgerald, and with only a hint of unsteadiness crossed the open space to his tent.

Chapter Twenty-nine

Tuesday, 24 December

Clattering sounds told Mariana that Dittoo had arrived with her morning coffee. Restive and awake long after she went to bed, she had finally slept, only to dream of endings and the loss of precious things.

'Memsahib,' Dittoo said as he dropped the tray noisily onto her bedside table, 'when will you marry Saboor's father? When is the wedding to be?'

Mariana opened her eyes. Her brain felt like lead. 'Don't talk nonsense, Dittoo.' She groped beside the tray for her timepiece. 'I cannot possibly marry Saboor's father. He's a *native*.'

Dittoo shrugged. 'Memsahib, I have not wanted to say this before, but if Saboor's father wants to marry you, then you should—'

'Dittoo, enough.' It was six fifteen. There was still time. She sat up and reached for her shawl. 'Bring me my writing box,' she said. 'I have letters to write before breakfast. I shall write first to Miss Emily, explaining everything. Then I shall thank Shaikh Waliullah for his proposal, and tell him that I shall feign illness in order to avoid marrying his son.'

'But why avoid this good marriage, Memsahib? So many ladies would like to marry the son of Shaikh Waliullah.' Dittoo shook his head as he put her inlaid writing box down on the table. 'I am sorry to say this, but you are very old to be getting married. No Englishman has proposed for you yet, not even the tall one with fair hair who wears a blue coat.'

Bent over to pull on her boots, Mariana winced. 'I do not want your advice, Dittoo,' she snapped.

When he had left, she sat down at her table and took her pen and inkpot from the box. She sighed, remembering the other officers avoiding Fitzgerald's eyes as the whispered translation of her speech flew from mouth to mouth around the Maharajah's canopied enclosure. Fitzgerald, too, believed she had ruined herself with a native man.

She reached for a sheet of paper. To explain the whole story of Saboor and his grandfather to Miss Emily before breakfast would be difficult, but it must be done. Without Miss Emily's forgiveness, she could never show her face in the dining tent again. Then she would write to the Shaikh, and after that, if there were time, she would send a note to Fitzgerald. He had loved her. He would understand.

As she dipped her pen into her inkpot, Dittoo reappeared. 'Memsahib,' he cried, breathing noisily, 'the sentry is here. He says some ladies have come for you on an elephant. They say they want to prepare you for your marriage.'

'Ladies? Elephant? Dittoo, how can that be? The wedding is not to be today, it is tomorrow. Someone has made a mistake. Besides, the Shaikh expects me to claim illness, the cholera or smallpox, to cancel the wedding. Why would he send an elephant for me today?'

Dittoo flapped his hands towards the red wall. 'I do not know, Memsahib, but an elephant is waiting on the avenue with ladies and an armed escort and many servants!'

She watched him go out and put on his shoes, then bent

again over her paper. *Dear Miss Emily, I fear that the events of last night have given a most unfortunate impression—*

Dittoo returned almost instantly, more breathless than before. 'Memsahib,' he puffed, 'the sentry says the ladies are insisting you go with them at once. They say they have come a long distance and that already there is very little time to prepare you for the wedding. I have looked out through a tear in the wall, and what the sentry says is true. Are you sure you are not marrying Maharajah Ranjit Singh? The ladies' elephant is so—'

Mariana slammed down the lid of her writing box. 'For heaven's sake, Dittoo,' she shouted, 'I am marrying no one!'

He looked so shocked that she changed her tone. 'Please, go and find Mr Macnaghten. Tell him that Shaikh Waliullah has sent an elephant for me. Say I wish to speak to him.'

When Ditto had gone, Mariana stepped outside. The compound was quiet, except for a few servants working near the kitchen tent. There was no sign of life at Lord Auckland's tent or at the tents of Miss Emily and Miss Fanny. Mariana crossed quickly to the red wall. After dinner, both Macnaghten and Byrne had looked at her as if she were the lowest form of dancing girl. What would Macnaghten do when she asked for his help?

She put one eye to the tear in the wall. There they were, a lavishly decorated elephant with a curtained howdah, liveried servants, a fierce-looking escort.

Up and down the avenue, the tents of the government secretaries lay silent, shrouded in the cold mist of morning. 'Please be awake, Mr Macnaghten,' she whispered as Dittoo appeared on the avenue, hastening towards the political secretary's tent. '*Please.*'

But Mr Macnaghten was not awake, and the servant who sat shivering beside his door was, Dittoo reported moments

330

later, under the strictest orders never to awaken him unless the Governor-General wanted to see him.

'The ladies,' Dittoo announced, rubbing his hands together, 'are saying you must hurry, Memsahib.'

'Perhaps the Shaikh wishes only to speak to me about cancelling the wedding,' she said as Dittoo followed her back to her tent. She pushed aside the blind and stood uncertainly inside the doorway. 'After all, it must be handled as gracefully as possible.'

She had seen Shaikh Waliullah only once, by torchlight, and yet she could still feel his powerful gaze upon her. What an extraordinary man he was. And someone else was at the Shaikh's house, someone she would give anything to see. *You will meet Saboor again*, the Shaikh had told her as the dawn light crept into his courtyard.

'Dittoo,' she ordered, debating no longer, 'fetch me my blue-and-white gown. I am leaving with those ladies for the house of Shaikh Waliullah. I shall return by ten o'clock. If anyone asks for me, tell them I am ill and am having breakfast in my tent.'

Instead of explaining everything to Miss Emily in writing, she would call on her in the afternoon while the men were away signing the treaty. That was a more sensible plan. Her explanations would surely sound better given in person.

She wrote a quick note to Miss Emily requesting a meeting after lunch and handed it to Dittoo with instructions to deliver it immediately. Then she dressed with care, determined to make a better impression on the Shaikh than her dishevelled appearance must have done last time they met.

The elephant knelt down to receive her, the velvet curtain of its enclosed howdah jerking and swaying. Like someone in a dream, Mariana watched herself scramble up the ladder, over the railing, and through the parted curtains.

Three ladies sat inside, facing one another on red velvet cushions. One, an attractive woman of indeterminate age with suspiciously black hair and many rings on her fingers, greeted Mariana kindly and pointed to the empty seat opposite hers. The woman's neighbour, a plain female with pockmarks and large features, stared at Mariana without blinking. A slight girl with an enormous pearl and ruby tassel hanging from her nose ring gazed out at the sliver of avenue visible between the curtains, without acknowledging Mariana's arrival.

Where was Safiya Sultana, the Shaikh's deep-voiced sister?

Mariana sat down and arranged her skirts about her feet. The woman with dyed hair had painted her eyes, perhaps even her lips. Between her rings, her fingers were stained with a delicate pattern that resembled brown lace.

'When,' asked Mariana as the elephant lurched to its feet, 'will we reach Shaikh Waliullah's house?'

'Shaikh Waliullah's house?' The three women stared.

'No, no, daughter.' The black-haired woman leaned across and patted Mariana's knee. 'We cannot take you to the Shaikh's house. His is the house of the bridegroom. We are taking you to the Citadel to prepare you for your marriage.'

Mariana's hand flew to her mouth. 'No!'

'Yes, of course.' The woman smiled and smoothed back her hair with a practised gesture. 'From now on, we are your family. It is we who will make you beautiful for your wedding.'

Mariana jumped to her feet as the elephant started to move. 'No,' she cried, clutching a curtain for balance. 'There has been a mistake. I cannot go to the Citadel. I want to get down!'

The three women leaned away from her, their arms raised in self-protection. 'Sit down,' ordered the black-haired one. 'You will fall.'

'But you do not understand. I must get down. There is to be no marriage. It is all a mistake!'

Gripping a handful of blue and white silk, the heavy-faced woman tugged sharply downwards, bringing Mariana back to her velvet cushion with a thump.

The sullen faced-girl turned from the gap in the curtains, her nose ornament swinging like a pendulum. 'There is no mistake,' she said, her pretty lip curling. 'No mistake at all. The Maharajah has given his *hukm* – his royal order – that you are to be prepared for your wedding tomorrow by his own ladies. What mistake can there be?' Her tone had an unpleasant edge.

'Quite right, Saat,' nodded the black-haired woman.

'No!' Fright edging away conscious thought, Mariana shot to her feet again. 'I *demand* to get down,' she shouted in a high voice that sounded like someone else's. She reached for a handhold, missed, and staggered against an upright pole hidden among the curtains. Again she was tugged downwards and this time the black-haired woman swung her open hand at Mariana's face.

The woman's slap left an imprint of each of her beringed fingers on Mariana's cheek. 'Sit down,' she rasped, 'before you injure one of us.'

Mariana subsided in her seat, tears of shock wetting the burning place on her cheek. No one knew where she was. What a fool she had been to get into the howdah!

She must wait. There would be some way to get out of the Citadel once they had arrived.

The Maharajah had given a royal order. What did that mean?

333

Perhaps there was to be no wedding. Perhaps the old king knew the truth about Saboor's disappearance and intended to punish her in some even worse way. Perspiration trickled down her neck. Were these the same queens who had murdered Saboor's poor mother? Had they been ordered to punish her? If so, what would they do? Would they beat her, starve her, torment her as they had tormented Saboor?

Swaying on her cushion in rhythm with the queens, Mariana raised her chin and hid her trembling hands in the blue and white folds of her skirt while the elephant, accompanied by the Maharajah's servants and his armed horsemen, moved ceremoniously down the avenue. Whatever happened, she would do as Uncle Adrian had instructed her – she would remember who she was.

Through the gap in the moving curtains, she caught glimpses of the red compound wall, of Major Byrne's silent tent, more tents along the avenue, the horse lines, and then the flat, dusty landscape.

Chapter Thirty

'I will *not* take off my gown.'

Mariana's voice seemed to come from somewhere else in the room. 'I will not take off my gown, and I will not wear those,' she declared, drawing herself up and pointing to the mustard-coloured satin clothes the black-haired queen held out to her. New hope quelled her fear. 'And I demand to see Faqeer Azizuddin.'

The queens stared.

'Are you mad?' The black-haired queen's painted eyebrows rose. 'Who are you to be meeting the chief minister? Charan, Vijaya,' she called, 'she wants to meet Faqeer Azizuddin!'

Mariana stiffened as the heavy-faced woman from the elephant and a thin one with frizzy hair nudged each other.

'Where do you wish to meet him?' The frizzy one moved forward, derision on her face. 'Will it be here at the Jasmine Tower, where no man comes, or at his own house in the city, where ladies never go?'

'She will do as she is told.' The first queen turned to the heavy-faced woman. '*Hai* Charan,' she complained, 'why must *I* be in charge of this foreigner? Why do these things always fall to me, while the others enjoy themselves, having their hair oiled and their legs massaged?'

Charan took a small green triangular packet from a tray. 'I

tell you, Moran, I never believed that story of the Maharajah wanting to marry her.' She stuffed the packet into her mouth and chewed noisily on something that spilled red dye over her teeth. 'He would never,' she said with her mouth full, 'marry one of these unclean women.'

'Nonsense,' snapped the black-haired queen. 'Everyone knows he has been trying for years to get a European wife.' She turned to Mariana. 'Take that blue-and-white thing off.'

'And if I refuse?' Mariana's cheek still burned where the queen called Moran had slapped her. Why did they want her to take off her clothes? Where was she in this warren of tower rooms? Surely the low door by which she had entered was not the only way out of this sinister place?

The women looked at one another.

Moran gave a loud sigh. 'We will send for the eunuchs and have them undress you. We will enjoy that.' She smiled, showing a row of perfectly white teeth.

Mariana swallowed. 'And if I do put these clothes on, what will you do then?'

'Then we will turn you into a beautiful bride.' A cool wave of relief rushed over Mariana. They had not guessed it was she who had taken Saboor.

'Who is she to marry? Who is the boy?' demanded a harsh-faced woman.

'The son of Shaikh Waliullah,' Moran replied curtly.

'Oh yes, of course,' said the woman, 'the one whose wife was poi—'

Mariana watched the woman redden and subside into silence under Moran's terrible stare.

Charan turned humourless eyes on Mariana. 'She will never make a beautiful bride,' she declared. 'She is too old. Her hair is a mess.'

'She will be good enough.' Moran turned to Mariana once more. 'And now, will you take those things off or shall I call the eunuchs?'

'We should not do it now, Moran. It is too late.'

An hour later, dressed in the long mustard-coloured trousers and shirt Moran had given her, Mariana sat on a bed while the black-haired queen and a stranger in red stood gazing down at her, their voices echoing in the little room. Her stays and chemise, her stockings and gown, her boots and her bonnet had all vanished, carried off by a servant to some unknown place. She tried to read the women's faces.

An hour ago, compared to torture and death, marriage to a stranger had seemed a small price to pay for her stupidity. Now as she watched the two women, unsure what they wanted of her, Mariana wondered whether the price was as small as she had thought.

'It will not heal in time. Her nose will be red and swollen tomorrow. It will look ugly.' The woman in red was tall. Her eyebrows had been reduced to two thin, arched lines.

'Don't be foolish, Vijaya,' replied Moran. 'Where are we to put the n'hut if she is not pierced?' She snorted delicately. 'How can she be a bride without a nose ring? There will be no swelling. I shall put a neem twig in the wound.'

'Wound? Nose ring?' Mariana started up from the bed, but was immediately pushed down again. As she struggled, other women appeared and more hands held her down. She fought an arm free and struck out blindly, catching someone's breast. She heard a grunt of pain above the tangle of restraining arms.

Moran gave an order, and in an instant two men appeared at Mariana's side. 'Do you want me to hold her head?' asked one in a high, smoky voice.

337

A pair of hands near Mariana's face worked on the end of a length of gold wire, filing it to a point. She shut her eyes against a sudden light. A powerful hand pressed down on her forehead. Someone had taken a threatening grip on her neck.

'Be sure to keep her still while I put it in,' someone said. At once, Mariana felt a burning pain on one side of her nose. She gasped and struggled, feeling fingers poking into her ribs. The hand on her neck grew tighter. Gritting her teeth, she lay still.

'Give me the neem twig,' ordered the same voice, and once again came the pain as something rough was thrust into the fresh wound.

The restraining hands were withdrawn. It was over. Mariana pulled up her legs and crouched, panting, on the bed, her back to a filigreed window, a hand covering her injured nose. Furious at her tormentors, angry at her own helpless tears, she glared at the crowd of interested women who had collected in the doorway. The women did not speak. They only looked at her, some holding their veils across their faces as if she were someone to fear. When they had stared for long enough, they departed on silent, bare feet, glancing over their shoulders as they left her.

'Drink this.' A servant girl knelt beside her moments later, a cup of red pomegranate juice in her hand. 'You must not be afraid,' the girl murmured. 'You must be a beautiful bride. It is beautiful to wear the n'hut,' she added wistfully.

'That's right, Reshma,' agreed Moran from where she lay, stretched out on the white-sheeted floor. 'We will make her beautiful, is that not so?' She yawned and got to her feet as gracefully as a cat. 'Let her rest until I return.'

Mariana felt her nose with her fingertips. It was very sore,

338

and something hard stuck out of the wound. Her upper lip tasted of blood. She had told Dittoo she would return at ten o'clock. It must be past that now. Why had she not brought her timepiece? Surely she would be missed at camp. Surely, sooner or later, the British party would learn that she had been taken away to the Citadel. What would happen then? Would they order a search party? Would there be outrage at her kidnapping? Sympathy?

She raised the cup to her lips, then choked on the juice. How could she have forgotten? They were coming here! The treaty was to be signed here, at the Citadel. She wiped juice from her mouth and lay back on her bolster, bathed in sudden relief. She had only to survive until her rescue this afternoon.

She looked about the room. Its door, the curtain pulled aside, led out onto a stone passage. Outside, she could see a male hand and a white sleeve: a eunuch, posted there to prevent any attempt at escape. If her situation were different, she would want to know every detail of life in this tower, with its narrow, circular stair and its population of women and eunuchs.

There seemed to be plenty to do while she awaited her rescue. Moran rustled in and out, organizing women carrying pots of sweet-scented mud, bending to run her fingers through a tray of seeds and pods that had been brought in for her inspection.

'Take these away,' she snapped at the child who squatted silently beside the tray. 'Do you think I cannot tell last year's reetas when I see them?'

A fat woman arrived to massage oil into Mariana's hair and scalp. As the woman worked, Mariana felt her eyes grow pleasantly heavy. When the servant had gone, she laid her cloth-wrapped head on the bolster and closed her eyes. She may as well try to rest until Lord Auckland came to save her. The thin mattress was quite comfortable, and a cool breeze entered through the window, shifting the air.

She was nearly asleep when she heard a small sound at her bedside. The little servant girl they called Reshma squatted on the floor, all face and knees. She tugged her grubby veil over her hair and glanced behind her. 'Memsahib,' she whispered, her face near Mariana's, 'have you seen the child Saboor?'

Mariana's breath stopped. *Saboor*. But no one else had mentioned him, and she had said nothing to give herself away. Why was the girl crying?

'No, I have not seen any child called Saboor,' she replied curtly, before turning her face to the window.

With the eyes of the Governor-General, the Misses Eden and Major Byrne upon him, William Macnaghten drew himself up in his folding chair. 'Miss Givens left camp at dawn,' he announced stiffly, 'before I was awake. There was no time to send the Maharajah a message that she was ill.'

He braced himself, waiting for Lord Auckland's response.

'Do you mean to say she vanished while everyone was asleep?'

'She did,' Miss Emily put in, 'but not before she had written asking to call on me after lunch. That is why I did not worry when she failed to appear at breakfast. Her servant reported at the time that she had a headache and would have breakfast in her tent.'

'It is not surprising that she chose not to come to breakfast,' Dr Drummond contributed darkly from his basket chair.

Miss Emily's forehead creased. 'It was only when she did not appear later that I sent to inquire, and discovered that she had gone off on an elephant at six o'clock this morning, promising

340

to return straightaway, and that not a word had been heard of her since.' Her hands tightened in her lap.

Lord Auckland tugged at his black brocade waistcoat. He looked unwell. 'Where did she say she was going?'

Miss Emily pursed her lips. 'Her servant said she intended to call upon the father of the man to whom she is engaged – that magician, Shaikh Wallawallah.'

'The Shaikh?' Lord Auckland snorted. 'She wanted to call on a native Shaikh at six o'clock in the morning?'

'But the servant did not believe it. He said that he tried to tell her the elephant had come not from the Shaikh but from the Maharajah, but she would not listen.' Miss Emily sighed. 'Apparently there were native women on the elephant who said they wanted to prepare her for her wedding; but Mariana said she was *not* to be married and she would be back before ten o'clock.'

'Could she have been kidnapped by someone else?' Miss Fanny looked up from her tatting needles. 'The elephant could have belonged to anyone, could it not?'

'No, Miss Fanny,' put in Major Byrne. 'The elephant's escort was wearing chain mail. That eliminates everyone save the Maharajah. The girl was a fool to believe she was going to the Shaikh's house. She really might have—'

'Then that is where she is,' interrupted Lord Auckland bluntly. He consulted his pocket watch. 'We shall be leaving soon, and then we can discover for ourselves.' He glared at Byrne and Macnaghten. 'I cannot have female members of this party vanishing without warning.'

'I fail to see,' said the doctor, brushing a fly from his coat, 'why the girl has done it. She is well bred, and reasonably good-looking. We all expected her to marry young Marks. Why has she developed this sudden passion for native

341

men?' He looked from face to face in the circle of chairs. 'How did she do it, and when? How did the man manage to—'

A subaltern arrived and whispered to Major Byrne, who nodded. 'The elephants are ready,' he said. 'The generals are on their way.'

'The treaty.' Lord Auckland got to his feet. 'The treaty at last.' He spread his arms. 'Within a few weeks we shall have control of Afghanistan, and of all Central Asia. What a proud time this is for England!'

Two hours later, Lord Auckland sat perched on a golden chair in the Maharajah's fine hall of mirrors. He cleared his throat. 'Before we sign the documents,' he said, a trifle too loudly, nodding to Macnaghten to translate, 'I must ask the whereabouts of a certain member of our party.'

Drops of perspiration ran down Lord Auckland's face, from his gold tricorn to his chin. Dark patches had appeared under the arms of his heavy brocade coat. His skin was turning grey. At a sign from Faqeer Azizuddin, who sat, as always, at the Maharajah's feet, two fan-bearers stepped forward through the crowd and waved peacock-feather fans in Lord Auckland's direction.

Macnaghten's face, flushing as he translated the question, turned still pinker at the Faqeer's reply.

'May I enquire as to which member of your party is missing?' The Faqeer's voice was bland.

'How I hate the man,' Macnaghten murmured to Lord Auckland. He raised his voice. 'No one is missing, Faqeer Sahib,' he said. 'Rather, we wish to confirm the arrival of Miss Mariana Givens, our lady translator, who left our camp for the Citadel early this morning.'

Perched on his golden throne, the Maharajah looked eagerly from face to face. Several of his sirdars smiled.

The Faqeer stroked his beard. 'Then let us enquire whether the young lady is gracing the Jasmine Tower with her presence.' At a motion of his hand, a pear-shaped eunuch materialized before them. 'Call one of the women servants,' he ordered.

'We shall soon be satisfied of Miss Givens' whereabouts,' said Macnaghten brightly. 'But, my lord,' he added, dropping his voice as the Maharajah bent to speak to his chief minister, 'as for our reclaiming the lady and forbidding this marriage to go forward, I have grave doubts. I know nothing about native customs concerning women, but after listening to some of the Maharajah's more colourful remarks about them, I have drawn the conclusion that they are not the subject of polite conversation. Since ladies are not to be spoken of, I do not know how to broach the subject of cancelling the wedding.'

Lord Auckland's face was the colour of putty. 'Well, Macnaghten,' he replied weakly, 'you will have to think of something.'

Macnaghten blew a long breath into the silence. 'There is still, of course, a very slight danger that he may not sign the treaty if we upset him.'

The eunuch reappeared, followed at a distance by a small, slovenly looking servant girl. 'This,' he said, stopping in front of the throne and waving a contemptuous hand, 'is Reshma.'

'Ah, Reshma.' The Faqeer spoke smoothly from his place at the Maharajah's feet, motioning the girl forward. 'Come closer, child. Tell us if there is an English lady visiting the ladies' quarters.'

The girl hesitated, fiddling with her shabby veil. 'Yes, Huzoor,' she said tremulously, 'there is an English lady in the zenana.'

343

'Good. Send for her at once.' Lord Auckland wiped his face as Macnaghten translated his command.

The girl, her eyes on her feet, did not respond.

'Speak, child,' prompted the Faqeer. 'You understand, do you not, that you are to call the English lady?'

'But I cannot bring her.' The words rushed from Reshma's mouth. 'She cannot be seen.'

'What? What nonsense!' Frowning, Macnaghten spoke directly to the girl. 'Tell her to come here at once!'

The girl's eyes were fastened on the carpet in front of the Faqeer. 'Huzoor,' she whispered, 'the lady is already wearing her yellow clothes. Her hair has been oiled. She cannot be seen. Soon they will put the ubtan on her skin.'

'What does it matter about her hair or her clothes?' said Macnaghten sharply. 'What has this ubtan got to do with it?'

The Maharajah's single eye was bright with interest. He leaned forward. 'Tell the girl to speak up. I can hardly hear her.'

The girl was near tears. 'Ubtan,' she quavered, 'is the spiced and perfumed oil they put on the bride's skin to make it soft and beautiful for the—'

'That will do.' His face reddening, Macnaghten coughed noisily.

Beside him, Lord Auckland wiped his perspiring face again. 'What is she saying? When is Miss Givens coming?' His voice had taken on a querulous note.

Macnaghten breathed carefully. 'She, that is Miss Givens, is apparently unable to come at present.' He avoided the eyes of the Maharajah and his Faqeer. 'She is indisposed.'

'I see. Well, we'll send for her later. Let us get on with the treaty.'

The Maharajah's golden table was carried in and set down

344

with ceremony. The Sikh courtiers closed ranks, and the British generals and senior officers in their dress uniforms stood at attention.

Lord Auckland's speech, although filled with compliments, was brief. Throughout it, he looked as if he was about to faint, but he did not. He lasted through the reading and translation of the two documents, line by line, one in English, one in official Persian. He survived the Maharajah's speech, which was not a speech at all but a paean of lush praise for the British, to which Lord Auckland listened, smiling gravely, while the dark stains spread on his official dress clothes. Twitching in his chair, Macnaghten translated it all.

At last, taking a quill from the velvet cushion held out by a stiff-faced officer, Lord Auckland signed the treaty. The Maharajah followed suit, embraces were exchanged, and it was over.

'My lord,' murmured Macnaghten after edging the Governor-General a little distance away from the crowd, 'I have doubts as to our ability to retrieve Miss Givens from the Jasmine Tower this afternoon.'

'Never mind the girl, Macnaghten,' replied Lord Auckland, gripping his political secretary above the elbow with a trembling hand. 'Take me away from here. I am going to be sick.'

Roused by the smell of food, Mariana opened her eyes to find Reshma once again squatting by her mattress. On the floor beside the girl stood a tray of bread, orange and yellow rice, and something strong-smelling that looked like a chicken stew.

'You should eat now,' the girl murmured, lifting the tray.

The light had altered. Below the window, trees cast long shadows across a wide, dry moat. Mariana sat up. 'My people, the British! Are they here? Have they come? I must speak to

345

them!' Loosened from its cotton bindings, her hair lay in oily ropes on her shoulders.

Reshma blinked. 'The British sahibs with their many soldiers and their strange-looking clothes?'

'Yes. Are they here?' Why did no one in this country answer a question directly?

'No, Bibi, they have gone. They came, but they have gone.'

'Gone? How can they be gone?' Mariana scrambled up and searched for a pair of shoes. 'They must be here. They must be asking for me.'

Reshma looked away. 'They asked for you, but we told them you could not be seen. After that, they went away.'

'You told them I was not to be seen and then they went away and *left me here*?' Mariana shouted into Reshma's face.

The girl shrank away from her, an arm upraised. The eunuch guard put his head round the door.

Mariana's chest hurt fiercely. 'Do not fear, Reshma,' she said wearily. 'I do not strike people.'

Reshma lowered her arm. 'Bibi, look at yourself.' Her chin trembled. 'You are a bride. A bride must stay in bed in her yellow clothes until the day of her wedding. You cannot even have your food upstairs with the other ladies.'

'Has she eaten?' Moran pushed through the door, followed by a slant-eyed servant woman. 'We will do her eyebrows and other hair now. Come,' she ordered briskly, signalling the second servant to approach.

Before Mariana could act, Moran had pushed her onto the bed again. Her head was immobilized by Moran's beringed fingers, her body pinned down bruisingly by other hands; Mariana struggled uselessly, tears of rage and pain leaking from her eyes as the slant-eyed woman pulled hair cruelly from her eyebrows with a cat's cradle of twisted string.

'Other brides do not behave like you,' Moran snapped after Mariana had twisted out of her grip for the second time. 'They know this is for their beauty.' She wiped her damp forehead as Mariana glared at her from the mattress. '*They* never complain.'

Her heart pounding, Mariana gritted her teeth when the women examined the fine down on her arms. But when they untied the drawstring of her loose, gathered trousers and pulled them down, she screamed until her throat rasped and she could scream no longer. While Moran and several other women argued with her wails, telling her that it was necessary, that it was beautiful, the silent servant woman pressed a ball of something stiff and sticky against Mariana's tender skin, then tore it away, while a crowd of silent spectators watched from the doorway. By evening, the woman had pulled out every hair on Mariana's body, from her ankles to her chin.

Chapter Thirty-one

Wednesday, 25 December

An angled shaft of sunlight shone through Mariana's window and lay hot against her eyelids. Still half asleep, she turned from the window and pulled the satin quilt over her face.

The ship of her dreams had returned again in the night, carrying her swiftly through ever thicker fog, as steadily as if it were indeed piloted by Noah himself.

Why dream of calm when she was in this state? Why not dream of clinging, terrified, to the ship's foremast while waves broke over the deck and loose rigging whipped through the air, and lightning clove the fog, revealing a ghostly, tattered shore?

Her wedding was to be tonight – Christmas night.

Her eyelids felt swollen. She opened her eyes and touched the side of her nose with its protruding sliver of wood. She moved uncomfortably, wincing at the memory of tiny drops of blood welling up in her softest places where the hair had been torn away.

She was not a bride. She was a lamb being prepared for the slaughter, a spectacle to be gaped at, touched and commented upon. Yesterday as the servant had raised Mariana's mustard-coloured shirt, women and girls had crowded about the bed, staring.

'She needs no ubtan,' one woman had cried as she stroked Mariana's midriff with painted fingers. 'Her skin is already white, and as soft as silk. No one in the Jasmine Tower has skin so white, so fine!'

Mariana's beating heart had drowned out Moran's sharp reply.

'She has long legs, too,' offered the woman with thin eyebrows.

Moran had sniffed. 'All very well,' she had retorted, gesturing for Reshma to fetch another pot of paste, 'but look at the size of her feet.'

Mariana flung off her covers and sat up. She would go mad if she did not keep her wits about her. *You showed quick thinking in a crisis,* her father had said to her once. If only she could do the same now.

She thought back to their discussions about the great battles, but found nothing she could use. What good were light cavalry or heavy artillery to her now? What use were flanking movements or crowning the heights when she was a prisoner, trapped alone behind enemy lines?

So far, resisting the queens had gained her nothing. She should save her strength and pretend to agree – allow them to pierce, pluck, oil and dye her as much as they wished. Sometime, perhaps this afternoon, this horrible preparation would surely end. What then? How was she to get away before the wedding tonight? The eunuch still stood guard outside her door. Somehow she must get away. No power on earth could force her to marry the Shaikh's son. She would marry a handsome, familiar Englishman, not some dusky-skinned native.

She wondered what the Shaikh's son was like. Was he fat like the little girl who had carried Saboor up the stairs at the

349

Shaikh's house? Was he raisin-faced, like his father? No, she would not think of it. It must never come to that. She dropped her face into her perfumed hands.

'Wipe that mehndi from her face! You will give her brown patches!' Moran's irritated voice reached Mariana as she lay on her back two hours later, her caked hair streaming over the end of the platform, her hands covered in a lacy design of drying mud.

She had not argued over the scented mud in her hair, or over the other things – the delicate tracings of the same mud now drying on her hands and feet, the bucket of slimy, boiled seeds with which they had washed the oil from her hair.

'Bibi,' said a voice, when Moran had gone. 'Look, I have brought your food.' It was Reshma. She set a tray on the floor and squatted beside it.

Mariana peered over the edge of her platform. A great, greasy round of bread leaked cubes of spicy-looking potatoes onto the tray. She shook her head, squeezing her eyes shut. It was Christmas turkey she wanted, and her mother and father, and Baby Freddie, and Fitzgerald.

'Please eat,' the girl whispered. 'You will need food today.'

Mariana opened her eyes. There was something haunted about Reshma. From time to time a sad, wounded look came over the girl. How frail, how underfed she looked, as if the very air of the Citadel were draining her life away.

'I cannot eat.' Mariana shook her head again and waved a dismissive hand at the food. 'You have it.'

The girl's eyes brightened. 'You are good,' she whispered, glancing first at the tray then, carefully, at the doorway. 'You are a good lady. That is why I am glad you are to marry the father of Saboor Baba.'

Mariana sat up.

'You will be good to Saboor Baba, will you not, Bibi?' the girl murmured as she folded her potato bread carefully. She raised her eyes, licking the grease from her fingers. 'He is such a good boy.' Her face, so eager at the prospect of her meal, filled suddenly with sorrow.

As Reshma concentrated on her food, Mariana measured with her eyes the distance to the door. What was outside this tower? A courtyard, a garden, porticoes, more guards? After she had been taken down the elephant ladder, her arm gripped painfully by the pockmarked queen, the palanquin she had been pushed into had threaded its way between many buildings. If she ran, would she find an open gate out of the Citadel before she was caught? If caught, how badly would she suffer?

She got up quietly, her mud-caked hair hanging heavily down her back, and crouched beside Reshma. 'How far is it,' she whispered, 'to Shaikh Waliullah's house from here?'

'It is not far,' said the girl between swallows. 'I think the Shaikh lives by Wazir Khan's Mosque.'

'Reshma,' Mariana murmured urgently, 'take me there. Find a way for me to get out of the Citadel, and then take me to the Shaikh's house.'

Reshma stopped eating.

'You must do this, Reshma.'

'I cannot, Bibi.' The girl's greasy fingers shook. 'You must not ask me to do this.'

'But why not?'

'Bibi,' came the answer, spoken so softly Mariana could scarcely make out the words, 'if you disappear as Saboor disappeared, they will punish me as they punished Saboor's servant.'

351

'What did they do to him?' Her heart thumping, Mariana watched Reshma's expression.

'They took a great, curved sword and with one blow they sliced his nose from his face.'

One by one by one, the elephants heading the British procession slowed, then halted. The marching band fell silent. Lord Auckland leaned from his howdah, his fingers tapping impatiently on the railing. 'Why must *every* journey to the Citadel be filled with interruptions?' He sighed. 'How I wish this ghastly wedding business were already behind us,' he told Macnaghten, who sat behind him. 'I am already exhausted, and it's only six o'clock.'

Staccato shouting erupted nearby. Lord Auckland straightened, abandoning his effort to see. Nothing was visible from his perch but the cavalry escort, an aimless crowd of liveried servants and the usual throng of excited boys from the nearest village, perilously chasing one another under the elephants' moving feet.

He frowned. 'I had hoped yesterday's treaty signing would be our last visit to the Citadel. What a wretched way to celebrate Christmas!'

A panting bearer loped past their elephant, a peacock-feather fan in his outstretched hand.

'I was sorry to hear that the bridegroom's father has refused to speak to us until tomorrow,' Lord Auckland said crossly. 'That is most inconvenient, Macnaghten. The man behaves as if we have nothing else to do, as if the Afghan Campaign were nothing at all.' He sniffed. 'Someone might have told us the old fellow was considered some sort of religious authority, that he held regular gatherings at his house. What fool told us he was a magician? Still, I don't suppose it matters now.

Our last effort at forestalling the marriage has come to nothing.'

The line of elephants, with the sombrely clad Lord Auckland and Macnaghten together at its head, started forward again. The Eden ladies, on the second elephant, bent their heads together in the soft light of dusk, one black crêpe bonnet nearly touching another.

'I would much prefer to take the girl away with us tonight,' Lord Auckland told Macnaghten, 'but since we have had no contact with the Shaikh, we shall have to leave her there until tomorrow morning.'

Beads of perspiration dotted Macnaghten's brow. He crossed his legs.

'I warned her.' Lord Auckland shook his head. 'When she first came to camp, I gave her my most stringent warning. Never, I said, show interest in the natives.'

The marching band had started up again. Macnaghten leaned forward to be heard. 'Who could have guessed at her excitement over native men? It is terrible to imagine how she will suffer tonight.'

Lord Auckland's only reply was silence.

Their progress slowed by a leaping, pushing crowd of native onlookers, they followed along the city wall towards the Elephant Gate. Steadying himself, Lord Auckland searched the floor of the carved howdah for his silver-topped cane.

'Whatever Miss Givens' intentions may have been,' he said as he sat up again, the cane in his hand, 'her revelation saved the day. Accidentally, of course.' His pale eyes brightened. 'What a diversion the girl created after the Maharajah's marriage proposal! We could not have done it better ourselves.'

'Quite so, sir,' Macnaghten agreed, bobbing his head. 'In fact, I have yet to think of a satisfactory response to that outrageous suggestion. Any refusal, no matter how well put, would have offended the old man and might easily have had the effect of undoing our alliance. One cannot fathom the native mind. But what baffles me the most is how Miss Givens formed her own alliance with the Waliullah family. When could she have done it? She never left our sight.'

Lord Auckland adjusted his top hat with precision. 'I haven't the faintest idea, Macnaghten, but I do not wish to think of such matters now. Let us enjoy our relief at not having to participate in tonight's ceremony. I cannot say how pleased I was when you told me that this barbarian exercise is to be conducted by natives, according to their custom, and that we may leave it to the ladies to join Miss Givens as witnesses to her "consent".'

Macnaghten frowned. 'I must say, I was most unpleasantly surprised at the behaviour of the girl's munshi when he came to explain their marriage proceedings.'

'Why?' Lord Auckland poked the end of his stick restlessly into the floor of the howdah.

'I found the man far too self-possessed for a servant, my lord. I did not like him.'

Lord Auckland nodded. 'Well, Macnaghten, this whole business is nearly over, thank God. I only hope my sisters keep their heads. They had some notion of getting Miss Givens to feign a swoon, then rushing her away on the pretext that she was too ill to give her consent.' He smiled tightly. 'It had not even occurred to them to wonder how they would manage this, with their only translator lying unconscious between them.' He shook his head bleakly. 'Why do we call this evening's spectacle a wedding? Why do we not call it what it will be, an oriental bacchanal? I can predict its course exactly, from deafening fireworks, to screeching dancing girls, to poisonous wine, and finally to red hot food.'

'A proper wedding takes place in church,' agreed Macnaghten. 'How well I remember my own wedding day, how anxious I was, how lovely my wife looked.' He smiled to himself and crossed his legs again.

'One thing is certain,' pronounced Lord Auckland. 'Miss Givens will never have a real wedding. We have tried everything to save her, and it is now too late. Tomorrow she will return to us in utter disgrace. For all that she is to blame, I cannot help but feel sorry for the girl.'

The fabled picture wall of the Citadel rose before them at last.

'Welcome, welcome, most respected Governor-General Sahib! Welcome to the Governor-General and his party!' The Maharajah's ambassador, a smiling man in a striped turban, started forward to greet them, torch bearers running beside his velvet-draped elephant.

As Macnaghten gave his prepared reply, a flock of white doves erupted suddenly from a hundred small apertures in the wall. Their beating wings made the rushing sound of a sudden windstorm as, flying together in a spiralling white cloud, they flew in an arc, then in a circle, over the English party, before vanishing again into the wall.

'Kindest greetings and salutations from the Governor-General and his party,' replied Macnaghten warily as the ambassador's elephant advanced.

Lord Auckland glanced up at the wall. 'If I were a native,' he said solemnly, 'I might believe the appearance of those birds to be an omen of some sort. But I am not a native. I, praise God, am English.'

355

Chapter Thirty-two

The thudding of artillery fire reached them through the filigreed window. Moran called sharply for silence.

'They have come,' she announced to the crowded room, as braying trumpets and rattling drums followed the sound of the guns. 'Send for the clothes.'

'Who has come?' Mariana loathed the wobbly sound of her voice.

'Your husband, his family. They have come to take you away.' Moran cocked her head and smiled. 'Your husband has come for you, dressed in beautiful clothes, riding a white horse.'

Mariana's throat closed.

Moran's eyes fixed on Mariana's face. She frowned. 'Bring a light, Reshma. I want to see how well her nose is healing.'

'This wedding is nothing,' said the sour girl from the howdah nastily, her nose ornament swinging like the tassel on a bell pull. 'She has no relations of her own, no jewels, not even a copper pot for a dowry. How do we know the bridegroom is wearing beautiful clothes? She has sent him nothing to wear.'

Murmurs of agreement filled the room.

Moran stopped peering at Mariana's nose and pointed at the girl. 'You, Saat, were you not a dhoolie bride, brought to the Maharajah's tent with no wedding dinner? Do not speak,' she snapped, as the girl opened her mouth. 'We have heard enough from you.'

Saat recoiled, her face reddening.

A maidservant stepped into the room carrying a shiny cloth packet, followed by a eunuch bearing a black velvet pillow on outstretched hands. An intricate emerald and pearl necklace, a pair of heavy gold earrings and other jewellery lay on the pillow, secured to the velvet with black thread.

'These are your wedding clothes, and your jewels,' said Moran. Turning away from the bright packages, she opened a mustard-yellow veil the size of a bed sheet. 'It is time for the nikah, the marriage agreement, now. We will take you upstairs.'

'Now? Like this?' As cramps of panic clutched at her, Mariana wrapped her arms round her middle. 'But my clothes are all oily and—'

Moran tugged her to her feet. 'You do not wear your wedding clothes yet. Lower the blinds upstairs,' she barked over her shoulder to a eunuch as she draped the veil like a tent over Mariana's head and face, 'and make sure the seating is ready. Come, be quick, and keep your head down.' She put a hand on the back of Mariana's head and pushed her forward. 'Do not walk proudly.'

'No.' Mariana stood straight and snatched off the yellow veil. 'I have already told you there has been a mistake. I have told you that the Shaikh does not wish this marriage to take place.' She held the veil at arm's length and dropped it on the floor. 'I cannot be married against my will. I will not participate in this wedding of yours.' She folded her arms.

Everyone began talking at once.

'Wedding of *mine*? Against *your* will?' Moran pushed her

357

face into Mariana's, her voice a loud, persuasive singsong. 'Against your will, when you announced aloud to a hundred men at court that you were betrothed?' She snatched up the veil and jerked it into place over Mariana's head. 'As for the Shaikh,' she sneered, 'you are wrong. He has just now arrived with his son to take you away. You are only feeling shy.' She raised her voice, as if speaking to a deaf person. 'Brides always feel shy. Tell the eunuchs to wait,' she said over her shoulder. 'We may need them to help her upstairs.'

Bodies crowded against Mariana. Hands pushed her head down. Bent over, she tottered helplessly up the tower stairs, propelled by chattering women. As she reached the head of the stairway, she was assaulted by a blast of music. Lights flickered through her veil as she was pushed outside and across a carpet, then nudged onto a platform like the one downstairs, this one covered with scratchy, metallic cloth.

Her breath dampening her face, she listened through her veil. Her attendant ladies were leaving. As their whispers faded, a rustling sound signalled the arrival of two other women who sat down, one on each side of her.

After a moment's silence, a familiar voice spoke into her ear. 'Mariana,' it said, in English, 'is that you?'

Mariana fought her imprisoning veil from her face. There, like two tardy rescuing angels, sat the Misses Eden. Both were wearing black, as if they were in mourning.

At the sight of Mariana's face, Miss Emily started, her eyes wide.

Mariana felt her mouth turning down like a child's. 'Oh, Miss Emily,' she choked out, 'please, I am so glad to see you. Please help me. They did so many things . . .' Should she describe her ordeal to a spinster lady of forty?

358

Miss Emily produced a handkerchief and pressed it mutely into Mariana's hand.

'But Mariana,' Miss Fanny whispered, staring, 'what have they done to your nose, to your hands? Why is your face all shiny? Why have they wrapped you up like a parcel? I must say mustard does *not* suit you. Are these your wedding clothes?'

Miss Emily found her voice. 'Perhaps there are things,' she said, 'that are better left unmentioned.'

Mariana looked about her. She and the Eden sisters were in a darkened enclosure connected by a covered passageway to the ladies' tower door. The sides and back of the enclosure were of thick canvas, while the front which faced the courtyard was a screen of thin cane lined with fine muslin. Through the screen, she could clearly see a brightly lit gathering of men, no more than ten yards away. Was that Lord Auckland in a silver chair?

'Can they see us?' she breathed.

'No, my dear, it is the oddest thing,' replied Miss Fanny. 'As we approached, we could see nothing at all. We had no idea what was inside this enclosure, and yet from here we can see the courtyard perfectly.'

'I am so glad you have come, Miss Emily,' Mariana said eagerly. 'I had thought no one would come to save me.' She hesitated. 'But why are you wearing black? Has someone died?'

Miss Emily tightened her black-gloved hands in her lap, then spoke rapidly, allowing no interruption. 'No one has died, my dear. We are wearing black, I am sorry to say, because we have *not* come to save you, although my brother and Mr Macnaghten have tried their best to prevent this disaster. This wedding business of yours has gone too far to be stopped. You must marry the man to whom you say you are engaged.' Black ribbons quivered under her chin. 'I cannot imagine how I shall explain this to your aunt and uncle after they trusted me to guard your safety and your reputation.'

Mariana swallowed. 'But Miss Emily, I cannot marry the Shaikh's son. It was never – Shaikh Waliullah never—'

'Mr Macnaghten is to call upon the Shaikh tomorrow afternoon,' Miss Emily interrupted. 'He did his best to arrange a meeting for today, but the Shaikh was too busy to see him.'

Too busy to see Mr Macnaghten and cancel the wedding? Impossible! Mariana shook her head vehemently. 'Miss Emily, I cannot possibly marry—'

'As much as it pains me to say so,' Miss Emily said firmly, 'you are the sole author of this dreadful situation. We *all* warned you to keep away from the natives. I shudder to think what you could have done to invite a proposal of marriage from one of them.'

Thundering in Mariana's brain joined the pounding of her heart. She could scarcely breathe. 'Miss Emily,' she almost shouted, 'I invited neither this proposal nor the Maharajah's!' Desperate, she turned to her other side. 'Miss Fanny, I—'

Miss Emily raised a finger. 'Do not appeal to my sister. She quite agrees with me. You, my dear, did not stop at soliciting a marriage proposal. You announced your engagement before the Maharajah's entire court, and then went away on his elephant. Had you not done those things, there might have been some way out.' She shook out her black skirts. 'As it is, nothing can be done until tomorrow morning when Mr Macnaghten will come to the Shaikh's house to collect you and return you, sadder but wiser, I am sure, to our camp at Shalimar.'

Mariana clamped her teeth shut to prevent herself from shrieking with rage and turned her face towards the crowd of glittering Sikhs and black-clad Europeans visible through the cane screen.

'What is that scent you are wearing, Mariana?' Miss Fanny enquired, covering her nose with her handkerchief. She shifted on the platform beside Mariana, her taffetas creaking. 'It has given me a headache.'

'The second thing we have come to say,' Miss Emily went on in a businesslike tone, 'is that no word of these events is to escape the British camp. My brother has issued instructions to all those who were present at the Maharajah's dinner and to all who are present this evening that no mention of this marriage is ever to be made in either personal letters or official dispatches. As far as we are concerned, these events will *never* have happened.' She coughed delicately. 'As far as he is able to do it, my brother has determined to preserve your reputation. It is not, of course, within his power to preserve your honour.'

Mariana did not take her eyes from the throng outside her enclosure. Of course they would gossip. They would all talk about her. She despised Miss Emily, Miss Fanny, Mr Macnaghten, every one of them. If he were here, she might hate Fitzgerald too.

A loud gasp came from the passageway.

It was the torturing Moran, now thickly decorated in jewellery, with layers of maroon silk rippling about her. Without pausing to acknowledge the English guests, she rushed through the entrance to the enclosure and cast the yellow veil for a third time over Mariana's face.

'Shameless girl,' she hissed. 'The court solicitor is coming to hear your consent! How foolish you are to uncover yourself!' She sat down on the platform, her jewellery clashing. Beside the now shrouded Mariana, Miss Emily rustled and sniffed.

361

'I do not wish to know what that rude woman was saying,' Miss Emily declared, 'and I shall be very glad when this absurd ceremony is finished.'

Mariana raised a corner of her veil surreptitiously and looked out. An elderly, bearded man in a knitted skullcap shuffled towards the ladies' enclosure, aided by a stocky person in plain-looking clothes.

Miss Fanny nudged Mariana. 'Is that square young man to be the bridegroom?' she whispered.

Mariana could not speak.

Another man followed the first two. He wore a tall head-dress. She dropped the veil, despair welling inside her. Why had the Shaikh spoken of her courage, and of the love she felt for Saboor, then cheated her of her honour and her life?

The trio of men waited uncertainly before the cane screen until two eunuchs appeared, carrying chairs.

'Ah,' said Moran, sighing gustily, as the three men seated themselves before the screen, 'it is time.'

Shaikh Waliullah raised his head and looked in her direction. For a moment, although she knew he could not see her, Mariana felt his powerful gaze reach through the screen, through her yellow veil, and pierce her heart.

'This,' murmured Miss Emily, 'seems more a fancy-dress party than a wedding. I must say that if I had ears like open carriage doors, I should not have chosen a costume involving a foot-high tubular headdress like that gentleman outside.'

Under her veil, Mariana stopped her ears with her fingers.

The sound of male voices drifted into the darkness of the ladies' enclosure. Someone cleared his throat and spoke. Mariana pushed her fingers harder against her ears.

She took them away when an elbow dug into her side. 'Answer him,' whispered Moran.

362

'Is she present?' an old man's voice asked.

'Yes,' Moran answered. 'I, Moran Bibi, declare that she is present.'

'And does Mariam Bibi,' rasped the ancient voice, 'give her free consent to marry Hassan Ali Khan Karakoyia?'

'What are they asking?' enquired Miss Fanny in her stage whisper.

'Speak,' ordered Moran.

Mariana breathed deeply. 'No,' she said grimly through her veil. 'I do *not* give my free consent.'

'What does "nay" mean?' Miss Emily demanded. 'Are you saying, Mariana, that you refuse to marry the man?'

Miss Fanny drew in a sharp breath. 'I think she is very brave, after all the things these people have—'

'*You will say yes,*' hissed Moran, her fingers gripping Mariana's arm painfully.

Mariana blinked. On second thoughts, to refuse would be a mistake. Moran would only return her to the rooms downstairs and inflict more punishment upon her. But if she consented, she would leave for the Shaikh's house within hours. Had it not been her plan to escape the Citadel at any cost?

'I consent,' she croaked.

'What did you say, Mariana?' asked Miss Emily and Miss Fanny in unison.

Mariana did not reply.

Bent over in her greasy clothes, she half listened as instructions were given and prayers recited in drawn-out Arabic. When clashing music started up in the courtyard, Moran tugged at Mariana's veil. 'Tell your ladies to join the other English people,' she commanded, 'while we dress you in your wedding clothes.'

Sick at heart, Mariana stumbled down the stairs again. What had the old man said? What was her husband's name?

Bathed at last, her hair dried, her eyes painted and her skin massaged with almond oil, Mariana stood as Moran tied the drawstring of her crimson wedding pyajamas and pulled a matching brocade shirt over her head.

'There.' Moran stood back. 'Now we are nearly ready.'

The watching women nodded.

'No, her hair is not right.' The heavy-faced Charan chewed as she spoke. 'Look. It is like a rat's nest.'

A rat's nest! Would she ever recover from the insults of the past two days?

Moran lowered a crimson dress of fine embroidered tissue over Mariana's brocade shirt. 'Why is everyone criticizing?' she muttered, as she broke the basting threads that held a heavy, fringed veil in a neat square. 'Pah! Do they all think I have never before dressed a bride?' With a snap, she freed the pearl and emerald choker from the velvet pillow. 'Be still,' she ordered, putting the necklace over Mariana's head and jerking the fastening cords tight. Then she rummaged in a wooden jewellery casket and pulled out a dozen straight ropes of pearls, each with a hook on one end and a large, lustrous pearl on the other.

'Here. These will help,' she said as she tugged at Mariana's hair. 'They will be our wedding present to you.' She stood back and narrowed her eyes. 'You look all right.' She nodded. 'You make a nice bride. The clothes they sent are good enough. They are not very elaborate, but after all, they have recently had a death in the family.'

What did Moran mean by not very elaborate? Mariana had never worn such fine clothes in all her life.

One piece of jewellery remained stitched to the pillow. Moran pulled it loose and approached, her eyes on Mariana's nose.

Backing away, her hands before her face, Mariana shook her head. 'No,' she cried. 'No!'

Moran let out a noisy sigh. 'Can you not hear the sounds from upstairs?' She gestured impatiently towards the window, her many rings flashing. 'We must take you there now. There is no more time to waste.' Gripping Mariana's chin, she tweaked out the neem twig and forced the gold nose ring through Mariana's nose with one sure movement. Her work accomplished, she nodded with satisfaction.

'Now we are done,' she said.

Mariana gazed at the brown tracery decorating her hands, as elaborate as the marble filigree of the window of the room in which she stood. She studied her four rings, two of rubies and pearls, two of emeralds and pearls, the enamelwork bangles on one wrist, the heavy gold circlets on the other, the seed pearls and gold thread decorating her sleeves. Other jewellery lay on her forehead. Her nose, having burned fiercely when the ring was first put in, now merely ached.

'Remember one thing, bleed heavily tonight,' Moran said carelessly as she unfolded the heavy fringed veil and draped it over Mariana's face. 'Bleed as much as you can, all over the sheets. It makes the family happy.'

On her platform in the ladies' enclosure once more, Mariana drooped with exhaustion. She made no effort to see through her new red veil. Outside, musicians nearly drowned the noise of male conversation.

Miss Fanny spoke from close by. 'A stout woman is coming this way. Who is she?'

365

'I don't know.' Mariana replied crossly, wishing they would all go away.

Bodies moved on the platform, making room for the new arrival, who promptly wedged herself into a too-small space beside Mariana.

It was not a queen. 'Peace, daughter,' intoned a baritone voice. Thick fingers grasped the fringed, crimson veil and raised it. Mariana glanced up into the satisfied face of Safiya Sultana.

'You are pretty, as I knew you would be,' said the Shaikh's sister, dropping the veil.

Mariana stiffened. Pretty she might be, married she might shortly be, at least according to them, but as soon as she was safely out of the Citadel, this charade must end. Her mother had never mentioned blood when she gave her terse, ugly description of the origin of babies. She had no intention of performing any wifely duty with the Shaikh's son, far less whatever grisly ritual they had in store for her. She would make that clear to Safiya Sultana this very instant.

As she opened her mouth to do so, Moran spoke beside her knee. 'We should let the foreigners see the bride.'

Mariana closed her mouth again. She had not realised Moran was there. There was no telling what unpleasant reaction her announcement would provoke from the queen. The Shaikh's sister would have to wait.

Someone lifted her veil again. Their black bonneted heads together, Miss Emily and Miss Fanny stared at her through a tunnel of crimson and gold tissue, their mouths forming perfect 'oh's' of mute surprise.

Mariana gazed steadily back. She would never speak to them again, never.

As Safiya Sultana's stout body shifted against hers, Mariana

366

fought off unexpected comfort and relief. When she had brought Saboor to the haveli, the Shaikh's sister had not hurt or humiliated her, she had only thanked her for the service she had performed. Safiya Sultana, at least, appeared to be kind and sensible, although who knew what cruelties she might subject a family bride to in the name of custom and tradition.

'We will complete the formalities and take you home as soon as possible,' Safiya Sultana said, wheezing a little. 'It is not our intention to spend time here. These men can have their drinking party without us.'

'The bridegroom is coming,' someone announced.

Everyone seemed to have gone away, save the Eden ladies and Safiya Sultana. In the middle of a tired yawn, Mariana was startled by a change in the atmosphere around her.

'Most extraordinary,' Miss Emily's voice declared. 'How can he see through that great tangle of beads and pearls?'

As someone sat down beside Mariana, Safiya Sultana began to recite something in a quiet singsong. 'Now the bride and groom must see each other,' she said when she had finished.

Miss Fanny gave a muffled cough as Mariana's veil was lifted again, this time all the way back, freeing her face.

Someone thrust a looking glass with an intricately engraved silver border before her. Leaning forward, she saw herself and gaped, astonished at her reflection.

Rimmed with black surma, the eyes that stared back at her were shapely and strange. Between unfamiliar arched eyebrows, a gold pendant set with jewels rested on her forehead, its pearl rope hidden in her hair. Her hair, no longer brown, but auburn, curled softly on her shoulders, interlaced with strings of pearls. A large ring of fine gold wire pierced her nose, its pearl and ruby beads touching her lips.

Was this creature really her? She made an experimental face and put out her tongue, just as the mirror was tilted to one side, and she saw, not herself, but a pair of shocked brown eyes. Holding his ropes of gold and pearl aside, the man looked briefly into her face before someone dropped her veil.

'May Allah Most Gracious bless you both and give you long life,' intoned Safiya Sultana.

An hour later, stiff with tension, Mariana sat upstairs at Qamar Haveli, surrounded by the Shaikh's family women. The Waliullah ladies, so benign when she last had seen them, now seemed like a crowd of vultures, staring, waiting.

'That is not the same girl who brought Saboor,' pronounced an old lady, dropping Mariana's now damp veil over her face again. 'The queens have sent someone else.'

'Of course it is the same girl,' said two other women at the same time. 'Look at her nose, her skin.'

The veil was pulled away again. 'So it is,' said the old lady, peering closely at Mariana. 'For all their malice, they know how to prepare a bride. I would never have believed she could look so lovely. That girl was as plain as a cooking pot.'

Half an hour ago, Miss Emily's voice had cut through the noise of the crowd as the two ladies were led away to their palanquins at the end of the evening.

'What an extraordinary transformation, Fanny,' she had said, her voice floating back over the marble courtyard. 'I find it astonishing that an ordinary-looking English girl could be made to look so exactly like a native. A white native, I mean, of course. What a pity the bridegroom was invisible under all those—'

'Yes, and I thought she made a very pretty native.'

'*Really*, Fanny.'

Mariana shifted. What were these women waiting for? Whatever it was, would it be even more horrible and disgusting than what Mama had described?

Her body felt clammy. She clutched her knees to her chest. Here in this upstairs room there were no eunuch guards, no armed men at the door. She imagined herself running through darkened streets in her bride's clothes, looking for the way to Shalimar . . .

Safiya Sultana sat in her accustomed place against the wall. Determined to tell Safiya of her refusal to continue this charade of a marriage, Mariana crawled to her side, dragging heavy embroidery and fringes behind her.

'I must speak to you,' she began as the other women murmured in surprise. 'I must tell you that—'

Safiya frowned. 'Not now, daughter. It is time to leave.' She nodded to a group of young girls who got to their feet and came towards them, holding their hands out to Mariana.

The only choice left was to fight, but Mariana had no more strength to protest or to struggle against restraining brown hands. Defeated at last, she got to her feet and let the girls lead her to a corner room at the end of a veranda. Inside were two string beds, both turned down, their sheets sprinkled liberally with red rose petals. An oil lamp glowed on a carved table. By its light, Mariana watched the girls run away, looking back over their shoulders, giggling through their fingers.

She sat down. The oil lamp looked like a reasonably dangerous weapon, but of course it was lit and would start a fire if she tried to use it.

There was a sound at the door. Ostrich-like, Mariana tugged her veil hastily down and peered through its fringe to see the curtain move aside and a figure in white pause before

369

entering the room. The bed creaked as the figure sat beside her. She did not turn her head. She could scarcely breathe. Attar of sandalwood scented the air. Where had she smelled that before?

'You didn't look foreign when I saw you, but then I couldn't see much in the mirror.' His voice was pleasant, like the Shaikh's, but without inflection, as if he were simply stating a fact. Beside her, a hand moved on his knee. It was a beautiful hand, perfectly shaped, with curved fingers. The hand lifted, pointing to a corner of the room.

'You should take off those heavy things and your jewellery,' he said. 'Put them on the trunk over there.'

No longer burdened by her elaborate clothes, she might be able to put up some resistance. In the corner, her back to him, she grimaced as she removed her nose ring and tugged at the pearl strands in her hair. How long could she avoid looking at him?

'I am glad to lie down,' he said. 'I have ridden forty miles today, from Kasur.'

She dropped her veil and dress onto the trunk, steeled herself, and turned. The Shaikh's son lay full length on the bed, his eyes closed, his hands behind his head, his lips parted under a full moustache. His beard was thick and neatly trimmed.

It was the tall man in the embroidered coat whom she had followed from the durbar tent, the same man who had later appeared, weeping, beside her near the howitzers, who had even then worn attar of sandalwood.

He did not look like the Shaikh at all.

His eyes remained closed. Still wearing her scarlet shirt and loose trousers, Mariana crept to the other bed. She lay down silently, arranged the quilt over herself and leaned over to turn out the lamp.

370

The bed beside her shifted and groaned. She froze, her arm still extended. Perhaps he was only turning in his sleep.

He was not asleep. His eyes met hers as he pushed himself up and sat on the edge of his bed.

Without speaking, he got to his feet. As he padded towards her, she twisted away from him and rolled her carefully prepared and perfumed body into a ball on the far side of the bed, her eyes screwed shut, her fist in her mouth. Her ragged breathing seemed to fill the room.

There was no sound from outside.

His weight came down beside her. 'Show me your face,' he said.

When she did not move, he took her by her shoulder and turned her to him.

She could only look up, her body clenched against invasion, too terrified to blink, too exhausted to move.

He studied her, his hand still on her shoulder, his eyelids drooping as Saboor's did when he was sleepy. 'They were right,' he said. 'You do not look foreign.' His eyes were ringed with dark smudges as they had been when she had first seen him a month ago. His expression altered. His breathing gathered speed. He dropped his gaze to her mouth and leaned over her, then pulled back when she flinched, her eyes wide.

'So,' he said softly, 'you are afraid of me.' He took his hand from her shoulder and turned away. 'There is no need for fear,' he said in a muffled voice, his back to her. 'You rescued my son. I am in your debt.' He stood. 'Sleep, Bibi,' he said as he returned to his own bed. 'Go to sleep.'

Chapter Thirty-three

Mariana swam to consciousness through a thick mist. As the events of the previous night returned, she lay still, holding her breath, and listened. Was he still there, in the other bed?

Silence.

She opened her eyes and put a hand to her neck. Forgotten when she undressed, her choker now hung loose, its scratchy cord wrapped about her neck, its pearls and emeralds entangled in her hair.

Daylight filtered into the room through closed shutters. On the trunk in the corner, her fringed veil and her jewellery lay where she had left them. Her tissue dress had fallen from the trunk and lay on the floor, its pearl embroidery gleaming in the striped light from the window.

She turned her head cautiously. The bed next to hers was unoccupied, its sheets wrinkled, its quilt thrown aside.

She drew up her knees, enjoying the cool air on her face and the warmth beneath the covers. Last night, when Hassan had left her to sleep, she had been too exhausted to feel the relief that now bathed her from head to foot. She was safe and unharmed. Mr Macnaghten was coming today. She was nearly free.

Someone pushed the door curtain aside. A small girl stepped shyly into the room, a set of clothes in her hands, neatly folded and held in place by basting thread.

Rose petals, crushed to a deep purple, marked the floor tiles, Mariana's pillow, the sheets of both beds. The girl looked at them, and then at Mariana, a question in her eyes.

Unable to think of anything to say, Mariana smiled.

'Come, Bhabi,' the child piped, returning Mariana's smile. 'I will show you where to bathe.' She held out the russet-coloured package and a soft-looking shawl of the same colour. 'You will wear these to meet the ladies. They are waiting for you in the big room.' Her face sobered. 'Of course you must understand that our house is still in mourning for poor Mumtaz Ba—' She pressed her lips together. 'I should not be speaking to you, a bride, of these things,' she added.

Mariana reached to untangle her choker. 'I would rather wear my own clothes. Please ask someone to bring my own things from the Citadel. They are my best clothes, you see.' Yes, her chemise, her stays, her stockings, her blue-and-white silk gown – wearing them again, she would feel entirely herself. She would look like an Englishwoman again when she met Mr Macnaghten.

The child was a birdlike creature whose thick, glossy braid fell below her waist. 'Your own things have not come from the Citadel, Bhabi.'

Resigned Mariana nodded. What did it matter after all? Her clothes were the least of her worries. In the past three days she had lost more than a borrowed gown and her good set of stays.

'Safiya Bhaji had these clothes made for you,' said the child. 'It will make her happy to see you wearing them.' She held out a silk, drawstring pouch. 'And see, she has sent you a beautiful gold necklace.'

Safiya Sultana. Mariana turned the necklace over in her hands. Did Safiya know what had happened, or rather not happened, last night?

Half an hour later, Mariana crouched naked in a small room with a drain in its tiled floor, watching hot water drain from a pipe into a brass bucket. Beside her, another bucket held cold water.

She dipped a vessel shaped like a teapot into the hot, then the cold bucket then shivered as she poured steaming water over her shoulders. Last night, when he leaned over her, Hassan's skin had smelled hot beneath the attar of sandalwood he wore, as if it had been scorched.

She put down the teapot. He would no doubt have felt within his rights to do whatever he wished with her last night, but he had not. He had given her one considering glance, and then left her alone. She would always remember that kindness, and the sweet, burnt scent of his skin.

Her washing finished, she took a Turkish towel from the small hand that came timidly round the door, dried herself, then put on the loose silks the child had given her. A short while later, she balanced nervously in the doorway of the big room, blushing as she removed her new embroidered slippers with their upward-curling toes, and added them to a pile beside the door. How odd to feel self-conscious over something that had not happened.

Safiya Sultana beckoned, pointing to an unoccupied place beside her on the cloth-covered floor. If she knew about last night, her face did not give her away.

The women whispered as Mariana made her way through

the crowd and crouched down beside the Shaikh's sister. A familiar-looking gap-toothed aunt patted her knee. On Safiya Sultana's other side, a very old lady smiled into the air.

Mariana's new clothes felt alien and voluptuous. Without stays and petticoats, her body felt unfettered and exposed. She reached up to touch the unfamiliar smoothness of her hair, now hanging down her back in a silken plait, so unlike her own flyaway hair that it could have belonged to someone else. Her oiled and hairless skin had a smooth, indecent texture.

There were children in the room. She looked for Saboor, and saw him near a doorway with a group of other children, too far away to notice her. His bubbling laughter reached her as a girl of six or seven, eyes alight, dragged him across the floor, her hands under his arms.

'An-nah!' He had seen her. He bounced, shouting in the little girl's arms, reaching out for Mariana. 'An-nah!'

The room stilled.

How sweet it felt to hold Saboor again! She kissed the top of his head and breathed his baby scent as he reached up to play with the gold buttons on her silk shirt.

A collective sigh enveloped her.

Safiya Sultana sniffed. Was she weeping? Still rocking Saboor, Mariana glanced up to see Safiya wipe her eyes with her white cotton veil.

'These are painful times,' she pronounced in her baritone voice. 'Painful times. We all remember that when our dear Mumtaz Bano died, her child was left alone among strangers at the Citadel, his life in danger.' She looked at Mariana. 'We also remember that, after this brave young foreigner saved Saboor, my brother, seeing her courage and her love for our child, determined that it was the will of Allah that she remain beside Saboor, to protect him from harm, and to help us raise

375

him to manhood.' She paused, clearing her throat. 'It is for this reason that we have joined her in marriage to Hassan.'

We have joined her in marriage. Mariana put Saboor down and turned to face the wall as nausea spread from her belly to her throat. Moran Bibi had been right. Miss Emily had been right. The proposal *had* been genuine, and she had accepted it in front of a hundred people, including Harry Fitzgerald, who had kissed her and made her happy. She had done all of this herself.

A worried voice spoke beside her. 'Is the bride ill?'

The bride. Fighting tears, Mariana watched Saboor scramble away. How would she face Mr Macnaghten and the British camp? How would she ever convince them that she had never believed the marriage proposal was genuine? And what of her family? Until this moment, she had not even considered them. Poor Mama and Papa were still waiting at home for news of her engagement to an Englishman . . .

'Allah alone,' Safiya Sultana was saying, 'knows the pain and confusion it has caused us to have our dear Mumtaz Bano's death followed so quickly by Hassan's marriage to this foreigner. We all suffer for Mumtaz's mother.'

A little distance away, a small figure rocked silently.

Mariana swallowed hard. These people did not want her. How could they? Of all of them, the only who really wanted her was Saboor. He was now in the arms of his fat cousin, who held him away from a dozen small, reaching arms. His eyes on Mariana, he fought to get down, and then hurried back to her and sat, with a sweet little thump, on her lap.

She wrapped her arms gratefully round his body and pressed her cheek against his head. If only she could take him away from here . . .

Safiya Sultana sighed. 'But we must remember how greatly

Hassan's new wife loves our Saboor. Her affection for him is plain to see. We have noticed her face soften as he approaches her; we have seen it fill with light. It gives us comfort to see her love for our motherless child. We all know of women who feign love for a widower's children in order to gain entry into his family. We pity the motherless child who must endure the hatred of his father's second wife.'

Mariana sniffed, wishing she had a handkerchief. She had certainly never wanted to 'gain entry' into this native family.

'Perhaps,' said one lady softly, nodding at the woman who sat trembling with age at Safiya Sultana's stout side, 'this foreigner will love Saboor as Bhaji Tehmina loved Safiya and Waliullah when they were orphaned as babies. Such love is rare indeed.'

Lured by beckoning children, Saboor slipped away. Mariana wrapped her arms about her legs and stared through the window at a cloudy sky, imagining herself back at the British camp. She pictured the camp preparing for the return journey to Calcutta, its bustling activity so different from the stillness of this room in the Shaikh's house.

Mr Macnaghten would arrive soon to call upon the Shaikh. There was no need to fear that she would miss him – he would be clearly visible, sitting beside the Shaikh's platform in the courtyard, and the ladies would rush to the windows to see the foreign gentleman. She would go down to meet him and insist that he take her back to the British camp. By the evening, disgraced or not, she would be in her own tent, standing over her trunks before she dressed for dinner, telling Dittoo which of her gowns to pack.

The ladies had fallen into contemplative silence. Outside, rain had begun to fall, splashing onto the windowsills, drumming on the flat, tiled roof over their heads.

The honour guard would have left already to join the march to Kabul. Fitzgerald must hate her now.

Mariana smoothed her russet silk over one knee. What if something happened to Mr Macnaghten and he never came? She shivered. What if he did come but she was somehow prevented from leaving with him? Would the British then simply leave her behind? No, surely not. They would not abandon her here for ever, never again to eat her own food, or hear the familiar cadence of her own language.

They had left her at the Citadel and gone away.

If only she knew her future!

She blinked. Someone here in the haveli knew her future. How could she have forgotten? Whatever her feelings about his marriage proposal, Mariana was certain that the old Shaikh possessed profound knowledge. When his eyes had met hers through the reed screen last evening, they had seemed to hold some promise she did not understand.

She leaned towards Safiya Sultana. 'May I please,' she said as sweetly as she could, 'offer my salaams to Shaikh Waliullah?'

'What?' Safiya Sultana looked startled. 'Why, daughter, you cannot see him today. He is not at home until the afternoon, and then he will have visitors.'

'*Nani, Nani!*' All the ladies looked up as a tall boy with the callow beginnings of a moustache rushed into the room and stood, breathing hard in the doorway, his eyes drifting to Mariana and Saboor. 'Armed men have come from the Citadel!' he said rapidly, jumbling his words. 'They are waiting in the courtyard. They say they have come to take Saboor and the European lady away with them. You are to have their clothes packed. They say Saboor and the lady are to live at the Citadel for ever, as guests of the Maharajah!'

No one spoke. Shutters creaked in the wind. Mariana felt the blood leave her face.

A question hung in the air. The boy answered it before it could be asked. 'There are no men in the house save Uncle Bilal and me.'

The woman beside Mariana shook her head. 'Only Safiya's grandchild and Bilal, the impractical one, the dreamer, the teller of tales. This is not good, not good at all.'

The children playing on the floor gaped at the tall boy, their chattering abruptly stilled. The little girl who had been reciting nonsense rhymes to Saboor stopped speaking and looked up.

A woman spoke from the corner of the room. 'It is wrong,' she said loudly, 'for them to take the child away. How can he go to the Citadel?' She stretched out her fingers. 'He is not the Maharajah's slave!'

Safiya Sultana turned a silencing glare upon the woman and looked up at the boy. 'Yahya, my darling,' she told him over the patter of the rain, 'go downstairs. Tell the Maharajah's men that it will take a little time to make Saboor and the lady ready. Tell them also that Saboor has a fever. Tell them we have had a case of smallpox in the elephant stable.'

The boy hesitated. 'But Nani—'

Anxious voices whispered around Mariana. 'Why can we not hide them? There are so many hiding places in this house. My children know them all. Surely we can—'

'Go, Yahya,' Safiya Sultana said sharply.

All eyes were upon the boy. He flushed, then turned stiffly away. Without looking back, he crossed the veranda and clattered down the stairs.

Safiya Sultana surveyed the room calmly, her eyes resting

379

on the only woman in the room who was dressed like a servant. 'Bina,' she ordered, her expression daring anyone to speak, 'bring us fruit.'

After the old maidservant had pushed her feet into her shoes and shuffled away, Safiya Sultana cleared her throat. 'Spies,' she said harshly. 'There are spies in this house.' She raised a hand, subduing the shocked cries that followed.

Mariana looked from face to face among the ladies. *Spies?*

'We do not know how many of our servants have been turned against us,' Safiya went on, 'but we must not blame them too much. They may have been tempted with gold, or they may fear for themselves or their families. But among our staff there are also those who can be trusted, even with our lives. Now, we have only a few precious moments to save Saboor. Under no circumstances can we allow him to fall again into the hands of the court. The Maharajah, as we have all heard, may die at any moment. Should he die, Saboor's life will be worth less than a cowrie shell.'

Blood thudded in Mariana's temples. She looked for Saboor, and saw him in the arms of a spindly girl who watched Safiya Sultana, her mouth open.

'When Mumtaz Bano died,' Safiya continued, searching the faces around her, 'we ourselves could not help Saboor. We could only wait here, praying with all our strength for his safe return. We did not know from which quarter help might come. Now, when he is once more in terrible danger, our circumstances are different. This time, with help from Allah Most Gracious, we ourselves will save him.'

A dubious sigh blew through the room.

'This time we have among us,' Safiya went on, drawing her audience with her, 'our bride, the young Angrezi woman who, disregarding the danger to herself, took Saboor from his

380

servant's arms at the Golden Temple and with her own hands brought him safely home to us.'

Heads swung from side to side in agreement. A shy-looking girl met Mariana's eyes for the first time.

Safiya's pudgy finger poked the air. 'She alone among all of us may leave this house in the necessary manner. Our bride has experience of the world outside, while we have only knowledge. She will do what is needed, will you not, daughter.'

This last was not a question; it was a deep-voiced command. Still, Safiya had left the way open for a refusal. Mariana's mind raced. Having never seen the street outside, she had no idea how busy it was. If a passerby had seen the Maharajah's men enter, an interested crowd, three or four deep, must already have gathered before the haveli's great, carved doors.

She and Saboor would never leave the haveli unnoticed. What would happen to them if they were caught? She did not need to ask. She knew enough of the Jasmine Tower. No one would protect Saboor from the wrath of the queens. No one would save her from the wrath of the Maharajah.

Rain entered a corner of a nearby window and trickled down the wall. Safiya Sultana waited, her eyes on Mariana's face. Sabooor watched her from across the room with the same round, expectant gaze that had melted her heart outside the Golden Temple, eleven days before. That gaze had made her feel capable of anything.

'Yes,' she replied, for the second time since yesterday. 'I will.'

Chapter Thirty-four

Safiya Sultana turned to the young girl who had come to Mariana's room. 'Zareen, go and bring me the oldest burqa you can find. Ah, here is Bina with the fruit,' she added in a warning tone as the elderly maidservant shuffled through the door bearing a tray of oranges and guavas.

All murmuring stopped. 'Spies,' said someone, under her breath.

Taking a guava and a sharp knife from the tray, Safiya Sultana cut out a wedge of rosy flesh with practised hands, dipped it into a little heap of salt on the tray and handed it with grave courtesy to the elderly lady beside her. 'Eat this, Ammi-jan,' she shouted into the old woman's ear.

The old lady took the fruit with a palsied hand, put it obediently into her mouth.

Safiya Sultana's face betrayed no anxiety. Mariana edged towards her on the floor, hoping to absorb some of her calm.

Safiya pointed to the door. 'Leave the tray with us, Bina,' she told the maidservant, 'and call Allahyar. Tell him to come up here at once. He is to stand outside the door for my instructions. Go, and close the door curtain on your way out.' She leaned over to Mariana. 'Look at these women before you,' she said quietly in her man's voice. 'They are my family. Some are wise, some unwise, all are good-hearted in their own way.' She put a hand on Mariana's knee. 'Together, we are about to undertake a journey as far from our own experience as an ocean voyage. Some of our ladies will not believe that you can succeed in the escape I have in mind. Others will see the sense in it and will have confidence. In any case, our prayers and our hearts will be with you.'

Mariana swallowed, trying not to think of the danger.

'I most certainly hope,' Safiya Sultana added more loudly, frowning around the crowded room, 'that none of you breathes a word of what we are about to do. Children, stand up.'

Mariana watched a dozen children straighten reluctantly and stand in a solemn brown-skinned row.

Safiya Sultana regarded them sternly. 'You must all leave the room now,' she said. 'Secrets can be difficult to keep. If you are not here, none of you can, by chance, betray your little brother.'

The whispering children rustled out, the larger ones carrying the smaller, leaving only Saboor. The ladies waited, moving only their eyes until a deep cough heard through the curtain revealed the presence of a man.

Safiya Sultana signalled for attention. The ladies leaned forward.

'Who is there?' she called out.

'It is I, Allahyar, Begum Sahib,' replied a male voice.

'He is Lala-Ji's personal servant,' one girl Mariana's age whispered to another.

'Allahyar,' ordered Safiya Sultana, 'you are to go to your uncle the storeroom keeper and get from him a small ball of opium.'

Mariana blinked. Opium?

A mumbled response came from behind the curtain.

'There is no use,' Safiya Sultana said firmly over the drumming of the rain, 'in trying to tell me that your uncle does not take opium. He has done so for thirty years.'

The ladies smiled.

'Ji, Begum Sahib,' said the male voice, after a pause.

'You will bring the opium here,' Safiya Sultana went on, 'and you will also bring a basket from the storeroom, the largest basket we have. You will then wait outside until a lady comes from this room and joins you. You will tell no one of these instructions. Do you understand me?'

'Ji, Sahib.'

'Go, then.'

Safiya Sultana looked at Mariana, studying her as if she were seeking something. 'My daughter,' she said, her deep voice softening, 'here is what you will do.'

Mariana returned the older woman's gaze. Unlike the malicious queens at the Citadel, Safiya had treated her like a daughter. Overcome with gratitude, Mariana felt a sudden urge to bury her head in Safiya Sultana's well-padded shoulder.

'I have sent for an old burqa,' the Shaikh's sister told her a little gruffly, 'the veil that our Punjabi women wear out of doors. We will put it over you, to conceal your face and hair, and your clothes. Wearing the burqa, you will go downstairs and, after passing through the kitchens, you will leave this house by the rear door. Allahyar, my brother's personal servant, will accompany you. He will walk a few paces in front of you.' She paused, her eyes moving from face to face, daring anyone to object. 'You will be posing as Allayar's wife.'

Mariana breathed in. But what of Saboor?

'The Maharajah's men may be watching the rear door,' Safiya Sultana warned, answering Mariana's unspoken question.

'Saboor will therefore not be with you as you pass out of the house. He will instead be lowered from that window.' She pointed across a tiled verandal to a window that gave onto the street below. 'In a basket.'

The women all tried to speak at once. Safiya Sultana held up a commanding hand.

'Do we not,' she asked the room in general, 'lower a basket to Vikram Anand, the sweetmeat seller, when we wish to enjoy his jalebees, his luddoos and his gulab jamons? And has not that same sweetmeat shop stood below our window for the past three generations?'

A thin lady near Mariana smiled as the room subsided. 'Of course, Vikram's best customer is Safiya herself,' she whispered.

'I have confidence that Vikram will help us,' Safiya told Mariana. 'He is known in the city for his charity and his level head.'

Mariana stared at the open window where Safiya had pointed. How did Safiya Sultana know what people in the city said about a sweet seller?

'Allhyar,' Safiya continued, 'will take Saboor from the basket. You will follow him as he carries the child towards the Delhi Gate. You will go through the gate after him, and on the road you will be overtaken by one of our palanquins.'

The gap-toothed aunt lifted her hands. 'Where is she to go?'

Safiya Sultana frowned.

'She should go to Kasur, to Hassan, of course,' contributed another woman. 'He is her husband. Where else should she go?'

Assent spread through the women.

Her heart thumping, Mariana shook her head. 'But Shalimar

is right here. Kasur is miles and miles away. Surely I must take Saboor to the British camp.'

Instead of answering, Safiya Sultana, signalled to the shy girl. 'Aalia, bring me a pen and ink, and some paper.' Turning to Mariana, she smiled grimly. 'The world is a strange place, Mariam, and the will of Allah Most Gracious is not for us to know. Wherever else you may wish to travel, this time you will journey, God willing, to Hassan's camp at Kasur.'

The burqa arrived. While Safiya Sultana wrote letters, Zareen gathered up the yards of cotton fabric that made up the burqa and fitted its embroidered cap carefully over Mariana's head. The dusty folds fell to her feet, causing her such a fit of sneezing that she did not hear what was being said through the curtain. Sniffing, she looked through the grille of cotton cutwork before her face, and saw that it offered a narrow, impaired field of vision. So this was what the women were able to see when they were out of doors. Could they see enough to avoid accidents? There was no side vision whatever. She moved her head experimentally to and fro, and saw the ladies nod their approval.

'Now,' someone said, 'no one will know she is foreign.'

Inside her cotton tent, Mariana sneezed again. No one would even know she was female.

She looked for Saboor, who had been sitting with one of his aunts. He was asleep, his body limp, a rim of something brown and sticky around his mouth.

Safiya Sultana pushed herself to her feet, the sheaf of papers in her hand, and took a book covered in heavy silk wrappings from the carved corner cupboard. She stood before Mariana, swaying slightly, her eyes half closed, murmuring something Mariana could not make out. Finished, she took a deep breath and blew three times in Mariana's direction.

386

'Take these,' she said. Reaching under the burqa, she pushed the papers into Mariana's hand. 'They are letters to our relations who live between here and Kasur. They will look after you and Saboor, and they will provide you with fresh bearers. Come, then.' Seizing Mariana's arm through the folds of cotton, she led her to the door, and held out the book, still in its wrappings. 'Kiss the Qur'an Sharif,' she commanded.

Mariana did not at all wish to kiss someone else's holy book, but Safiya Sultana pressed it against her lips through the cotton veil, then held it up, allowing her to pass under it on her way out of the room. Mariana would have preferred Safiya to embrace her, but there was no time for that. There was no time to be afraid, or even to bid the ladies goodbye.

'May Allah Most Gracious guide you.' Safiya Sultana's deep voice followed Mariana along the tiled veranda.

Through her peephole Mariana made out the slight figure of a man with orange hair, the same servant who had guided her to the Shaikh the first time she had come. He nodded and started for the narrow stairway that led down to the great kitchens below. The stairway was dark. She felt her way carefully down, holding the dusty burqa away from her feet.

The kitchens were hot and smelled of cooking fat and spices. Women squatted on the floor, away from the fiery heat of three massive stoves, slicing onions and crushing a yellow ball of paste between two stones. Through an open door, Mariana could see rain splashing onto a small brick courtyard. This was the way out that Safiya had described.

Allahyar signalled. Mariana stepped into the courtyard after him, and within a few moments was drenched to the skin. Across the courtyard, a low door led into a narrow cobbled alley with an overflowing gutter running along one of its sides.

Had she been able to extricate her hands from the sodden burqa, Mariana could have touched the houses on either side of the alley at once. Icy water ran down inside her fitted cap and dripped from her cutwork peephole.

Allahyar strode past an armed man loitering halfway down the alley. Was that one of the Maharajah's men? As she hurried to catch up with Allahyar, Mariana failed to see a loose cobblestone. Falling, she reached forward to save herself, and instantly doubled into a ball as her trapped hands forced the heavy burqa to drag her head downward. The gutter beside her stank. One side of the burqa had fallen into the running water and was now drenched in filth. As she scrabbled for the papers she had dropped, a pair of hands grasped one of her arms through the soaked cloth. Allahyar's disgusted face passed close to hers as he hauled her to her feet, then disappeared as he moved off.

The bustling, familiar British camp had never seemed so distant, but Mariana no longer cared. If Safiya Sultana had carried out the other part of her plan, Saboor waited, drugged and helpless, in a sweetmeat shop below Safiya's veranda window, while other armed men patrolled the city lanes, ready to pounce on him and drag him away to the Citadel.

She must hurry. Ignoring the wet and the cold and the stench of sewage, she toiled along the alley and past the armed man, hugging the wall opposite the gutter, her whole being intent on escape. Reaching the alley's end at last, she shuffled out onto a wider cobbled lane, and found herself beside a small shop that had been built into a corner of the Waliullah haveli's wall.

I would not mind having you beside me in battle, Papa had said after she rescued Jeremy Harfield from drowning. That, like this, had been a desperate situation, partly of her own making. What would he say to her now?

Vikram Anand, maker and seller of sweetmeats, was accustomed to seeing a basket lowered from the upper windows of Qamar Haveli. The ladies upstairs enjoyed his cooking, none more so than Safiya Sultana herself, who sent for his wares by this simple method at least once a week. He had it on authority that this important lady had described his jalebees as the best in the city. He was therefore unsurprised when a basket appeared from above and dangled near his elbow.

He pushed aside a bowl of flour and wiped his hands on his clothes.

'O, Vikram,' called a deep, familiar voice from above. 'Do not sit idle when there is work to do. Take our basket and do the necessary.'

Vikram leaned from his sheltering overhang and pulled the soaking basket towards him. It was heavy. He pulled the sides apart and looked inside. There, with rain lying like tears on his face, lay Saboor Baba, the child sought by all of Lahore. There was no mistaking the child's identity. Vikram knew of every betrothal, wedding and birth in the city. Hadn't he himself made the luddoos, each covered in a gossamer sheet of silver, that had gone to all the great houses, announcing the birth of this very child?

Had anyone seen? Glancing anxiously about, he reached into his shop for a banana leaf, and covered the laden basket, hiding its contents from view. Working as rapidly as he could with the wet rope, he untied the basket and put it behind him, out of sight. That done, he arranged himself once more in his usual place, and breathed deeply.

It was said in the city that Shaikh Waliullah's grandson had brought the Maharajah luck. Perhaps that explained the curious desperation the child's disappearance had caused the old man. How many times since Saboor Baba's vanishing had

389

the Maharajah sent high officials into the streets to investigate his disappearance, to ask the same questions each time
they came?

Vikram stirred his vat of boiling milk. Even after everyone
knew that the child had somehow found his way home to the
haveli, the visits had not stopped. Only this morning, a showily
dressed eunuch had come, asking for the child. Vikram had
been unwilling to answer then. Now he knew the truth. A
daring escape was to be made. He nodded to himself. One
glance had told him the baby behind him was drugged. For
that, he was grateful. There was no knowing how long they
would have to wait. He frowned with pride as he stirred his
milk, feeling the weight of the Waliullah family's trust upon
his thin shoulders.

A man who sits all day frying sweetmeats on one fire and
boiling down milk on the other has patience, but Vikram Anand
needed to wait only a short time before an orange-haired man
appeared, standing beneath the dripping canopy in front of
his stall. Allahyar was well known to Vikram. He came
several times a month to collect sweets for the men's side
of the household and often stopped to pass the time of day,
enjoying a moment to watch the life of the city pass by the
little shop.

'Have you a package for me?' asked Allahyar cautiously,
without preamble.

Vikram noticed the female in a filthy burqa who stood
behind Allahyar. Confused, he looked silently at his hands.
Do the necessary, Safiya Sultana's voice had said.

Allahyar's eyes darted to a pushing crowd by the main
entrance to the haveli, not thirty feet away. 'I believe the
lady Safiya Sultana has sent something for me.'

Vikram Anand made up his mind. 'Ah, yes, the lady

Safiya Sultana has sent something. Shall I give it to you in the basket?'

The tense face before him relaxed slightly. 'No, I do not want the basket.'

Vikram reached behind him and lifted the banana leaf from Saboor's sleeping form.

Allahyar's face creased into a smile. 'I am to tell you,' he told the sweet seller as he hoisted the sleeping baby to his shoulder, 'that in consideration of your trouble, there is something for you in the basket.'

After Allahyar strode off, the woman shuffling after him, Vikram Anand felt in the bottom of the basket. His fingers found a coin. It was a gold mohur.

Nodding gravely, he tucked the treasure into his clothes. The Waliullah family had a sense of occasion that distinguished them from the other families of Lahore. A few copper coins would have been enough, considering the small work he had done. But that would have devalued the child. To put the coin on Saboor's body where it could be seen would have devalued Vikram. By hiding the gold coin under the child, Safiya Sultana had, in one gesture, complimented Vikram and demonstrated her family's love for their baby.

'Vikram, are you expecting to keep my basket?'

He should have known someone was watching. He started, jerked from his musing by the deep voice two storeys above him.

Chapter Thirty-five

'Move out, move out!' By the time the Maharajah's armed men forced their way into Qamar Haveli, Yar Mohammad the groom had been waiting in a doorway opposite Vikram's sweet shop for nearly three hours.

An unsatisfactory meal of dry bread forgotten in his hand, he had watched the soaking horses clatter past, their riders' shouts interrupting his thoughts. Now he watched their leader pound on the haveli door, demanding admittance for his men and for a carved palanquin carried by bearers wearing scarlet loincloths and turbans.

These armed men, he knew, could be on no errand of mercy. He remembered the previous afternoon at the British camp, when he had hurried from the horse lines to Shafi Sahib's neat tent.

'I have seen something,' he had said as he entered, his eyes roving to a new feature of Shafi Sahib's tent, a string bed in one corner where a man lay, breathing heavily, his face covered in a poultice of boiled leaves.

'Speak,' Shafi Sahib had replied from where he sat on his own bed near the door, his prayer beads dangling from his fingers. He gestured towards the figure on the bed. 'You may speak in front of him. That is Ahmad, Saboor's servant.'

Yar Mohammad willed himself not to stare at the injured man who, if he lived, would for ever wear the mark of shame on his face. He imagined himself in the man's place, with rough hands holding him down and other hands jerking his head back by the hair while the swordsman prepared to bring down his blade. Who could not have respect for such a sacrifice?

'I have seen a great dust cloud enter the city and surround Shaikh Waliullah's haveli,' Yar Mohammad began.

Shafi Sahib's beads ceased their clicking. 'Go on.'

'After that, the vision became unclear. Something seemed to come from the haveli and pass out through the cloud. I am almost sure there was a snake somewhere nearby, but all I can say for certain is that I saw the dust cloud.'

Shafi Sahib frowned at the wall of his tent, his eyes moving as if he were looking at something Yar Mohammad could not see. Yar Mohammad allowed himself a glance towards the man in the corner. Faced with such a punishment, would he, like Saboor's servant, have refused to speak?

'As you know,' Shafi Sahib said, 'a cloud of dust signifies an emergency.' He closed his eyes and rubbed his forehead. 'As it happens, Shaikh Waliullah will be absent from his house all tomorrow morning. I suggest you go into the city at dawn and keep watch outside the haveli door until Shaikh Sahib returns.'

Yar Mohammad stiffened. 'Will there be danger?'

'Of that I am not certain. But, Yar Mohammad,' Shafi Sahib had said with a smile, 'it is you, not I, who received the little vial. If it is His will, Allah Most Gracious will keep you safe.'

A crowd had begun to collect as the horsemen pounded upon the carved door of Qamar Haveli. Tightness in Yar Mohammad's chest told him that this was, indeed, the emergency of his dream. These men had certainly come in search

393

of the child Saboor, intending to take him as a hostage to the Citadel. They must intend to take Memsahib also, as she was now the child's stepmother. Why else would an elegant palanquin with a team of bearers have followed the horsemen inside? The horsemen had carried swords and matchlocks. Armed with only his curved kukri knife, he would be useless.

The crowd at the door grew larger. Raised voices argued over the family's response to this new crisis. Would the Shaikh perform magic again? Would the Maharajah punish him? As Yar Mohammad listened, coils of terror wrapped themselves about his heart. What unknown, dangerous work had he undertaken? What if, unsure of his mission, he made a mistake so terrible that he endangered them all?

Coolies passed his doorway, bent beneath heavy loads of charcoal and rags. Horses trotted by, their riders wrapped in dripping shawls. A picture rose in Yar Mohammad's clouded mind of Shaikh Waliullah and Shafi Sahib seated side by side in the upstairs room at Qamar Haveli. *You and no one else*, the Shaikh had told him, while Shafi Sahib nodded his agreement, *will know when the time has come to act*.

Yar Mohammad stepped onto the wet stones and started towards the Delhi Gate. He would go back to Shalimar, to Shafi Sahib. Someday, perhaps, he would be braver, would know how and when to act, but today he needed advice.

He had not taken three steps before a familiar-looking red-haired man hurried past him, followed by a stumbling figure in a stained burqa. The man's eyes shifted from side to side as he walked, as if he were afraid of being observed. On his wet shoulder lay a sleeping baby.

The man was Allahyar, the servant who had taken Yar Mohammad to meet the Shaikh and Shafi Sahib on a day still vivid in Yar Mohammad's memory. The baby was, without question, Saboor Baba. And if he was not mistaken about her manner of walking, the struggling figure in the filthy burqa was the English memsahib.

As she hastened past Yar Mohammad towards the great stone gateway, the woman lifted the edge of her burqa away from a pair of ruined slippers. Oh, yes, it was Memsahib. No woman of the city would reveal her ankles like that. He must warn her not to give herself away! Uncertain no more, he fixed his eyes on her back and lengthened his stride.

Men and animals crowded the street near the old public bath, blocking his way. Afraid he might lose sight of the odd trio, he elbowed other men aside, bruising his shin on a fruit seller's stall, jostling a blind man's hand from his guide's shoulder. Then he was through the gate and past the heaving crowd at the entrance to the caravanserai, the rest house of travellers. The crowd thinned, and there they were again, the red-headed man, the lady and the sleeping child.

As he drew breath to call out to Allahyar, Yar Mohammad found himself flung aside by an outstretched arm as a wide old palanquin drove past, its bearers shouting warnings as they ran. Recovering his balance, he looked ahead in time to see it halt and Memsahib's burqa-clad figure climb inside. As he began, panting, to close the distance between them, he saw Allahyar hand the baby inside and slide the door shut.

Still running, he watched helplessly as the bearers lifted the poles to their shoulders and started off again in the direction of the Delhi road. Desperate, he searched the crowd for a sign of Allahyar, but the red-headed man was gone. As the chill downpour soaked through his thin clothes, Yar Mohammad began to trudge along the road behind the speeding palanquin, his shoulders hunched against the rain.

* * *

So intent had Yar Mohammad been on following the three figures before him that he failed to notice the smartly dressed eunuch who stood in the crowded shelter of the Delhi Gate, staring in surprise after Allahyar and his companions. He missed seeing the eunuch turn to a lanky, sallow-faced young man, and gesture with long arms towards the sleeping bundle on the man's shoulder.

'I know that child,' Gurbashan said excitedly, ignoring the water dripping from the end of his nose. 'I would know him anywhere.' He put his mouth next to the young man's ear. 'It does not matter how he has come to be on the road in the company of servants,' he whispered. 'That is the child Saboor. I am telling you, it is he. How could I fail to know him after I spent four days taking him to the Maharajah's camp? I recognized him once before, whatever they may say, and I have now recognized him again.'

'Shall we follow them?' asked the young man, staring after the stumbling woman.

'No,' replied the eunuch. 'I know where they are going. Why give only information when we can present Saboor himself to the Maharajah and get the full reward? I know exactly how to get the brat. Come with me.'

It was late afternoon when the eunuch Gurbashan and the sallow young man made inquiries at a mean house in a narrow alley in the city. Then they stood and waited for the man they sought, jostled by noisy strangers, while music floated from the adjoining houses and the pungent smell of perfumes mixed with the filth of the street.

'I do not like this,' the young man said, his feet dancing nervously on the stones. 'I do not like this at all.'

'If you do not like it,' snapped Gurbashan, looking hastily

396

behind him, 'then be gone. I will keep all the reward for myself.'

A narrow-faced man appeared and stood before them, studying them with lifeless eyes. Although he was not old, he had no front teeth. Behind him stood a boy whose face was round and ruddy beneath a layer of dirt. Both were dressed in rags. The narrow-faced man and the boy waited, saying nothing, gazing hungrily at the eunuch's clothes.

'I understand,' said Gurbashan, drawing himself up, 'that you are well-versed in the stealing of children.'

The man offered no reply. The boy behind him stared.

'I want to know how good you are.' The eunuch lowered his eyes and poked the ground in front of him with a sandalled foot. 'We desire the services of someone who can do what we need.'

The man drew his lips back, revealing more missing teeth. His hair was matted and dusty. The ruddy-faced boy smirked.

'I have stolen more than thirty children,' the man replied, his lisping voice as flat as his eyes. 'I sell them for labour, or I sell them, especially the girls, to these places.' He tilted his head towards a row of open-windowed houses, the only ones in the city where women were not hidden but displayed. 'Some,' he added, 'I sell to the beggars.'

Perspiration gleamed on the sallow forehead of the eunuch's young companion.

The dead-eyed man gestured, palm up. 'Why is your friend so afraid? He is too old for the market I sell to. And it is not I who deforms the children.' He shrugged, pointing with his thumb at an impossibly twisted man lying in a doorway. 'It is others who break their bones to arouse the sympathy of the pious. They know how to—'

The eunuch hastily raised his hands. 'How do you work?'

'The work takes skill,' the man answered. 'I know how to enter a house silently, in the darkness. I can drug a child without killing it.' His half-smile disappeared. 'The children I steal do not cry out.'

Gurbashsan's companion swallowed noisily. The eunuch scratched his head, his eyes on the cobblestones. After a time, he nodded. 'All right,' he agreed, 'but remember, if the baby is not delivered in perfect condition, you will get no money. Now, listen while I describe him, and tell you where he may be found.'

'You told me you would frighten the child thieves with threats,' whispered the sallow-faced boy later as Gurbashan propelled him away, a long arm about his shoulders. 'You said you would warn them that they would be tortured to death by the Maharajah's soldiers if Saboor Baba died.'

'When did I say that? I never said such a thing,' replied the eunuch, turning to look quickly behind him as they reached the alley's end and rounded the corner into a wide lane.

'*What?*' Lord Auckland's face, reflected in the silver table ornaments, had turned crimson. 'You say that the girl was not there when you called at the Shaikh's house? You say she had gone off without a word on some native errand, when she knew perfectly well that you were coming to fetch her?' He glared at Macnaghten. 'They must have hidden her somewhere in the house. Why did you not protest, demand that they produce her? If she was not there, why did you not insist on having someone take you to her?'

Macnaghten speared a piece of fish with his fork before replying. 'Your lordship may have forgotten that natives of the Shaikh's class seclude their women. It was therefore impossible for me to go to Miss Givens. It also seemed to me that the Shaikh was telling the truth.' Macnaghten chewed deliberately. It was true. Surprised though he had been at the girl's absence, he had not questioned the Shaikh's promise that Miss Givens would, God willing, present herself at the British camp four days from today. The man was clearly someone of importance among the natives. He had spoken with authority.

'Shaikh Waliullah has given me his word that Miss Givens will call on you and your lady sisters four days from today when this camp reaches the city of Kasur.' Macnaghten watched Lord Auckland push potatoes angrily onto his fork. 'I therefore take full responsibility for her safe arrival, barring, of course, some unforeseen accident upon the road.' He raised his hands. 'I assume that she will then remain with the camp for the return journey to Calcutta.'

Aides murmured at the far end of the table. 'Four days from now,' observed Lord Auckland darkly, 'you will not be at this camp. You will be partway to Kabul with the army.'

Macnaghten's appetite left him. It was no use talking to Lord Auckland; the man was an ass. He put down his knife and fork and refused the rest of the dishes. His toes curling inside his shoes, he waited for dinner to end.

Shafi Sahib let out a gentle sigh. 'Yar Mohammad,' he repeated, 'you must take the road to Kasur.' The string bed creaked under him. 'I am certain that Memsahib has taken Saboor Baba to his father. She must have done so – there is no sign of her here.'

Yar Mohammad said nothing. At a loss, unable to keep up with Memsahib's palanquin, he had followed the road as far as Shalimar, then stopped at the British camp, hoping to find her there. He had waited for hours, posting himself near the guarded entrance in the red wall. As night fell, he had gone to the back of the red compound and entered by the kitchen gate, to discover Dittoo, sleeping by a cooking fire.

'No,' Dittoo had said, shaking his head, 'Memsahib has not returned.'

Yar Mohammad was tired. His head ached from trying to decide.

'Go, brother,' Shafi Sahib told him. 'Go now. You must travel all night. With luck, you will find a bullock cart that will carry you. But you must go. Otherwise, you will not find them on the road tomorrow morning.'

Chapter Thirty-six

In a corner room at the Citadel, the Maharajah leaned from his low bed and spat into an engraved silver bowl.

He spoke with effort. 'What am I to believe, Aziz? Is Saboor at his house in the city, ill with smallpox as his family claims, or is he at the British camp, as the eunuch insists?'

'Only Allah knows,' replied the chief minister gently.

The Maharajah coughed weakly, his eye closed. Azizuddin drew closer to the bed.

'I hope he is not at his house,' the Maharajah said. 'If he is anywhere on the road or even at the British camp, Gurbashan's child stealers will be sure to find him.'

'Child stealers?' Aziz's neck went rigid. 'You have allowed the eunuch to hire child stealers?'

'I am old, Aziz. I am weary of everything.' The Maharajah shivered a little. 'Today I have not the heart even to tease the British. I need my Saboor.'

'Ah, Mahraj,' Aziz said softly, a hand on the bedcovers, 'you are tired only because you are unwell. Why, only two days ago we were—'

'Leave it, Aziz,' his king interrupted, turning his head away. 'Without my Saboor, I will not live another three months.'

After some time, the old man's laboured breathing became regular. Aziz signalled for a servant to take his place beside the bed, then he stole quietly away.

'Stop, stop!' Mariana pounded with her fist on the planquin's roof. She could wait no longer to relieve herself. 'Get off, Saboor,' she snapped, pushing the little boy from her lap. 'You're making Mariana feel worse.'

He crawled away, his face puckered into a baby glare. She slid open the panel and looked out. They were passing a place where thorn bushes grew thickly along the road. This was exactly what she needed. 'Stop, I say,' she repeated, pounding again. 'Stop!'

She shifted her body on the thin mattress. Yesterday, after their escape from Qamar Haveli, she had balled up her filthy burqa and hurled it from the moving palanquin. Since then, dressed in the rust-coloured silks Safiya Sultana had given her, she had entertained Saboor in this creaking box with no view of the passing landscape and no idea where they would stop. This was not at all like the long journey from Calcutta to Simla with Uncle Adrian and Aunt Claire. She missed Uncle Adrian's arrangements — tea and coffee, and regular opportunities for the ladies to retire discreetly into stands of bushes along the way.

Dear Uncle Adrian. She had not thought of him for some time. So much had happened since she had last written. How would her aunt and uncle respond when they learned the truth? She imagined Aunt Claire being carried unconscious to her room, leaving Uncle Adrian to sit alone, shaking his head, her letter in his hand.

But for all its fright and discomfort, what a time this had been! Surely Uncle Adrian would understand the adventure of it. No Englishwoman could ever have been prepared for marriage by Indian queens, or seen a case of snake bite being cured by a Shaikh. No one Mariana knew had stayed with natives while travelling in India, but she had, although that had certainly been the worst part of her journey so far. Last night, Safiya's female relatives had crowded around her in the large village house where she had been taken. Some had asked indecent, prying questions about Mariana's clothes and habits, and some had stared, veils drawn over their mouths and noses, as if she were some evil fairy. One narrow-eyed woman had even shooed her children away, looking fearfully over her shoulder, as if Mariana's presence were enough to poison everyone in the house. How could Safiya Sultana be related to people like that?

The palanquin stopped at last. She looked out again. Her bearers had understood her needs, and chosen well. She wished she had something to give the nameless sirdar bearer. He had stopped in a neat clearing where upturned stones had been arranged near a heap of cold ashes. Surrounding the clearing, thorn trees and bushes offered protection.

'Go to the bearers, there's an angel,' she said, patting Saboor on his back as he clambered after her out of the palki. 'Take him to do soo-soo,' she ordered, as she started for the bushes.

Like all the bearers along the route, the men had turned their backs the instant she emerged, but they welcomed Saboor when he danced over to where they had squatted down to rest. She stepped carefully, skirting the largest of the bushes, looking for a good hiding place.

The bearer's voices filtering through the bushes grew faint.

She crouched down gratefully. This evening, if all went well, she would arrive at Kasur. There she would ask the palanquin bearers to wait, she would kiss Saboor goodbye, and then hand him over to his father. She shifted her feet among the leaves. There would be no need for conversation with Hassan, or any long farewells. She would simply climb back into the palanquin and find the British camp. Once there, she would somehow live without Saboor.

She must also live without Fitzgerald, who had already departed for Afghanistan with the army. She could hardly bear to think of him now, knowing the pain she had caused him, but in spite of everything, she hoped for his forgiveness. Surely when she had written the truth to him he would understand what she had done, the terrible risk she had taken to save the Afghan Campaign.

Oh, please let him love her still, if only in one tiny corner of his heart.

The British camp should not be difficult to find. After leaving Shalimar, it would, like her, have followed the road to Kasur. Proceeding over much-travelled terrain with no rain since the downpour on the day of her escape with Saboor, it would most likely arrive there when she did, in three days' time. Heaven alone knew what the British party would say to her when she reappeared, out of nowhere, four days late, having missed Mr Macnaghten at the Shaikh's house.

A squirrel leaped from branch to branch above her head. It was too late to worry about what people would say. Of course, the Shaikh's family expected her merely to call upon the Eden ladies in order to assure everyone of her good health, and then return to the haveli without Saboor. But once she was safely at camp, she had no intention of leaving again. Sixteen days of adventure seemed more than enough. Not even Safiya Sultana could persuade her to spend the rest of her days in a walled city house with a group of native ladies.

Mariana sighed. Her departure from the haveli had not

been graceful, but it had been effective. The queens, Shaikh Waliullah, Safiya Sultana and the aunts were behind her now. Soon, even her lovely little Saboor would be only a memory. She watched a column of ants march past her, towards the carcass of a beetle. What would a palanquin ride be like without Saboor's edgy little self, all elbows and feet, scrambling over her, trying to open the panel, insisting that she bounce him on her lap?

As she half stood, fumbling with the waist cord of her loose trousers, shouting erupted from the clearing. Something was wrong. Silently, she moved towards the edge of the bushes. She stopped.

A man's voice spoke with gritty authority. 'We want her gold. That is all.'

Thieves! Where was Saboor? She leaned forward, desperately afraid to make a sound.

Another man spoke, closer by. He punctuated his words with hollow thumps, as if he were slapping the top of the palanquin with an open palm. 'You are our mother, our sister,' he said, his voice a tenor whine. 'We wish you no harm. We only want your money and your jewellery. If you throw them out of the palki, we will leave you in peace. Give us your gold. That is all we want, nothing more.'

'You fool,' barked the first voice, 'she is not in the palki. You are talking to yourself, Suraj.'

Mariana held her breath.

'Begum Sahib,' the first man called. 'Come out of the bushes.'

Could he see her? Which way was he looking? She peered through the foliage, but could see nothing. She kept still, all of her being focused on quieting her breathing.

'Come out. We will not harm you.'

405

Sounds of scuffling and grunting were followed by a sharp male cry. 'If you come out now,' the first man said, the roughness in his voice turning to poison, 'we will not harm the child.'

Saboor's wail started on a low note and rose swiftly to a high pitch, where it remained, drawn out, wavering like an infant version of the call to prayer. *Allah-hu-Akbar*, God is great.

A long thorny branch lay at Mariana's feet. She jerked it from its place, braced her slippered foot against it, and with one sharp motion snapped it in two. It was not much of a weapon, but it would have to do.

Holding the branch over her head, she rushed, screaming, from her hiding place and into the open, just as an agonized shriek from one of the thieves drowned out the sound of Saboor's voice. The bearers huddled in a terrified circle on the ground, their arms protecting their heads. Beside the palanquin, his weapons clanking, a small man in dirty clothing had turned towards the sound of the cry, Saboor in his arms. Two more thieves, one of them bloody and sobbing, backed away towards the road, flailing their arms as if warding off an invisible demon. The injured one began to run jerkily, bent double, clutching at his leg. Shreds of red-stained cloth hung from his shoulder. Blood ran into the dust from behind his knee.

'Put the child down,' shouted a voice Mariana knew well. 'Put him down and be gone! Sons of shame. Pigs! Dogs!'

The thieves did as they were ordered. The small man beside the palanquin dropped Saboor and fled across the clearing and onto the road without stopping to help his friends. The third man turned and followed him, dragging his gabbling and wounded companion with him.

406

Mariana threw down her stick, knelt in the dust and gathered Saboor, still howling, onto her lap. When she looked up, the thieves had vanished. The bearers now gaped at someone sitting on one of the upturned stones, his head buried in his hands.

It was Yar Mohammad, of all people, the tall groom from the British camp. Beside him on the ground lay a heavy, wicked-looking knife, the blood on its curved blade filmed with dust. He was weeping.

Yar Mohammad did not look up at the sound of approaching feet, but he saw before him the mud-stained slippers of the memsahib, guardian of Saboor, whom he had last seen clothed in a filthy burqa at the Delhi Gate, and who had just now run, wild-faced and screaming, from the bushes, her veil fallen to her shoulders, a thorny branch in her hands. The slippers were pointed towards him. They waited.

He would not weep before a woman. Heavy with shame, his eyes on the ground, he got politely to his feet. Perhaps she would go away soon and leave him to his grief. He needed to forget the sickening feeling of the knife as it cut the flesh of the brigand's shoulder, separating muscle from bone. To Yar Mohammad's hand, the act had felt like an execution. Worse, while sweeping his knife sideways and out of the way, he had cut again, this time slicing the tendons at the back of the man's leg.

The memsahib seated herself on a stone. Her face, still grey from fright, was now filling with curiosity. From her lap Saboor Baba, quiet now, regarded him intently.

'You have done a brave thing, Yar Mohammad,' she said in Urdu, 'but how have you come to be here? Why are you not at camp, at the horse lines?'

Wrenching his mind to the present, Yar Mohammad coughed.

407

He wiped his face. 'I have followed you since yesterday,' he said, then hesitated. 'I thought I had lost you until I saw the palki, then the baba.'

She looked puzzled. 'Why have you followed us? How do you know Shaikh Waliullah's palanquin?'

How should he answer? He had walked most of the night and part of the morning, searching the road for that very palki.

'Sit,' she said. 'Speak.'

He lowered himself to the ground and extended his arms over his knees. His fingers picked indecisively at each another. She was the Guardian. After what she had just done, he could have no doubt of that. Perhaps it was his duty to tell her of his dreams, of his wondrous meeting with the Shaikh. He blinked. The story would take some time to tell, and he was not a teller of stories.

'There is so much to tell,' he said.

'There is time,' she said kindly. 'Begin at the beginning.'

He would not begin at the very beginning, for Shaikh Waliullah had forbidden him to speak of the vision in which he received the small ceramic vial.

'One morning at the British camp,' he began, watching a beetle hurrying over a dried leaf, 'I had a dream of smoke, and of a lioness . . .'

When he had finished, the Englishwoman stared off into the distance for a long time without speaking.

'A lioness,' she said finally, her voice sounding far away. 'Shafi Sahib, interpreter of dreams. That is why I felt I was being watched . . .' Her voice trailed off. 'Tell me one more thing,' she said, sitting straighter. 'Why were you weeping?'

Yar Mohammad bit his lip. 'I did not mean to hurt the thief so badly.' He glanced to where his kukri knife still lay in the dust. 'He will never walk again. If he had been a horse, I would have been forced to cut his throat.'

The British camp had done its travelling for the day. Teams of coolies had erected the durbar tent and the red compound wall hours ago. Since then, the dead-eyed man and the ruddy-faced boy had waited, squatting beside the avenue in the shade of the durbar tent, watching the folded entrance to the red compound.

The boy spat into the dust. 'We should have made that eunuch come with us, Jagoo,' he said. 'He would easily recognize the child. How do we know we have not missed him?'

'Be quiet.' Jagoo sucked air through the gaps between his teeth and turned his flat gaze on the boy. 'We haven't missed him. The eunuch swore that he is here. Stop giving advice and watch for that bent-over manservant the eunuch described. He will lead us to the brat.'

Since yesterday, they had travelled with the camp, walking towards Kasur, unnoticed among a crowd of labourers and baggage animals. Yesterday, as soon as the camp had been erected, they had posted themselves at the back of the compound and watched the kitchen entrance. They had not seen even a glimpse of the child.

'Perhaps he is ill,' Jagoo said. 'Whoever has him is being careful, keeping him out of sight.'

They had stolen their food by day and slept in the open at night, making their own small fire with pilfered charcoal. Now, as they waited by the durbar tent, all sorts of people passed them on the avenue. Some were children, ripe for stealing, but none answered the description of the child Saboor for whom the eunuch was willing to pay such a high price.

'We have missed him,' insisted the boy.

'You know nothing.' Jagoo's voice was less certain than before.

The boy scratched himself. 'I know some things,' he said as they watched a passing bullock cart. 'I know that Hassan Ali Khan, the father of Saboor, has been sent out of Lahore on the Maharajah's work. And I know where he is.'

Jagoo stopped chewing his wad of betel and tobacco. 'What have you not told me?'

'The child's father is at Kasur. Before we left the city, while you were asleep, people were talking outside our door. They said Hassan Sahib, the son of Shaikh Waliullah, has gone to Kasur to get tax money for the Maharajah. He is not more than ten miles from here.'

Jagoo's blow caught the boy cruelly on his temple, knocking him sideways against the canvas of the durbar tent.

'The eunuch is a fool,' he rasped as the boy crawled to his knees, a hand to his head. 'And so are you!'

Chapter Thirty-seven

Sunday, 29 December

It was dark by the time Mariana's palanquin stopped outside the little walled city of Kasur. She half listened, yawning, while her bearers asked a passerby directions to Hassan's tents.

'An-nah!' Saboor murmured in her ear as he tugged at one of the enamelled bangles on her wrist.

Soon she would be back at the British camp, although nothing there would be the same as before. How exciting, how filled with promise even the dullest camp day had seemed only a short time ago. Now, after the scandal, even the White Rabbit would find it hard to take her part. Lord Auckland, she knew, was lost to her for ever. She was not speaking to the Eden sisters. With luck, Major Byrne and the doctor would ignore her. If not, they would make unkind remarks. Mr Macnaghten, thank goodness, would already have left for Afghanistan to be chief political officer there. But there was no sense worrying about it. For all the unpleasantness it promised her, she could not deny that the British camp was where she belonged. At least she would be spared any more lectures about avoiding the natives. And she could always count on Dittoo, Yar Mohammad and Munshi Sahib. There was another ray of hope too. According to Yar Mohammad, the great Shafi Sahib

411

was staying at the camp. How maddening that the interpreter of dreams had been there all along, attached somehow to the army or the government, in the curious way of natives, and she had not known! Perhaps he would interpret her dream of the guided ship. He might give her hope for the days to come.

'Come here, Saboor,' she said, beckoning the child who had crawled to the foot of the palanquin. 'See?'

When he crept back, she dropped her thin silk veil over his face, and then pulled it off in a quick gesture, watching his smile broaden, waiting for his chirping laugh.

It was Shafi Sahib, of course, who had sent the message, delivered by Yar Mohammad, on the night she had taken Saboor. *You have done well. Wait for your instructions. Tell no one what you have done.* She tried to imagine his face. Did he, like Shaikh Waliullah, radiate a mysterious power? According to Yar Mohammad, Shafi Sahib was a Punjabi, and the old Shaikh's childhood friend. But what if he had remained behind in Lahore after the departure of the British camp? She would be so disappointed.

The palanquin began to move. Tired of Mariana's game, Saboor had climbed onto her lap in order to pull on her gold necklace. Cooing to him, she unwound his fingers from the gold links, imagining Shaikh Waliullah's house, and the view from the ladies' upper window. Perhaps, at this moment, the Shaikh and Shafi Sahib, both wearing tall headdresses, were conversing in his courtyard by the painted portico, while the Shaikh's family ladies sat together on the sheet-covered floor of the upstairs room. She sighed. Safiya Sultana had been so strong, so motherly, she would have liked, just once, to have wrapped her arms about Safiya's bulky form.

Perhaps it was a good thing that it would take months and months for the camp, now without its army, to return to

Calcutta. She needed time to decide on her future. Should she return to England and live quietly with her family, or should she remain in Calcutta and brave the inevitable gossip?

She *must* write to her mother and father. It was no use putting the letter off any longer. She had already rehearsed it a hundred times. *A dreadful thing has happened, for which I must take the blame. I did something I thought was right, but the storm of events that followed has left me in serious trouble . . .*

Would they forgive her?

The palanquin thumped to the ground. With a little groan, Mariana swung her feet out through the open panel and stood, waiting while Saboor, who liked to do it himself, clambered out on his own.

The night was cold, the air sharp. Stars made a dazzling tapestry overhead. A large tent with a curving roof loomed before her. Outside, by a flickering fire, two men leaned on bolsters, smoking a hookah on the carpet between them. Seeing her, one of them stopped speaking in mid-sentence.

Servants stood around her palanquin, each one wearing the same shade of blue she had seen on the servants at the Shaikh's house. As Mariana hoisted Saboor to her hip, they all gaped in momentary astonishment, then spun about, turning their backs as men everywhere had done since she left Lahore. 'Saboor Baba,' she heard one of them murmur. 'The memsahib has brought Saboor Baba.'

Ordering her bearers to wait, she paused by the entrance, then, coughing to announce her presence, pushed aside the door hanging and entered.

The tent was vacant and icy cold. Sandalwood hung in the air, igniting her memory. She hesitated. Someone had followed her inside, a lamp glowing in his hand. She turned.

Hassan put the lamp down and approached her, his hands

413

extended to take Saboor, his face a mask of tenderness. When Saboor wrapped his arms round his father's neck, Hassan kissed him several times, then frowned at Mariana, one hand stroking his son's small back. 'Why have you brought him here? What has happened?' His gaze was as intense as it had been the night of their wedding. She saw that his naked feet were long. They were not as beautiful as his hands. He was lighter-skinned than she remembered. She saw that his nose was crooked, as if it had once been broken.

'Four days ago, after you left the haveli,' she answered, shivering from the cold, 'armed men came from the Citadel to take Saboor away. To save him, your Aunt Safiya had him lowered in a basket from an upper window.'

A string bed stood in one corner of the tent. Hassan sat Saboor on the bed, then bent over a trunk at its foot. He straightened, a length of embroidered woollen cloth in his hands. He held it out. 'From a window? Then what happened?'

She wrapped the shawl round her shoulders. It smelled of tobacco leaves. 'The basket was lowered to a sweetmeat shop, where your father's servant Allahyar picked him up. Pretending to be Allahyar's wife, I followed them through the Delhi Gate. Then your family's palanquin came and I got into it with Saboor.'

He picked Saboor up again, and pointed to the bed. 'Why don't you sit down?'

'No.' Mariana backed away. Let this moment be over quickly. Later there would be time to grieve for Saboor, to remember. 'I must leave.'

Hassan, too, wore a shawl. Thrown over his long coat, it fell in elegant, finely embroidered folds over his shoulders and down his back. He jogged Saboor gently up and down, his nose

414

against his son's cheek. 'You should rest,' he said, as if he had not heard her. 'And I must ask you, what has happened to your burqa? Why was your veil not on your head just now when you got out of the palki?'

'My veil? My burqa?' She stared. What did her clothes matter?

His tone developed an unpleasant edge. 'You were not properly concealed. My servants saw you. My friend saw you.'

She had worn no burqa on the journey. That explained why the women had stared so, why the men had turned away from her. Palki bearers and servants had seen her without it. Safiya Sultana's friends, her relatives, her *male* relatives had all seen her uncovered.

It was too late to argue over etiquette. Besides, none of those people would see her again. 'I fell down on my way out of the city,' she said tersely. 'The burqa was soaking wet and filthy. I threw it out of the palanquin.'

Elongated by the lamplight, his shadow loomed over her. 'You cannot walk about uncovered.' He fixed his eyes on her as if he were teaching her something important. 'You are my wife. If you behave like a foreigner, you bring shame on me, on my father, on my family.'

'*Shame?* But I *am* a—'

'Foreigners allow their women to wear indecent clothes, like that thing you wore at the Maharajah's dinner when you made that shocking announcement before the court. People are still laughing . . .' His voice trailed off.

Mariana's cheeks warmed as she remembered the deep curtsey she had made to the Maharajah in that low-cut gown. 'I do not care what people think of me,' she snapped, putting out her chin. 'I care only for Saboor.' All she wanted now

415

was to be left alone. She stepped towards Hassan, and touched Saboor's cheek. 'Goodbye, my lambkin,' she murmured. She had said the same words to her little brother when she kissed him for the last time. Like Saboor, Ambrose had been asleep, but his face had been dry and hot, not moist like Saboor's. Forcing grief away, she stood back and faced Hassan.

Her tongue felt thick. She sniffed, wanting to wipe her nose on her veil, aware that her face was smudged with dust from the road. 'I am leaving now,' she said stiffly. 'You will not see me again.'

As she started away, he took a step towards her and caught her arm. 'It's night,' he said sharply, pulling her from the doorway. 'You cannot travel now.' He blinked at her over Saboor, as if uncertain of what she might do next. 'Call on your people tomorrow on your way back to Lahore.'

'Lahore? No!' Mariana pulled her arm away. Her braid had unravelled. She raked her hair back with her fingers. 'I am not going back to Lahore,' she said loudly, glaring at him. 'I am going to the British camp right now!'

'Do not attempt to leave this tent.' His voice was level, his eyes as unreadable as closed doors. 'I am dismissing your bearers and setting a guard outside. You will go nowhere until tomorrow morning.' He lifted the door hanging. 'A servant will bring you food and hot water.'

'You cannot make me stay behind while my people return to Calcutta! You—'

The hanging closed behind him with a dusty thump.

The little lamp bathed the tent in a dim light. Mariana's bones ached from four days of palanquin travel. Still wrapped in Hassan's shawl, she sat down on the bed. How dare Hassan criticize her and tell her what to do! She had hoped to leave before there was time to feel the loss of Saboor, but now hurt overwhelmed her. Why had she given her heart to a child who was not, and could never be, hers?

Voices murmured outside the tent. Hassan must have taken Saboor outside to his friend. She would never let him hear her weep. She pushed a fist into her mouth and bit down on her fingers, her face crumpling as Saboor's had done that first evening in her tent.

She wanted to go home. It was green in Sussex. She would have to face her mother's mortification and her father's disappointment, but after that she would be safe from the anguish and frustration she felt here. She would find things to do. She would help Papa with his sermons, and fight imaginary battles on paper in his study. She would visit Charlotte and Spencer and baby Freddie. She would sketch or study singing, or the pianoforte. She would not mind changing the flowers or the library books, whatever Mama might say. Half married to someone she would never know, she would learn to live without a nice English husband or fair-haired babies of her own.

'Memsahib, Memsahib!' The hoarse voice of a servant came from outside, accompanied by the sound of a tray being put down. 'Your food has come!'

Yusuf Bhatti did not look up when Hassan returned to the fire, his son in his arms, nor did he mention the raised female voice that had come from Hassan's tent. Poor fellow, married by his father's command to that odd foreigner who had already behaved so badly in front of the court. Everyone knew about the woman, about her speech to the Maharajah. Now she had shouted at Hassan loudly enough to be heard by the guard and all the servants.

When she had entered Hassan's tent, her face uncovered,

417

her veil falling, her body moving suggestively under her thin silks, Yusuf had looked away, mortified for his friend. Even now, he could not meet Hassan's eyes. But there was one thing he should say. As a friend, he must tell Hassan what he had heard.

'Did you see the hill-man waiting outside?' he asked, gesturing with his chin towards a long man who crouched silently by the doorway.

Hassan, who had been murmuring to his son, raised his head.

'His name is Yar Mohammad. He is a groom at the British camp. He is acquainted with Shafi Sahib and with your father.'

'He is?' Hassan turned to look.

Yusuf pulled a bolster towards him and leaned against it. 'After Saboor and the foreign lady left your house four days ago, someone sent Yar Mohammad to protect them on the road. He says he followed the palanquin carrying Saboor and the – ah – lady all the way from Lahore to Kasur.'

His face averted, Hassan leaned over the child in his lap and idly drew a finger along a pattern in the carpet.

Yusuf watched him. He was probably thinking of the trail of shock and embarrassment his foreign wife would have left behind on that journey. Yusuf chided himself. He should have left her out of the story until the end.

'On the road, Yar Mohammad heard shouts coming from a clearing,' he continued. 'He went to investigate, and found three armed brigands robbing your family's palanquin. One of them had laid hold of Saboor and was threatening to hurt him if the lady did not turn over her jewellery, but the lady was not in the palki.'

Hassan's finger froze.

418

Yusuf grunted in sympathy. 'The other two thieves were standing with their backs to the road. Yar Mohammad ran up behind them and pulled a knife. As he was dealing with them, the lady charged, screaming, from the bushes, a length of thorn bush over her head. Without hesitating, she ran straight for the man who was holding Saboor.'

Hassan let out his breath.

When the food came, they ate without speaking while the child drowsed beside his father. Later, when Saboor was asleep and Hassan's eyes had grown heavy, Yusuf signalled a servant to cover them with a quilt where they lay.

Yusuf stared into the fire. It was clear that the Englishwoman's bold action in taking Saboor from the Golden Temple had not been accidental. She might be shockingly behaved, but she had courage. Like a wild animal, this woman would kill to protect those she loved. He called for another quilt. Still, he thought as he stretched out, his head on the bolster, it was a mystery to him why the honour of guarding Saboor had fallen not to him, Hassan's soldier friend, but to this uncivilized female.

'Foreigners,' he said softly, shaking his head. 'Foreigners.'

'Get up!'

Something bumped against the string bed, tugging Mariana from sleep. 'You must get up.' The voice above her was urgent. 'Something has happened.'

Except for the starlight that shone in through the open doorway, the tent was perfectly dark. 'Go away,' she muttered. 'Leave me.'

He sat down on the edge of the bed, pinning her beneath the quilt. 'Listen,' he said, his words almost too rapid to understand. 'Two strangers from Lahore have been asking

419

for my camp. A villager overheard them talk of stealing a child. He says they are dangerous-looking men. He has come to ask for our protection for his own children, but it is not a village child they want. It is Saboor.'

Awake now, Mariana stiffened under her quilt. 'How can that be? No one knows he is here. Everyone thinks he's at Qamar Haveli, ill with smallpox.'

'Not everyone,' Hassan said harshly. 'Why else would child thieves be looking for this place?'

She pulled her arms from the covers, then crossed them hastily over her chest to avoid touching him. 'Why worry when your camp is full of armed men?' She felt his eyes on her.

'Child stealers hide during the day and work at night. They are silent and dangerous. You must take Saboor to the British camp tonight.'

'The British camp?' She felt a rush of hope. 'To stay? For how long?'

He turned away from her, towards the starlit doorway. 'I don't know. If these child thieves fail, more will come. As long as the Maharajah lives, they will come.'

She remembered him weeping silently beside her in the crowd at the durbar.

Hassan leaned across her body and rested his elbow on the bed. 'My son,' he said softly, 'is more precious to me than my own life.' His face was near her breast. His tense weight and the burnt scent of his skin made her dizzy.

'Do not fear,' she said shakily, putting a hand carefully on his embroidered sleeve. 'I will take Saboor to the British camp.'

He sat up and gripped her shoulders. 'Go now, before the child thieves come. Take him across the Sutlej, to British territory. Hide him even there, especially when the camp is moving. Do you understand?'

His face was now very close to hers. She took a ragged breath, then nodded.

He stood, and started for the door. Mariana found her slippers and followed him in her dusty silks, Hassan's tobacco-smelling shawl over her shoulders. He stopped her with an outstretched arm and gave an order. Then he let her step from the doorway and moved off to fetch Saboor. Soldiers and servants stood at attention, their backs to her. Even the bearers squatting beside the Shaikh's palanquin had turned away. She recognized the silent, shadowy figure by the doorway as Yar Mohammad.

'I will try to visit you,' Hassan told her as he handed Saboor to her. 'This time, you will have an armed escort, so there will be no need for you to be attacking brigands with sticks and branches.' He made a sound that could have been a laugh. She could not read his face. 'Go,' he said to the bearers.

The fire outside Hassan's tent had long been cold by the time Jagoo and the ruddy-faced boy arrived. It was nearly dawn. Motionless, the boy strained his eyes in the darkness, waiting for Jagoo to return from his work.

He winced when an icy hand clamped his neck. Jagoo gestured silently to the clearing where they had set their own small fire, and the two of them walked towards it. Jagoo's hands shook from cold as he lit the fire. A rancid smell came from him. His clothes bore fresh grease stains. He raised his lifeless eyes to the boy's. 'The child is not there. Nor is the woman.'

For the boy, any failure was painful, no matter who was to blame. He tensed his shoulders against a blow.

But Jagoo moved closer to the flames instead. 'When I did not find him with his father,' he said, rubbing his arms, 'I

421

searched the tent.' He drew back his lips and pointed through the scrub trees. 'Go now, and see if the child sleeps with the servants.'

Reluctantly, the boy stood, pulling his ragged shawl over his shoulders. 'And if the child is not in the camp?'

The fire sputtered. 'We will find him.' Jagoo spoke without looking up. 'Not tomorrow, but soon. We know where the father is. That is all we need to know.'

'All we need to know? Why?'

Jagoo spat into the flames. 'You ask too many questions. Go. If the child is not here, I will leave in the morning. While I am gone, you will watch for anyone leaving this camp.'

Without another word, he stretched out on the ground and closed his eyes.

Chapter Thirty-eight

Monday, 30 December

'What will you tell your friends now?' Mariana asked, an hour before dawn, as Dittoo, smiles wreathing his face, reached into the palanquin for Saboor. 'You did say, after all, that you had sold him to Sirosh, the tailor.'

'I will tell them, Begum Sahib, that Baba cried all the time and annoyed Sirosh's wife.' Dittoo's grin broadened as Saboor reached up to pat his face. 'I will say Sirosh forced me to take Baba back and return his money. My friends will not question me – they will only call me a fool.'

'Be careful,' Mariana called as Dittoo set off towards the line of servants' cooking fires, Saboor under his arm.

She sat up and swung her feet out to the ground. Dittoo had called her Begum Sahib, a salutation reserved for married women. She had never seen him so happy. Was he happy for Saboor, or for her?

At one o'clock the next afternoon, she stood in the middle of her tent, fumbling her way into one of her gowns.

She had arrived well after midnight, and had then marched with the camp at 6 a.m., which had given her reason enough to sleep through breakfast. But now, much though she dreaded

423

it, she must go to lunch. She could no longer put off meeting the camp.

She bent stiffly, her stays biting into her, to tie her boots. Last night, with Saboor beside her in the palanquin, she had dreamed that she had stolen him from the Maharajah only moments before. In her dream she had regarded her future with a fearless calm. If she could bottle that feeling of calm, she would take a spoonful of it every morning.

Her skirts smoothed, her bonnet tied, she stepped from her doorway and started towards the dining tent. It would be all right. Whatever they might say in private, the Eden ladies would never be unpleasant to her in public. She, on her part, would be civil, even though she was still not speaking to them after they refused to rescue her from her wedding.

'Miss Givens, how delightful to see you!' The White Rabbit did not look as delighted as he tried to sound. He swallowed, his Adam's apple bobbing, as he straightened from his bow. 'May I escort you to the dining tent?' He offered her his arm.

Government officers murmured and elbowed one another as Mariana approached the dining table. When the Rabbit pulled out her chair, Major Byrne stood abruptly and stalked out, his exit punctuated by a quiet but distinct honk.

Seated near one end of the table, Mariana surveyed the company with growing unease. Dr Drummond was there, and Lord Auckland; but of Miss Emily and Miss Fanny there was no sign. A few empty seats from her, Dr Drummond glanced in her direction without meeting her eyes. 'It is a pity,' he declared, 'that the Eden ladies are both so unwell with coughs and fevers.'

So she, the pariah, was to be the only woman at table. How would all these men behave without the Eden sisters? Mariana searched the faces around her. Eyes moved rapidly away from

hers. A servant offered her a platter. Thankful for something
to do, she helped herself to a mutton chop. What a lot of
cowards these people were!

At the head of the table, Lord Auckland cleared his throat
noisily. 'Would you mind, Miss Givens,' he said, addressing
her at last, speaking through his nose, 'wearing a pair of gloves
the next time you come to a meal? I am finding it difficult to
enjoy my lunch in the presence of such dirty hands.'

Mariana looked down at her hands. The delicate tracery
from her wedding was still there, now faded to an unpleasant
yellow, incongruous against the lace edging on her sleeves.
She had forgotten all about it.

Someone sniggered.

Mariana dabbed her mouth with a faded napkin. 'Certainly, Lord Auckland,' she said clearly, before pushing back
her chair.

Fury made her strong. In one motion, she rose to her feet
and swept from the tent, her chin high.

Yusuf stretched his legs on the carpet, careful to avoid knocking
over the dishes from their afternoon meal. He raised a greasy
hand. 'Hassan, your cook has been resourceful, as always.'

His curiosity about Hassan's wife wanted satisfying. What was
she really like, this wild European? Did Hassan care for her?
Yusuf took an orange. 'At least Saboor is safe. It seems,' he
added carefully, hoping a compliment would elicit the truth,
'that some of these foreigners have good hearts.'

Beside him, Hassan stared southward, towards the Sutlej
River. 'Yes,' he replied absently, disappointing Yusuf, 'some
of them have good hearts.' He pulled himself upright. 'Yusuf,
I must visit my son.'

Hassan had seen his son only last night. Yusuf swallowed a

mouthful of orange. 'Well then,' he answered, 'go today. By tomorrow the English and their camp will have crossed the Sutlej. Twenty miles is already a long way for you to return if your negotiations here unexpectedly succeed. After all, you have these people in a tight noose.'

Hands outstretched over a basin, Hassan nodded to his servant to pour water over them. 'What do I care for these Kasuris and their treasure?' He shook droplets from his fingers. 'Saboor may spend months in the British camp. He has already suffered at the hands of strangers. I must see for myself that he is comfortable and safe.'

Yusuf nodded. He might be a soldier, but he was not stupid. Hassan clearly wished to see his new wife again, although he would never say so. Safe the child would certainly be, with that wild woman for company. As for his comfort, a child could grow accustomed to anything. He, Yusuf, certainly had, raised in the cold of Kashmir by two uncles and a grandfather, with his mother dead and his father away, serving in the Maharajah's army.

'I am leaving now,' Hassan was saying. 'If Allah wills, I will enter the British camp by nightfall. If I find my baby comfortable and safe, I will bid him Godspeed and return here.'

Yusuf rubbed his face. 'Be careful, Hassan. Stay off the roads. If someone follows, you will lead him straight to your son.'

'No one will follow me,' Hassan replied, glancing sideways at Yusuf, 'if I'm wearing your clothes and riding your horse.'

Yusuf gave a snorting laugh. 'And if you wear my clothes and ride my horse, then whose clothes am I to wear and which horse am I to ride when I accompany you?'

Smiling at last, Hassan reached out and gripped Yusuf's outstretched hand.

*   *   *

An hour later, the sun had dropped behind the branches of a dusty tree. Under the tree, Jagoo, the ruddy-faced boy, and a gaunt stranger with matted hair bent over a jumble of hoof and footprints in the cracked soil.

The stranger straightened up and squinted into the distance. 'And these are the tracks you want me to follow?'

'Yes,' the boy told the stranger. 'This is where the two men mounted before they rode away.' He pointed south, in the direction of the river.

'Well?' Jagoo turned his dead gaze on the stranger. 'Can you track them?'

'Of course,' replied the stranger. 'I can track a stolen cow through the walled city of Lahore. I told you that. There is no one in this area who can follow tracks as I can.' The tracker squatted over the prints again. 'I can tell you this,' he said, looking up. 'There are two riders. Both are gentlemen. Their shoes are not patched, and their footprints are regular. These are not low-caste men accustomed to carrying heavy loads. The first one has a slim foot. He is thinner than his friend, who is heavy. The heavy man's right foot turns in. As to the horses, one has a small cleft in its right rear hoof, and the other has a variation in its gait, tending to advance sideways from time to time.'

Jagoo and the tracker, trailed by the ruddy-faced boy, walked rapidly towards the southeast, their eyes on the ground, their unclean cottons flowing around them.

Chapter Thirty-nine

Monday, 30 December

Just before sunset, Hassan and Yusuf reined in their horses. Hassan stared ahead, a hand shading his eyes, then nudged his mare close to Yusuf's. He pointed to a horizontal cloud of smoke and dust that lay over the flat line of the horizon. 'There,' he said.

Both men were armed. Hassan's pistol was serviceable, but his sword was better for show than for fighting. Yusuf had his own pistol, his triangular-bladed dagger with the hunting hawk engraved on its blade, and his heavy curved sword hanging at his side. His sharpening stone lay in his saddle bag. If it came to a fight, he preferred hand-to-hand.

Hassan breathed deeply as they kicked their horses and moved off again.

'First we will find Shafi Sahib,' he said as they passed the outskirts of the camp, 'and then I will see my son.'

An hour later they had found Shafi Sahib's tent and been invited inside. 'I have come, Shafi Sahib, to assure myself of Saboor's safety,' Hassan said politely. He had begun speaking as soon as he entered the tent and was still standing before the string bed and its elderly occupant. Behind him, Yusuf looked about

428

him for somewhere to sit. An empty bed stood against one canvas wall.

Shafi Sahib read his thoughts. 'Ahmad, Saboor's servant, has gone out,' he said. 'He is recovering very well from his wound.'

For all his toughness, Yusuf could not help wincing at what the man had suffered.

When his servant boy entered, dragging a canvas chair, Shafi Sahib got up from his bed and sat in the chair. 'It will be difficult,' he told Hassan gently, 'for you to enter the compound openly. Unfortunately, you are not welcome there.' He crossed his legs and reached for his beads as his two visitors lowered themselves to the string bed.

Hassan stiffened. 'Why, Shafi Sahib?'

'I fear,' answered the old man, 'that the English people have been gravely displeased by your marriage.' He pressed his lips together. 'They do not look upon us as their equals. Your wife,' he went on, ignoring Yusuf's snort, 'may be suffering as a result, although her suffering will not affect Saboor. The English are unaware of his presence here.' He raised his chin, warning Yusuf not to speak. 'But it is not anyone's feelings that will keep you from entering the Governor-General's compound by ordinary means. It is the two well-armed sentries who are forbidden to allow strangers past the gate.'

'What then?' Hassan's voice had flattened. 'Must we kill both sentries before I may see my child again?'

At his side, Yusuf smiled grimly.

'Oh no, my boy, that will not be necessary.' Shafi Sahib leaned back in his chair. His beads clicked softly. He turned to Yusuf. 'If you will give us permission?' he said politely, his eyes straying to the door.

It took Yusuf a moment to understand that what Shafi

Sahib wanted to say was for Hassan's ears alone. Grunting an apology, wondering whether it had to do with one of the Shaikh's spiritual tricks, Yusuf pushed himself to his feet and left the tent.

The tracker bent over the dust of the avenue. 'It's too dark,' he said, straightening. 'I cannot see the hoof prints any longer. As soon as it is light we will return and continue from here.' He pointed to where smoke rose from a ramshackle bazaar, just visible beyond the avenue's end. 'I am going to get food.'

The ruddy-faced boy shrugged. 'The child isn't in this camp. We have been here already. We—'

'Quiet!' barked Jagoo. He jerked his chin towards the horse lines. 'And what if the horses are there now? Among so many other mounts, how will you find their tracks tomorrow?'

The tracker smiled, cracked teeth large in his gaunt face. 'You do not know my skill.' His voice held confidence but his eyes had become wary.

The three men were crossing the avenue when two riders came into view, passing among pack animals and groups of coolies, a tall groom on foot beside them.

The tracker started, then snatched at Jagoo's shirt. 'Look!' he whispered.

One of the horsemen turned in his saddle to look back at them, a hand on his sword. 'One man is slim, the other heavy,' the tracker murmured as the riders continued down the avenue. 'Both are gentlemen. One horse likes to move sideways from time to time. They are now with a groom, but that is the only difference.' Signalling the others to follow, he crossed the avenue.

The avenue was broad and crowded. The air held the scent of charcoal fires and cooking. A bullock cart heaped with firewood

430

passed, led by a boy singing at the top of his voice. Laughing groups of young men pushed one another. Englishmen strode past carrying carved wooden walking sticks, lips pursed, their black clothes smudged with dust.

The two horsemen and the groom continued along the avenue until they reached the same high, red canvas wall where Jagoo and his companion had waited fruitlessly only four days previously. His eyes on the riders, the tracker strode along the edge of the avenue, followed by Jagoo and the boy. When the horsemen stopped at the guarded entrance, the three men faded into the blackness beside the wall. The uniformed sentries stood at attention by the gate, ignoring the lively activity in front of them. Jagoo pushed past his companions and edged up to the red wall, near the two horsemen who had stopped a little distance from the sentries. There he bent over and feigned a fit of coughing. The two riders had begun speaking to each other. Jagoo stopped coughing and listened.

'He said to turn left as you enter,' Yusuf Bhatti was saying. 'Her tent stands alone in the corner, there.' He pointed to his left, where the red wall turned away from the road, thirty yards away.

Nodding, Hassan dismounted.

'May the Most Gracious guide you,' Yusuf offered, reaching for Hassan's hand. 'I'll stay here in case, Allah forbid, something goes wrong.'

Hassan waved, then started towards the entrance, his lips moving as he walked.

As Hassan moved away, Yusuf leaned from his saddle, his eyes on the groom beside him. 'You are allowed through the gate, are you not, Yar Mohammad?' he asked.

'Ji, Sahib,' he replied.

'Then go inside and guard Memsahib's tent.'

431

Jagoo had crept up to hear the two men's words. When he turned back to look at the road, he stopped short, eyes wide. Beside Yusuf Bhatti's horse, Yar Mohammad froze where he stood. Yusuf jerked upright in his saddle, blinked, then blinked again.

In the time it had taken for the onlookers to glance away, Hassan should have covered ten or twelve feet of the distance from his horse to the red wall. But he was not there. Yusuf, Yar Mohammad, the tracker, Jagoo and the ruddy-faced boy all searched the avenue with their eyes, but Hassan was nowhere to be seen.

Yusuf smiled to himself. Now he was sure of it. Shafi Sahib had told Hassan one of the secrets of the Karakoyia Brotherhood. He also knew for certain that he would never know what that secret was.

'Light the lamp, Dittoo, it's too dark to read.'

Inside her tent, Mariana sat up, propped on several pillows, an open letter in one hand, Saboor's arm in the other.

'Saboor darling, sit down,' she pleaded as he pulled away from her. 'See, you can play with Mariana's ribbons. They are there, on the bed.'

'An-*nah*.' He pronounced the last part of her name carefully, his eyes fixed on hers, then dropped down and, digging his hands and knees into her lap, crawled towards the little bedside table. She pulled him back, holding her letter safely out of the way, as he reached for the tinderbox.

His little body felt so soft under his clothes. She retrieved him, kissing a little hand that smelled of babyhood and dust. He pulled it away and wrapped his fingers round the neck of her dress.

'And take Saboor away,' she told Dittoo, unclasping the small fingers. 'He is everywhere at once.'

Dittoo shambled into the tent, wheedling as he came. '*A-jao*, Baba, come, I will find something very nice for you, yes, very nice.'

'An-*nah*, want An-*nah*!' Saboor complained as Dittoo carried him, kicking, across the floor.

His health had certainly improved. Mariana made a kissing sound. 'Shhh, Baba. There, there, my love, it is only for a little while.'

She held her letter to the light, while Dittoo's singsong nonsense floated in from outside corridor. She wanted to read it and reread it until her mother's firm handwriting faded from the page. Three months old, yet new to Mariana, it carried with it the very air of home.

We all missed you dreadfully at Freddie's birthday party. A few of the neighbours came and Freddie rushed about with their children until he became overexcited and had to be put to bed.

He spends more and more time with Papa. I pray that he will, in time, take Ambrose's place in your father's heart.

As for you, my darling, remember that you are not bound to marry in India. If no young man there makes you happy, you are to come home. Do not rush into a misalliance in order to please us.

If you should return unmarried, our shoulders are broad enough to bear whatever society has to say.

Those reassuring words did little to take away the jolting pain Mariana had felt while reading another letter that had arrived that afternoon along with her mother's. *It saddens me immeasurably*, Fitzgerald had written from the army camp, *to*

433

know what scandal, what utter *disgrace you have brought upon yourself. I excuse myself after dinner each night to avoid hearing the shameful things our officers are saying about you. How could you have associated so recklessly, so indecently, with a native man? Who will dare to be your friend now?*

Of course, they all thought her indecent. After all, she had spent a night alone with Hassan after her wedding. No explanation of hers could change that fact. Fitzgerald was gone for ever. Who *would* be her friend now? Mariana's call on Miss Emily had been as unpleasant as she had expected.

'You have not only ruined yourself for marriage,' Miss Emily had declared flatly from her pillows, 'you have ruined yourself for society. You have also grievously wronged Lieutenant Marks. We shall not easily forgive you,' she had continued, as she adjusted the ribbons on her bed-jacket, 'but we shall not mention it again. You must accept your just desserts. Wear gloves to meals and do not attempt to join the conversation. Only pray that, one day, you will be forgiven.'

'It would have been better if you had not come to India, Mariana,' Miss Fanny had said mournfully, an hour later. 'You are much too adventurous for this country.'

Although Fitzgerald's letter had made Mariana weep with near-despair, no one, not the Eden sisters, Lord Auckland, or all the government and army officers combined, could frighten her. But there was one thought that brought her ambushing panic. Once the scandal reached England, it would break her family's heart. She could bear being an outcast in India, but the thought of her family at home suffering for her mistakes was too miserable to endure. Lord Auckland had given orders that her story should not be repeated, but there had been a hundred witnesses to her declaration before the court, and to her wedding. Such a tale was too dark, too exciting not to be told. Within days of the camp's arrival at Calcutta, it would certainly escape Lord Auckland's censorship and reach every drawing room in the city, to be embellished with false, damning details of her enticement of native men. From there it would spread, carried by every ship bound for England.

Her mother's letter lay on the bed beside her. Mama and Papa loved her. They would go on loving her no matter what she did, no matter what society thought. She longed to sit down to Sunday lunch with them all, even the always critical Aunt Rachel . . .

Why not leave now? Why not arrange to travel by palanquin ahead of the camp? Lord Auckland and his sisters expected to stop at Simla for several months on the way back to Calcutta. Even after they resumed travelling, they would be expected stop all along the way, to allow local Rajas to entertain Lord Auckland. It might be a year before the camp arrived in Calcutta. If she left within a few days and travelled without stopping, she would reach there many months ahead of her story. If she were fortunate, a passenger ship would be waiting on the Hooghly River. She might well be on the high seas long before her story was told. Uncle Adrian would arrange everything, of course he would! She would write to him at once. The mail pouch was sent to Calcutta every day. In England, she would have time to explain, to prepare her family and their friends. It was, perhaps, too late to worry about society, but she must protect her family from hearing her story from other lips.

Outside, a pacified Saboor squeaked with pleasure. Mariana pushed away sadness. She had always known she would leave him. He would be happy without her. As long as he had

435

someone to guard and love him, he would be safe. Hassan's fear was surely exaggerated.

Someone scratched at the door blind. Dittoo stopped singing and stood before it, Saboor in his arms, then turned and rushed towards the bed, his feet thumping on the striped rug, and thrust the child at Mariana.

'I have come to see Saboor Baba,' said a male voice from outside.

Who was that? Who knew Saboor was here? Mariana held her breath and pushed Saboor down beside her on the bed, and covered him with her shawl. 'Quiet,' she cautioned softly, a finger to her lips. '*Chup*. Do not speak.' She nodded to Dittoo.

'Who is it?' he asked, his voice cracking with nerves.

'It is Hassan Ali Khan,' said the voice with some annoyance. 'Open the blind.'

Mariana sucked in her breath. Beside her, Saboor struggled to sit up.

Dittoo flung aside the blind. Hassan stepped in from the darkness outside.

'Abba! Abba!' As Dittoo stooped his way backwards out of the doorway, Saboor scrambled off the bed and danced to Hassan. His face tilted upward, he braced himself against his father's knee.

Something about Hassan reminded Mariana of Saboor. It was the candour in his expression perhaps, or a softness in his eyes. He looked strained. His coat smelled of horses. Rings gleamed on his hands. Behind her, Mama's open letter lay on the bedspread.

She hardened herself against him. 'As you can see, Saboor is safe here, but there is something I must tell you.'

Hassan did not look at her. Instead, he surveyed her tent.

'How can you live like this?' He poked a long finger at her sparse furniture. 'Where do you sit?'

She pointed to her upright chair, wobbly now from hard travel. 'There, but that is not—'

'Where are your furnishings? Your carpets? I can't have my son living in these conditions. For all we know, he may be in this camp for months.'

'I—'

'You need better arrangements,' he interrupted, frowning as he lifted Saboor into his arms. 'I must make them tonight.'

Saboor wrapped his arms about Hassan's neck. Father and son regarded Mariana with identical gazes.

'A letter has come for me,' she said firmly, changing the subject. 'I must return to Calcutta at once.'

Hassan waved a dismissive hand. 'It is late, Mariam,' he said abruptly. He put down his son. 'I must hurry.'

'But I—'

Before she could finish speaking, the door blind had closed behind him.

Chapter Forty

Saboor stared past Mariana's face, refusing to meet her eyes or acknowledge her kisses. Hurt and mystified, she handed him to Dittoo. 'Why has he become like this?' she wailed. 'He could not have gone deaf in one minute. What is the matter with him?'

'I do not know, Begum Sahib.' Dittoo bounced the passive, unsmiling child, then shook his head. 'I have never seen such a thing before.'

Saboor's sudden change of mood had begun the moment his father had left them. As the door blind shut behind Hassan, Saboor had gone still. It seemed as if his whole being had turned suddenly inward, out of Mariana's reach. For an hour she had rocked him, crooning, searching her memory for a cause. She had examined him with nervous fingers, looking for signs of a spider or scorpion sting that might have paralysed him somehow. Finding nothing, she had crooned his name and tried to force him to look at her, but he would only stare past her, his energetic, affectionate little self replaced by a stiff, unloving stranger. What could they have done or said to change him so? Surely he had not divined her plan to leave him and return home? But if he had not, why had he retreated into silence, as if his heart were crushed?

'Please, Dittoo,' she implored, 'do something.'

A bath did not help, nor did Dittoo's arguing or Mariana's embraces.

Later that evening, Mariana sat up, still dressed, with Saboor asleep beside her. Hassan would return soon. When he did, she would find words to explain her leaving. For now, all she could do was sit while the clock on her bedside ticked away the passing time.

Mariam. He had called her Mariam.

On the starlit avenue, Jagoo nodded to the boy and moved along the red wall near where the two riders they had been following had stopped to talk. Here the canvas sagged and billowed. Jagoo sat down again and stretched his body out, as if readying himself for sleep. But he did not sleep. Instead, he began gently, unobtrusively, to smooth away stones, twigs and small obstructions from the ground under the wall.

It was nearly midnight. The traffic had died on the avenue. Bats swooped overhead. Hollow coughing came from nearby servants' quarters. In the distance, men laughed. Someone was singing. The tracker yawned.

'I want to eat,' the boy whispered. 'I can smell cooking over there.' He jerked his chin towards the horse lines.

Jagoo ignored him and began to take things out of a cloth bag. First came something that looked like a greasy leather pouch. Next came a ten-inch knife. Jagoo motioned to the boy, a silent, significant gesture. Then, the pouch hidden in his clothes, the knife between his teeth, he slid in one smooth, nearly soundless motion under the red wall, and was gone.

Horses approached on the avenue. The boy stiffened instantly, his breath hissing as the same two riders come into view again, this time followed by a laden donkey cart.

The tall rider dismounted and started towards the guarded entrance. From where the tracker sat, he could make out that the man's lips were moving. The tracker turned his head and glanced at the boy beside him, who stared back at him, his eyes wide and worried. When the tracker turned again to look at the place where the tall rider should have been walking, the avenue was empty.

The tracker shook the boy's fingers from his arm and stood. Keeping his body flat against the wall, he crept away, leaving the guarded entrance, the donkey's driver and the second horseman staring at the empty avenue behind him. Breathing hard, he hurried to the corner where the red canvas wall turned away from the avenue. Once round the corner, he fled through the dark, his clothes billowing and flapping around him, his sandals slapping on the hard clay ground.

Attending to a personal need, Dittoo crouched behind the thicket of guy ropes that supported Memsahib's tent, his face turned to the red wall. He looked over his shoulder, his dhoti draped discreetly about his legs, considering for the hundredth time the extraordinary fact of his memsahib's marriage.

How would his life change after this event? Time would tell. One thing was certain. No wife of Hassan Ali Khan Sahib would be allowed a male servant. But with no maidservants for Memsahib, how could he escape going into her tent? Without him, how was she to have her morning coffee, or her bed made, her lamp lit or her side table dusted?

The canvas beside him trembled. He looked along the wall in time to see an arm, then a leg, then a whole man appear silently from under the wall near Memsahib's tent.

Dittoo hastily adjusted his clothes and crept closer. When

he was near enough to see the man clearly, he stopped and held his breath.

The man had not seen Dittoo. He stood, half visible in the starlight, and reached with a swift movement under his shirt. His loose cotton trousers dropped to the ground. He stepped out of them and then, naked under his long shirt, began to smear something from a greasy pouch onto his legs and buttocks. That done, he pulled off his shirt.

Yar Mohammad had come, hours ago, to guard Memsahib's tent. Ghostlike in his grey shawl, he now sat gazing into space beside her doorway, unaware of the naked intruder who had finished smearing his chest and back. As Dittoo watched from the shadows, the man bent over, his skin gleaming faintly, and withdrew something from his discarded clothes.

It was a long, cruel-looking knife. Dittoo went cold.

Too terrified to move, Dittoo crouched by the canvas wall as the intruder, silently, slowly, his eyes fixed on Yar Mohammad, crept forward, the knife ready in his hand.

Dittoo found his voice. At his yell of warning, Yar Mohammad jerked his head up. He saw the man and reached, scrabbling, for his own weapon.

At that instant, a third man appeared. Before Dittoo could make another sound, the man began to run towards them. Dittoo held his breath. Whoever this was, he must have seen what was happening beside the tent door. Was he a guard or another assailant?

He was neither. It was Hassan Ali Khan Sahib himself, breathing hard, running full tilt at the intruder. His hands gripping his face, Dittoo watched Hassan Sahib throw himself forward past Yar Mohammad. Ignoring the raised knife, he drove the intruder into the doorway of Memsahib's tent, bringing the door hanging thumping to the ground.

441

Gasping and spitting, the two men grappled in the dust. Fighting to gain a purchase on the greased body, Hassan Sahib cried out as the naked man slid from his grip and darted towards the red wall. The intruder flung himself down, caught the canvas wall with one hand and began, lizard-like, to slither under it, still holding his knife; but Yar Mohammad was too quick for him. Throwing himself at the man, he caught one greased ankle, then another; grunting with effort, he dragged the intruder from beneath the wall and across the ground to the tent.

Naked, bleeding and covered with dust, the man wept aloud as Hassan grasped him by the hair.

'Piece of filth,' Hassan rasped, and beat the man's head on the ground. 'You dare to attack my wife, my son!'

'Oh Sahib, have pity!' the man wailed. 'I am only a small thief in search of trinkets. Had I known it was your family—'

'Pig! Son of shame! I know who you are, what you want. Yar Mohammad, get his knife!'

Dittoo shivered as he watched Yar Mohammad turn the man roughly onto his stomach and force a knee into his back. What a pity he himself was too old to help!

Shouting came from the entrance. Someone was arguing with the sentries, trying to get in. A moment later, a guard appeared, followed by a well-armed burly man who strode behind him, dragging a frightened-looking boy.

'I know nothing, Huzoors, nothing at all.' Arms over his head, the boy cowered before the sentry, babbling with fright.

'Be quiet. See, guard, I told you there were others,' said the burly man, fingering the hilt of his curved sword. 'I only wish I had caught the one that ran away.'

As the sentry poked at the greased man with his bayonet,

Dittoo suddenly remembered Memsahib and Saboor Baba. He stepped over the fallen door blind and went into the tent.

'Memsahib, Memsahib,' he whispered, uncomfortably aware that Hassan Sahib would likely shout at him for entering, 'Are you all right?' He fumbled across the floor in the darkness, found his way round the bed to the little table in the corner, and lit the lamp.

Awakened by Dittoo's frightened shout, Mariana had reached for her boots. Then, her heart pounding, she had seized the lamp and dropped to her knees beside her bed. 'If someone has come to harm you,' she had whispered to the sleeping Saboor as she wrapped him in one of her shawls, 'they must kill me first. Oh, Saboor, if only I had a sword . . .'

Now as she sat upright on the edge of her bed, her dressing-gown skirts spread widely about her, she could see Hassan by her open doorway, his back to her, his shoulders heaving.

An authoritative male voice spoke. 'You take charge of them. Say you caught them yourself. Yes, yes, of course, that is what a sentry is supposed to do. Now be gone and goodnight.'

Dittoo came towards her, holding the lamp aloft, shortly followed by Hassan, smelling foul, his face and clothes streaked with grease and dirt. Hassan looked at her without speaking, his whole soul asking for Saboor. Behind him Yar Mohammad craned to see inside.

Mariana pushed her skirts aside and got down on her knees. While Dittoo held up the lamp, she lifted the edge of the bedspread. There under the bed lay Saboor where she had hidden him, wrapped in a nest of shawls, his head turning towards them, his eyes open.

'An-nah.'

'There, darling, it's all right now.'

As she took hold of the shawls and pulled him towards her, she felt someone strike her violently from behind. Her back arching involuntarily, she let go of the shawls and clutched at her spine with both hands.

'Why, why?' she stammered, her face crumpling in pain, searching the surprised faces above her. Panting with shock, she tried to crawl away from her attacker. Then Yar Mohammad's urgent voice pierced the ringing in her ears.

'A snake has bitten her. That is what happens when a viper strikes. They think someone has struck them in the back – look at her hands!'

A snake! She struggled to speak, to tell them she had looked under the bed, that she had even brought the lamp, but her voice had left her.

Still on all fours, she watched Hassan, his hands outstretched, snatch his son from the terrible nest of shawls. As her sight dimmed, she saw her four-poster bed upturned and Yar Mohammad pounce, a heavy blade flashing in his hand.

Someone took her wrists. 'There. Two puncture wounds.'

Her bitten arm was on fire. She felt herself being dragged across the floor. 'Lift her from the other side,' someone said. 'We must get her to Shafi Sahib.'

'No,' another voice said, 'she'll be unconscious soon. Yar Mohammad will fetch Shafi Sahib. Go, Yar Mohammad, take my horse.'

Shafi Sahib. Friend of the magical Shaikh, interpreter of dreams. Why would the great Shafi Sahib come to her? Who was sucking at her wrist, spitting and cursing? Who prayed aloud, while a baby wailed hopelessly?

An alien creature had invaded her body and was scorching

her from the inside. Too weak to cry out, she could not tell them of her agony, or beg them not to touch her. She thrashed, gurgling, and there was rustling and silence and a voice began to recite in an undertone.

She sank into blackness.

The ship rocked. She could not see rigging above her, but she could feel the rolling of the deck. She strained to see ahead, and there, through the fog, glimmered a brilliant light. The waves beneath her murmured something she could not understand. Longing to reach the light, she tried to stretch out her hands. The ship was taking her there, taking her there . . .

She could breathe. The burning, although fierce, had abated, and she could breathe, shallow breaths at first, then deeper, sweeter ones. As she drank in the air, the voice went on, soothing and healing her. There was no sound of a baby crying. Light shone through her eyelids.

When she opened her eyes, she saw a blur of faces. As she began to focus, the light went out and the singsong murmuring ceased. 'Get another light,' said someone. 'I must be able to see her.'

Did she know that voice?

'Who must see me?' she murmured into the darkness. What was this dark place? What language were they all speaking?

Several voices spoke at once. 'Are you all right? Have you recovered? Can you breathe?'

'Yes.' Her voice sounded curiously distant. Something unpleasant had dribbled from the corner of her mouth. Her hair was drenched. The pain in her arm was nearly gone.

'Can you sit up?'

'Yes, but I do not wish to,' she said weakly.

Someone sighed. She heard the rustling sound of someone

standing up. 'Since she is now all right,' said the familiar voice, 'I shall go back. Yar Mohammad will see me to my tent.'

When she opened her eyes again, the lamp had been re-lit. The interior of the tent looked odd from where she lay on the floor near the desk. Her dressing gown had bunched itself uncomfortably around her legs. Her empty chair stood a few feet away. Her four-poster lay onto its side, spilling bed linen over the striped floor. Dittoo, holding Saboor, sat motionless in the corner. Hassan crouched beside her, a hand to his head. Near the door, his eyes fixed on the sky outside, stood a heavyset stranger, a long curved sword hanging at his side.

'I think,' she said, 'I would like to go to bed.'

Dittoo got to his feet and began to pick up the bedclothes. Saboor trotted towards Mariana. Sitting carefully down beside her, he reached out, round-eyed, and patted her arm. Her eyes stung.

At a rustling outside the door, she raised herself on one elbow. In the doorway, their feet on the fallen blind, stood the Misses Eden, their two faces fixed in horror as if they had come suddenly upon some fearful accident or scene of torture.

For a moment, there was silence. But for the quivering of Miss Emily's skirts, Mariana would have believed the figures in the doorway to be a delirium-induced tableau.

She cleared her throat. 'I hope I have not caused a disturbance,' she said weakly.

Hassan pointed meaningfully at his mouth, then at hers. Mariana wiped her mouth with a corner of her dressing gown, and found it covered with something pink and slimy. She closed her eyes and subsided to the floor, doomed, but too ill to care.

Miss Emily found her voice. 'We have been called here, Mariana,' she said, ignoring everyone else, 'by the servants, who heard some very unexpected sounds coming from your tent. Get up at once. You are coming with us.'

Hands raised Mariana. Illuminated by the torches of Miss Emily's servants, she was marched, her head lolling, past Hassan, past Dittoo and Yar Mohammad.

'Fanny,' she heard Miss Emily say, 'call the sentries.'

'We shall not ask you to explain now,' said Miss Emily crisply, as she tucked Mariana into her bed, now hastily reassembled in her own large drawing room. 'There will be time for that when you are sufficiently recovered. You shall sleep here until we march tomorrow.'

Through half-closed lids, Mariana could make out Miss Emily's little sofa, her bookstand and several tables, each with an oil lamp. Someone had put a cold compress on her forehead. Miss Fanny stood beside her sister, her lips tight.

'My sister and I,' Miss Emily declared, turning to Miss Fanny who nodded without speaking, 'are determined to mention this to no one, at least for now. We request that you do the same, until something has been decided. In the meanwhile, you should rest. Whatever you have been up to,' she added darkly, 'is certain to have been most exhausting.'

Mariana nodded as she floated into sleep.

Chapter Forty-one

'Do not be foolish, Yar Mohammad,' Shafi Sahib said, shortly after dawn, from his seat on a borrowed mule. 'How can you not see the importance of your work?'

The groom strode silently at the animal's head, Shafi Sahib's reins in his hand. Around them, the brass ankle bells of the camels chinked and sang.

Perhaps he should have kept quiet and not bothered Shafi Sahib with his troubles, but his sense of failure had been too great. What had he done to earn the little ceramic vial that had been put into his hand? What had he found to offer those about him in this strange and powerful time?

'Of course your work is important,' the old man said, letting go of the saddle with one hand to search for something among his garments. 'What would have happened if you had not been there to stop Yusuf Bhatti from slaying the madman on the road to Lahore when these events first began? Without your intervention, the man would have died, I would not have received his message, and we would not have guessed at the identity of the Guardian.'

Encouraged, Yar Mohammad looked up.

'It was you,' Shafi Sahib continued, gripping the saddle

one-handed, his beads held in his free hand, 'who delivered our messages to the Guardian Memsahib, you who provided the child's first morsels of food after his rescue. You fought for them on the road to Kasur and sat guard over Saboor's place of refuge when the child thief came to steal him. It was you who recognized the viper's bite, and summoned me to save the Guardian's life.' The old man smiled down from his swaying perch. 'You, Yar Mohammad,' he said, his voice lifting, 'have been given the duty of protecting the Guardian. Your little vial was full when you showed it in your dream to Shaikh Waliullah. I believe it is full even now.'

Shafi Sahib was tired. His head drooped. Yar Mohammad walked on, breathing deeply of the morning air.

'I understand we had some excitement last night,' remarked an aide-de-camp as he helped himself to omelette aux herbes Indiennes in the dining tent. 'It seems that two men tried to rob this compound.'

Lord Auckland looked up, frowning. Mariana stared down at her plate. The Eden sisters made a point of looking neither at each other nor at Mariana.

'Yes,' said another aide. 'One of them tried the old trick,' he coughed delicately, 'of covering himself with grease.'

The first aide smiled broadly over his buttered toast. 'I heard one of them actually got past the guard and tried to get into the tents, and——'

'Absolute nonsense!' Major Byrne's face had reddened. He cleared his throat noisily. 'Nothing of the sort, nothing of the sort.' Avoiding the Governor-General's eye, he inclined his head gallantly towards the Misses Eden. 'Your compound is impregnable, ladies. You must have no fear on that account. Both men were caught by the sentries well before they attempted to get in.' He glared at the aides. 'Do not let these young men frighten you. They have no idea what they're talking about. And now, ladies, Lord Auckland,' he said with a decisive little nod, 'if you will excuse me.'

Miss Emily regarded him silently over the rim of her coffee cup as he strode away.

Lord Auckland nodded vaguely in Byrne's direction, then pushed back his chair. 'Emily, my dear, it seems that we are to be relatively safe from the natives this morning. I thought we might take a drive before lunch. There may be some interesting ruins on the way to Kasur.' He smiled hopefully at his sister from beneath dusty eyebrows.

'I am so sorry, George,' said Miss Emily, glancing reproachfully at Mariana, 'but Miss Givens was quite ill last night. I cannot go out until Dr Drummond has seen her.'

Mariana pushed smoked fish onto her fork. Miss Emily, she ordered silently, take the drive, take the drive!

'I had hoped, Mariana,' Miss Emily said as they waited in her drawing room for Dr Drummond, 'that we had heard the last of your extraordinary behaviour.'

Mariana touched the healing puncture marks on her wrist. She would not explain or apologize, whatever they said to her.

'But not at all.' Miss Emily rose from her seat and crossed the tent to her little bookshelf. 'Since then,' she went on, turning back to Mariana and folding her arms across her bosom, 'you have not ceased to astonish us. Is there any point in my asking why we found you last night lying on your floor in your nightclothes in the company of not one but two strange native men?'

Mariana's bed, now tightly made, stood on one side of the tent. No one looked at it.

'If you are going mad,' Miss Emily pronounced as she lowered herself to the sofa beside her sister, 'your behaviour can be explained, although of course it can never be excused.' She opened her hands. 'Why, Mariana? Why the foul-smelling native men? Why the unexplained baby? Why the overturned bed, the general disarray?'

'There was a viper,' Mariana said as coolly as civility allowed, 'under my bed.' Why did she bother to tell them anything?

A servant bowed in the doorway. 'Doctor Sahib has come,' he said, in polite, accented English.

Dr Drummond strode in and stood over her in his old-fashioned clothes, smelling of tobacco. He nodded a greeting to Miss Emily and Miss Fanny on the sofa, and then turned to Mariana.

'Now, Miss Givens,' he said, bending to look cautiously at her over the tops of his spectacles, 'how are we feeling today?' He pursed his lips. 'I understand that the arrival of these good ladies at your tent last night prevented your meeting a most unpleasant fate. What none of us can grasp is how these things keep happening to you. Do you know, Miss Givens? Hmmmn?'

They already believed her a lunatic. Nothing she told them would change their minds. She turned over her wrist. 'A snake bit me last night.' She pointed to the marks. 'I was very ill then, but I am much better now.'

'Now, Miss Givens,' the doctor said reprovingly, looking not at her but at Miss Emily, 'we all know there is no cure for poisonous snake bite.'

'Yes, Dr Drummond, but—'

'No cure at all,' he repeated in a firm tone, smiling falsely. 'You had a narrow escape last night to be sure, but we all know that it was *not* from poisonous snake bite. Nonetheless, if it will make you feel better, I will have a look at those marks. 'She could, of course,' he said to the Eden ladies, taking Mariana's wrist in his hand, 'have been injured by one of the men. Miss Givens, do you mind coming to the light?'

Injured by one of the men, indeed! If Miss Fanny had not been watching, Mariana would have made a face behind the doctor's back.

He turned her wrist this way and that, looking down his nose at the two marks. After a moment, he nodded. 'You may sit down now, Miss Givens. These are clearly puncture wounds. They do resemble marks left by the fangs of a snake, but if they are bite marks, the snake must have been of a rare, nonpoisonous variety. In any case, as they have nearly healed they are obviously not recent and can have nothing whatever to do with the events of last night.' He shook his head. 'I really do not know what to make of all this.'

'May I please,' Mariana asked, struggling to keep her tone level, 'tell you what really happened last night?'

Greeted with silent surprise, she took a deep breath. 'The thieves we discussed at breakfast this morning,' she began, 'were child stealers. They did indeed get into the compound. In fact, they nearly got into my tent.'

Miss Fanny's mouth opened. 'Nearly got in? But Emily and I saw them clearly!'

'No, Miss Fanny,' Mariana said patiently. 'That was the bridegroom from the wedding, and another man I have not seen before.'

Miss Emily's face turned pink. 'Are you trying to tell us,' she cried, 'that the filthy creature beside you was your *husband*?'

Mariana glared at her. 'I said I would not marry him. I am certain you heard me say so, Miss Emily. In any case, he was dirty because he had fought with a child thief who had got

452

into the compound. They were trying to steal his baby from my tent.'

'Baby?' Dr Drummond's jaw hung open.

Miss Emily was now scarlet. 'You will not speak to me like that, Mariana,' she snapped.

'Whose baby?' The doctor looked from face to face.

'I think, Dr Drummond,' said Miss Emily, her eyes narrowing, her tone a potent combination of charm and force, 'that we have no further need take up your valuable time.'

'But Miss Eden, we have not yet discovered—'

'Thank you so much, Dr Drummond.' Miss Emily smiled thinly. 'Fanny, please see the doctor out.'

Mariana caught the doctor's disappointed expression as Miss Fanny ushered him from the tent.

Miss Emily's gaze was inescapable. 'The baby, Mariana, is the key to this entire, disgraceful story, is he not? Your father-in-law is Shaikh Waliullah, the magician grandfather who was said to have spirited the Maharajah's baby hostage from the Golden Temple.'

Mariana nodded.

'The missing baby, therefore, is now your stepson.'

Mariana nodded again.

Miss Emily's voice would have been triumphant if it had not been so deadly. 'In that case, the child in your tent was Maharajah Ranjit Singh's hostage, whose disappearance caused the Maharajah to fall ill, thus delaying our treaty negotiations. Delaying, in fact, the very Afghan Campaign for which we have all come so far and worked so hard.' Her eyes bored into Mariana's. 'It was not magic that caused the child's disappearance, was it, Mariana? It was a conspiracy in which you played a part. Are you or are you not the thief who stole the child from the Golden Temple?'

Miss Fanny gasped.

It was pointless to deny the truth. 'It was I who stole him, Miss Emily, but there was no conspiracy.' Mariana raised her chin. 'I tried to tell you so, after the Maharajah's dinner party, after I got up and spoke—'

'Later, you lied to us repeatedly on the subject. When questions were asked, you deceived and betrayed us.'

It was true. She had lied to them.

'I should have guessed before now.' Miss Emily shook her head. 'It was all in front of me. Your disappearances and your sudden headaches all began after that baby vanished. You fell asleep in your palanquin the morning after the rice test.

She sighed. 'When I consider that awful scene last night—'

She closed her eyes. 'Call someone, Mariana,' she said, shaking her head. 'I shall not say another word until I have had tea.'

'*I* think,' remarked Miss Fanny a little while later as she stirred sugar into her cup, 'that we should allow Mariana to tell the *entire* story.'

Miss Emily stopped pouring the milk. 'Absolutely not, Fanny. I cannot bear any fresh horrors.'

'There may be details we have not understood.' Miss Fanny bent forward. 'But even if there are not, I should like to hear Mariana's side. It is, after all, a most *interesting* story.'

Miss Emily sniffed, but did not argue.

'The baby's name is Saboor,' Mariana began, responding to Miss Fanny's nod. 'His mother was poisoned by the Maharajah's queens. He has been ill-treated by the queens *and* by the Maharajah. He was forced on me suddenly by his own servant, who feared he would die. I returned him secretly to his family on the night of the rice test.'

454

The ladies stared at one another. Mariana took a sip of her tea to steady herself. 'The Shaikh then proposed that I marry his son. I was horrified, of course, but when the Maharajah announced that he wanted to marry me himself, I used the Shaikh's proposal as a means to refuse him. I honestly thought the Shaikh's proposal was not serious, that it was meant to save me from the Maharajah. I was tricked into going to the Citadel.'

Miss Emily sat immobile, her teacup partway to her lips. Mariana plunged on.

'The morning after the ceremony, the Maharajah sent armed men to the Shaikh's house to fetch the baby and me. I was forced to take the baby away in the rain, in disguise.' She shivered at the memory. 'Then child thieves came to steal him. The one who nearly got in was covered in grease. He had a knife.'

'Grease?' Miss Fanny's eyes danced naughtily over the hand at her mouth. 'You mean he had no—'

'Fanny!' Miss Emily put her cup down sharply.

'Saboor's father caught him just in time, but the struggle was messy because of the grease. That is why he smelled so awful.' Mariana sighed. 'He had been wearing nice clothes.'

Miss Emily drummed her fingers on the arm of the sofa. 'Who, then, was the man with no neck?'

'I don't know. A friend of his, I think. He was not supposed to look at me, as I am married. He and a groom and someone else came in to help after I was bitten by the snake.'

'Ah, the snake.' Miss Emily sighed pointedly.

'I *was* bitten, after the fight.' Mariana touched her wrist. 'I thought I would die from the pain. I fell down, something horrible poured from my mouth, and then I fainted. They sent for someone who cures snake bite by reciting verses.'

'I see.' Miss Emily raised her hands. 'All polite behaviour

455

was flung away as soon as you were to be seen rolling on the floor and foaming at the mouth. More native men were summoned, mumbo-jumbo was recited and you recovered.' Her hands dropped into her lap.

Mariana refused to look away. 'I know it sounds fantastic but it's true.'

Miss Fanny let out her breath. 'And we all believed camp life was dull!'

'I blame myself.' Miss Emily shook her head. 'I should have had your tent put closer to mine. I should never have allowed you to be pushed off alone into a corner of the compound with only a native manservant and no woman to confide in. That is precisely how young girls get into trouble. And you, Mariana, have a genius for trouble.' She folded her hands in her lap. 'This wild behaviour must stop at once.'

'But Emily,' Miss Fanny protested, 'she only—'

'First,' Miss Emily announced, ignoring her sister, 'the baby is to be returned to the Maharajah. The child's welfare is no concern of ours. I will *not* spirit the Maharajah's hostage out of the Punjab like a thief in the night. And as for you, Mariana, our only choice is to send you to Calcutta at once. You are a danger to yourself and all of us. I shall speak to my brother this afternoon.'

The air around Mariana seemed to go cold. Her training and manners forgotten, she jumped up. 'No, Saboor cannot go back! If you send him to the Maharajah, he'll die of grief, and it will be all your fault!' She started for the doorway, leaving the two sisters agape on the sofa.

There was no time to be lost. Before Miss Emily went to Lord Auckland, she and Saboor must escape once more. With only Yar Mohammad and Dittoo for company and nowhere safe to take refuge, she and Saboor must become gypsies, travelling at night, hiding from people who did not care for them, who thought only of rewards or politics.

To her shame, last night she, too, had chosen England over India. In her haste to forestall her own ruin, she had put her troubles above Saboor's. In the hours before the child thief came and the snake coiled itself beneath her bed, she had chosen Mama and Papa over the Shaikh and Safiya Sultana, Freddie over Saboor, eau de cologne over attar of sandalwood. How could she have failed to see that, willingly or not, at every fork in the road she had taken the path leading to India? How could she have failed to notice that each choice had been made as if she had, indeed, been on a ship piloted by someone else? Now, when she was about to lose him, she knew for certain that she was Saboor's true guardian, as Yar Mohammad's dreams had foretold.

How could she ever have thought of leaving India?

'Mariana, sit down. Emily, I am *shocked*.' Mariana had never heard Miss Fanny use that tone. 'Whatever we may think of her, Mariana is the child's stepmother. It is for her to decide what is to be done with him.'

Before a startled Miss Emily could reply or Mariana return to her seat, a bumbling sound came from outside.

Unshaven and untidy as ever, Dittoo nodded apologetically as he pushed his way inside, out of place in Miss Emily's grand tent, a freshly bathed Saboor wriggling in his arms. 'He gave me no peace,' he explained. 'No one saw us,' he added as he lowered Saboor to the carpet. He tipped his head carelessly at the two ladies. 'They had already seen him, had they not, last evening?'

'An-nah, An-nah.' As Mariana sat down, Saboor danced, chirping, to her. Gripping her skirts, he tried, panting with effort, to climb onto her lap. She felt herself flush with pleasure as she reached for him.

His clothes were starched, his cheeks newly washed. He sat straight on her lap, his thumb in his mouth, gazing at the two English faces before him.

'These are Angrezi ladies,' Mariana said instructively, kissing the top of his head.

'Rezi,' he said seriously, then got down and marched, not to Miss Fanny who was already holding out her arms, but straight to Miss Emily, who sat very still, her hands clasped tightly in her lap. He leaned against her skirts and peered into her face, his head tilted back, his little red coat bunched up, a small, familiar fist resting on her knee.

'Well,' she said at last, looking down, her mouth beginning to turn up, 'well, well, well.'

'He must,' declared Miss Fanny, as Miss Emily took Saboor under his arms and lifted him, still sucking his thumb, to her lap, 'come to my tent and stroke the spotted deer.'

Mariana lay awake at midnight, enjoying her solitude, relieved that her bed had been returned to her own tent, that she was safe at last from the scrutiny of the Eden ladies, their ladies' maids and assistant ladies' maids.

Her head felt heavy but her body felt as light as air. The sisters had not sympathized, but they had been fair.

'We shall not, for the moment,' Miss Emily had said later, 'and I emphasize for the moment, mention to anyone the whereabouts of Saboor or the events of last night.'

'Do not tell her I said so,' she had murmured to Miss Fanny as Mariana listened behind them on the way in to lunch, 'but I fear we may have done the girl an injustice. She is young, after all, and the baby is very sweet.'

Mariana looked across her tent. The furnishings Hassan had brought after the fight looked quite comfortable arranged along one wall – the thick carpet from which Dittoo had beaten clouds of dust, the pair of bolsters, the low carved table.

She got out of bed, and, after making sure there were no snakes about, lowered herself uncertainly to the carpet, loosened her hair and leaned back on a purple bolster. Hassan had provided a satin quilt. She pulled it to her chin.

What a comfortable arrangement! It was a pity she had never had her own native furniture before.

She yawned. She had wanted to call on Shafi Sahib today but there had been no time to find his tent. Munshi Sahib had given her a wonderful lesson. The poem he had brought her had been beautiful, but difficult to translate.

I gave my heart to three qualities I found in you.
To be taken from these has caused my torn heart pain.
But if you suffer, it is worse for me.

I do not fear for you,
Alone on the field of battle.

'Dittoo,' she called, 'raise the door blind.'

This moment was perfect enough to make one wish to travel for ever. The sky through the open doorway was awash with stars. A plaintive melody drifted in from the distance. Saboor slumbered peacefully on the bed.

She had seen Hassan through the same doorway after the fight, his back to her, his shoulders heaving, his beautiful coat stained and torn. She had not said goodbye to him, or thanked him for saving her life. Glancing behind her as she was marched away, she had caught a glimpse of his exhausted face. He had met her eyes, then looked away.

She pushed a tangle of curls from her face. By this time he must be on his way north to Kasur. The British camp, now moving south, would cross the Sutlej tomorrow morning. Every day the distance between them would grow.

Dittoo greeted someone, then backed hurriedly away.

Hassan stepped quietly in through the doorway. He stood there, his gaze travelling to the bed where Saboor lay sleeping, then to her. He had a cut on his cheekbone. His ruined coat had been replaced by a shawl.

He sat beside her on the carpet. 'Let me see your wound,' he said without preamble, pushing the quilt out of the way and reaching for her hand. An uncut emerald set in gold gleamed on one of his fingers as he raised her wrist to the light.

'I must thank you for what you did last night,' she said a little weakly, distracted by the pressure of his fingers. 'I might have died. Was it you who sucked the poison?'

He did not answer. Instead he released her wrist and sat back against a bolster, his face turned from hers. The shawl across his chest moved up and down.

'I have received an urgent message from Kasur,' he said. 'I must start back tonight. I had hoped to cross the Sutlej with your camp, but I cannot.'

'It *was* you,' she whispered, her fingers on the healed wounds, remembering the agony in her wrist and the voice praying by her side.

He said nothing, nor did he look at her, but a wave of feeling seemed to come from him, as if he were speaking to her without words. It crossed the space between them, gaining power, mixing with the scent of sandalwood, reaching every part of Mariana's body. Her breathing deepened.

A small sound came from the sleeping Saboor. Hassan glanced towards the bed. 'When people ask us where you are,' he said softly, turning to Mariana, 'we will tell them you have gone to stay with your relatives.'

'With my relatives,' Mariana repeated. That would imply that she had run away from his family, from him. But it was suddenly far more complicated than that. 'No,' she stammered. She ran her hands over the satin quilt, searching for the right words. 'No.'

He rose to his feet. She could see by the way he held his shoulders that he was about to leave her. She stood up beside him.

'The Maharajah will most likely die soon,' he said. 'After that, the succession, Allah willing, will be smooth.' He moved to the bed and lifted Saboor. 'If it is not, there is a chance you may not see us again. If you do not, have courage, and remember me and my family.' His eyes closing, he hugged his son. 'Shafi Sahib will remain with you and my son.' Hassan stepped closer to her and handed her the child. 'Even while he is small, Saboor should be instructed in the ways of the Brotherhood. One day, God willing, he will be a great man.'

She could not speak.

'Yar Mohammad also will stay. He is now in our pay. I am sure he will think of a way to hide Saboor during your journey.' He paused. 'When it is safe, I will come for you.' His voice had thickened.

'You will come for *me*?' she repeated, searching his face.

'Yes.' With a sharp intake of breath, he bent and caught her mouth with his.

She did not try to escape him. She stood, trembling, the sleeping child in her arms. His mouth was harder than Fitzgerald's had been. His eyes were open.

Approaching footsteps broke the silence around them.

Hassan released her and looked out through the doorway. 'Shafi Sahib is coming,' he said in a different voice. 'He must have come to say goodbye to me and to talk to you of your journey.' He smiled apologetically. 'I must go out and meet him.'

He stepped through the doorway, then turned and looked hard at her. 'Khuda hafiz,' he said. 'May God protect you.' He raised his hand, just as his father had done when she left Qamar Haveli after returning Saboor.

Mariana stood still, holding the child tightly against her.

A moment later, Hassan's respectful greeting drifted into the tent. She looked about her. Shafi Sahib, the mysterious interpreter of dreams, was nearly at her door. She must do something. She laid Saboor on the bed and wiped her palms on her skirts. What would she say when they met? She could not touch his knees or his feet as the natives did, but she must make some gesture, however subtle, to show her respect. She could not treat Shaikh Waliullah's friend as if he were an ordinary person. Until she saw them again, Shafi Sahib would be her link to Hassan and his family.

Someone was removing his shoes outside the door. Brown fingers grasped the reed screen and held it aside. Her munshi stood before her, blinking a little in the half darkness.

'Peace, Bibi,' he said mildly. 'I trust you are well?'

That night, she half woke as a light wind sighed around the tent. The fog of her recurring dream had lifted at last. Over water that sparkled and shone, her ship now sailed parallel to a rocky shore, an energetic little dinghy bouncing on the waves behind her.

They were not alone. Ahead of them, a plain and powerful Arab dhow moved purposefully through the water, its lateen-rigged sail creaking in the wind. Beside the dhow and a little behind it, a narrow, gondola-like boat moved smoothly through the waves, propelled by oarsmen, its graceful prow carved to resemble a bird. Between Mariana's barque and the dangerous-looking shore was a long, serviceable barge, piled high with leather and straw.

She searched the distance. There, above the horizon's edge, rose the graceful masts of an Indian river yacht.

It was not, after all, Yar Mohammad but Dittoo who found a way to hide Saboor as they travelled. 'No one will look for him at so great a height,' he had said, nodding fiercely to emphasize the cleverness of his solution. 'We need only take care that Saboor is not seen when we bring him across the avenue.'

The next day he had tramped away, a newly hemmed cotton shawl in his hand, to make Saboor's travel arrangements.

Later, as she rode beside Miss Emily in one of the carriages, Mariana caught sight of Motu the elephant behind them in the distance, a large, swaying shape among a dusty sea of carts and baggage animals, the tiny figure of his mahout, Hira Lal, seated on his neck, carrying the Governor-General's great durbar tent and the grandson of Shaikh Waliullah of the Karakoyia Brotherhood to Calcutta.

YVONNE ROBERTS

A History of Insects

It is early 1956 and the British Empire is crumbling. But for nine-year-old Ella, living with her parents at the British High Commission in Peshawar, Pakistan, the walls of class, snobbery and racism are still intact. Growing up is a lonely, painful exprience, and Ella withdraws, recording the hypocrisy of adult behaviour in her diary, *A History of Insects*, where she hides a secret that could shatter the lives of the people around her.

Written from the perspective of a young girl, and with all the charm of *Behind the Scenes at the Museum* and *The God of Small Things*, this is an illuminating and evocative account of the loss of innocence. It heralds a radical departure in Yvonne Roberts' writing, and has been critically acclaimed:

'Unputdownable . . . wonderful novel . . . A mesmerising tale of death and love and passion' *Times Educational Supplement*

'The intricacies of class and the social life of the British High Commission are beautifully observed, and Ella's confusion over race, politics and religion mirrors a society where nothing is quite what it seems' *Bookseller*

'Tells with charm and delicacy the story of a girl's unwitting collusion in her own loss of innocence' *Independent*

'Moving and intelligent' *Publishing News*

'The style is lucid, the plot absorbing and the characters engaging . . . an engrossing read' *Metro*

0 7472 6126 1

review

You can buy any of these other **Review** titles from your bookshop or *direct from the publisher*.

FREE P&P AND UK DELIVERY
(Overseas and Ireland £3.50 per book)

The Seventh Son	Reay Tannahill	£6.99
Virgin	Robin Maxwell	£6.99
Bone House	Betsy Tobin	£6.99
Girl in Hyacinth Blue	Susan Vreeland	£6.99
A History of Insects	Yvonne Roberts	£6.99
The Long Afternoon	Giles Waterfield	£6.99
The Journal of Mrs Pepys	Sara George	£6.99
Still She Haunts Me	Katie Roiphe	£6.99
Vienna Passion	Lilian Faschinger	£6.99
Earth and Heaven	Sue Gee	£6.99
Stolen Marches	David Crackanthorpe	£6.99
The Last Great Dance on Earth	Sandra Gulland	£6.99
Scheherazade	Anthony O'Neill	£6.99

TO ORDER SIMPLY CALL THIS NUMBER

01235 400 414

or visit our website: www.madaboutbooks.co.uk

Prices and availability subject to change without notice.